SUDDEN THREAT

A. J. Tata

Published by Washburn Books, LLC

Published by Washburn Books, LLC (USA).

Cover illustration: Larry Rostant

Cover layout: Jeremy Robinson and Stanley Tremblay

Interior layout: Stanley Tremblay

Map: Jackie McDermott

IN MEMORY OF:
Command Sergeant Major Jerry Lee Wilson
Captain Bill Jacobsen
Major Doug Sloan

This book is dedicated to the memory of three soldiers killed in combat, two in Iraq and one in Afghanistan. These men are role models for all of us.

CSM Jerry Wilson was command sergeant major during my last six months of command of the Second Brigade, 101st Airborne Division. A tall, strong man from Thomson, Georgia, Jerry was killed in Mosul, Iraq in 2003 during Operation Iraqi Freedom. Jerry's heart was as large as he was tall, and as I said at his funeral in Thomson, we must all endeavor to earn his sacrifice.

Bill Jacobsen, who also served with me in the 101st Airborne Division, was killed the next year during the devastating attack on a dining facility near Mosul, Iraq, while serving as a Stryker Brigade company commander. Bill was a six-and-a-half-foot-tall devout Mormon who loved his soldiers. In the streets of Mosul, he was an icon among both his troops and the Iraqi people. He was the best officer with whom I served.

Doug Sloan served with me in the Eighty-second Airborne Division and Tenth Mountain Division and was killed by an improvised explosive device in Afghanistan in 2006. It happened three months after he was scheduled to leave company command, but his soldiers had asked their commander to keep him in place. I was proud of Doug's courage and the fact that he had achieved the highest praise a man can seek: subordinates who demanded his leadership.

Jerry, Bill, and Doug were the kinds of leaders soldiers loved to follow. They were selfless men who courageously and valiantly answered the call to duty. Men and women like them are not uncommon in our military. They are a reflection of our society and the values of our nation, and their sacrifices should galvanize all of us to recognize the reality that we have enemies who seek to destroy our way of life and indeed, freedom is not free.

Sudden Threat is the first in a series of books that follows the paths of two brothers, Matt and Zachary Garrett, CIA paramilitary operative and U.S. Army officer, respectively. Any thriller must have a stage on which to play out, and that stage must be based on current events. In addition to the disclaimer that this book is, in its entirety, fiction, including all of its characters, I want to add that *Sudden Threat's* purpose is to entertain. It is not a political statement and in no way, shape or form represents any official opinion of the United States government. If you choose to read on, this work of fiction also attempts to show the grittiness of combat against a realistic geopolitical backdrop.

As for me, I am a soldier. I believe in and endeavor daily to accomplish the country's strategic aims, I despise and have fought the enemies of our nation, and I know the threat we face. Late at night, as thoughts of combat and training spin through my mind, I'm always left with the images of Jerry, Bill, and Doug. So, if I've been able to capture a little bit of the qualities of men such as these in the characters of the main protagonists, then I will have succeeded.

ACKNOWLEDGEMENTS

The publication of this book would not have been possible without the friendship and guidance of Rob Hobart and Brad Thor. Rob's professionalism and years of dedicated, selfless service are the foundation for a character readers will discover in *Rogue Threat,* the sequel to *Sudden Threat,* and books beyond. Rob introduced me to Brad, who has simply been an unbelievable mentor through the publication process, not to mention a first-class friend and best-selling author.

To my entire family, who has been so incredibly supportive of me over the years during military deployments and the usual roller coaster of life, I say thank you. My parents, Bob and Jerri Tata, in particular have been steady supporters of my writing even when life seemed to get in the way.

And to Jodi Amanda, as you say, *all ways and always.*

PROLOGUE
Nangahar Province, Afghanistan, December 12, 2001
Matt Garrett

Matt Garrett pulled his white Gore-Tex hood over his forehead, warding off the biting winds that sliced downward from the 14,000-foot peaks of the Tora Bora Mountains and rifled through his layered Afghan garb like invisible sheets of ice. As he turned his head slowly to check on his three other men, the snow felt more like pellets firing sideways at his face by enemy weapons.

Holding in position a mile inside the Pakistani border overlooking a small, nameless village, he studied the hand-held monitor and watched the grainy, barely discernable Predator video feed as it followed the ambulance that had passed through Torkum gate, the fabled Khyber Pass. The ambulance turned north on a small road out of Peshawar and then the video feed was lost due to the blizzard.

Matt had just led his team from Jalalabad through the rugged, snow-jammed trail north of the pass separating Afghanistan from Pakistan while the Eastern Alliance, fortified by a consortium of special operators and some of his cohorts from the CIA, had attacked Tora Bora. The night before, Matt had stared at the map hanging in the small shack near the Jalalabad airfield as he listened to the fight raging in the windswept mountains.

Then he heard the announcement of a cease fire from the Generals in the Pentagon.

"Bullshit," he had said. "Head fake."

Matt figured that with all of the intelligence assets watching and listening to Al Qaeda in the mountains, he would form a supporting effort. His study of Bin Laden always had led him to the small village in Pakistan that he now viewed through the scope of his M24 sniper rifle.

Before leading his team into enemy terrain, Matt had pointed at the map with his team and said, "If he doesn't go the back way out of Tora Bora into Parachnir, he's going there." His finger had smacked the map north and west of Peshawar. "We've got enough dudes up in the mountains; this is where we're going."

Then as they were about to move, an Eastern Alliance checkpoint reported the pearl of intelligence to General Ali. An ambulance had appeared from nowhere in the snowstorm and was passing through Torkum Gate, heading east.

"That's him," Matt had said to his men. "Get Pred feed over it now." The Predator was unarmed and could only monitor. Headquarters had not believed in Matt's hunch, which made Tora Bora the focus and therefore had received the balance of the armed assets.

Matt, his three teammates, Bones, McKinney, and Macrini, and two mules had walked all night from a drop-off point near the border. They shivered and struggled to keep their bottled water and Camelbak hydration systems from freezing. After a quick recon, Matt had selected this rocky crevice with superb fields of fire into the village. They were perched high above the village nearly 500 meters away.

Matt plugged a cable from his sniper scope into a USB port in his small handheld satellite communications device. He was transmitting his sight picture back to Langley, but he also knew that the National Command Authority in the White House Situation Room and the National Military Command Center in the Pentagon routinely tapped into the CIA video, all in the name of post-9-11 intelligence sharing.

Matt could not give a rat's ass about who was watching the video feed.

They want proof? They can watch the bullet pass through his brain.

The driving snow provided ample cover, especially with their white ghillie suits that lay atop them. Two of his men were faced outward, securing their position from any passerby. Tony Macrini, known as X-Ray, lay next to him peering through a larger scope, confirming what Matt was seeing while providing redundant digital confirmation of the kill.

"Pred lost them, but they're heading this way," Matt said, confidently.

"Roger," Macrini said, then spit some tobacco into the bone-white snow. The brown juice disappeared almost instantly beneath a fresh layer.

Bones and McKinney tapped Matt every fifteen minutes. One tap meant all ok; two taps meant there was a problem. Better with minimal talking.

Matt's heart quickened. Though he was experienced, knowing he may have the shot on Al Qaeda senior leadership elevated his nervous system slightly. That was good, he thought. He wasn't anxious, but there was something nagging at him about headquarters not listening to his report.

He had been told to call in approval for any sniper shot on AQ senior leadership. *It's okay to drop a bomb on a cave and kill the dude*, Matt thought, *but I can't pull this trigger without approval?*

"Movement," Macrini said.

Matt shifted his scope marginally and picked up two men with AK-47s slung across their backs standing outside in the snowstorm. Pulling into the view of his scope was a makeshift ambulance with a large, red cross on either side. It slowly wound through a defile and pulled to a stop in front of the larger adobe structure in the nine-building village.

"That's it," Matt said. Men clambered out of the ambulance and opened the back door, extracting a stretcher. After the AK-47-clad stretcher bearers pulled the litter from the back, a short man wearing wire-rim spectacles stepped carefully from the compartment into the snow.

Matt watched as the spectacled man rapidly ushered the precious cargo into the large building. Momentarily losing sight of his target, Matt was pleased when they placed the stretcher on a table juxtaposed to an open window.

"I've got the shot," Matt said.

"You've got the shot," Macrini affirmed.

Matt deliberated. *Make the call, not make the call?*

"You've got the shot," Macrini said again, emphatically, as if to say, *screw the call.*

Before Matt could ruminate any further, his earpiece crackled with the sound of a distant incoming radio call.

"Garrett, stand by."

"Don't answer it," Macrini cautioned. "I don't like it."

"Headquarters can see my feed; they know we can talk."

"Garrett, standby, acknowledge immediately." Matt didn't recognize the voice through the wind and static, though he assumed it was some bureaucrat 17 times removed from Matt's low level status as an operator. He registered that the voice could be coming from any of the outstations: Langley, the White House, the Pentagon, and God knows whoever else might be watching. The 8,000-mile screwdriver was going cordless.

"I'm telling you, man," Macrini warned. "You know anything good to ever come from headquarters?"

Matt looked at his friend, a former Marine Force Recon scout. Macrini's beard, like his own, was thick. He wore a pakol and tan and green blankets beneath the white sheets they had used to conceal their position.

He turned back to his sight picture and lined up the black dot of the cross hairs on the middle of the patient's torso. The medical team had stripped the man, a very tall man, down to his long johns. The white shirt was stained red on the left side. Shrapnel, maybe a bullet, Matt figured. The scope traced the body and then the black dot landed on the bearded face, actually just to the side of the elongated nose and just beneath the dark, brooding eyebrows. The eyes, though, seemed compassionate, or perhaps he had the faraway look of a wounded deer.

Matt nodded to his battle buddy, exhaled steadily and placed an exposed trigger finger on the trigger mechanism. He found that spot where he would have no pull on the weapon, just straight back, not moving the weapon, sending the bullet directly where the cross hairs were resting. He closed his eyes briefly, retreating into that inner sanctuary that allowed him complete focus. Opening his eyes, all he saw was the black dot and the man's face looming large in his sight picture, the way that a slow-spinning curve ball might look to Tony Gwynn, the greatest batsman of all time.

"Homerun," Matt whispered.

"Homerun," Macrini confirmed.

"Do not fire! Do not fire! Kill chain denied!"

"What the hell?" Macrini said. Matt marginally noticed him rolling away from the scope and yanking out his earpiece.

But Matt didn't move. He was in his zone. Everything was in slow motion: his breathing, his trigger finger beginning the squeeze, the movement of the patient's head turning toward him, exposing the worn prayer callous on his forehead.

"Take the shot!" Macrini growled.

"Do not fire! Kill chain denied!"

"Take the shot!"

With the good angel on one shoulder, Macrini, and the bad angel on the other, the anonymous voice, Matt closed his eyes.

I've got the shot.

"This is a direct order. Entry into Pakistan was not authorized. Kill chain denied. Violation will be prosecuted."

I've got the shot. I'm close.

"Take the shot!" Macrini demanded.

Matt exhaled again, keeping his sight picture, and squeezed the trigger at the same time a JDAM missile exploded perilously close to his position.

"Holy shit!" Macrini shouted, covering his face. Bones and McKinney turned toward Matt, who was still in his zone.

The bomb's detonation created a bright orange fireball that mushroomed into the sky nearly 100 meters from his position.

"Closer to us than the shack," Matt said to his three teammates.

He looked at Macrini, who stared back at Matt and shook his head.

"HQ punked us."

"Roger that," Matt said.

"Kill chain denied, Garrett. Return to Jalalabad for new orders," came the headquarters voice into his earpiece.

CHAPTER 1
Thursday, April 25, 2002, 1900 Hours (Local)
Davao City, Mindanao, Philippines

The one time my country asks for a head on a platter, Matt said to himself as he recalled the nightmarish scene in Pakistan. He let out a heavy sigh, watching the sun dip behind Mount Apo, just to the west of Davao City, Republic of the Philippines, on the island of Mindanao. From the freezing snow to the humid backwaters. From the epicenter to the periphery.

I had the damn shot!

Disappointed in himself, he shook the memory from his head and crushed a smoldering butt under the sole of his dingy work boot.

Keeping his gaze fixed on the gray evening, he noticed a few destitute but industrious Filipinos scurry around the concrete fishing piers that abutted Davao Gulf, a horseshoe expanse of water adjacent to the Celebes Sea.

Pulling the ratty Dodgers baseball cap down over his forehead, Matt shook off a bit of his clinging anger and discreetly strode next to a shack, watching the activities—nothing out of the ordinary. He had been cycling between Zhoushan Naval Base, China, and Davao City for over two months. Tonight, he had been given instructions in the form of a text message from his handler to meet a dockworker who would provide him information.

A few short months after being mysteriously yanked from Pakistan while in hot pursuit of Al Qaeda senior leadership, Matt was now trying to locate a large number of unmanned aerial vehicles (UAV) called

Predators. They were just being put to good use in the War on Terror, and it appeared that someone in the United States had traded this technology to the Chinese for financial motivations. Either that, or the Chinese theft of top secret information at Los Alamos had contributed to the satellite imagery that indicated the Predators were being built and tested near Zhoushan, China. Matt had developed a lead in China when he had suddenly received a message from his handler that there was a significant find in Davao City; and so here he was. *Every time I'm close, I'm moved*, Matt thought to himself.

Matt was large, a college shortstop, and despite his inner angst focused on appearing at ease in his cargo pants and khaki shirt. He tugged at the Dodgers baseball hat again and hid his eyes behind Oakley sunglasses.

"Muggy," the dockworker said to him in Tagalog.

"Always in the evening," Matt said in Mandarin.

A hazy mist rolled off the bay, distorting the presence of hundreds of fishing vessels. A gull stood guard atop a pylon and flapped its wings as if shivering, though the temperature was in the nineties.

"Got any cigarettes?" the man asked, this time in Mandarin also. That was the key, he had been told.

He turned and looked at the slight Filipino. Matt, standing over six feet, towered above the diminutive man, who was shorter than five and a half feet. The contact had black hair and brown eyes, the norm in that part of the country.

"Sure. Here." This time in English. Matt grabbed his rumpled pack of Camels and held it out to the source, who took two, glancing at him for approval. Matt nodded.

"Running out of time," Matt said. He watched the man put a cigarette between yellow teeth and strike a match. Once he had lit the cigarette, the man shook the match and tossed it on the pier. He looked in both directions, then nodded at a ship across the harbor.

"See that tanker?"

Matt looked past the rows of red and gray fishing ships in the direction the man had nodded. He saw several tuna rigs and could make out a large black-and-red merchant vessel. It looked more like a container ship or an automobile carrier. He guessed the contact had mistaken it for an oil tanker.

"What about it?"

"Japanese. Leaves tonight. Didn't off-load anything, but Abu Sayyaf put something on it."

Matt continued staring at the ship and read the name on the side: *Shimpu.* That name registered with him, but at the moment he couldn't remember why.

"What was it?" Matt asked, still staring at the ship.

With his peripheral vision, Matt saw the guard remove the cigarette from his mouth and begin to speak. What followed happened quickly: the orange tip of the cigarette fell from the man's hand and dropped at Matt's shoes as his contact's body shuddered. Instinctively, Matt pulled his Glock 26 from beneath his untucked shirt and jumped onto a floating dock running perpendicular to the pier on which they had been standing.

As he leapt, he saw that the contact was prone on the pier and bleeding from a head wound. He also felt the hot wash of a bullet pass uncomfortably close as he ducked behind a junked generator, which he presumed was used as an auxiliary power unit for some of the ships. The generator pinged twice from gunshots, and Matt eyed a large Bangka boat with a roof, a ferry of some type, backing away from the dock.

The ferry helmsman was removing a weathered bowline from a rusty cleat about 30 meters away. There were a few passengers that he could see, mostly fishermen, probably making their way home to Babak on the eastern side of the gulf. Matt waited until the captain gave the boat a slight shove. As he watched the boat separate from the pier, he sprinted as if he were stealing third base against a catcher with a rifle arm, then did his best long-jump imitation, his feet cycling through the air.

He landed with a thud on the roof of the boat, which promptly gave way and dumped him on the floor, which held.

The helmsman had put the engine into forward, and the ferry was moving slowly away from the pier.

No more shots followed him, but he thought that the ship captain might decide to take over where his other attackers had left off. The wizened man stood above him and was screaming at him and baring his teeth, throwing his arms up in the air. Matt understood most of what he was saying and stood, brushed himself off, and pulled five hundred dollars from his wallet.

"Sorry about the roof. Buy a new boat," he said in Tagalog.

The man took the $500 and considered it, shaking his head. "My boat. Had for 25 years. New roof."

Clearly the man was bargaining with him, so Matt pulled two hundred dollars more from his pocket and handed it to the man but didn't release it. The helmsman tugged on the money with a weathered hand.

"Drop me off at the next pier up near the airport, and we're even," Matt said.

The man yanked the 200 dollars from his hand and nodded.

Much later, true to his word and the seven hundred dollar payment, the captain of the ship pulled into the pier normally used for fruit transshipment. Night had fallen, and Matt effortlessly leapt from the bow of the Bangka ferryboat onto the concrete pier.

He reassured himself by patting his Glock, which had stayed firmly in his hand through the fall, and which he had quickly placed in its holster while still on the floor of the boat. He walked a kilometer to the room he had rented, grabbed his gear, then discreetly moved another kilometer and a half toward the airport and checked in at the nondescript Uncle Doug's Motel.

Matt presumed that "Uncle Doug" was Douglas MacArthur, patron saint of all things Philippine.

He tossed his duffel on the floor, locked the door, and pulled out his satellite Blackberry to send a text message.

Check out Shimpu. Contact KIA. New location. Standing by.

Matt sent the dispassionate note as if having contacts killed and being shot at were akin to signing an office memo or sitting in a meeting to discuss the next meeting. He removed the Baby Glock from its holster, ran his finger along the extractor and felt the reassuring bump indicating he still had a round chambered.

Almost immediately he received a text message from his handler.

Airport. Midnight. More to follow. Feet and knees together.

Matt looked at his watch. It was 0200, or 2:00 am. *Like I'm on a wild-goose chase*, he thought, and shook his head.

Matt forwarded the text to his personal secure e-mail account; it was his way of keeping a journal.

"Feet and knees together" was paratrooper code for the best way to survive a parachute landing. Matt understood that if you kept your feet and knees pressed firmly together, you stood a chance of not breaking an ankle or leg. If you reached for the ground with only one foot, all of your weight would come barreling onto one spot on one bone, usually resulting in a fracture.

He typed back: **Roger.**

Sitting on his twin bed with no box springs, he stared at his pistol, cycling the events of the last few hours through his mind. He snapped his head upward and whispered, "Shimpu." Remembering the meaning of the obscure Japanese word sent a chill up his spine.

"Divine wind," he said to himself. *It's what the kamikaze pilots had called themselves.*

CHAPTER 2
Mindanao Island, Philippines

Matt spent the day resting, doing a few push-ups, and chowing on combat rations. One thing about a parachute jump that Matt knew for certain was that the jumper rarely landed in his intended location. Therefore, he needed to be rested and well fed in preparation for the energy he would need once on the ground.

He cinched the parachute straps, tightening them against his legs and across his back. He patted the Duane Dieter Spec Ops knife he had taped beneath his cargo utility pants, then tapped his Baby Glock and visually inspected his SIG 552 Commando rifle. He felt the reassuring weight of his 9mm and 5.56mm ammunition in his outer tactical vest. All seemed to be in good order.

What was not in good order, in Matt's mind, was the new text he had just received, stating that a group of Filipino Rangers had just been shot down somewhere over the island of Mindanao. Matt's handler had sent a text indicating that one C-130 was a catastrophic loss, meaning everyone was killed, while the lead airplane had some paratroopers successfully jump.

His mission was to determine if there were any survivors and to send their location to headquarters. There was no expectation that he could save them alone.

I come here looking for Predator connections, and now I'm looking for dead Filipino Rangers, Matt thought, shaking his head. It was not that the task was a nuisance; just the opposite. He knew damn well that the soldiers who had just died were fighting in the name of freedom.

The Casa 212 airplane bounced along the runway and lifted easily into the sky. Matt was jumping a square parachute so that he could steer it to a precision landing. He had asked the pilots to put him over the wreckage site, and he would work from there. The reported crash site was 30 kilometers east of Compostela.

Through a map recon, Matt had selected a drop zone about a kilometer away. It was the best he could do, and even at a kilometer, he believed that the blank level-looking spot on the map was probably a banana plantation or worse, a recently harvested sugarcane field. Either way, he stood a good chance of being impaled on a freshly cut banana tree or sugarcane stalk.

The flight from the Davao City airfield to his drop zone took about 90 minutes, even though the release point was only 80 kilometers north of Davao. Matt had asked the pilot to fly south over the water, then to circle around the island and approach the drop zone from the north, which doubled the flight route. He would be jumping from ten thousand feet above ground level, which would put the airplane at about sixteen thousand feet above sea level. The plains of Mindanao were surrounded by jagged volcanic mountains that ran parallel along the west and east coasts. The heat and rainfall had, over the course of time, spawned lush tropical rain forests on both the windward and leeward sides of the island. Matt would be jumping in the bowling alley between the two ranges, which topped out at about fourteen thousand feet, but he would be cheating toward the eastern range, where the airplanes had last been sighted.

Once the pilot made the turn to fly from north to south, using his goggles Matt saw the city lights out of the front right of the airplane. He was standing between the pilot and copilot seats, observing through the windscreen, and assuming the city was Compostela.

"There," Matt said, pointing to his left front. He saw the faintest evidence of fire. Stepping away from the cockpit, he walked over to the open port personnel door and held onto the rails on either side, leaning out of the aircraft but staying out of the slipstream.

When he looked more closely, he could see the smoldering remnants of two spots of burning wreckage.

Seems right, he thought.

He walked back to the cockpit, lifted his goggles, and said, "Just get me over those two hot spots. I'll open at about a thousand AGL and find a good location. That's where I need to be."

Paramount in his mind was the fact that there might be some survivors. He was jumping in with a small rucksack, which included a first-aid kit. He would be able to treat a few patients, but that was all. Unfortunately, Matt knew, a few might be all that were left from the two planes that carried sixty paratroopers each.

"Okay, sir, we're over top. Anytime now," the copilot said, leaning back and looking at Matt.

"Roger. Thanks, guys."

Matt checked his gear once more, then walked off the back of the open ramp, fell forward into a swan dive as if he were going to do a belly flop, and flared his arms to stabilize his free fall.

Initially he was unable to detect the two fires he had seen from the airplane, and as he checked his altimeter, he saw he was approaching 1100 meters above ground level. He spun once, then again. On his second spin, he saw the wrecks and adjusted his airflow to direct his fall toward them.

At just above one thousand feet, Matt pulled the rip cord on his parachute. It opened cleanly and he had good silk above him. The cool air offset the typically warm Philippine nights and rushed past his face.

He retracted his goggles from their pouch, steered them to his face, and placed the harness on his head, securing it with a chin strap. The "dummy cord" flapped against his windbreaker but would prevent him from losing the goggles should they come loose.

Through the green-shaded world of the goggles, he studied the wreckage. At the southernmost airplane he saw hundreds of people milling around the burnt remnants. Making a snap decision at about six hundred feet above the ground, Matt pulled hard and steered about a kilometer away from the southern airplane and toward the northern wreckage.

He couldn't see anywhere to land.

"Oh shit," he whispered. Then, thankfully, he caught an updraft and rode it over a small ridge. The terrain was severe, which he reasoned must have been why there were no people near the northern fire. They might arrive soon enough.

At 100 feet above ground level, he could see the fire burning, and its ambient light gave him enough visibility to conclude that the only place he could land, if at all, would be in the middle of the plow field of the wreckage. So, his two options were to land either in burning, twisted metal or in a stand of sixty-foot high oak, chestnut, and mahogany trees.

His goggles refracted the glint of something elongated running perpendicular to his axis of descent and he realized, perhaps a bit too late, that it was the moon reflecting off water, which in those mountains could even be a waterfall.

Just as his feet were skimming the tops of the trees, he miraculously found a small clearing and toggled hard into a spiral that took him into the hole. Beneath the jungle canopy, his goggles were less useful but still better than the naked eye.

His parachute caught on something, and he swung forward, suspended in air and oscillating back and forth as if on a playground swing set. He had his rucksack on a twenty foot lowering line, so he pulled the quick release and heard his rucksack thud into the ground.

Matt flipped his goggles back onto his head, removed a flashlight from his vest pocket, and shined it beneath his feet. He was a mere two meters off the ground.

He removed his Duane Dieter Spec Ops knife from its ankle sheath, cut one riser, grabbed above his intended cut on the remaining riser, cut it and held on with one arm. He flipped his knife into the ground, heard it stick, then let go, keeping his feet and knees together as he landed. Collecting his rucksack and knife, Matt pulled a compass from his vest, set an azimuth north, and began walking quickly to the wreckage.

CHAPTER 3

Just to move one kilometer took him nearly an hour. Where the terrain was moderately level, it was choked with dense undergrowth. Where there was less vegetation, there seemed to be impossibly jagged and steep volcanic rocks and cliffs.

Matt took a knee on the rock ledge that he had just ascended. His beacon had been the bright spot in the offing, like town lights reflecting off the clouds. His goggles, though, provided the clarity to remind him that the light was a burning airplane on the face of the mountain.

Finally, he removed his goggles from his eyes and saw without technological assistance the smoldering ruins of half a fuselage. Looking to his left, he could see the direction from which the aircraft had flown, or tumbled, and cut a wide swath of destruction. To his right it looked like the debris field continued on another 50 meters or so until a flat wall of rock had blocked any forward progress.

Matt stood and walked carefully, again scanning with his goggles in both directions as he stepped lightly over hot chunks of metal scattered about. He had seen airplane crashes before, and they were never remotely comprehensible. Could anyone ever imagine the terror or horror of plummeting in a plane into the ground? In a way, he hoped that someone could tonight; it would mean they were still alive. On the thought, he touched his rucksack, feeling for the first-aid kit inside.

He stepped over a full propeller, knelt next to it, and touched the blade. It was warm, but not hot. The friction of the crash and the jet-fuel spillage had created fire and heat, but not everything was burning.

All I'm asking for is one person to be alive, Matt thought to himself. *Just one.*

He moved toward the blackened hull of the aircraft, which was surprisingly intact but split wide open, like a lobster tail. He entered the fuselage from the rear. The heat and smell pushed him back outside. For the first time he noticed the crackle of the fire still burning rubberized pieces of material.

Then he noticed a body.

Matt saw the man's hands first. It was an odd visual display as the body was actually outside the aircraft, tethered by a deployed parachute.

The flashlight that Matt shined on the scene revealed a charred static line tracing from the door of the aircraft to the rock ledge. From there Matt saw the metal ring at the apex of the parachute and some charred parachute nylon. His eyes followed the suspension lines to the risers, the straps connecting the parachute to the paratrooper, which were surprisingly intact.

The hand was splayed upward toward the riser as if reaching to pull a slip. Matt moved the flashlight beam farther down the body and could see a U.S. Army combat uniform.

Shit. He sighed.

He moved quickly next to the man and saw the name tag: Peterson. Matt checked for pulse and airway but got negative reports on both accounts. He visually inspected Peterson and saw that he had been rigged to jump and that the airplane must have crashed as he was trying to exit.

Matt saw the arrowhead patch of the U.S. Army Special Forces on the man's shoulder sleeve with airborne and Special Forces tabs above. *No one told me Americans were in this thing,* he said to himself. *What the hell is going on?*

Returning to the moment, Matt shook his head. The seconds between life and death were so arbitrary. Why did Peterson not make it, while apparently everyone else did? His search of the surrounding area had yielded two pilots and a loadmaster, meaning the paratroopers from this aircraft had made the jump and were somewhere in the jungle. As tragic as the pilot and loadmaster deaths were, Matt knew they were Filipino, which mattered, but somehow did not have the same impact on him that kneeling there looking at Peterson did.

"Who are you, Peterson?" he whispered. *And why wasn't I told about you?*

Again, he checked for pulse and any sign of life, shining the flashlight into Peterson's wide eyes. The pupils were nonresponsive, so Matt used his thumb and forefinger to slide the eyelids shut. Peterson had not been burned badly; really, just the heat from the fire had burned his parachute. The man must have died from blunt-force trauma during the crash or as he was flung from the rear cargo door.

Matt looked up and saw that the starboard wing had been sheared off and was probably a kilometer or so back in the debris field. He stood and made another lap around the airplane and into the split fuselage, then moved the bodies of the two pilots and the crew chief onto the rock ledge near Peterson's body. He pulled a GPS locator beacon from his rucksack and put it in the mouth of each man, then shut each jaw tightly. Human scavengers would be picking the place clean in less than twenty-four hours, and the last place they would look was in the throat of a dead man. Filipinos were not known for their gold fillings.

Regardless, he would send a report back to the station chief in Manila and get word to the Armed Forces of the Philippines that they had three men located in the jungle.

He could only carry one.

He carefully removed the parachute harness from Peterson and checked him one last time for signs of life.

Again, he was denied. Climbing his way out would require two hands, and so he took three twelve-foot ropes from his rucksack and slid them under Peterson's upper back, lower back, and buttocks, leaving enough rope on either side for his purposes. Next he laid himself face up on Peterson's body, wrapped Peterson's arms around his chest, and tied the ropes around their bodies. He rolled to all fours with Peterson on his back and then pulled his hands down and tied them with the trail ends of the lower rope. When he stood, he felt the full weight of his rucksack, which he had secured to his chest, and Peterson on his back. But his arms were free to move and pull his way out of the wreckage. To the casual observer it would appear that Matt was conducting a tandem jump or giving Peterson a piggyback ride.

Looking up at the cliff he needed to scale, Matt silently wished it were a tandem jump.

Matt heard a noise below the crash site, perhaps one and a half kilometers away. He had been at the site for an hour and knew it was time to move. He would go to high ground, as he would surely run into opposition if he went lower.

With Peterson on his back, he stepped into the first of many foot ledges in the rock wall that angled away from the crash site. While Peterson's weight was almost unbearable, Matt determined that it was the least he could do.

"Never leave a fallen comrade," he whispered to himself. And while he wasn't an Army officer like his brother Zachary, whom Matt had last seen while undergoing Langley's immersion training in preparation for his current assignment, he thought that was a pretty good credo to live by. And he knew damned well that if it was Matt Garrett at the end of that parachute harness and Peterson had found him, Matt would expect the same thing.

He pulled and scraped his way out of the crash site until two hours later when he had to stop.

The sun was beginning to crest the ridge in the east, and he had reached some sort of plateau by climbing almost straight up. Earlier, he had spotted a hole in the forest canopy through which a helicopter would be able to lower a jungle penetrator. He determined he would stop there, make contact, then figure out his next move.

He sat down awkwardly with Peterson on his back and untied the ropes. Peterson had gone to full rigor and looked strange sitting there, dead, as if he were driving an invisible car, his arms and legs outstretched.

Matt pulled his satellite Blackberry from his backpack and sent the following message:

One U.S. KIA. Peterson, Ronald W. Current grid location at beacon 13; airplane crashed at grid location of beacon 12; 3 AFP personnel dead at location. Status on other U.S. personnel? Why not told?

He wolfed down a combat ration and a power bar, downed two bottles of water, and changed out of his sweaty T-shirt.

Sitting on the grassy mountaintop, his anger resurfaced. *First, I'm pulled from Pakistan. Next, I'm moved from China. Then, I find a lead in Davao City but have to leave. Every time I'm close, I'm moved. Now, I've got a dead Special Forces soldier.*

What is going on? He inhaled heavily and blew out the air. "No use in whining," he whispered.

He looked east, then stared down at the map on his GPS that had appeared once he'd established satellite triangulation. The visual display showed that Matt was on a volcanic ridge just southwest of Cateel, a fishing village on the windward side of Mindanao.

He repacked his rucksack, checked his rifle and pistol, and stood. He could see the ocean and was momentarily struck by the beauty of the sun nosing its way out of the blue sea.

He was distracted, and he did not hear the echo of the bullet before he felt its turbulent wash through the air next to his head. A few more shots zipped in his direction.

Peterson's body took two shots to the chest while Matt's backpack took one. Matt spun and aimed his rifle. The shooter had been careless to miss, because now Matt could see two men trying to scale the cliff he had just climbed. In full daylight, Matt was awestruck at the cliff he had climbed with Peterson on his back as he leveled his SIG SAUER on the lower man and pulled the trigger. The man tumbled backward...a long way.

Matt then shot the lead man, who had been on all fours trying to scale the cliff. After confirming the second shot, Matt studied the lead man through his sight. He was black-haired, young, and dead. He wore a red bandanna and had ammunition strapped across his chest like Rambo. A few sparse hairs were growing along his chin, and his skin seemed smooth, almost oily. He had to be part of the Al Qaeda splinter cell, Abu Sayyaf or New People's Army.

Matt decided that he could probably defend his current position better than any other, so he made only a minor adjustment by moving 200 meters to the south, where he found a series of boulders behind which he could set up a defensive perimeter The canopy was still open in the area and he had good visibility. It took him two trips, but he finally got his equipment and Peterson's body into the rock formation.

He opened his rucksack, pulled out his Blackberry, and stared at the blank screen.

There was a bullet hole between the T and Y buttons, as if someone had been aiming at the device.

He pressed a few buttons to no avail. He pulled his cell phone out of his cargo pocket and saw that there was no reception. No surprises in the middle of this uncharted rain forest.

Matt thought quickly. Had his handler received his last text? Assuming Peterson was not alone, there had to be some American GIs that had survived and fled...unless they were on the other plane. But that didn't make sense. Peterson would *not* have been alone, and they would have at least split six and six, so that means at least five were still alive. Something told Matt that the helicopter would not be arriving and now he had no way to confirm his instinct.

I'll bury Peterson with a GPS, Matt thought, *then try to find the remainder of the team.*

"Besides, they'll probably need my help," he said aloud.

After snatching Peterson's ID tags from the beaded chain lying against the dead man's chest, he placed some rocks on top of Peterson. They would be too heavy for an animal to move. Then he placed a GPS in the dirt about ten meters from the rock formation. He pulled out his compass, shot an azimuth to the south, and determined he would follow the ridgeline of the mountain he had scaled.

As the sun rose, Matt picked his way carefully along the rocky ledge.

Looking over the eastern side of the mountain range, he saw modern tanks being loaded onto railcars.

CHAPTER 4
Previous Night, East China Sea
Taiku Takishi

Knowing that Matt Garrett was on the island of Mindanao, former Japanese Naicho agent, the equivalent of CIA in the United States, Taiku Takishi had shut off his satellite phone and begun his portion of the plan.

While his Mindanao sniper had missed Garrett and actually hit the informant, Takishi would be on the island soon enough. At the moment though, he held on tightly to a metal rail as the Taiwanese-built and Japanese-operated Kuang Hua VI attack ship cut through the dark sea with purpose. Its gray hull burst from the swirling fog and tracked against the racing thunderheads above—a ghost ship emerging from another time and suddenly finding its way.

A storm was approaching from the north. The worst kind. The wind kicked the ocean into white-peaked swells, testing some of the small crew. Takishi's worried face reflected weakly off the cabin window as the GPS navigation device flashed that they had passed their mark. He had just completed a 24-hour flight schedule and was weak from travel. Now this.

He cast a skittish glance at Admiral Saigo Kinoga, thinking, *We've come too far.*

"Admiral?" Takishi barked, watching the radar device.

Kinoga ignored him. Takishi knew that the admiral had commissioned the craft just two years ago. It was the newest of the Japanese attack boats. Her two Mitsubishi diesel engines and gas turbines turned the two screws, getting her about 35 knots in the rough seas. He felt the ship churn through a massive swell, pitch to the top, and ride the crest downward, only to bore through another wall of water.

Takishi doubted that Kinoga appreciated a politician such as him riding shotgun on his mission. In a way, Takishi admired the admiral, who had been a young officer in the Imperial Navy before Takishi was born. Takishi saw his own face reflecting off the windscreen in the dim cabin light; he tried to hide his fear, forcing a passive countenance.

Having performed his duties as a teenager in the Japanese Self Defense Forces, Takishi had eventually become a clandestine operative with Naicho, then ventured into the banking business, where he had amassed a fortune. He was an expert marksman, mountain climber, and viewed himself as the ultimate Renaissance Man. He believed that there was nothing of which he was not capable. How many times had he climbed Fuji, he wondered? Why not Everest? Perhaps his ascent up his personal Mount Everest had begun two years ago over a few beers with an old Harvard Business School classmate. That classmate was now a senior official in the American Defense Department.

Kinoga shut the engine. The boat yawed, listing hard. Takishi stumbled in the cockpit and saw Kinoga smile.

"What do we have for defensive measures, Admiral?"

Kinoga took measure of Takishi briefly and said, "Four Hsiung-Feng II missiles for ship-to-ship combat. If our strategy is successful, they will not be necessary."

Takishi's dual purposes came to fruition as Kinoga's modified vessel sat silently in the wind-whipped sea. They rocked aimlessly in the churning water. His anxiety mounted as Kinoga ordered the helmsman to turn the bow to the east.

"What makes you think we can get this close, Admiral?" Takishi asked. It sounded like an accusation.

"Mind your own business, politician," Kinoga spat. "They think we're fishing."

"Fishing? I see," Takishi said. His deal with China had increased their fishing rights along the 12-mile border. The fishing vessels had made the People's Liberation Navy's defenses less sensitive to boundary incursions.

"Are you worried about your Chinese friends?"

"Do not accuse me of conflicting loyalties," Takishi countered, showing the first inkling he was getting his sea legs.

Takishi examined Kinoga, who was a very different man from himself. Kinoga was a career seaman, waiting for the day his country could erase past embarrassments. Takishi was a stockbroker turned politician turned special agent, hoping to rule Japan sometime in the not-too-distant future. They were two men with different aspirations, but they had the same goal tonight: to cause the Chinese to focus their intelligence assets on Taiwan. Their demonstration tonight was to convince the Chinese that Taiwan was probing their waters.

"Initiate jamming," Kinoga said harshly into a gray microphone, his voice transmitting to his crew of six. Takishi stepped back as the jammers sent bursts of radiation to momentarily short-circuit the Chinese radar and interrupt communications systems. It was a silent attack, and he wondered if anything had worked.

"Fire the pods," Kinoga said. Takishi held firmly to the dashboard of the attack ship as fire bellowed from the foredeck. The rockets burst away, burning brightly, momentarily silhouetting the ship against a bright fireball, then dove quickly into the water five hundred meters off stern. Nine others followed. Takishi knew that these "Pods" would create the electronic signature of attack ships. Chinese radar would record multiple vessels threatening their sovereign territory.

"Admiral, they have launched two bombers and a reconnaissance plane with the rest of the squadron to follow," Kinoga's Chinese linguist remarked, lifting one earphone away from his head.

Takishi snapped his head toward the admiral.

Kinoga had only two 20mm guns and four useless ship-to-ship missiles to protect his vessel. Even though the guns could fire 300 rounds a minute, they would be ineffective against the high-tech Chinese aircraft.

"Full ahead," Kinoga said. Takishi felt the boat move slowly almost immediately after the admiral's order.

Takishi saw Kinoga watching the radar. The Chinese aircraft pursued his vessel as it strained for the safety of international waters and ultimately, the southwestern shores of Japan. Takishi knew that success depended entirely upon the avoidance of conflict or capture in Chinese seas.

Takishi settled into a calming routine, part of his jujitsu training. He watched Kinoga and his crew. In his dark blue utility uniform, Kinoga looked like any other sailor. His eyes seemed closed as he watched the radar screen. He periodically looked over the bridge of the vessel and into the black night.

"Scared, Takishi?" Kinoga prodded.

"The only thing that scares me, Admiral, is taking unnecessary risks. What happens if they capture our ship?" Takishi muttered.

"Then we die. Remember, or did the prime minister forget to tell you, that we are rigged with explosives?" Kinoga grinned.

Takishi looked away, shaking his head. He began to wonder if he was in too deep, but he had made commitments to his prime minister and to others. He had no option but to continue, and there were more dangerous tasks ahead. The prime minister had guaranteed him that the emperor would promote him upon successful accomplishment of the entire plan. Thinking of this seemed to motivate him.

There were no beacons or lighthouses to guide their retreat through the dangerous seas. Black water crashed against the angled hull, spraying a thick, salty mist high into the air that clouded the cabin glass. It was like trying to look through a thin veil of milk. The ship accelerated, riding the swell, then slowed, boring through the mass of water at the bottom of the pitch, only to repeat the process every few seconds.

He pushed it too far, thought Takishi.

Kinoga smiled at Takishi, as if reading his mind.

Takishi smiled back, denying the admiral satisfaction. Yes, indeed, Takishi would be getting satisfaction soon.

But right then he was infinitely more concerned with Kinoga's ability to outrace the rapidly approaching aircraft.

By Takishi's calculations, they had to be close to international waters and their relative safe harbor from Chinese attack. The plan was for them to turn southeast and aim toward the island of Yonaguni, whose port would provide shelter and whose proximity to Taiwan would offer the intended ruse.

Then it happened. Takishi heard the steady, high-pitched sound of radar lock screeching through a speaker in the cockpit.

"What's that?" Takishi asked nervously.

Ignoring Takishi, Kinoga studied the night sky, watching the two bright flashes punch through the cloud cover and streak through the blackness, searching for an illusory target: his ship. He reached down and pressed a gray button, employing countermeasures. He released three SIREN electronic chafflike rockets, hoping to confuse the missiles by sending a strong electronic signal from a battery-powered amplifier floating beneath a parachute. The SIREN rockets screamed into the air, quickly deploying their parachutes and high-technology merchandise below.

"What the hell is going on, Kinoga? You went too far! Now we are in combat!" Takishi screamed.

Kinoga lurched at Takishi and grabbed the lapels of his heavy jacket. He moved his face within centimeters of Takishi's, who could smell the captain's stale breath.

"Don't question my authority on my ship!" Kinoga hissed. "I am the captain. I am in charge. Now shut up before I throw you overboard and grieve your accidental loss before the prime minister!"

Takishi's body was limp in Kinoga's powerful grasp. His back against the wall, Takishi ran one hand lightly over the pistol inside its holster beneath his jacket.

Kinoga stepped away and returned to his duties, smiling as he watched the rockets seduce the enemy missiles, breaking the radar lock on his vessel.

Takishi silently urged the ship forward, not wanting to know how close they had come to being hit. *Let's move*, Takishi thought, as the missiles veered away and screamed ineffectively into the water, which quickly drowned their potency.

Kinoga pointed at the radar screen, which showed multiple dots moving rapidly toward the radar images of the Chinese jets. "Taiwan. Those are F-16s confronting the Chinese Air Force."

Takishi nodded. "Mission accomplished...provided you get us safely out of here."

Takishi watched Kinoga pilot his ship as they continued to tunnel through the black, salty night. They finally split the lighthouses of Kubura and Irizaki, which guided them into a port tucked safely behind the rocky bluffs of Yonaguni, the southernmost of the Japanese Ryukyu Islands and a short seventy miles from Taiwan. As they arrived at the small pier, Takishi pondered the night's activities. Their actions had given the impression that Taiwan was probing, if not provoking, China by attacking its fighter jets in Chinese airspace.

Takishi was a master strategist, and he was certain that Prime Minister Mizuzawa had chosen the proper course for his native land. With North Korea and China possessing both the capability and the intent to dominate the Pacific Rim militarily, Japan could not let the 9-11 attacks and a few radical Muslims divert the world's attention away from what really mattered: the geopolitical balance of power in the Pacific.

With the Taiwan deception mission nearing completion, Takishi's thoughts turned to his secret alliance with the Americans. That, he thought, was merely a means to an end. One that would one day make him Prime Minister.

Nobody planned wars in a vacuum, Takishi knew, and he was no exception. His instructions from the prime minister had been as clear as they were vague.

"Exploit this window of opportunity to our advantage. We have China, Taiwan, and North Korea salivating now that the U.S. is focused on their upcoming war in Iraq. And we have pressing resource-related and economic issues to confront. You are a Harvard man. Help me solve them."

Takishi knew that most people recognized a window of opportunity by the sound of its slamming shut; it was always in hindsight. But not Mizuzawa and especially not him. Takishi was proud of the phased operation he had begun planning right after 9-11. As the Americans focused on the Middle East in the wake of the 9-11 attacks, Takishi would lead Japan to the natural resources it so desperately needed to survive.

Takishi felt relieved as he spied his Shin Meiwa US-1A float plane, a Japanese air-and-sea craft with four Rolls-Royce AE 2100 engines that drove the amphibious craft's four propellers, tethered just one pier away. The sun was already spreading its morning glow on the rugged terrain of the atoll, where Japanese explorers claimed to have found a city that sank when the island broke away from the continent in the twelfth century.

A sinking Japan, Takishi thought, was exactly what they were trying to avoid.

"Satisfied, Takishi?" Kinoga asked as he walked to the starboard ramp with Takishi, the morning brightness hurting his eyes.

"Yes," said Takishi. "I was much too bothersome to you during the mission, Admiral." He snapped from his reverie as he held a stanchion at the top of the ramp.

"It is good that you are not in my line of work. Don't ever pretend you could handle it."

Seagulls circled nearby, hoping for the ceremonial dumping of the ship's slop bucket. Their loud squawks hurt Takishi's ears, causing him to flinch and narrow his eyes. The fresh morning air returned some coherency to his thoughts.

"If you could gather your crew, the prime minister has given me the authority to award you and your men the Imperial Cross."

Kinoga hesitated, perhaps ever suspicious. But the Imperial Cross was the highest military decoration, and Takishi was sure that Kinoga believed his men had earned it.

"Why are you so generous, Takishi?"

"It's not my idea, Kinoga. Our prime minister instructed me that if you successfully completed the mission, your men were to receive the Cross," Takishi said, avoiding eye contact.

"Do you not believe we deserve the medal?" Kinoga scoffed.

"What I believe is irrelevant. Your men accomplished the mission, and they deserve the prime minister's compliments."

"Very well, I will be in the cockpit debriefing the men."

Takishi looked over his shoulder as Kinoga assembled his six men. Then, Takishi debarked and walked to a black limousine waiting near the pier. As he returned, Takishi overheard the admiral complimenting his men.

"You performed a difficult and sensitive mission for your motherland last night. You should be proud," Kinoga said. "Whether you know it or not, you all have taken part in the first of a series of activities that will lead our great nation back to its rightful place. Because of your actions last night, the Japanese Empire will rise again."

The sailors, all hand-chosen by Kinoga, were weathered seamen who Takishi was sure only wanted the best for their country. They all nodded with approval at Kinoga's words.

Kinoga then individually congratulated them, reminding them of the secrecy of the mission.

"Your prime minister will reward you highly for your accomplishments," said Kinoga, facing the table with his back to the door. He heard the door open with a metallic squeak.

Before he could turn around, a whisper shot through the room. Kinoga fell forward at his men's feet, bleeding from the skull.

Standing in the doorway was Takishi, holding a silenced machine gun at his side.

He smiled and finished his business, killing the rest of the crew.

"And it is good you are not in my line of work, Admiral," he said, stepping over the bodies.

Leaning over the admiral's corpse, he whispered to the man's lifeless face, "Politics? This is about national survival, my dear friend."

Takishi, who had been given the codename, "Charlie Watts," pulled out his satellite-enabled phone and sent a text message to his contact, who had demanded he use the ridiculous alias, "Mick Jagger."

Satisfaction.

A moment later "Mick Jagger" sent a return note:

Let it bleed.

Indeed, Takishi laughed. *But not how you might think.*

Takishi boarded his Shin Meiwa as the men in the black limousine moved to dispose of the attack boat.

CHAPTER 5

Immediately after slaughtering Kinoga and his crew, Takishi flew nearly twelve hundred miles from Yonaguni to Davao City, Mindanao, to meet quickly with the Abu Sayyaf leader there.

Now, he stooped and stepped down the ladder of the Shin Meiwa airplane. With its upgraded Japanese computer avionics and GPS technology, the craft was perfect for Takishi's purposes.

As he stood on the steaming runway, the bright sunlight and intense Mindanao heat rapped him in the face. He was tired from the previous night's seafaring activities and the humidity further sucked his strength. Yet, he was more at home here than bouncing around the cockpit of Kinoga's attack boat. Dismissing the memory of killing the admiral and his men, Takishi focused on his next task. *So much to do.*

Meeting Takishi on the tarmac was Commander Douglas Villanueva, a snake-eyed man who led the entire Al Qaeda sub unit of Abu Sayyaf in the Philippines, having engineered several attacks and kidnappings of Western aid workers and U.S. military personnel over the past decade. The more spectacular, the better, because Al Qaeda money would pour into the Abu Sayyaf coffers once they were able to post onto the Internet the images of death and destruction. Villanueva was unusually tall for a Filipino, nearly six feet, and he wore an Australian bush hat with one side flipped up. Takishi looked at him and thought the man at least had some style.

That an emerging Muslim extremist terror network existed in that remote southern isle of the Philippine archipelago was no surprise to Takishi. He knew that Al Qaeda was seeking areas that lacked governance, and the hundreds of islands that constituted the Republic of the Philippines were nearly impossible to govern effectively. The remote islands presented the perfect sanctuary ingredients: desperate, uneducated peasants, isolated terrain, and clandestine routes of ingress and egress. The ingredients were perfect for Takishi's plan as well.

His sunglasses shielded his eyes from the bright sun and the Filipino commander. The prop wash from the four propellers of the Shin Meiwa blew hot air against his back as he bowed. Fortunately, Takishi had worn his lightweight khakis for his final meeting with the Al Qaeda knockoff group.

Villanueva returned the bow and said in broken English, "Good news. But first, Takishi, I should show you our plans for the entire operation again."

"I only have a few minutes, Villanueva, but I wanted to make sure all was on track."

"Yes, yes, no problem," Villanueva said quickly with a heavy accent. "All operations are no problem. All good. Good news, too."

"What news?"

"We have destroyed two ranger C-130 airplanes. My deputy, Pascual, is securing them now."

Takishi reflected a moment, glad his eyes were hidden by sunglasses. *The Rolling Stones work quickly*, he mused.

"Yes, that is good news. Do you have all of the information and ammunition you require?"

"We have most of what we need. Luzon will attack the Subic ammo point. No problem. They get the ammo from Subic for us and to keep the Americans from having it. No problem."

"Okay, you run your operation however you see fit. I'm here to make sure you have what you need. And congratulations on the victory."

"No problem. And Takishi, I have been inspecting your operation as well. It appears you have no problems also?"

Takishi lowered his sunglasses and stared at Villanueva, whose face was rigid with sincerity.

"No problems." Takishi smiled.

He offered his hand to the Filipino as they approached his aircraft.

"Yes, it is all good. And remember, Villanueva…"

"Yes?"

"When you are done, you will be justly rewarded. Perhaps president?"

"We want Muslim nation; that is all." Villanueva appeared nonplussed.

"One final thing," Takishi said.

"Yes? But hurry, I must meet with Pascual."

"There is an American somewhere on this island. It would be good to catch him and…do as you please with him." Takishi looked down the long runway, away from Villanueva, wondering if they caught the significance of what he was saying. "Matt Garrett. He's CIA. He may have a jump mission tonight."

"I understand, Takishi," Villanueva said. "We will capture this man and make an example out of him."

"But no other Americans, clear?"

"No problems," Villanueva smiled.

Takishi bid Villanueva farewell and boarded his plane. He fit a set of headphones over his ears as he sat in a strapped jump seat between the pilot and copilot, and told them to head to Cateel Bay.

The Shin Meiwa pulled away from the runway with a short roll, its four powerful Rolls-Royce engines easily lifting the aircraft off the concrete.

Ascending above Davao City, Takishi looked down upon the impoverished metropolis of Davao City. There were a few modern buildings in the downtown area, like pearls in a rotten oyster, but they quickly gave way to adobe structures, then to the thatch huts that dominated the outskirts of the city. Banana plantations and rice paddies formed odd geometric shapes beneath them, in stark contrast to the thick triple-canopy jungle of the highlands.

His pilot cut the trim of the tail rudder, and the plane leveled into a smooth glide. Cateel Bay was only 45 minutes away, just northeast of Davao City on the eastern coast of Mindanao.

They then flew above the tropical rain forest that dominated the mountains, which cut a jagged north-to-south path over the eastern portion of the island. A series of small agricultural and fishing villages dotted the east coast, where Takishi could see groupings of thatch huts every 12 kilometers or so. Parked on the sandy shore were small wooden boats that the fishermen used for short ventures beyond the coral reef to harvest the rich waters of the Philippine Sea.

He tapped the pilot on the shoulder when he saw the horseshoe of Cateel Bay. The pilot knew the route and nodded at Takishi. They began their descent, circling down from above as the tropical blue hue of the water greeted them. The pilot banked the Shin Meiwa, then leveled its wings parallel to the water. With its protective coral reef nearly a kilometer offshore, Cateel Bay was the perfect area in which to land an air/seaplane. There were no waves and the beach was sandy, allowing the craft easy ingress and egress.

The plane skidded as it always did, spraying fine mist in either direction. Another skid, and the water's friction against the pontoons grabbed the craft, causing its passengers to lurch forward for a typical landing. The pilot steered the plane to the beach, where it found purchase with a gentle nudge into the sand.

Takishi turned and spoke in his harsh Japanese tongue to his 18 passengers, telling them to stand and exit the airplane.

They came crawling from the back of the plane toward the side door in single file. Movement was difficult, as each man had his hands and feet chained together. Like a clumsy centipede, they clanked together down the ladder of the airplane, stepping into the shallow water.

To a man, they shut their narrow eyes, balking at the brightness of the noonday sun. They were relieved, however, to be out of the airplane, as the temperature had reached an unbearable 120 degrees inside the steel frame of the craft while they were waiting for Takishi in Davao City. Outside it was only 105 degrees. Much better.

Takishi stood on the beach, envisioning himself as a futuristic MacArthur, with his gold-rimmed sunglasses and wicked smile. He pulled a revolver from his trousers and checked its payload with a quick flip of his wrist. At the familiar sound of unlatching metal the prisoners looked up, squinting in the bright sun. With his thumb, Takishi popped the cylinder back into the New Nambu revolver. Takishi liked it because it made him feel like a cowboy. It was different from the military automatic pistols, and the curved, custom-made pearl-handled grip fit his hand rather well.

He smiled at the gang of prisoners, all Chinese, Korean, or Indonesian carpetbaggers as far as he was concerned; they had infiltrated his homeland as byproducts of the fractional criminal element in Japan. While the black market was a nuisance to the country, these illegal immigrants were perfect fodder for his purposes. Remnants of an overcrowded judicial process, the prisoners came Takishi's way through one judge, whom Takishi had handsomely rewarded.

He marched them off the beach, past the thatch huts of the fishing village and onto a trail that led almost two kilometers into the jungle. Takishi relished this post-9-11 window of opportunity. The Americans' fledgling effort in Afghanistan and their obvious intentions toward Iraq opened the door for geopolitical chess moves that would overwhelm and stymie the Americans. He was part strategic military planner and part pragmatic economist: a modern-day Machiavelli, who would take Japan to its Imperialistic heights of yesteryear.

As they walked, Filipino peasants waved at Takishi. He always brought them packages of food from his country. This time was no different as he had the pilot drop three boxes next to an elderly woman. The peasants were unaware that the food was nothing more than military combat rations. It was nutritional and filled their children's stomachs.

The Filipinos stood from cleaning fish along a straw mat and watched the entourage. Takishi looked at the children in bare feet, their legs dirty and riddled with fly bites. He smiled and waved, though it was an insincere gesture. He had no sympathy for them. The food though tended to buy their silence and this would be the last deposit of both prisoners and food.

They soon entered the dense jungle and followed a worn path up the spine of a ridge to the south of a river that would lead them to a brown and green structure. There was a road that came from the north, but the shorter distance to the factory was directly through the jungle.

Once there, Takishi would introduce his fresh laborers to Mr. Abe, the manager of Plant Number Three, who could surely use the help. The other three Rolling Stones knew about Plant Number One, which manu-factured small arms for the Abu Sayyaf insurgency.

But they had no clue about the other three plants, which built weaponry of a different type.

With things moving along smoothly here, Takishi called the captain of the *Shimpu* and ordered him to begin moving his vessel and its lethal contents toward the United States.

CHAPTER 6
Japanese Weapons Production Plant #3 Cateel, Mindanao, Philippines
Kanishi Abe

Kanishi Abe both dreaded and welcomed the arrival of Takishi-san with fresh prisoners. It meant that his time here in Mindanao was almost over, but he also detested the abuse of the men he transported. But Takishi had arrived and was resting for his travels.

"Unit number seven needs more hydraulic fluid in its lower lathe," Kanishi Abe said to the production supervisor.

"Mr. Abe," Mr. Kuriwu began, pronouncing it *Ahbey*. "We are operating well beyond the capacity of these machines. They are less than two years old and we have exceeded the quality-control time lines on all replaceable parts."

"I understand," Abe said. "We have almost met our production goals, and a new team will come in a few days to replace us. Then it will be their problem." Abe knew his reply was out of character. as he considered it unprofessional to pass along unresolved problems. But this was different. He continued. "Please patch the tubing and replace the fluid before we lose hydraulic power in number seven and exceed the parameters for safe assembly."

"Yes, sir."

Abe walked along the assembly line, watching his robots perform assembly of minor parts of a tank chassis. Wearing a white smock, he looked like the automobile engineer that he used to be. Graduating with honors from the University of Tokyo, Abe had immediately gone to work for Mitsubishi, designing most of their current line of automobiles. Recently, he had participated in developing—hell, *he* had developed—the Mitsubishi AH-X helicopter with the new 2900-horsepower turbo shaft engine.

He spoke briefly with a technician and moved along the brightly lit production facility. Robots moved in short, hydraulic spurts, placing a widget here or a gadget there, and at the end of the line came a tank or a helicopter. The sound of men speaking Japanese was evident above the constant clanking of the assembly line.

How the Japanese engineers had ever constructed this plant was a mystery to Abe. Carved into the side of a mountain, it seemed more like a huge white cave to him. He was impressed but not surprised by the abilities of his countrymen. His particular plant was built into an old mining quarry, and it was his understanding that there were three other similar facilities spread over the remote island. In essence, the Japanese had simply laid down a floor on the bottom and a big roof on the top. But the guts were state-of-the art robotics, pushing tanks and attack helicopters along two separate assembly lines.

He was curious how the Philippine government could afford such a massive increase in their armed forces. He surmised that the Americans were paying for all of it, and construction of the facilities was another "peaceful" way for Japan to contribute to security in the region and contribute to the Global War on Terror. It made sense, and Takishi-san had told him that the United Nations was exploiting the strengths of member countries to create a stronger world that could fight terrorism at its roots.

"Manufacturing is our strength," Takishi had said. Abe did not personally know Takishi other than the fact that he appeared roughly every couple of weeks with 18 new workers for him, mostly foreigners: Chinese, Korean, and a few Japanese mafia. He knew that Takishi landed his float plane in Cateel Bay, walking the prisoners up the spine of the ridge to his plant location.

But still Abe wondered, why the secrecy?

The facility was located in the eastern mountain province of Mindanao just northwest of the small coastal town of Cateel and astride a river that provided waste runoff from the plant into Cateel Bay. He and his production team had rotated to Mindanao from Japan six months ago, replacing a team that had already been working six months. In three days, another team was to replace them, and he could go back to his family.

He paused at a water cooler and drained two cups. He pulled a picture of his wife and two girls from the breast pocket of his smock and stared at it. He missed them. He wondered if his two children, ages five and three, would remember him. He had not been allowed any phone or email contact with his family and was only permitted outside of the biosphere environment to exercise for 30 minutes daily.

Abe jogged during that time, as it was the only real stress relief he could find. He wore a bright orange Nike jogging suit when he ran. That way, no Filipino hunters would mistake him for a wild pig running through the jungle. The Japanese construction team, two years earlier, had built an exercise path through the jungle above the old quarry. It was perversely anachronistic—a modern arms-production facility with an executive jogging path in the Mindanao hinterlands, through which indigenous tribesmen occasionally wandered. The dense tropical rain forest made it seem like the facility and path both were out of place, not that the area had failed to modernize.

The top of the plant was covered with dirt, and tropical growth had flourished over the past two years. The running route was a dark tunnel of trees through the thick jungle, consisting of a circular kilometer and exercise stations every couple of hundred meters where the five or six high-level technicians could do push-ups, pull-ups, sit-ups, stretching, and balancing exercises. At each station was a sawdust pit off to the side of the gravel track, with signs that described how to use the equipment correctly. For Abe, the exercise had become the only thing he looked forward to since his plant had gone to round-the-clock production. He couldn't remember being so tired since Mitsubishi increased production in the mid 1990s in order to flood the American market.

It was nearly five in the morning and time for Abe to get four hours of sleep before checking the nine o'clock shift. During his next shift he would sneak out and relax his mind and body, he told himself. He summoned his vice president of operations and told him to take charge while he rested. The man dutifully obeyed. Abe walked past the constantly moving assembly line, looking at the many tank chassis and marveling at the technology they were employing on these modern weapons.

He knew very little about the military. He was a pacifist, having been raised in Japan's post–World War II era. He advocated Article Nine of the Japanese Peace Constitution. He saw no need for Japan to be strong militarily when they could effectively compete in the world through economics. But he understood the need for other nations to have strong militaries, particularly countries such as the Philippines, where insurgency impeded government headway.

He opened the door to his cubicle of a room. As the plant manager, his accommodations were less spartan than the others', but they were not luxurious by any stretch. Still, he had no television or radio. He was isolated from the outside world. The walls of the sterile facility were as white as Abe's smock and traditional Japanese folk work music from Japanese tapes poured through speakers in the work area.

Before he entered his room, he paused and looked down the pristine white hallway toward the glass door and guard station that separated the living quarters from the production area. Beyond his door in the other direction was the heavily guarded entrance. Abe felt secure with the guards there. Takishi-san had warned him about the rising tide of Islamic insurgency and had assured him that the insurgents would try to steal everything at the slightest sign of a security weakness. It was good, he thought, that there were Japanese soldiers protecting his plant. He agreed that trucking the tanks at night to the port city of Davao was best, also, because it was then that they would be most secure from the wandering Abu Sayyaf bands.

He closed and locked his door behind him. His room was about seven meters wide and five and a half meters deep. He had a bed, sink, shower, and toilet area; desk area with nearly thirty books; and a closet and chest-of-drawers area. It was not unlike his dorm room at the University of Tokyo. Littered about his desk were pictures of his wife and girls. His wife, Nagimi, was a beautiful woman in her late thirties. She had black hair and a huge grin that produced dimples in her cheeks. In one picture, she was kneeling, looking up at the camera and wearing an oriental robe. Sitting at his desk, he got out his notebook to make another entry in his journal.

"April 2002. I have only three days remaining until the next team arrives to plant number three. Soon, I will joyously return home to my lovely wife and children. I can't wait. But I must. I can feel the spirit of my family every day.

Oddly, we have continued to increase production of tanks at a rapid pace. We are making nearly 20 a day now. I hope and pray that these weapons bring peace and security to the Filipino people and help the fight against terrorists. If in some small way, I have made the world a safer place through the production of these weapons, then I will have fulfilled a duty that I always wanted to pursue. If these weapons, however, only add to the fighting and suffering in the world then I will be ashamed and will, of course, be responsible for my actions. At the very least, I have fulfilled an obligation to my prime minister, and I am happy about that. A new poem:

The path is my way
A way to peace I say
The path is my guide
My temple to pray

It moves past me
As only I can see
My motives pure
To make these people free
Gravel beneath and green above
It is the dove, I hope
And not the fisted glove
That comes flying toward
These people so moored
To their misery.

Three days and counting."

Abe closed the book and placed it in his desk drawer. He had religiously written similar thoughts in the journal every night since his arrival. He thought he might try to publish his collection of poems. It was an escape for him, like writing the fabled poison-pen letter that never gets sent to whom it is directed—at least it makes me feel better, he thought. He walked to the sink area and washed his face. Looking in the mirror, he noticed new wrinkles. He was aging quickly. Perhaps all of the stress and worry had gotten the best of him. After brushing his teeth, he urinated and climbed in bed. He set his alarm clock for 6:30 am. That would give him enough time to wake up, shave, shower, dress, and report for the 7:00 am shift and then go for a quick run. He enjoyed running just before sunrise.

Lying in bed, he thought of his two girls and wept silently. He had to be strong. Even though he was only a few days away from rejoining his beloved family, the battery in the clock seemed to be weak, dragging the second hand more slowly each day. Sometimes, it almost seemed to stop.

When the alarm rang, Abe awoke and efficiently changed into his running clothes.

To Abe, transitioning from the state-of-the-art factory to the path was like stepping into a time machine. One minute he was the classic Japanese manufacturer, the next he was an orange-clad aborigine dashing through the rain forest.

Placing the picture of his wife and two girls into his bright orange jumpsuit, he informed the vice president for operations that he was going for a quick jog. He walked out of the electronic doors, passing the guard, who had fallen asleep leaning against the building. They pulled hard shifts, and he decided not to wake the member of the Japanese Defense Force.

He stretched briefly, then hopped onto the railroad-tie stairway that led out of the old quarry and onto the jogging path. Over his shoulder he could make out the beautiful blue waters of Cateel Bay. The beach had a pinkish hue as the sun began to nudge above the horizon. With a joyous smile, he broke into a gallop into the darkened tunnel of the path.

Today, I am free.

As he ran, he dashed into the jungle and followed the trail until he saw the first exercise pit. He dropped and began doing pushups, his breath laboring.

He slowed when his eyes caught a glimpse of a young Filipino boy.

Abe had had little contact with the Filipino people during his stay in Mindanao. He had read much about them and their history and truly felt sorry for his country's past treatment of their people. In part, he felt good about producing weapons for the Filipinos so they would no longer have to rely on other powers for their own security. He believed the time had come for them to forge their own history instead of always being the pawn of some higher power's struggle.

So, as he reached out his hand, he was reaching in compassion to a people for whom he held great pity. He wanted to talk with them and experience at least some of their culture. He wanted to be able to tell his family about the Filipino people and how they were struggling in a world that recognized only raw power. True to his liberal beliefs, Abe reached his hand toward the young boy, obviously hurt, lying there like a wounded deer maimed by a hunter's bullet.

His next poem would be about him, he was sure.

He heard shots being fired and military men running toward him, as the Filipino boy locked his arm around Abe's neck and dragged him through a fresh cut in the security fence.

CHAPTER 7
Matt Garrett

Matt Garrett woke, ate another power bar and peered through the night scope of his SIG SAUER and tried to assess everything he was watching.

As dawn approached, the forest remained dark. Animal chatter filled the air, the menagerie anticipating the sun's imminent arrival. He also spotted through his night vision goggle, a man running on a gravel path as if he was exercising, which was strange enough out here in the pristine jungle highlands. Then he saw the man drop and do some push-ups. Matt watched as a young Filipino soldier approached the Japanese man through a cut in a well-maintained chain link fence.

Adjusting his sight ever so slightly, Matt was able to pick out the faces of two well-camouflaged American soldiers just beyond the fence.

They must be part of Peterson's team that jumped in last night.

Matt was on ground higher than any of the other participants in this uncoordinated drama, and he could plainly see that the situation was headed for tragedy. The Japanese man could be a martial-arts expert. The Filipino could be Abu Sayyaf. The Special Forces soldiers might be wanting to kill anything because of their loss last night. There were multiple combinations and algorithms that could play out, yet none was what he would consider to be positive.

Just when he thought the strange situation could not deteriorate any further, he saw three Asian soldiers running up the path from the east. They were brandishing weapons that looked like small machine guns.

Quickly assessing the situation, he shot the three guards, who were wearing Japanese Defense Force uniforms and sprinting toward the man in the orange jumpsuit. His silenced Sig Sauer rifle made mechanical sounds mute to the guards, and the three men dropped to the ground, dead. Though as he swung his weapon's sight back to the American soldiers, he saw them scanning with their own weapons. They had heard or seen something and were spooked.

Matt did what he always believed was best to do in that type of situation; he remained perfectly still. If they saw him, they might shoot him. He presumed he had just saved someone's life...by taking three. He didn't want to think of the other possibilities, perhaps that the three men he had killed were simply doing rifle physical training and joining their commander on a jog.

No, the men were reacting to something, most likely the Americans who had cut the fence, which was probably wired with sensors. That triggered the response, and the guards were coming to close up the hole in the wire.

Matt reasoned that if that were truly the case, then they might have remote-viewing cameras and monitors around whatever facility the fence was protecting. That caused him to wonder just what the hell was happening there.

Could this compound be related to the Predator drones, the location of which was his original mission here in the Philippines?

Matt had made three precision kills with his silenced weapon, then watched the two Americans disappear to the south into the dense jungle with the young Filipino and their hostage.

So Peterson was part of a special forces team.

His position afforded him a view of the action that had unfolded beneath him and that of an unnatural flattened expanse of land to the east, his left. He was well protected by an assortment of large rocks and tall pines. The climb down the back side of the mountain had been less difficult than the climb up the western slope, yet knowing Peterson's body was still up there weighed on him.

He tried to understand what he had just seen. Obviously, there were survivors from the jump, and they had taken captive a jogger. Three Asian men, who he now realized were Japanese soldiers, had quickly responded to the breaching of the metal fence. As he watched now, there were about 10 soldiers standing at the location from which the man had been abducted.

One man in particular seemed to be in charge. He was in civilian clothes and wore a pearl-handled revolver on his hip, like a cowboy. An old officer's hat, like MacArthur's, shielded much of his face, making it difficult to ascertain all of his features, but Matt could see that the man in charge was taller than any of the others.

His information on the Predators had led him to believe that China was developing the unmanned aerial vehicles for clandestine use against the United States or its allies. Originally his mission had been to find out whether that was true. Then his mission had morphed into locating the wreckage of the aircraft and any survivors. Now here he was in some uncharted rain forest of a remote, yet strategically vital, Philippine island, and he was watching Japanese soldiers and businessmen move about what appeared to be an old mine.

Knowing he had no chance of catching the Special Forces team that had bolted into the jungle, Matt eased away from his perch and moved to the north, away from the gaggle at the fence.

As he approached the fence on the northeastern side of the compound, Matt saw that there was a sensor wire running through the chain link, and every fifty meters or so there was a solar panel and battery pack that powered each sensor. Matt suspected that some enterprising villagers had probably toyed around with stealing the batteries for their own purposes, so he continued walking along a minor path along the fence, looking for a weak spot.

Sure enough, when he reached a spot that afforded him a view, albeit darkened, of Cateel Bay, Matt saw that not only was the battery and solar assembly missing, but there was a small tunneled area beneath the fence. Either an animal had burrowed underneath, or an industrious villager had evaded the sensors.

Matt scraped some loose dirt out of the hole, slid his rucksack underneath, then snaked his way under the fence, the barbs of the chain link scratching at him as he burrowed. Once inside, he grabbed his rucksack and weapon and continued downhill until he saw the clearing he had spotted from his firing position.

Kneeling behind a tree, Matt placed his night vision goggle to his face and scanned the area like a pirate searching for land. He saw the Special Forces team rounding the corner about 75 meters southeast of his position.

He noticed a rail spur that led to a concrete ramp at the mouth of what appeared to be a large complex set in the mountainside. What looked like an old mine shaft actually was some type of well-concealed facility. On the rail spur sat five flatbed cars and four armored vehicles or tanks. Japanese soldiers seemed to have stopped in the middle of driving what looked like a German Leopard tank onto the last railcar, as the mammoth machine was perched precariously half on the last car and half on the ramp. It seemed to Matt that everyone was moving in the direction of the abduction, so he moved to the line of railcars and observed the tanks, committing to memory every detail possible: six wheels, the two in the middle almost touching, an armored skirt, and what appeared to be a 120mm main gun.

This is the Japanese Type 90 Main Battle Tank.

He heard a sound less than 50 meters away and looked up. He noticed the tall, bush hat wearing man with the pearl-handled-revolver break away from the gathering and begin walking to the east with two armed personnel.

Interesting.

Matt backed toward the fence, stepping past generators and telescoping lights like one might see at a Little League facility in the middle of a cornfield in Iowa. As he reached the perimeter fence, Matt followed the pearl-handled-revolver man in parallel and watched as they exited a small gate that was guarded by at least four soldiers. He had moved along the fence about 200 meters from where he had started. Not wanting to lose time by heading back to where he had gained entrance to the compound, Matt retrieved his Leatherman and cut the fence. He pushed out a small section, scooted through it, then pushed the section back in, as if someone had just cut his way *into* the compound.

A siren immediately began wailing in the background, and searchlights, those telescoping lights, began crisscrossing as if he were a prisoner escaping from Alcatraz. Behind him he heard the harsh commands of a Japanese guard team. His sense was that they had a general idea of his location but did not yet have a bead on him.

The trail on which he ran pushed him in a due easterly direction, and he could at last hear the water of Cateel Bay lapping at the shore. Two shots ricocheted through the leaves above his head. *Probing. Spray and pray. They did not have a fix on him yet,* he thought.

He reached the beach, kneeling next to some chest-high scrub. Thankfully, he was in superb physical condition and his breathing remained calm. He smelled the faint odor of dead fish, as if he was near an area where they were either dumped, cleaned, or both.

Matt heard the men's footsteps a few feet from his hiding place. They were talking in Japanese.

"I'm getting a report of another break-in."

"Have the defenses go to full alert. We cannot afford a compromise at this point." There was a rustling as one man seemed to move away.

"Where are you going?" asked the other.

"I told you. To refuel and to inspect the fleet. I have already called for another engineer to take Abe's place. I will talk to Villanueva about him. Abe is not to survive. Clear?"

The conversation continued, but a coughing airplane engine drowned the voices.

Matt looked all around, then into the bay, and for the first time he noticed the float plane sitting about 10 meters to his front. The tail of the airplane faced the beach and the prop wash blew directly onto him.

He looked to the west along the trail he had traveled and saw the faint beam of flashlights sweeping and the disturbing sound of search dogs barking.

Operating mostly on instinct, Matt took his next steps under cover of the sputtering engine. He tightened his rucksack on his back and moved parallel with the shoreline until he could enter the water near a grouping of Bangka boats. As he stepped into the bay, he could see the three men handling the small Zodiac boat, and by then all four turbo propellers of the airplane were spinning loudly. Matt waded behind a Bangka boat in which he had placed his rucksack and rifle. To the naked eye, the boat would appear to be drifting slowly toward the airplane, as Matt's shoulders were just above the level of the warm water, but his head was below the rim of the boat.

As he entered the backwash area of the plane's propellers, he was blasted with salt water and hot air. He grabbed his ruck and rifle and pulled himself up onto the floatplane's landing gear well.

He released the Bangka boat and it blew onto the beach. Matt could still see the Zodiac making its way to the starboard side of the aircraft, so in one deft movement, he leapt inside the port cargo door and rolled to the floor. He brought his weapon up to eye level but only saw the darkened hull of an airplane and an open cockpit door.

In his periphery, he saw the Zodiac approach. He hid behind two pallets of combat rations in the rear of the plane.

The tall man with the pearl-handled revolver boarded and strode to the cockpit, where he entered and took a seat.

Matt saw the man's head swing around and stare at the rear of the airplane, directly at him. Matt tensed as he watched the Japanese man step out of the cockpit and walk toward him. The man pulled a long knife from a sheath opposite his holster as Matt cradled the SIG SAUER, his trigger finger firmly in place.

The two pallets were about five feet high, filled with tan boxes of rations and other supplies. As Matt pressed his body into the back of the pallet, trying to make himself as small and invisible as possible, he noticed that flexible white binding straps secured each box. He was unable to see the man now, save for the toe of a cowboy boot that was pointing in his direction.

Matt felt the pallet tug and heard a "pop" followed by some rustling noises. Soon the boot toe turned in the opposite direction and he heard both cargo doors close on either side of the airplane.

Confident that the man had not seen him, Matt peered around the corner and saw him stepping into the cockpit holding a combat ration in one hand.

Soon thereafter, they were speeding along the smooth waters of Cateel Bay until they were finally airborne.

CHAPTER 8
Kanishi Abe

Upon waking, Abe sensed he was still bound and gagged, his back smarting from a fall and the tips of his fingers bloody and sore. The climb through the treacherous mountains had nearly killed him. The only thing keeping him alive, he knew, was the physical-conditioning regimen he had been doing for the past six months. The same path that had led to his capture had prepared him to survive the kidnapping.

He had heard of Islamic extremists capable of such actions, but he'd never expected anything to happen to him. He wondered if he could reason with them. A Filipino voice spoke to him in broken English, occasionally mixing in a couple of Japanese words. A hand tore off the gag and placed a cup of water to his lips. Abe thanked the provider, using slightly better English. The Filipino asked him questions, and he responded. Still blindfolded, Abe had the sense that others were around him, listening.

"What you doing here?" the voice asked him.

"I manufacture," he replied. "You Abu Sayyaf?" Abe's weak voice asked.

"Abu Sayyaf! I spit on Abu Sayyaf!" the man said. He sensed the man move, as if to elevate, perhaps preparing to strike him.

"What you make?"

Abe told him that they were making helicopters and tanks for the Filipinos so they could achieve independence from foreign powers and fight the insurgency.

"Traitor!" the Filipino screamed, slapping him across the face.

Abe felt others move quietly around his questioner, perhaps pulling him back.

The man regained his composure, though, and continued questioning.

"Japanese?"

"Yes," Abe responded.

"Other Japanese with you?" Again Abe responded in the affirmative.

"Name?"

"Abe. Mister Kanishi Abe," he said slowly.

The questioning continued and Abe gladly told them everything. He mentioned the number of Japanese in his plant and the number of plants, as well as how long the facility had been operating. One plant produced small arms, such as rifles and pistols, he believed, while his and two others made tanks, infantry fighting vehicles, and attack helicopters. He kept reiterating that the weapons had been ordered by the recognized government of the Philippines. At least that is what Mr. Takishi had told him.

Abe simply did not understand what all of the confusion was about. Needless to say, he was scared. Despite his fear, he realized that his situation was definitely good material for a poem; something to do with the blinded man groping to see reason.

Images of his family tumbled through his mind as a wave of sadness settled over him. He was tired and hungry, and he had no quarrel with his captors. It would be so simple to let him go. The hand placed a bowl of rice in his lap and he ate voraciously but awkwardly, with his hands still cuffed.

"Let him eat," a voice said.

"I think he's telling the truth," another spoke.

"Agree, but keep him tied up."

They were Americans.

What were Americans doing kidnapping him from his main battle tank production plant on Mindanao? The Americans, as far as he knew, had authorized and paid for much of the construction.

Major Chuck Ramsey

Believing that they had stumbled onto something significant, Special Forces Major Chuck Ramsey had Sergeant Jones set up the satellite communications antenna so that Ramsey could call in the information to his headquarters in Okinawa. They only had one satellite radio remaining, as the other was packed in Ron Peterson's rucksack. Watching the radio operator, Jones, play with the antenna brought images of Peterson rushing back through his mind, but he stopped the emotional onslaught, erecting a barrier in his mind, telling himself, *Not now, save it for later.*

"Son of a bitch," Jones said in his distinct Boston accent, toying with the radio and repositioning the antenna. What had been a consistently reliable means of communication failed for the first time. It was not that Ramsey didn't expect it to happen, because it always did; but the timing could not have been worse. It might be something about their new position, Ramsey thought, but Jones kept insisting that everything was functioning properly until he remembered that Abe had fallen on him during their climb away from the capture point.

"Son of a bitch."

"What do you think it is?" Ramsey asked.

"Don't know. I'm getting power, but I can't reach anybody. Last time I used it was to keep comms with your fox mike when you captured this guy," Jones said, pointing at the captive and referring to standard frequency modulation radio communications. With the flip of a switch, the tactical satellite radio was capable of performing routine FM short-distance communications or long-range satellite communications.

"When he fell on me, I landed on my ruck. Sounded like the radio took the blow, but I'm getting a signal. Can't figure it out. Son of a bitch!" Jones exclaimed again.

"Okay, but the helicopter pick up at Cateel Beach is today. Let's get that thing working so we can communicate," Ramsey said. The prearranged pick up time was this afternoon and then they would be mission complete on their way back to Manila then Okinawa.

Sending his men to perimeter positions in the triple-canopy jungle, Ramsey began to think of options to communicate.

But his thought process was interrupted by machinegun fire.

CHAPTER 9
Palau, South Pacific Ocean
Matt Garrett

Matt was surprised first when he heard the landing gear of the aircraft come down. He had been expecting another water landing. Second, he was surprised at how soon the landing gear had been extended—maybe three hours since takeoff from Cateel Bay.

The pearl-handled-revolver man had mentioned something about needing to refuel, so Matt surmised that was why they had landed. Then, inspecting "the fleet." What fleet?

During the flight, Matt had begun to have serious reservations about his decision to follow them. He was a passionate, driven decision maker, and also a calculating man. Most importantly, perhaps, everyone worked for someone, and he had a boss who was no doubt furious right now. He hadn't sent an update for hours, and he had little to no chance of making contact after his satellite communications had been disabled. Most likely, his cell phone would not work until he got to Davao City.

But Matt had sensed that they were flying east. They had taken off straight out of the bay, he was sure of that much, and he had felt very little banking in one direction or another until he'd felt the landing gear deploy.

He gathered himself and his equipment as they were leveling off for the landing, which came suddenly with a loud report and bounce. Obviously the pilot was more adept at water landings than runway approaches. As the aircraft taxied and began to slow, Matt worked his way toward the cargo door, which he opened and leapt from. He conducted a combat roll as if performing a parachute landing fall. The concrete runway smacked his rib cage and his head bounced slightly off the tarmac.

He stood, quickly assessed his surroundings as the plane braked about 50 meters away, and began running.

He saw a warehouse, a fuel pump, and what looked like an old dump truck etched against the night sky. There appeared to be a single Gulfstream jet parked on the tarmac at the terminal. He was moving too fast to determine the origin of the Gulfstream, but noticed that on either side of the runway was low brush similar to that he had just seen near the beach in the Philippines.

Could they have taken the long way around to Davao? He didn't think so.

Guam? Too far; they could not have made it in under three hours.

Luzon? He didn't believe that either, as they had not banked hard enough.

He heard a voice call out to him in Japanese.

"Yamete!" *Stop.*

Opening the cargo door while the plane was moving had obviously triggered an alarm in the cockpit, but he had chosen getting out over being cornered in the airplane.

He ran across the runway and threw his bag over the chain-link fence that abutted the length of the airfield. He heard several shots above the din of the propellers, and his luck didn't hold.

As he flipped over the fence, a bullet ricocheted off the top post and grazed his shoulder. A few centimeters to the right and the lead would have caught him square in the face.

Despite the pain, he kept moving into what he thought looked like scrub oaks. Unfortunately, they weren't large enough to provide cover or sufficiently conceal his movement. Nonetheless, no more shots came close and he continued to run like a tailback with no blockers, ducking, weaving, spinning, and lunging.

His plan was first to survive…then to circle back and ask some questions of whomever he found.

He found a dirt road and followed it to its end, then sprinted into the woods, which were again sparsely populated with scrub oaks. Soon he found himself standing on a blacktop road from which he could see the faint outline of lights to the north. He jogged in the direction of the lights and rounded a bend, stopping when he saw buildings less than a half a kilometer away.

There was something familiar about this place; either that, or he was experiencing déjà vu. But as he studied the terrain and the buildings, he suddenly knew he was on the island of Palau, about five hundred miles due east of Mindanao. He recognized the road to the Airai View Hotel, where American diplomats sometimes stayed on their way to Australia or other Pacific Rim nations. Matt remembered the road and the bright lights from the hotel because he had on occasion used a safe house in the small village near the airport.

He remembered that the Palau CIA contact's name was Pino, and he moved in the direction of the swank resort, despite the fact that his bleeding was worsening, he smelled like a stable hand, looked like an assassin, and clutched the dog tags of a dead American soldier in his right hand.

If he could find Pino, he could make contact with his handler and alert him to everything he had witnessed in Mindanao.

Japanese tanks on Mindanao and the Shimpu docked in Davao City meant two things to Matt. First, the tanks meant the Japanese had found a way to violate their constitution and produce an army that could go on the offensive.

Second, the Shimpu, the Divine Wind, meant only one thing to Matt: that Japan had a kamikaze mission planned somewhere.

Taiku Takishi

As Taiku Takishi stood at the fence line where the stowaway had climbed over, a spot of damp blood on the top rail convinced him that one of the four bullets he had fired had wounded the fleeing man.

Who was he? Was he just some local seeking a better life outside of Cateel Bay, or was the man connected to the two security breaches at the plant earlier that day? Takishi's instincts told him that the man was not some ordinary stowaway, but he couldn't linger. He had business to do and time lines to keep.

He retrieved his satellite phone from his pocket and dialed a number.

"Do you have anyone snooping around Mindanao?"

"Well, hello, to you, also," the voice replied.

"Answer my question, please, because we've had two breaches in one day and I just had an uninvited passenger on my airplane," Takishi said. He turned and watched the refueling truck pull up to his Shin Meiwa. Next to his aircraft he saw two men walking around a U.S. Government Gulfstream jet.

"Don't get terse with me. We've given you everything you've asked for. That was Matt Garrett gathering frequent flyer miles with you."

Garrett? That's not possible.

"Slippery little bastard," Takishi said. But he hid his surprise.

"I told you. The real question is, what did he see?"

That was tricky territory for Takishi. First, he didn't know what Garrett had seen. Second, if he'd caught sight of, for example, the main battle tanks on the railhead, then Takishi had a problem. The Rolling Stones had been led to believe that they had purchased a small-arms-manufacturing facility.

They didn't know that Takishi and Prime Minister Mizuzawa had taken the funds and, with true Japanese efficiency, created the facilities to make tanks and helicopters for their own strategic plan. That would, Takishi determined, come as a surprise to his musician buddies.

"All I know is he saw the inside of my airplane," Takishi said. *They'll know soon enough what he saw,* he determined.

"We need the insurrection to start quickly," the voice on the other end of the phone said.

"Don't worry about my end of the deal." Takishi laughed. "If Garrett saw anything, he's probably confused as hell anyway. I've got soldiers down there guarding the plant and even a couple of armored vehicles." *Perfect,* Takishi thought.

"Okay, then. Let's get off this phone. Any further questions?"

"Roger. Good-bye."

Takishi flipped his phone shut and continued to watch the men conducting a preflight inspection of the Gulfstream. By needing the insurrection to start soon, it appeared that the Americans were on schedule. *But if Matt Garrett was indeed on my airplane, what should I do,* he wondered? *Is Garrett a threat? Possibly. Do I have anyone on this island who can kill Garrett?*

Of course.

Over the course of the past two years, he had worked on clandestine operations with the man code named Keith Richards, the only member of the Rolling Stones to span two administrations. The money had begun flowing nearly a year ago, money Takishi partly began funneling to Villanueva and his loose band of Muslim insurgents.

Better than Iran-Contra, Takishi thought. *At least the Contras were on the American side.* Now, the Rolling Stones would start a war in the Philippines by funding Abu Sayyaf, pulling them away from Iraq where his three conspirators believed the United States should never have been in the first place. Takishi didn't care what his co-conspirators motivations were, because he and the Prime Minister had pivoted off the American conspiracy and created their own.

"Makes sense to me." Takishi chuckled.

The smile left his face as he thought of Garrett. Yes, he would take his chances and ask Keith Richards to take care of this new nuisance.

He needed the Americans to kill Matt Garrett so he could get on with his own conspiracy.

CHAPTER 10
Matt Garrett

Matt knocked on the wood door of the small A-frame house that served as a manager's residence on-site at the Airai View Hotel. He heard heavy footfalls and the sliding of a chain against metal.

A pistol poked through the gap in the door as a voice said, "You rang?"

"Pino, it's Matt Garrett. Put down the pistol."

"I could shoot you and have you stuffed like one of those bears," Pino said, laughing as he opened the door. Matt watched him as he flipped a cell phone shut and stuffed it in his pocket.

"I wouldn't be too comfortable to lie on," Matt said. "And the thought of your fat ass humping some chick on my back makes me want to puke."

"Now that you have given proper bona fides, I will let you in." Pino laughed again. He was a short man, nearly as wide as he was tall. His thick black hair was cut just above his ears, which were small compared to his rotund face. "Cherubic" wasn't the right word, but it was close enough.

They hugged, and Pino backed away.

"You're shot?"

"Just a nick," Matt said, entering the small residence. "Is the missus home?"

"She's working the floor tonight. Do you need a doctor?"

"I might," he said absently, touching his wound. "There are Americans here tonight, right?" He guessed that the Gulfstream was an official U.S. Government aircraft. The country of Palau had become a U.S. protectorate after World War II, and the American government had just signed up for another 50 years of providing for its defense.

"Yes, Rathburn's here. Are you here to see him?"

"Yes," Matt said, searching his mind for the name Rathburn. He thought he might be in the Department of Defense. "I need to see him tonight if possible."

Pino looked at him with suspicious eyes.

"Here, have a seat," the Palauan said. Pino's house was an odd mixture of rattan island furniture, photos of high-ranking U.S. officials hanging on the walls, and furniture that looked as if Pino had purchased it from a 1970s Sears and Roebuck catalog. *Lived in*, Matt thought.

Matt sat in an old corduroy La-Z-Boy recliner while Pino took a bottle of astringent and a damp paper towel to the open wound on Matt's shoulder.

"Son of a bitch." Matt grimaced at the stinging.

"This is more than a graze, Matt. I need to call the U.S. doctor. Is it okay?"

Matt looked at his arm, and said, "Call Rathburn's assistant and get him over here. Then we can talk about the doctor."

Pino looked at Matt.

"You have no idea who Rathburn is, do you?"

"Not a clue. Defense?" Matt offered.

"Yes, and his assistant is a 'she,' not a 'he.'"

"Whatever, I need to talk to her. My comms are broke. I've got some huge shit to give her."

Pino sat across from Matt on the sofa, and said, "I'll call her if you let me get the doctor."

"Okay, whatever. Get the damn doctor. Hang it on your Web site that I'm here. Whatever. Just get me Rathburn or his assistant."

"Hey douche bag, you came to me for help, remember?"

Matt felt himself fading. Between the lack of sleep for two full days and the loss of blood, he knew he needed help.

As his mind spiraled, his last thoughts were that there were others who needed aid more than he: while it was too late for the dead Special Forces officer, Peterson, Matt thought, the rest of his team desperately needed some assistance.

After an indeterminate amount of time, through the fog in his brain, Matt heard a female voice.

"How long has he been out?"

"About an hour," a man said. "I gave him four full IVs, cleaned his wound, and pumped some antibiotics in him. That he lasted this long is amazing."

The woman said, "I've got it from here, thank you."

Matt opened his eyes and saw a man with a white lab coat walk out of Pino's guest bedroom. An attractive blond woman sat in the chair next to the bed. She looked at her watch. He could see the face of it show that it was past midnight or noon, he wasn't sure how long he had been out.

Through half-lidded eyes, he felt her study him. The wound on his left shoulder just above the clavicle bit at him and helped him awaken to her presence.

Matt opened his mouth and she leaned forward.

"If I'm dead, are you one of the 72 virgins?"

The woman cocked her head, laughed, and said, "No, but I am a Virginian."

"Even better," Matt replied. "Are there 71 others?"

"I think I'm quite enough for you right now, Mr. Garrett."

"Well, with a blond Virginian as my gatekeeper, I must be doing something right."

The woman smiled. "Actually, to be lying here in fat Pino's sweaty bed sheets with your shoulder shot up is not an indicator you have done something right."

"Aw, man, did you have to put it that way?" Matt chuckled. "I'm okay with the gunshot wound, but who knows what's beneath Pino's sweaty sheets?"

Matt opened his eyes again and, though a bit hazy, saw a young Meg Ryan facsimile staring back at him. She was wearing a blue cotton shirt and light blue denim jeans.

"Name's Meredith. You okay to talk?" Meredith asked.

"I need to talk," Matt said, sitting up. "But I want to get out of this bed first."

Pino entered the room, carrying a large pitcher of water.

"Hey, bro, doctor said no getting up. Just no wet dreams in the sheets, okay?"

"Pino, these sheets are so stiff and nasty I could use them as body armor," Matt countered.

"Listen, brother, I washed those sheets two months ago. They are fine."

"I'm getting up," Matt said.

He sat up and collected his thoughts, then fished a clean Under Armour T-shirt from his bag. As he wrestled it over his head, Meredith held one sleeve for him. Grimacing, he pushed his arm through the hole, then stood and walked from the guest room into the family room, where he sat back in the recliner.

He watched Meredith approach him. She had a nice figure and was at least five and half feet tall. *Very attractive,* he thought. It had been a month or two since he'd seen a real, live American beauty up close. Sure, he loved Asian women, but there was no replacement for a girl-next-door American knockout such as the one standing in front of him right now.

"What is it you need to talk about?" Meredith asked. "And why are you here?"

"Can we go for a walk?" Matt said. He knew that Pino was on the payroll of the Agency and other departments within the U.S. government, but still he preferred to keep his information held within as tight a circle as possible.

"Paranoid?" Meredith asked.

Matt shrugged, and soon they were walking the trail Meredith had followed from the hotel to Pino's cottage. Vault lights were located every 10 meters or so, illuminating the flagstone path.

"I need to see your credentials," Matt said. The doctor had given him enough Percocet that the pain was numbed, but not so much that he couldn't think straight.

"Sure," Meredith said. She pulled out a circular ring with about five different identification badges on it. Matt flipped through them. One was for the Pentagon, another for the State Department, a third was for the White House Situation Room, and a fourth was for the Central Intelligence Agency.

"What's this one?" Matt asked of the fifth.

"Pentagon Athletic Club. Is that the one you need to see?" She smiled.

"Just checking to make sure you're in shape." He handed the credentials back to her. "If indeed you are the first of 72 Virginians, then I'm assuming there was some type of competition."

"Pretty sure of ourselves, aren't we?"

Matt ignored the rebuke and asked, "Clearance?"

"Top secret, special compartmented information."

She seemed to know the right combinations of words, and the pictures on the identification tags certainly looked like her.

"Okay, I've been working a project down in the Philippines," he started. Then he told her the entire story about the *Shimpu*, the contact's getting shot, his handler having him jump in to the plane crash, and what he had seen in Cateel.

By the time he was done, they were at the main hotel and had taken a seat by the dimly lit pool area.

"We need to get somebody to Mindanao quickly to help those guys and recover Peterson's body," Matt emphasized. "And the tanks. What the hell could they be doing with tanks on Mindanao?"

"When he wakes up, I'll let Secretary Rathburn know immediately and call back to the Pentagon," Meredith said, worry etched across her forehead.

Matt had lain back on the poolside recliner, exhaustion getting the better of him again. He watched cars over the bluff crawl along the coast road. When he saw a small sports car snake around the corner, he thought of his 15 year-old Porsche 944, an outdated sports car he had purchased at the same junkyard in which he'd found his pitching machine. Having played shortstop on the University of Virginia baseball team, Matt often swatted away his demons in the solitude of his makeshift batting cage in his Loudoun County home. Given his career, his love life was less than he had actually hoped for, the multiple "friends with benefits" opportunities out there notwithstanding. Sometimes reluctantly, Matt always rejected the hook-up only offers because women to him were more than a quick fix. His last serious relationship was a two-year college girlfriend and the ensuing two years after graduation as she moved to New York City for a high-profile investment banker job. For Kari Jackson, the love had faded with the distance. Her beauty and brains had vaulted her into a different, more elevated social circle, something which Matt could not or perhaps cared not to enter. Time and distance had sawed at their connection from the other end, then there was nothing.

Though on his short break between Afghanistan and China/Philippines, Matt had received a message from Kari on his home phone.

It had started, "Hi Matt, this is Kari, and I just miss…"

He didn't know any more of what she said because he had punched erase and gone out to his batting cage and rifled nearly one hundred fastballs traveling about ninety miles an hour. The blisters on his hands had started bleeding against the stained athletic tape wrapped around the grip area of his Pete Rose 34-inch bat. Better to have bleeding blisters than to revisit four years of a slowly dying relationship.

That was Matt. All or nothing. Either you had him or you didn't. And while he understood shades of gray just fine, his personal moral guideposts prevented him from operating that way. He could tell a straight-faced lie to a source he was trying to turn, but deceit in his personal life was out of the question.

Matt's mind spiraled and followed a path toward that day only a few months ago when he had been behind the sniper scope.

Why?, he wondered. *We had them in our sights.* His relentless, haunting conflict over the missed opportunities to kill Al Qaeda senior leadership was overcome by pure physics. His body had shut down, but not before a thought had scrolled through his swooning mind. It came back to him now: *Every time I'm close, I'm moved.*

He could make amends, though. What he had found in Mindanao was earth shattering.

As his mind shut down, he heard Meredith stand and turn her back. She was making a phone call.

"Yes. He's here. I've got him."

CHAPTER 11
Orange County, Virginia
Secretary of Defense Robert Stone

Secretary of Defense Robert Stone looked at his friend as they relaxed in his Orange County, Virginia home. He contemplated what he had set in motion as the backdrop of the war in Afghanistan played out on the nightly news. Bin Laden's trail had gone cold and the country seemed to be on the bullet train to Iraq.

As he had watched and listened to the administration quickly move their focus from Islamic extremism to ousting Saddam Hussein so soon after 9-11, he had gathered three other men to rapidly develop a scheme to counter the movement into Iraq. He personally believed that invading was a good idea, but not just yet. He believed that the specter of another threat akin to Al Qaeda along the South Pacific shipping channels might provide grist to slow things down just a bit. He wanted more time to confirm the threats and finish Afghanistan. Not that he was altruistic at all about U.S. vital interests. He was most concerned with Robert Stone's vital interests.

And they had to be clandestine. Or he'd be fired, of course.

Given his surname and his penchant for classic rock music, he had labeled their group "The Rolling Stones," choosing for himself the nom de guerre of Mick Jagger.

His assistant secretary of defense for international security, Bart Rathburn, had latched onto the name of guitar ace Keith Richards. Japanese businessman and former Naicho operative, Taiku Takishi, had been summoned and handed the cover of drummer Charlie Watts.

Stone looked across at the man he had given the name of bassist, Ronnie Wood, whose participation in the scheme was the ultimate high-risk gamble, given his government position. The men had made a pact to use only their rocker aliases when communicating over phones or texts, but all realized the importance of keeping Wood's name a secret forever, like buried pirate treasure never intended to be found.

What the four men had in common was a desire to keep America focused on the root causes of 9-11 and its associated enemies. This was in distinct opposition to the sleight of hand of the likes of policy advisors and media pundits, Saul Fox and Dick Diamond, who were using the attacks on America as a causus belli in Iraq.

With Rathburn in Palau and Takishi already on the ground in the Philippines, Stone was confident that the plan was off to a good start. He puffed on his cigar, looking at Ronnie Wood sitting across from him. The floor-to-ceiling windows provided a view of rolling terrain that somewhere on the horizon gave way to James Madison's Montpelier.

Ronnie Wood returned Stone's gaze as if he was awaiting a status report. The tune "Wild Horses" played in the background, the real Mick Jagger belting out "...*couldn't drag me away...*"

They each took a sip of a local Merlot from Donna Kendall Farms, the best winery in Virginia. A bowl of venison jerky sat on the mahogany Queen Elizabeth table between their two burgundy leather chairs that were canted inward at 45 degree angles. They faced a stone hearth fireplace, handcrafted with rocks from the Rappahannock River. A musket hung on brass hooks above the mantel. A bugle and powder horn adorned either side of the cavernous fire pit, hanging like Christmas stockings. Stone broke the silence.

"Takishi seemed to take the news of Garrett's presence in stride, no?"

"A little too cool for school," Wood said.

"Takishi's good. Bart Rathburn vouches for him," Stone said.

"I was never sure about bringing in Takishi," Wood said.

"Needed him. No doubt about it. Where would we be without him?" Stone asked.

"That remains to be seen," Wood said.

Stone paused, considered the comment and decided upon a new line of discussion.

"So the first phase has gone okay, true?" he said.

"Well, we've got Matt Garrett right where we want him," Wood said.

"True, true," Stone noted. He swirled the merlot as he stared through the windows of his Orange County estate. Two bay windows framed the fireplace, giving him a view of the distant Blue Ridge Mountains. Dozens of ash, oak, and birch trees dominated his prominent grounds.

"Just a brief conversation with Takishi and, I mean, wow, Garrett is perfect. He's all pissed off about being pulled out of Pakistan…"

"He was close, you know," Stone said. "And I would know."

The man hiding behind the moniker Ronnie Wood agreed. "This is really all about Iran, in my point of view."

"Agreed. If we dismantle Iraq, Iran becomes the Middle East power with nothing to balance it."

"Without balance of power in the middle east, we're screwed. Nuclear Armageddon is not far behind," Wood said.

"Roger that," Stone said.

"There's the blackmail from Fox, of course, which has my attention, also. Garrett's a good operator. Part of me hates to see him used in this fashion."

"It was just one move. Fox has his limits and he works for me," Stone said. "Besides, don't you think this continuous thread of insecurity has given us some wiggle room, so to speak? I mean, if we had crushed Al Qaeda, would we be able to use the notion of a global threat for our purposes in the Philippines right now? It preserves our flexibility."

"Yes, but it is this same strategic flexibility that has allowed the notion of invading Iraq to gather momentum. One move always leads to another. For every action, there is a reaction, and so on," Wood said. "For example, Garrett is pissed off now, which turns out to be a good thing. But tomorrow, who knows? Thankfully, Takishi's on to him. Garrett's the one guy who could blow this whole thing up for us."

"Yes, a good thing," Stone said. "Rathburn will get him up to Manila and feed him back into this thing. He won't stand a chance. You get his reports?"

"Yes. Not sure what to make of the Japanese tanks he reported. Takishi says that it was just his security. What do you think? I mean we only paid for small arms for the insurgents, right? Takishi's job was to manufacture enough rifles and rocket launchers to support a full-scale insurgency in the Philippines. To boot, we didn't sell enough Predators to China to finance tank production. I have two thoughts, though. First, they may have gotten the money from somewhere else. Second, what the hell do they need tanks for?"

"I don't know, but here's how we'll proceed. We need to keep the man-ufacturing bit secret. We don't need any attention on site, like satellites or press. But we do need to get some media coverage of this insurgency, con-nect it to Al Qaeda and show how the real threat is in the Pacific."

"We can do a press conference saying that we've started diplomatic, informational, military, and economic initiatives in the Philippines," Wood said. "It's the Asian arm of Operation Enduring Freedom. We'll call it OEF-P as opposed to OEF-A for Afghanistan."

"That's good. The eastern anchor of Bin Laden's Caliphate. Plus, tur-bulence for the Asian markets would not be good for our economy. Not to mention China, North Korea, and Taiwan in that general vicinity. It's a freaking powder keg."

"All that combined should make the case that Iraq is a red herring," Wood said.

"We can't forget to mention that we had some soldiers killed there," Stone said.

"Yeah, almost forgot," Wood agreed. "Peterson, right?"

"Think so. Might be Patterson. Anyway, what do we do with Garrett?" Stone asked.

"What if his cover is blown?"

"While he's there?" Stone asked. And answered, "Not a bad idea."

"I wasn't making a proposal, Bob," Wood added. "He could wind up dead."

"That works for us too," Stone said. "A dead Matt Garrett becomes a martyr for the cause. Woe is us. We pulled out of Afghanistan too early. Al Qaeda got away. We found them again in the Philippines. Now our number one Al Qaeda hunter has been killed. And our other problem goes away: he can't talk about being pulled off that shot in Pakistan." Stone theatrically waved his hands as he talked, as if he were rolling out one point after another.

"I don't know," Wood said, tapping his lip with his finger. He crossed his legs and sat back, sipping his Syrah and popping a bite of venison jerky into his mouth. Then he laughed. "You're crazy enough to do this, aren't you, Bob? We're talking about a bona-fide American hero like he's a chess piece."

"Well, that's because he is. We need the flexibility to pin all of this on him if it goes south," Stone said, concluding the point. "You can't abandon us now."

"No, but a dead Matt Garrett, other than through legitimate means, like combat, was never part of the bargain."

Stone moved past his partner's objection.

"Okay, so our next move is to get some forces flowing to the Philippines and that's my job. So, I've got that ammo detail I mentioned that is about to kick off. They'll be leaving shortly under the guise of OEF-P," Stone said. "I'll do a press conference later today and announce Patterson was killed, express our sorrow, the usual tap dance. Hold him up as a hero and our game changer. If Garrett is killed, then I think that seals it."

"We're running on the edge of a razor blade, Bob. We don't get this right--" Wood said.

"—we're all screwed."

Secretary of Defense Robert Stone had made the hour-long trip from his estate to the Pentagon. Now he stood at the podium in the Pentagon pressroom. The round Department of Defense symbol hung on the laminated wood of the lectern and another one hung behind Stone on the wall. If the camera were to move in for a close-up, there would be no confusion.

"I've received many questions from the media in the last few days about some recent developments in the Philippines and about Operation Anaconda and other U.S. and international actions in Afghanistan. Today I'd like to first offer a few observations about the war in Afghanistan, which is going extremely well, then outline our global effort to eradicate terrorism, which is taking shape not only in Afghanistan but in the Philippines, our next necessary front."

Of course, the subtext was intentional. As he'd stated, the only reason he was giving a press conference that day was in kind compliance with media requests. He had set up the possibility of action in the Philippines as simply a necessary response to American lives that had been brutally cut short, as opposed to an aggressive act of war by the United States on an ally republic. Today as always, Stone spoke without notes or a written script. It drove his public-affairs officers crazy, but there was no way they could know what he would say beforehand because they weren't privy to his plan. Sure, he let them build some talking points, and sometimes he read the work that his staff prepared for him, but usually what he said was what the Rolling Stones had agreed upon.

He wasn't one to yield the power of his words to anyone. After all, he was the one who had formed the Rolling Stones and their vision. It had been his desire to use more force in Afghanistan, yet Fox had presented him with documents that were more powerful against him than krypton-ite was to Superman. Essentially, he was a bought man. His options were to either lose his job, career, and reputation in one fell swoop, or to be Fox's pawn.

He'd accepted duties as the pawn in late 2001 but quickly tired of Fox's manipulations. So he had pulled together Rathburn and Takishi, two Harvard Business School classmates, explained the situation to them, and they agreed he was screwed.

But they had proposed an option. Actually, it was Takishi's idea. Japan had a few mineral and manufacturing plants on Mindanao and in a few months, if not weeks, they could retool those structures to produce some small arms. Takishi had the contacts that could feed the weapons to the insurgents, who would overthrow the government of the Philippines and voilà, America would have to manage an insurgency in the South Pacific as opposed to a full-scale, bloody, intractable situation in the Middle East. Further, the enemy in the Philippines would be the Abu Sayyaf, an Al Qaeda chain, of sorts. It would fit nicely with the overall theme of their plan. He continued his statement, ignoring the questions that were already firing and hands that were shooting into the air.

"We have intelligence that Abu Sayyaf in the Philippines has become a significant threat not only to our close ally, the Philippine government, but also the shipping lanes, and by extension, the Pacific Rim region. We are becoming increasingly concerned with the information we are getting from our JUSMAG, the Joint United States Military Advisory Group, in the Philippines, and I regret to inform the American people that a Special Forces soldier was killed in combat against an Abu Sayyef cell in the Phil-ippines recently. We will release his name pending notification of the next of kin."

Reporters were now practically howling. Why weren't they informed of the military operation? When could they know the soldier's name? What did this mean for the possibility of war in Iraq? Just how many fronts could America keep up at once? Chaos reigned briefly until Stone called on a reporter with whom he had a brief conversation prior to the press conference. The question was a plant.

"Mr. Secretary, so to make sure I understand what you are saying, can you tell me what the U.S. defense priority is right now? Is it Afghanistan? Iraq? Philippines? Where are our vital interests?"

"That's a great question, Mark," Stone said, grimacing, then quickly correcting it into a close-lipped smile. His public affairs officer had told him to be pleasantly present. Not sad, but sober. Just there. Competent and friendly, but concerned. "Our priority is to crush Islamic extremism wherever we find it and to counter the proliferation of weapons of mass destruction. That remains our priority and is exactly what we're doing. Operation Enduring Freedom-Philippines is our Pacific front in this war."

Stone saw his public-affairs officer cringe when he used the term "front," but it was deliberate on Stone's part. He wanted to alert the world that he had started another front.

A shapely red head from the back of the room raised her hand and shouted, "Do we have enough force to do all of this?"

Stone lifted his hand to his face as if in a salute, peering over the throng of reporters as if trying to see who had just spoken but really giving him time to formulate his answer.

"Oh…hi, Betsy. Of course, capacity is always primary concern of ours. We, in fact, are working to determine how best to allocate the force we have and where."

How's that for saying nothing? Stone smiled.

On cue, a staffer handed him a note and his public affairs officer, Johnny Smithwick, replaced him at the podium to handle any further questions.

And it *was* time to go. He left the press room, walked to the National Military Command Center, and called the Pacific Command Admiral in charge.

"Have you deployed that rifle company to Subic Bay to guard the ammunition stockpile yet, and are they prepared for further combat operations?"

CHAPTER 12
Schofield Barracks, Island of Oahu, Hawaii
Zachary Garrett

"Blow me, McAllister," Captain Zachary Garrett said to his close friend, Captain Bob McAllister.

"I don't have time to form a search party," McAllister shot back in his Boston accent.

The two company commanders sat in squeaky gray chairs in Zachary's office on Schofield Barracks, an Army base in the middle of the island of Oahu.

"I'll give you a lead—start searching near my ankle."

"Listen, Zach, all I'm asking for is an introduction," McAllister said.

"Yeah, right. You'll follow that up with a dinner at a cheesy restaurant, or worse, the O-Club, some drinks to loosen her up, then a quick slam at your place."

McAllister looked confused, waiting for Zachary to continue. "So what's your point?"

"That's exactly my point. I've only been close with Riley a short while, she's an admiral's daughter, and you want me to introduce you to her sister just so you can pounce on her—forget it."

"Look, I saw this girl—she's gorgeous. She is the future Mrs. Robert M. McAllister—"

"A fate worse than death. I'll buy her a one-way plane ticket to the mainland."

"I can't quit thinking about her. She's in my every thought," McAllister said with mock theatrics, his Boston accent sounding almost like a Cagney impression. "This morning at PT doing push-ups—"

"Forget it."

"Come on. What do I have to do?" McAllister asked. Zachary thought that perhaps he was, despite the joking, serious. The two men were dressed in Army combat uniforms and had their feet up on Zach's desk. They could see the Waianae Mountain Range through Zach's window.

"Promise me you will not touch her on the first date," Zachary said.

"Promise," McAllister agreed, "But what if she goes for the big guy herself?"

"Forget it—"

"Okay. Okay. I understand. We can double-date—"

"Yeah right, so Riley can see what kind of morons I hang out with."

"The best kind." McAllister laughed. "Call her now, hero, or I'll tell Riley how you let Ballantine get away."

Zachary studied his close friend and laughed. He'd known all along he would set them up but couldn't pass up an opportunity to give McAllister some grief. Jacques Ballantine was the Republican Guard commander Zach had personally captured in Desert Storm when he'd been a lieutenant. But after delivering the prisoner to the interrogators, Zach had learned that the fabled commander had been released in a prisoner exchange shortly after the cease-fire.

"I'll call her tonight, now beat it."

"No, I'll let *her* do that." McAllister laughed, stepping out of Zachary's office. He successfully dodged the brass paperweight that flew past his head and struck the adjacent wall.

"Get out of here!" Zachary yelled.

"Call me tonight," McAllister said as he walked across the lanai and into the Hawaiian afternoon heat.

Zachary and his company had been back in garrison nearly a week after an arduous field-training exercise and relaxing company party at the beach. Even though he had no family on the islands—he was divorced—it was nice to be able to enjoy "the Rock," as he called the island of Oahu. Zachary was a little over six feet, with dark brown hair. Despite the square jaw and green eyes, when his tan was deep the locals sometimes confused him with one of their own. Regardless, he associated well with the native Hawaiians.

He was a few years older than most of his fellow company commanders because he had taken a break in service. Graduating from West Point in 1989, he had seen combat duty in early 1991, fighting with the 101st Airborne Division in Operation Desert Storm. After a few years of peacekeeping duty in the mid 1990s, Zachary had taken a slot in the Army reserves and pursued some civilian interests. He had earned a master's degree in business from the University of Virginia before trying his hand at farming on the family property just north of Charlottesville. With no combat in the offing, Zachary had resigned himself to life on the farm.

The Army had already cost him a marriage. Glancing at the photo of his daughter sitting on his desk, Zach recalled how he had completely focused on hanging on to the thread of a relationship with her when one day, she had just quit communicating. His efforts toward Amanda had been so all-encompassing that they had prevented Zachary from developing any meaningful adult relationships.

But still, he kept trying.

Then, on the way out of his divorce hearing, he had met a child psychiatrist from Charlotte, Riley Dwyer, who was now coming to visit Zach in Hawaii for a week.

"Coming to see me or Diamond Head?" he had asked, smiling into the phone.

"You have rattlesnakes, there?" Riley asked in mock horror.

"Those are diamondbacks—wait a minute."

"I had no idea Hawaii was so dangerous," Riley joked.

"Just get your pretty face over here." He laughed. "It's been a while."

"It has," she whispered into the phone.

And it had been a few months since he had spent any time with Riley. When 9-11 occurred less than a year ago, Zach was on the phone to the Army Personnel Command immediately. The assignment officer had opened the gate for Zachary, given his outstanding record in combat and the fact that he had continued to drill with the reserves. The Army brought him back on the active rolls as a captain, which was fine with him. It meant he would have be a company commander, the best job in the army, in his view.

Not only had he been assigned to company command, but the assignment was in Hawaii's 25th Infantry Division, the quick-response force for the Pacific region. While he'd been initially disappointed that he had not drawn what he considered a more prestigious unit such as the 82nd Airborne Division, he was nonetheless satisfied to be back in a combat unit when it looked like there was some fighting to do. Besides, with combat in Afghanistan or even Iraq as a possibility, he would surely get back into the fight soon. Operation Anaconda had wound down, only whetting his appetite.

Sitting at his desk, he opened and read the most recent letter from his sister, Karen. The glint from his West Point class ring caught his eye as he read that his brother Matt was off on another assignment somewhere in Asia, she wasn't sure where, and Matt certainly couldn't say. He smiled warmly, thinking of Matt and the great times they had lived growing up on the farm hunting and fishing.

Zach's company phone rang and he heard the CQ answer the phone in typical fashion, "B Company, 30th Infantry, this line is unsecured, how may I help you, sir?"

The soldier in charge of quarters knocked on his door.

"Sir, the battalion commander wants to see you in his office ASAP," he reported.

"Look, Jackson, if I get relieved, you can be in charge," Zachary joked.

Jackson was a new recruit and pumped his chest out proudly, saying, "Can do, sir!"

"I bet." Zachary laughed.

He made the short walk to the commander's building. The Hawaiian afternoon sun hung over the jagged green Waianae Mountains. He stopped at the battalion adjutant's desk to try to discern the reason the old man wanted to see him. Glenn Bush, the adjutant, was talking on the phone while sitting at his desk, which was positioned in an office just outside the battalion commander's door.

"Hey, Glenn, what's up?" Zachary said, ignoring the fact that Glenn was on the phone. Glenn held up a hand while he finished his conversation. Zachary liked Glenn, who had a reputation as someone who hustled to get the job done, and as a staff officer who supported the company commanders regardless of the circumstances.

Hanging up the phone, Glenn stood up, leaned toward Zachary, and said in a low voice, "I don't know, but the brigade commander called five minutes ago with a blue-flash message. I answered the phone, heard someone say "blue flash," and immediately buzzed the old man. Not a minute later, he told me to get you up here right away."

That was good news to Zachary. Blue flashes meant real missions. Real missions meant high morale for his troops. In the post-9-11 world, everyone was seeking to fight the enemy. With that thought, he knocked on the commander's door and entered the spacious office.

Lieutenant Colonel Kevin Buck was a young battalion commander. The division commander had frocked him from major to lieutenant colonel, meaning he wore the insignia but didn't get paid for the rank yet.

Buck was a short man, only about five foot six, which always surprised Zach when Buck stood. He had his black hair neatly cropped
around his ears but did not wear a high-and-tight-style crew cut. He
had a youthful face that belied his 36 years. He wore freshly pressed
army combat uniforms to work every day and possessed all of the req-
uisite badges an infantryman should have: airborne, Ranger, air assault,
and the expert infantryman's badge. Buck had missed the action in
Panama and Desert Storm like so many of his peers, who were in jobs
classified as "away from troops." Accordingly, Zach knew that Buck was
slightly jealous of the combat infantryman's badge and right shoulder
101st Airborne Division patch that he wore, signifying his service during Desert Storm. Additionally, Zach was just a few years younger than
the "fast mover" battalion commander, making their relationship awkward for Buck. Zach was fine with it, perhaps even enjoyed pushing the
commander's buttons a bit.

He stood in front of Buck's desk, assuming a relaxed position of
parade rest as he reported to the battalion commander. The office was
situated at the corner of the quad that housed the battalion's troops. As
such, he had almost a panoramic view of Waipahu. The commander
had decorated his office with the customary plaques, mementos, and
pictures of him with VIPs, as so many officers tend to do.

"Zachary," the commander said, standing from behind his desk, "we
got a blue-flash message from brigade for you to deploy to the Philippines in 24 hours. It's an ammunition guard mission. Sounds pretty
straight forward. Guard the ammo until a ship comes in and picks it up
in a day or two."

Zachary let the statement hang in the air briefly, expecting Buck to follow up with further instructions. There had to be more to it than ammunition guard. He realized that there was an Al Qaeda splinter group in the
Philippines and wondered if his mission somehow involved the Abu
Sayyaf. He also knew that the Department of Defense had closed Clark Air

Base and Subic Bay in the mid-nineties. He had also heard the Secretary of Defense's speech on the radio. This was good, Zachary thought.

"That's good news, sir," Zachary reacted. "Do we have any word on other missions?"

"You'll get a full mission statement at the N+2 meeting." "N" stood for "notification." So, Zachary would receive his mission in two hours. "You understand that this is a company deployment?" the commander continued.

"Yes, sir. We're the quick-reaction force this week for the battalion, so all of my men are within two hours' return time," Zachary said, looking at his watch. He cursed beneath his breath as he remembered that the first sergeant had just released them for the day. It was 1700 hours.

"Good. Get back to your unit and start the alert. The embassy knows you're coming. At the staff meeting in N+2 we will discuss initial requirements and where your unit stands as far as processing for overseas movement."

"Thanks, sir," Zachary said, snapping a quick salute, turning an about face, and exiting the commander's office before anymore discussion could take place.

As he walked, he made a mental checklist of things to do. They had to be wheels up in less than 24 hours. It was a test of his unit's preparedness; there would not be time to go back and fix things that were broken, either systemic or mechanical. It was basically a come-as-you-are operation.

Reaching his company area, he summoned the first sergeant and the executive officer. First Lieutenant Marcus Rockingham, "Rock," and First Sergeant Isaiah Washington, commonly called "Top," as the highest enlisted soldier in the company, quickly arrived at the commander's office, sensing something was happening. Zach closed the door behind the two men and spoke without emotion.

"Good news, guys. We've got a blue-flash mission to the Philippines. We have to be wheels up in 24 hours. Top," he said, looking at Washington, "I want you to activate the alert roster. The message is SOP. Have the CQ say, 'this is a blue-flash message—report to the unit immediately.' Write it down for the CQ so he doesn't mess it up." The Executive Officer, or XO, and First Sergeant were frantically writing on hand-size notebooks that Zachary required every soldier to carry.

"XO, I want you to activate the N-hour checklist, ensuring we make all of the proper reports to headquarters. Don't fudge the numbers, just give the staff the facts. This is no time to try to cover up mistakes. The earlier we identify deficiencies, the better chance we have of making them up before we fly. First Sergeant, as the troops begin to come in, I want them to line their gear up outside in formation and start drawing weapons, night sights, binoculars, and so on. Everything goes, guys. We don't have any idea what type of mission this is or how long we will be staying. I'll be in my office getting my personal gear straight; then I'll be periodically checking company operations and hounding the battalion staff for information.

"It's now 1705. I have a meeting at 1900 with battalion. I want a quick meeting with you two and the four platoon leaders at 1845. At that time everyone should be here, and I want a written, but concise, listing of the number of personnel missing, any problem areas, and issues for deployment. The first thing I can think of right off the bat is that we need maps of the Philippines. Any questions?"

The two simply nodded, salivating to get the train rolling. Both the XO and first sergeant were task-oriented in their own right. Rockingham was a Virginia Military Institute graduate who had starred as a tailback on the football team. He looked every bit the part. Washington had served as a Ranger platoon sergeant during several combat missions and knew how to soldier. They were warriors in the finest tradition.

"That's all," Zachary said.

Zach turned to his wall locker, retrieved his duffel bag and rucksack, then walked outside. He placed his gear on top of the letters CO. As commanding officer, he was leading by example by having his equipment ready first.

As he was reentering the headquarters, he saw that the arms room was already open. He walked up to the split door, the top half of which was open, and said to Private Smith, the arms-room chief, "Hey, Smitty, need my M4 and nine mil."

As Captain Garrett signed for his weapons, an ominous feeling settled over him. He pulled back the charging handle of his M4, looked in the chamber, then slammed the bolt shut.

As he reentered his office, the sound of soldiers dropping their gear in formation resonated throughout the quad.

He picked up his phone and called Riley.

"I won't be coming home tonight," he said. "And that's all I can say."

After a moment of silence, Riley said, "I understand."

He prayed that she would one day understand. He visualized her kinked, auburn hair held back in her scrunchie, dark blue eyes, and broad smile. He was lucky to have her in his life. If anything, she had helped him deal with the pain of his daughter Amanda's estrangement.

He tucked those unwieldy emotions tightly into a compartment in his mind and began studying the map of Subic Bay Naval Base.

CHAPTER 13
Subic Bay, Luzon Island, Philippines

The loud hum of the four propellers had kept Zachary awake for most of the flight. With the rush of the rapid deployment behind him, he could contemplate what lay ahead. Bound to his nylon-strapped seat, bouncing with the C-130 as it fought the Pacific trade winds over the Luzon Strait and racing toward the forgotten islands of Asia, Captain Garrett mentally ticked items off his checklist.

He had nearly forgotten to give Riley's number to Bob McAllister so that Bob could get in touch with Riley's sister; or perhaps he just loathed doing so. Regardless, his friend said he would "square them away." Whatever that meant.

They were to make two refueling stops, one each at Wake Island and Guam, then land at an old airstrip on the Subic Bay Naval Base. Zachary had been keeping up on developments in the Philippines and knew that there was an Al Qaeda offshoot called Abu Sayyaf, which operated in the island chain. They were closely linked with the New People's Army, or NPA, many of whose members had seamlessly merged with Abu Sayyaf. As global insurgencies went, Zach surmised, these splinter groups probably wanted to coalesce and tap into bin Laden's funding stream. He did wish that the intelligence officer had given him a decent update because it wasn't clear to him whether the locus of the insurgency was on the main island of Luzon or in the southern island of Mindanao. Furthermore, they had received precious little in the way of maps.

Looking at his soldiers, the weight of his responsibility settled over him. There would be no one to check his decisions or give advice. It was a commander's dream, yet he felt a bit like he did in his old West Point collegiate wrestling days, when it was him out there to succeed or fail…in front of everyone.

Amidst his tumbling thoughts of isolation and responsibility, it occurred to him that a West Point classmate of his, Major Chuck Ramsey, led a Special Forces A-team based out of Fort Magsaysay in the Philippines, and thought perhaps he could catch up with him if time permitted.

As the aircraft began to descend, Zachary unfastened his seat belt and stood to look out of the window. He could see bright city lights below. It was an enchanting sight, reminiscent of flying into Honolulu International Airport and seeing the bright yellow lights twinkle from below. The song "Honolulu City Lights" played briefly in his mind until the aircraft took a sharp dive. The movement threw Zachary back against the stanchion supporting the webbing. He held on to the red strapping tightly. It seemed that they were almost in a delta dive, in which a free-fall parachutist tucks his body to achieve maximum aerodynamics.

Suddenly the aircraft leveled with a jerk, and Zachary could see out of the window that they were no more than 200 meters off the ground. The plane then banked sharply, turning its wings almost perpendicular to the ground. By now, all of the troops were awake and wondering what in the hell was happening. The aircraft shot up into a steep pitch and banked hard to the right, pinning Zachary against the frame. As soon as he could, Zachary sat down again and refastened his seat belt. The aircraft reverberated as the pilot was obviously stressing it beyond its design capacity. Another steep drop made Zachary's stomach fly up into his throat. The subsequent leveling slammed it back down into his stomach. Zachary smiled grimly and shook his head at First Sergeant Washington, who seemed to be enjoying the ride. The plane's turbo propellers whined and craned, trying to carve into the night air and defy gravity.

Zachary envisioned the C-130 in the middle of a Blue Angels or Thunderbirds aerial show. Perhaps the pilot was a frustrated fighter jock. He did not care as long as all the wheels touched the ground safely.

The aircraft jolted, causing a loud bang underneath, and Zachary could hear the familiar sound of all of the engines going into reverse. More jolts followed until the plane rolled to a hot landing using nearly the entire runway. Regardless, they were on the ground safely. One of the pilots came into the back of the aircraft wearing night-vision goggles, smiling broadly. It suddenly occurred to Zachary that they had been doing Nap of the Earth, or NOE, flying where the pilots follow the contours of the ground. If the pilot used night-vision goggles, the technique was especially dangerous. *Well,* Zachary thought, looking at the pilot with a wide grin, *half of my troops puked in the back of your airplane, so we're even.*

The ramp dropped, giving way to an eerie darkness as a blast of warm, sticky air rushed into the hull of the plane. The men poured into the dark expanses of the runway and surrounding scrub grass. The airfield was deserted except for the two C-130s, a forklift, and a lone white Chevy Blazer with U.S. government markings on it. Inside the Blazer, Zachary presumed, was his contact. The forklift was to unload the pallets of duffel bags.

Meanwhile, the troops had taken up security around the airfield. Each platoon leader had a green metal can full of 5.56mm ammunition locked and stored in his rucksack only to be issued to troops on the personal direction of the commander. Those were the rules of engagement that had been wired from the JUSMAG to the 25th Division headquarters. Zachary was not happy with it and had every intention of distributing the ammunition once he got settled.

He walked over to the vehicle to meet his contact, his boots cracking the crusty shell of dried lava from the Mount Pinatubo eruption several years earlier. He had never seen anyone play it so close to the vest, thinking the guy would at least come and talk to him. Looking through the window from a distance, he saw a lone man wearing Army battle dress uniform. On the dashboard was his black beret with the silver oak leaf cluster indicating that he was a lieutenant colonel. The beret meant one thing to Zach: that the U.S. military in the Philippines was in administrative mode rather than combat mode.

Zachary walked around to the driver's side to talk to the man, who had not yet looked at him. In fact, the colonel was motionless. The closer he came to the window he instinctively began to raise his M4. Something was wrong. The colonel was leaning against the door, and as Zachary began to reach for the door handle to open it, a hand grabbed his arm and pulled him away.

"Sir, don't touch that," Washington said, urgently, pulling his captain away from the vehicle and turning his glistening black face from side to side. He saw for the first time the bullet hole in the center of the colonel's forehead.

"See these wires, sir?" Washington said, pointing through the windshield at a taut silver wire connected to a small credit-card-like object that was clamped between the teeth of a metal clothespin. Zach got it immediately. Open the door, the wire pulls the card out, and the clothespin snaps shut, completing the electrical circuit, which would then trigger whatever explosives had been assembled. Someone had shot the man and rigged the Blazer with explosives. "Jackson from First Platoon had a report of a local running fast along the other end of the runway. I got suspicious and came over here and saw this shit. Improvised explosive device—IED. Sir, this is some spooky shit," Washington said.

Zach took control. "Might be IEDs around here, so let's move out. Top, find someone who can run a forklift. I'll come back over here with our engineer after we've secured the perimeter. You can get the forklift moving the duffel bag pallets to those buildings back that way." He pointed in the direction of some white barracks huts about three kilometers across the runway. There were a few operational streetlights around them, and he figured that would be the safest place for the equipment in the interim.

As they jogged away from the vehicle, Zach continued. "Have the loadmaster roll the pallets off the planes now and tell the troops to make sure they have all their crap off the aircraft because I'm sending them away from here. Then we will cover the airfield until we can secure the buildings over there. Get the ammo issued out immediately and put out a net call for everyone to stay away from the Blazer and to be alert for other IEDs."

Zachary pulled his night-vision goggles out of his rucksack, snapped them onto his helmet mount, and flicked the metal *ON* switch. It was a deep black night with ample starlight to give the goggles adequate illumination. As Zachary scanned his surroundings, he came to the grim conclusion that his troops were in a valley. There was high ground to his north, east, and west. Obviously, the water must be to the south.

He heard the pallets slide off the back ramps. Zachary explained to the pilots that it was not safe for an airplane in that location. They agreed and said that they still had enough fuel to make it to Andersen Air Force Base on Guam. Zachary thanked the pilots, as the aircraft would only make them a bigger target.

The equipment was unloaded, the forklift had safely cranked, and Slick, the commander's radio operator, handed him the radio handset, saying, "Let's get down to business, sir."

With that, Zachary began controlling the movement of his four platoons, leaving Kurtz's platoon to cover to the north while Taylor's platoon provided flank security to the east. The XO led the headquarters platoon while the first sergeant floated between the other three platoons, keeping the men alert. Second Platoon led the way for the company as it followed the beacon of the streetlights.

As the Air Force pilots were maneuvering the ancient beasts, images of the disaster in Iran at Desert One popped into Zachary's mind. He had mixed emotions as he watched them quickly turn, bump along the runway noisily, then float into the silent night sky. In a sense, he wished that he and his men could be flying away with them. On the other hand, he had a mission to do, and the soldier in him thrived on situations like this one. After the deafening roar of the two aircraft had gone, the silence was acute.

The three-kilometer walk to the barracks was uneventful, which Zachary attributed to the unit's security level during the move. They found four white Quonset huts unlocked and ready for their occupancy, with metal-frame beds, mattresses, and sheets in boxes. A row of three streetlights illuminated the buildings. Zachary had the sapper inspect the buildings for bombs or other booby traps as he searched the area.

To Zachary, they seemed positioned in the middle of a desolate wasteland. By now, he could see Subic Bay to their south. It was not far away, maybe another 300 meters. But other than a pier to the south, the barracks were not remotely close to anything that resembled a naval base. Walking with Slick, his radio operator, to the pier, he saw what appeared to be a more complete facility across the water. Mists of salt water stung his eyes, and he returned to his company and decided to move them another 200 meters to the west, away from the buildings. *They're magnets,* he thought. This portion of the closed Navy base was a ghost town, complete with tumbleweed rolling through the spotlights of the streetlamps like lost children searching their way home.

At that moment, Zach reaffirmed every commander's mantra. *All my men are coming home.*

CHAPTER 14

The night was strangely silent except the low muffled sound of crates opening, 5.56mm ammunition speed loaders zipping the rounds into magazines, and the assorted metallic clicks and clanks of equipment distribution and inspection. Zachary had his company form the standard triangular patrol base. It was the most secure position for his troops since he did not trust the buildings.

He probably could have reached the embassy from Subic Naval Base using standard frequency modulation communications, but he wanted to test the Single Channel Anti-jam Man Portable (SCAMP) radio and saw this as the perfect opportunity. Slick, the radio operator, knelt on the hard-packed dirt and popped open a white metal suitcase about the size of a gym bag. It weighed thirty pounds altogether. One half of the suitcase lid separated from the other and served as the radar dish. It was square and pivoted on a metal frame with four legs that angled out from each corner of the chassis. The other half of the suitcase contained the voice and data sending units. The SCAMP operated on extremely high frequency (EHF), using the Military Strategic, Tactical, and Relay Satellite Communications System (MILSTAR). A satellite positioned somewhere over the Pacific Ocean would receive the message and relay it to the receiving station in Hawaii.

Zachary tucked his map into the cargo pocket of his pants while Slick performed the standard radio-telephone operator, or RTO, habit of blowing into the mouthpiece after turning on the transmitter. He delivered the handset to the captain.

"JUSMAG, this is Bravo six," Zach said.

They waited in the darkness as his men either slept or performed security tasks such as scanning and patrolling. Zach had one patrol, led by Second Lieutenant Mike Kurtz, the Second Platoon Leader operating under the call sign "White six," checking the perimeter 200 meters to the west.

"JUSMAG, this is Bravo six," he tried again, "we have crossed phase-line October and are awaiting further instructions. Your liaison was incapable of communicating with us, and we had enemy contact on the objective. Request immediate link up, over." JUSMAG was an adjunct to the U.S. embassy in Manila. A small military team coordinated all Department of Defense activities within the country, and Zach had been instructed to contact the JUSMAG immediately upon arrival.

"Bravo six, this is JUSMAG," a voice came back. "I'm the only one awake here at the moment. I will inform the colonel as soon as possible, over."

"JUSMAG, this situation requires immediate notification of your leader, over." *No one is awake? What kind of excuse is that? I'll bet that lieutenant colonel with a bullet in his head wasn't awake either.*

Zachary's feeling about the mission did not improve when the voice came back, "Bravo six, this is JUSMAG. Your instructions are to continue with the mission, over."

"Continue with what mission, over?"

"Wait one." After a minute or two pause a different, harsher voice came on the line, "Bravo six, this is JUSMAG six, what seems to be the problem?"

Finally, Zachary thought, *someone with authority.* The six suffix was the designator for the commander, so he knew the voice belonged to someone in charge.

"Your liaison was incapacitated prior to our arrival. We need link-up with a member of your team for further instructions."

"Incapacitated in what way?"

"Shot through the forehead before we got here," Zachary said, violating what he considered to be operational security. There was a long period of silence.

"What is your status?"

"We have secured our equipment and moved across phase-line October. We are awaiting further instructions."

"Roger, I'll be at your location ASAP. Anything else?"

"Negative, over."

Zachary and Slick looked at each other, wondering how long ASAP would be. A warm, moist wind pushed across their faces. Slick left the SCAMP operational as Zachary used his night-vision goggles to get a glimpse of his unit's security. From one knee he could see all three platoons, tightly joined in a triangular formation. The platoons were a bit close together for his liking, but considering the circumstances, and the fact that he had three new platoon leaders, he was satisfied. The sun would rise shortly, giving him a clearer vision of what looked to him to be a wasteland of hardstand surrounded by mountains on three sides and water on the fourth.

Vulnerable, he thought again.

As the morning sun crested the eastern mountains, scattering its rays through the jagged peaks, Zachary slept sitting on his rear end, leaning against his rucksack. He was tired and floated in and out of a dream state, vivid images of his parents' farm in Stanardsville dancing through his mind.

"Sir?" Slick said. "Sir, there's a helicopter coming in."

Zachary pulled out of his dream slowly. It had been a rough two days for him since the alert notification back in Hawaii. The only sleep he had managed was a shaky three hours on the airplane. The rest of the time he had spent making plans, reassuring soldiers, and thinking about his family. His mind rose out of the dream like a fighter pilot pulling out of a dive, spinning rapidly across the Blue Ridge near his home in Virginia, the continental United States, Hawaii, and landing with a thud in the Philippines. He rubbed his eyes and, in the wafting heat of the morning, looked at Slick, who was pointing at a UH-60 Black Hawk helicopter flaring as it landed.

A portly man in solid green jungle fatigues stepped out of the aircraft, holding his flop hat in one hand. His pistol holster slapped his thigh as he ran from under the prop wash. Zachary looked at his watch. 0830. *So, ASAP meant three hours.*

Some of Zachary's soldiers challenged him before allowing him to enter the perimeter, and by the time the Lieutenant Colonel stood before Zachary, he was fuming.

Zachary saw his nametape read "Fraley." Lieutenant Colonel Fraley stood there in front of him with all of his soldiers watching in the dawn mist. Finally, it occurred to Zachary that Fraley was awaiting a salute.

Sure, give this dude a sniper check. Zachary smiled, then snapped a sharp salute. The overweight lieutenant colonel performed a sloppy half-salute. Zach smirked and considered it the lieutenant colonel's good fortune that none of his men had shot him as he blew into their perimeter. He was doubtless a garrison officer. He had a thick, bushy mustache that hung over teeth stained from smoking, and his hair, while balding, was long by Army standards.

Earlier, Second Lieutenant Andy Taylor, going by the call sign "Red Six," and his First Platoon had moved back to the airstrip where the colonel had been shot to secure the body they had left behind. Taylor had radioed back that the vehicle and the body were nowhere to be found.

"Whaddya mean you don't have the body?" Fraley lashed out at Zachary in the middle of his company perimeter, troops watching.

"Sir, the vehicle was rigged with explosives. My immediate concern was for the safety of my troops," Zachary responded with authority.

"You ever think he might still be alive?" Fraley barked, his mustache catching spittle as he talked. Zachary looked awkwardly at the man, then his own soldiers, who were hovering around the two men and staring at the ground. He had always followed the leadership maxim to "praise in public and punish in private," but he kept his thoughts to himself.

"And who the hell do you think you are sending those two airplanes away? They were supposed to backhaul some equipment."

Zachary did not feel badly about his call on that score. He was keeping his men safe, and he might have saved the government two airplanes. But the dead colonel was another matter. He was sure that man had a family somewhere and would at least want a proper burial, and he felt a pang of guilt. However, he took consolation in the fact that he still had all of his troops and remained poised despite Fraley's ranting.

"I'm calling your division commander and telling him not to send another hothead commander in charge of a ragtag unit to my islands," Fraley said, launching rockets of spit at Zachary.

"Sir, any intel you think you can give us in light of what happened last night?" Zachary asked, ignoring the rebuke.

"Your clearance ain't high enough, son. Now move your shit into those buildings, lock up your ammo, and don't breathe unless I tell you to," Fraley ordered. "The ammo's over there, and the boat will be here tomorrow to pick it up. Not hard, Captain."

"Sir—"

"At ease, soldier. Come down here itching for a fight, are ya?" Fraley said. "Well, you just better back off it, son, and do exactly what I tell you to do. Are you sure you saw a dead body, I'm beginning to wonder—"

"Yes, sir. I'm positive." He couldn't stay quiet any longer. "Sir, I've stood here and listened to you rag me out in front of my troops, but I will not allow you to question my integrity," Garrett shot back.

Fraley did not budge.

"Listen here, Captain. This ain't no game, and you ain't in charge. I'll have your ass locked up for insubordination next time you talk to me like that."

Zach stared at the officer. It was easy. He decided to employ the method of voluntary disobedience; in short, he would do exactly the opposite of what the colonel had told him not to do.

As Fraley remounted the Black Hawk, Slick looked at the commander, holding the radio handset in one hand and his M4 in the other, saying, "Boy, what an asshole," he said.

Fraley's head turned, as if he heard Slick.

"You said it, my friend," Zachary said to Slick, who knelt back down and continued to monitor the SCAMP, his FM radio, and the phone line that he had run to each platoon command post.

Zachary watched as the Black Hawk pulled away from the ground, sucking twigs and dirt into the air and spitting them back down upon his troops as the pilot flew low over his company perimeter, blowing hot dirt onto the men.

"Go to hell," Zachary said under his breath, watching the aircraft fly away. Slick looked up at his commander and smiled, as did some of the other headquarters platoon troops who had overheard the ass chewing. Nobody gave their commander shit and got away with it. They were sure of that.

He called his platoon leaders and platoon sergeants in. This was a time for both commissioned and noncommissioned officers to receive the word straight from the commander. He briefed them on exactly what had transpired between him and the colonel. They shook their heads and offered words of support to the commander, which he quickly hushed.

"Here's the deal. We will only rotate one platoon at a time into the barracks. The other two will dig fighting positions and defend the primary avenues of approach into your area of operations. Headquarters, you'll set up in one of the buildings also, but we will change barracks every night to avoid presenting a stationary target. If we have to, we'll even pilfer the ammunition stockpile. If you haven't already done so, I want leaders to distribute all of the ammunition we brought to every soldier. I'm talking everything we've got," Zachary directed.

As the commander talked, the group coalesced. They became more cohesive as a result of the simple altercation between an outsider and their commander. In all, Zachary figured, things had actually worked out for the best.

"Platoon leaders, you need to sight weapons and give me your sector sketches so I can develop a company fire plan. We want aggressive patrolling within the confines of the base and you have my order to take anyone who appears to be scouting us captive for tactical questioning." He did not know if his directive was within the rules of engagement, but he did not want strays roaming around the vacant, windswept base.

Zachary finished the meeting by saying, "As long as we are in this ghost town, B Company is the sheriff." His leaders smiled and crowed with a few "hooahs," the standard infantry signal of approval. One of the troops even barked out the name "Garrett's Gulch," which would stick. They had to call their new home something.

His briefing had been more like a halftime pep talk at a football game. Indeed, Zachary recognized that part of his job was to motivate, and he was satisfied that tonight he had.

Quickly, they moved out to perform their missions. They checked ammunition, dug foxholes, and determined the location of their machine guns.

Zachary stood in the middle of the activity in the same way a head football coach directs a practice session. He gauged his playing field and assessed his position's strengths and vulnerabilities.

As the day wore on, he approved of his men's progress and was beginning to feel the slightest bit of comfort until Slick turned toward him.

"Sir, we've got a report of military age males moving in the jungle carrying small arms weapons and mortars."

CHAPTER 15
Palau, Pacific Ocean
Matt Garrett

Matt bolted upright in the bed and was momentarily confused by his surroundings. He was in a plush hotel room, swaddled in thousand-count Egyptian cotton sheets and resting on a bed that seemed to swallow him. In addition, there was the blond woman again, hovering over him.

"My Virginian," he said, turning and looking at her. She was dressed in a navy blue business suit.

"Time to go," she said curtly, stuffing her Blackberry into her purse.

"Did you file my report?"

She looked away, then back at him. "I did, with Rathburn, who called back."

"So, can you give me a status of what's happening in Mindanao?"

"Well, I also called the military commander of the Joint U.S. Military Advisory Group in Manila. He is sending a Blackhawk helicopter to the latitude and longitude that your GPS tracker is providing. They have Peterson's location."

Matt thought for a moment. That was good information. He gained a bit of respect for the woman that perhaps he had not given her credit for earlier. She had done the right thing.

"Thanks. That was good thinking. I'm glad the beacon is working. Does the special forces team know where the pick up is?"

"They had a prearranged pick up in Cateel that was supposed to occur today. The helicopter will check both places. Cateel beach and the beacon where Peterson's body is."

"Thanks. What else?"

"We'll discuss the rest in the car. The secretary wants you to fly to Manila with him. It's a short trip, and you can update him on everything during the flight."

Manila? That would put him in the thick of things, he realized. He would get back to his assigned country and could perhaps pick up the trail of the Predators again his original mission. On that thought, he asked Meredith, "Any status on the Japanese float plane?"

"It departed quickly after refueling and has not been sighted since," Meredith replied.

"Anyone check the refueling logs?"

"Let's go," Meredith said impatiently. "You've been out of it a day now, so you should be well enough rested to make a short plane flight."

"Who are you, Florence Nightingale?" Matt laughed. It was a defensive mechanism for him. An attractive woman was in his hotel room, and he had the distinct impression that she was bothered by something. "By the way, how did I get naked?"

Again she averted her eyes. "Pino undressed you…and I'm not sure what else he did."

"Not again. C'mon," Matt said, standing and wincing at the pain. She was flashing a movie-star smile back at him, chuckling.

"Thought that might get you moving. Here's a bio on Rathburn. You two will be going to Manila, then you'll be further assigned from there. We talked to CIA about you."

"Further assigned?"

"I assumed you have a better feel than I do for what that means," she said, smiling.

He looked at his shoulder, which felt okay.

"You really don't remember, do you?"

"Remember what?"

"It's just as well," she said. "Ten minutes. Be dressed and downstairs."

"Okay. One question?"

"One."

"Are you going to Manila?"

Meredith walked to the window, which provided an expansive view of the Pacific. Closer in were palm trees and beautiful horseshoe beaches that appeared as a series of semicircles beneath the bluffs.

"No. I have to get back to DC. I was the advance team for Mr. Rathburn's Asia trip. I have briefed him on everything he needs to know, the trip is set, and I'm heading back."

"You don't sound too happy about it," Matt said.

"How would you like to be the expert on the region and get punted by a bunch of other people who are there for the politics?"

"What people?"

She turned and looked at him.

"You ever hear of the Defense Advisory Committee on Women in the Service? DACOWITS?"

"I'm not even going there with that acronym. And no," Matt said, pulling his washed and pressed cargo pants over his legs.

"They are going with Mr. Rathburn to Manila, Okinawa, South Korea, and Hawaii on the way back in order to assess the status of women in the military."

"You're a chick, why can't you do that?" Matt was pulling his shirt over his bare chest, but needed some help with the shoulder.

Meredith walked over, lifted his shirt, and slid it over his arm so that Matt didn't have to raise it above shoulder level. He felt her place her soft hand on the small of his back as she used her other hand to manipulate the shirt.

"We talked, didn't we?" Matt asked.

Meredith moved around to his front once her chore was complete.

"Yes. You were doped up, but we talked," she said.

"That's about the only way to get me to talk. Did we watch Oprah, too?"

Meredith laughed. "No, but you told me about your brother Zachary and how much you love him and your sister, Karen."

Matt shrugged. "As long as I'm not remembering stuff, you're in my room watching me get dressed. How was I?"

"I'm not smoking a cigarette, am I?"

"Ouch."

"Time is of the essence here, and you didn't respond to two phone calls and five minutes of knocking on the door."

"So you picked the lock?"

"Maid let me in." She smiled, picked up his rucksack, and said, "C'mon. We've got an assistant secretary of defense waiting on us."

"Who gives a shit?" Matt said. "He's just a dude who sucked up to the right guy at the right time. Give me a minute to do some personal hygiene here."

Matt did his business in the bathroom, brushing his teeth with the gratis incidentals that came with the room. He studied his four days of growth and decided not to shave. If he was riding shotgun with a defense department assistant something or other, he wanted to look either like security or galley help.

As he exited the bathroom, Meredith turned and began walking at a fast clip along the hallway. They took the elevator down to the lobby and immediately walked out and got into one of two waiting Suburbans.

"He in the other one?"

"Yes. I should warn you that he's got a bit of a temper."

"That doesn't bother me," Matt said, a confused look on his face.

"Then what does?"

"That you're not going."

Matt's compliment seemed to stagger her for a moment, but she regained her composure, and said, "Thank you. I wish I was going, too. I haven't been to Manila or Okinawa, though I've been to Korea."

"Just been awhile since I've seen a beautiful woman." Matt smiled. He followed up his awkward comment with, "Do me a favor. When you get to DC, if you have the chance, tell my sister I said 'Hi' and that I'm okay. She worries, and sometimes I'm not as good as I should be about keeping up. Mom and Dad are getting up there, you know, and she's trying to hold everything together." He pressed a phone number into one of Meredith's hands.

Meredith looked at him, then at her hand, and said, "I will."

"But before you do that," he said, looking at her, "take these and make sure his family knows he died a hero, and I want you to close the loop on where his teammates are and make sure that they're okay."

Matt placed Peterson's dog tags into her other outstretched palm as they bounced along in the back of the Suburban. Her eyes dropped to the two metal strips with Peterson's name and other identifying information. He closed her hand around them and held it.

"I can joke around with the best of them," he said. "But I never forget my mission, which was to determine if there were survivors. There were, I confirmed that, but Peterson died."

Meredith nodded and said, "I understand."

CHAPTER 16

As the plane taxied along the Palau International Airport runway, Matt's thoughts reflected back to his foggy day with Meredith. He honestly couldn't recall much about their conversation, though much of it had occurred poolside, where he remembered falling asleep. How he had gotten the room, or even to the room, was anyone's guess. Meredith had probably done so.

He was facing the rear of the airplane and seated across from Assistant Secretary of Defense Bart Rathburn. The U.S. Air Force Gulfstream 5 jet ambled along the runway and lifted slowly off the ground, then banked hard to the right, turning from south to west to northwest as it climbed to its target altitude.

Matt had actually been mistaken for security by one of the female officers on the advisory committee Meredith had mentioned. The woman had handed him a bag to carry as she ascended the steps to the aircraft. Once he saw she was inside the airplane, Matt walked over to a local, who was toying with the auxiliary power unit for the Gulfstream, and said, "On behalf of the President of the United States, please accept this as a small token of appreciation for all that you do for us."

The man smiled back at him with what teeth he had left in his mouth, took the shopping bag, and nodded. For all Matt knew he had just given the man a bagful of thongs.

Secretary Rathburn and Matt sat on opposite sides of a foldout table in the forward cabin. The female delegation was in the aft cabin, which was separated from theirs by a pocket door. Rathburn placed a Blackberry phone into his briefcase, leaned back, and slid the door shut, saying, "They tell me I'm supposed to look happy that I get to travel with a bunch of nosy feminists looking for things to whine about," he said.

Matt said nothing.

"Meredith told me about your mission in Mindanao. Fascinating," Rathburn said.

Matt couldn't see what was so fascinating about a dead American soldier and chaos in Mindanao, so he didn't take the bait. He remained silent.

Rathburn continued staring at him. When Matt didn't respond, Rathburn, "She also told me you were a tough nut to crack. I'm assuming her assessment is based on reading your dossier as opposed to personal knowledge."

Matt didn't like where the conversation was headed. He had believed he was going to get an update on the *Shimpu*, the situation in Mindanao, and the floatplane that had both carried him to safety and deposited him in the lap of a mystery.

Matt said nothing.

"Why don't you tell me what you saw in Mindanao, Matt?"

He paused.

"Sir, I quite frankly thought I was getting an update from you," Matt replied. "I gave a big dump of information to Meredith, and now I'm on an airplane headed to Manila with no update on my current mission. What do we know about Mindanao?"

"We can always open the door and let you out, you know." Rathburn smiled. Matt looked through the gray morning at the dark ocean thirty thousand feet below and said, "Give me a parachute and I'm out of here."

Rathburn paused and said, "We're not sure what's happening in Mindanao. We got the report of the two Philippine C-130s shot down and were unaware that any Americans were on either of them until we got your confirmation from the Agency. I think this was a bit of the left hand not knowing what the right hand was doing."

"How do you mean?"

"There weren't supposed to be any Americans in Mindanao," Rathburn said flatly, and left it at that. Something registered in Matt's mind that Rathburn was wrestling with something, perhaps a decision he had to make. Or one he had already made.

"How do you mean?" Matt posed the question to flesh out his own instincts that Rathburn was doing mental gymnastics Maybe it was just the fact that Rathburn was sitting here with his manicured fingernails, well-coiffed hair, pinpoint cotton shirt, and silk tie while across from him sat Matt in his nondescript dark shirt and olive cargo pants, muscles pushing at the seams of his sleeves, four days of growth on his face, and a bullet wound in his shoulder.

Rathburn ignored Matt's question and paid homage to Matt's CIA bona-fides by saying, "Pretty ballsy move going into Pakistan last December. Many of us were cheering you on."

Why not everyone? Matt wondered.

"I've got a saying," Matt commented. "When you're right, don't worry about it."

"Your conscience is indeed clear, but you landed you in the Philippines. What do you make of that?"

"I go where they send me. But I don't know why they stopped me," Matt said, looking over his wounded shoulder through the oval window. The ocean passed silently beneath them.

"Ever think it might be this Iraq thing? We need bin Laden alive?" Rathburn asked.

"That's an interesting theory, sir," Matt said.

"Not biting I see. Anyway, I'm concerned about something you told Meredith," Rathburn said. "Something about Japanese soldiers on Mindanao. Can you tell me more?"

Had the situation been reversed, with Matt as the senior defense official, he would have asked first about Ron Peterson, then about the

Special Forces team and the young Filipino, then about the *Shimpu* or the abduction of the Japanese man. Sure, the presence of Japanese soldiers on Mindanao was curious, but a man had to have his priorities.

And he presumed Rathburn did.

"They were guarding something. It was a facility with civilians. It's something they are trying to hide. I told it all to Meredith," Matt said.

"Why would the Japanese government have soldiers in Mindanao?" Matt wasn't sure if Rathburn was asking him or talking to himself, so he remained silent for a moment.

Indeed why? And more importantly, why was that Rathburn's primary concern as opposed to a dead American soldier?

"You know, Ambassador Kaitachi came over the other day to talk to the secretary. Something about China-Taiwan. Wants us to put some eyes up there."

Matt swirled the Diet Coke that had been delivered by a young airman.

"Doesn't really make sense."

"I know."

Rathburn leveled his hawkish eyes on Matt.

"Ever hear of *Bridges to Babylon*?"

Matt shrugged. He faintly recalled a movie, he thought. "Film?"

"Stones. Where have you been? Their last album of the nineties," Rathburn chided.

Confused, Matt hunched his shoulders, and said, "So?"

"We're on that bridge now, and it's a one-way road to Iraq. China-Taiwan won't get any traction."

"We could always back up," Matt said.

"Ever try to back your way out of a traffic jam?"

"This isn't I-395, sir. It isn't that hard," Matt said.

Rathburn stared at him for a long moment as if he was considering saying something. Matt noticed his countenance actually become softer, less tense, the way a patient might look before finally talking about that one issue to his therapist. Matt thought he might actually hear the man say something he meant.

Just as quickly, though, Rathburn's face tightened again as he instead asked, "What do you know about Japan?"

Back to Japan again. Matt wondered why. "Not really my specialty. Philippines, Korea, China, and missing Predators; those are my fields, along with some unique field craft." Matt took a sip of his Coke and ate some peanuts, consciously not bringing up Afghanistan and Pakistan again.

"We're on this airplane together for the next few hours. We'll land at about 0800. My sleep cycle is all screwed up, and you seem like a knowledgeable guy. So, humor me and tell me what you know about Japan," Rathburn said with an edge in his voice.

"On one condition. Can you guarantee me that my report on Mindanao has been filed and someone is working that intelligence and going to rescue the soldiers?"

"Guaranteed," Rathburn said, slapping his palm on the table.

Matt racked his brain and lined up some points to make for the man, searching for a logic flow.

"Okay, Japan. Like a country report that might lead to clues as to why they have soldiers in Mindanao?"

Rathburn nodded.

Matt ran a hand down his face, stalling for time. He finally started talking. "Okay, I'm not sure if this is what you want but I'll free-associate. Stop me if it's not what you're looking for."

Rathburn nodded again. "Don't worry, I will," he said. "I don't suffer fools or bullshit, which is why you're still sitting here with me and not in that viper's nest back there." He pointed over his shoulder at the aft cabin, where the sound of chatter and laughter could be heard.

Matt smiled thinly and said, "Well, Japan has a population inversion. They have more old people than young people and the gap is growing. Meanwhile, they've got this economy that needs X number of people to keep it running. Today their unemployment rate is just over one percent. So, we've got a labor shortage in the world's fastest-growing economy. What are they going to do, farm out their jobs and markets to other countries that need the work? Takishi did for Japan just that last year with the China agreement."

"Why not? We do it with Mexico *and* China," Rathburn said.

Matt caught a flash of surprise in the political appointee's face at Matt's use of Takishi's name, but he hid it quickly. "Yes, sir, you're right in many cases; the U.S. has done exactly that with the call centers in India and Pakistan, for example. We do it because it makes short-term economic sense in our almost purely capitalist system. But to the Japanese, who have more of a state-directed capitalism and a circular vision of life instead of the Western linear view, to seek labor outside of the country would be anathema; which makes Takishi's move so…interesting. For them it is like exporting their success while devaluing their own net worth."

Rathburn nodded.

"So then, add that to the fact that up until 9-11 the United States had become economically protectionist and practically reduced Japan's available financial and trade markets by 10 percent in the last few years. The European Community has done the same thing, and they've only started. Nearly 60 percent of Japanese exports head either to the EU countries or the U.S. Chop that number in half and Japan loses one-third of its trade. We've already decided that they can't sustain their economy with current labor projections. So that's two strikes against them already. Remember, the Japanese have staked their entire future on their economic prowess. So in a sense, their national security revolves first around the economy, *then* goes to the basics of the vulnerability of their geographic positioning, which is alleviated in part with our post-World War Two agreement to intervene if they are attacked. Of course, with Afghanistan and Iraq in the mix, we would be hard pressed to assist Japan if she needed it."

Rathburn nodded and indicated for Matt to continue. The plane ran into a brief period of turbulence and Matt looked up at the ceiling assessing whether or not there was a threat,. Convinced it was nothing unusual, he looked back at Rathburn and proceeded.

"Now we've almost got something to think about," Matt said, grabbing the matchbook out of the glass ashtray on the table. The flimsy white cardboard book had the Department of Defense symbol on it, an eagle with its head turned and claws holding three arrows. He pushed up his shirtsleeves over his thick forearms and decided how to demonstrate his newfound idea.

"See, this represents the labor shortage," he said sliding the matchstick across the table toward Rathburn. "This is the fall in trade from U.S. and EC protectionism." He dropped both sticks into the ashtray.

"Now let's talk energy policy. Japan has reduced its dependence on foreign oil much better than most other countries by pursuing alternative means of energy. They've got everything ranging from geothermal to windmills to nuclear power. They have big plans to build 20 or so more new nuclear plants, adding to the 50 they already have. But every time a shovel hits the ground, students and radicals are protesting and blocking construction. Imagine how we'd feel with 60 nuclear plants in California."

"Not a bad idea." Rathburn smiled, the first indication of connection.

"Agreed." Matt smiled in return. "The point is that they have no oil or natural gas deposits, and they cannot expect their energy needs to keep pace with their economic expansion. So there's another match. In fact, I'll give that issue two matches," he said, tossing a third and a fourth stick to the pile with a confident flick of the wrist.

"I've already mentioned that the U.S. is almost solely focused on the Middle East, reducing its security presence in the Pacific Rim. This has a proportional effect on Japan's perception of its own security. The more we pull back," he said emphatically, "the more insecure they feel. More sulfur." He dropped a fifth match into the ashtray.

"Now we can count, if you want to, all of the intangible and esoteric stuff like the fact that they are a strictly closed Confucian society with almost a purely homogenous people. Confucianism operates on three levels. First, Confucian societies have a strong sense of identity with their heritage and ancestry. Second, Confucianism breeds a sense of exclusivity. That is, it produces the closed Japanese society that only someone born in Japan to a Japanese family can belong to. In essence, racist. Third, Confucianism stresses that the family is the critical unit of a society and that government should simply be an extension of that family. This reinforces the exclusivity of the society and also produces an "us versus them" mentality. That equals nationalism. Another match.

"They've been putting up with our bullshit since the end of World War Two. Americans wrote their constitution and set up their government. We have a base or two on their land. While 99 percent of American troops are the best our nation has to offer, there's always that one percent of bad apples who have committed crimes against the Japanese. I think there was a rape in Okinawa not too long ago. So, the wounded pride of having to kowtow to the Americans and the distorted perception created by the few bad apples calls for a seventh match." It fell from his fingers, landing in the ashtray.

"Taiwan was formerly called Formosa before it was granted to China in the post–World War II settlement. It had belonged to the Japanese for 50 years before that. They bargained with the Russians for the Kuriles to their north. Imagine how they feel about something like Formosa to their south. Territorial claims," he said bluntly, dramatically dropping an eighth match into the pile.

"And if we go big time in Iraq, it's even worse," Rathburn said, more to himself than to might. Matt nodded.

"True. And so we've got a Japan poised for economic downturn, minus its former security umbrella, and with some territorial disputes and longstanding grudges against the United States. Its traditional enemies are challenging Japan on the economic level. Korea's pursuit of markets is very aggressive, and China is the eight-hundred-pound gorilla about to rip free from its chains. As you know sir, economic competition is just another form of warfare, only on a lower level. Competition is competition. So, traditional enemies and an unwillingness to mediate historical differences calls for another match."

Matt looked at Rathburn, whose eyes were fixed on his. He seemed uncomfortable, almost nervous.

"Then, there is the idea of *henka*. It's a Japanese process of accepting new, radically different positions. It's a Japanese social tradition. Simply put, it formalizes new decisions that are dramatic departures from old positions, allowing them to change their minds without having to explain why and to completely shift social or personal direction without any forewarning. That accounts for the ease with which they moved from a militaristic society to a democratic one after World War II. Similarly, it accounts for the shift from a Samurai society to the Tokugawa era."

Matt looked at Rathburn, and said, "Governments can 'do' henka and people can 'do' henka. The only constant in Henka is that it always serves the common Japanese good."

He dropped the last match. The sticks crossed in the ashtray, looking like a pile of bones.

"So that is 10, I believe. The only question is, will there be a spark? Or is it already smoldering and we just don't see it?" he asked himself, thinking, then pulling a match out of the book and striking it. The flame burned eerily bright in the darkened cabin of the aircraft as he held the match above the ashtray. "So, do they seek to shed the implications that Western thought set their society on the correct path? Or to do even more?"

"I thought you didn't know anything," said Rathburn dryly.

"I know some stuff," Matt said.

"How does that square with Kaitachi's Taiwan-China issue? That we need to protect Taiwan?"

"I don't know, sir. Let me ask you, what do you make of all of this? And why did you ask me about Japan instead of my real areas of expertise?"

Rathburn looked away. "We've got intelligence that China and Taiwan are rattling sabers again. China claims there was an attack two nights ago. We can't find any evidence of it, but the Chinese Navy is prowling."

"I guess that is an exclamation point, then," Matt said.

The plane droned along and Matt dropped the lit match into the ashtray.

Both men fixed their gaze on the flame, which continued to burn a fluorescent white, then faded to orange. The plane etched a trace across the sky, arching toward the Philippines where a government delegation, and God knows what else, would meet them.

As Matt drifted to sleep, a thought nibbled at his mind, spiraling into the black void that brought rest. What was it? There, he had it for a moment. Something about watching fires.

Some fires were intentionally lit, like the pirates of the Outer Banks who tried to create ersatz lighthouses so that ships would get stranded on the shallow shoals. In their flat-bottomed boats, the pirates would then steal everything from the stranded and defenseless ships.

Was Japan lighting a fire that they wanted the United States to watch, landing the American foreign policy ship high-center on the rocky shallows of international brinksmanship?

CHAPTER 17
Subic Bay, Luzon Island, Philippines
Juan Ayala

Juan Ayala's mission was to kill Captain Garrett.

He stuffed his cell phone into his pocket. Villanueva, his mentor, had given him the word to execute his mission. Ayala had made two subsequent calls: one to his assault element at Manila International Airport and one to his support team leader at the naval base, where he was located as well. Ayala was about half a kilometer from the team that would create the diversion before he personally led the attack on the American position.

As he cleaned the Shansi pistol he had carried with him through 10 years, he smiled thinly at the opportunity to kill more Americans. He had been only twelve at the time an Abu Sayyaf veteran had given him the Chinese mock-up of the broom-handled Mauser C96 semi-automatic pistol from an Abu Sayyaf veteran. As a young boy living in the wastelands of Olongapo, a city of brothels just outside Subic Bay Naval Base, he had come to hate Americans.

He carried four 10-round stripper clips of .45- caliber ammunition for the 30-centimeter-long pistol with attachable buttstock, the broom handle, which allowed Ayala to shoulder-fire the weapon or use it in pistol-grip mode. It had served him well when he'd used it on the stupid American sitting alone in his truck on the naval base. That had almost been too easy. He had asked the man for a cigarette.

"Hey, Joe, any smoke?" he had said to the man sitting in the white SUV. Images of 10-year-old Filipino girls who had turned to whoring for the American sailors had been running through Ayala's mind while he spoke, but he'd kept his tone nonchalant and friendly. The man, with his elbow propped on the frame of the open window, had not been alarmed at the sight of the short brown man with a deep scar running from his right ear to his chin. The fool had shut off the ignition and reached into his pockets, acting without hesitation.

From less than a meter away, without hesitation or remorse, Ayala had leveled the pistol and pulled the trigger. One shot was all he had required. The .45 caliber bullet had struck the *Yanqui* in the forehead, just above the nose, causing bright red blood to spray outward and onto the windshield of the Blazer.

Surprising Ayala, the man's forehead had remained largely intact. The bigger hole had been in the back of his head, where the exit wound had removed a quarter of his cranium. Ayala had then taken his roll of M186 demolition charge and taped pieces in strategic locations on the vehicle. The M186 consisted of pentaerythrite tetranitrate (PETN), a highly sensitive and powerful explosive that he had acquired from the last ammunition raid they had conducted at the naval base. He had rigged the blasting caps so that they would ignite when the driver-side door was opened triggering a metal clothes pin to snap shut, completing an electrical circuit to the vehicle battery. Proud of his work, he had then faded into the darkness moments before two airplanes landed not a half kilometer away. Watching as soldiers disembarked from the aircraft and moved aggressively to the outer reaches of the runway, he had padded into the night, having accomplished his mission.

Killing Americans or high-ranking Filipino government officials had become his specialty in the Abu Sayyaf organization. He had organized his own sparrow squad, and like policemen writing tickets they were expected to reach a weekly quota of either assassinations or intelligence gathering. On that night, he had done both by himself and had been awarded a command in the final coup.

Now, two days later, at 0400 hours, he slid the pistol into the attachable wooden shoulder stock, a unique feature of this weapon, wrapped it in plastic with the .45 caliber ammo, and jammed the deadly ensemble into his back-pack. He leaned over, grabbed his Chinese Type 68 assault rifle, and looked at the 75 men he commanded, all huddled tightly in the dark, steamy jungle just northwest of Subic Bay Naval Base. They carried a mixture of Type 68s, a Chinese version of the Russian AK-47, M16s, and AK-47s. Through years of pilferage from U.S. ammunition storage locations and from their own resupply efforts, they had accumulated a healthy stockpile of contraband. They had 5.56mm and 7.62mm ammunition, explosives, mortar rounds, and light anti-tank weapons. Ayala's men had three 81mm mortars they had stolen from the Army of the Philippines over two years ago.

Working with Villanueva's guidance, Ayala knew the airport raid he would direct at 0500 hours would be coordinated with similar attacks across the islands. An air traffic controller friend had given him a tip that an American government airplane was scheduled to arrive that morning. Destroying it and killing the passengers would reap huge financial gains for the movement.

The Abu Sayyaf network had issued broad guidance and, through the Internet, the small cells scattered across the Philippine Islands had developed the plan to overthrow the central government. Ayala's mission involved capturing the airport and the ammunition that had been unloaded from the American barge yesterday.

His plan was to have the mortar teams lob rounds away from the ammunition dump, drawing the American unit away from the real target. Then he would sweep from the west into the rear of the American position, shooting and killing them all.

Zachary Garrett

Zachary Garrett walked the company's defensive positions wearing his night-vision goggles. His men were alert and wide-eyed, having learned of the American ruthlessly shot through the forehead two days ago.

The ammunition was stacked on a pier to the south of the white barracks. According to a major at the U.S. Embassy, the navy ship had been delayed a few days, even though the ultimate destination of the ammunition was Afghanistan, where combat was raging. Despite the delay and the knowledge of their vulnerable position, Zachary had received no updated orders.

Doesn't make sense, Zachary thought to himself.

He had stuck with his original plan to use two platoons for perimeter defense and let one platoon "relax" in the barracks every 12 hours. The constant movement was designed to confuse any enemy that might want to target them or the ammunition, and it had worked so far. He looked at his watch, popped a cracker from an MRE into his mouth, and continued to survey both his position and the defensive array of his company. It was 0415 hours. The sun would soon rise, and he would want to be on full alert when it did so because "that's when the bad guys always attack," as the saying went. He furrowed his brow.

Lieutenant Taylor's platoon was nearly 500 meters from the command post, defending the eastern approach to the base. They had developed a good defense in depth that protected the main mounted avenue of approach into their position. The Olongapo gate had a four-lane road going through it that the enemy could use to make a mounted assault. Taylor had positioned his three squads of 11 men throughout the depth of the road as it led to the dock area, and they had constructed an elaborate barrier plan to prevent car bombs and such from splitting their defenses. Stan Barker's Third Platoon, "Blue six," was to the north, covering the route that they had taken from the airfield that first night. His right flank was tied in with Taylor's left flank, and they had mutually supporting lines of fire. His sector sketch back in the Command Post (CP) reflected the array. Barker's men would intercept anyone coming out of the valley along the runway.

Zachary was accepting risk in the west along the waterfront. He felt that Barker's left flank could accurately observe any movement into that area and reposition to defend against any attack from the docks. Success, however, would depend upon Barker's initiative, something that concerned Zachary.

Zachary had one squad of the reserve platoon guarding the stockpile of ammunition. That foggy morning, Kurtz's men were in the barracks, most sleeping soundly. Their primary mission was to act as the company reserve, a sort of quick-reaction force. Zachary had them sleep with their boots and uniforms on, so that the only thing they would have to do was grab their weapons, which were in their cots with them, and move to the location he ordered them to. The CP was also in that area, so they could pass the word quickly.

He walked, kicking at the dirt and dried lava that would soon be hot dust in the raging Philippine sun. He had worked on several flex plans in his mind. With no vehicles to move his troops, they would have to run if they were to get into alternate positions to handle other avenues of approach.

Sampaloc Point, a high volcanic rise, guarded the mouth of the bay and dominated the Western terrain just outside the base. Beneath the jagged, cross-compartmentalized feature was a barren flatland that gave way to the hardstand upon which they currently operated.

Zachary had worked on several contingency plans, none of which seemed sufficient. He was yearning for information. He turned and watched the fog tumble off the soundless bay, lifting and separating in the light breeze.

His mind shifted back to the problem at hand. Regardless of the Embassy's reassurances that "there is no credible threat," he did not want some assassin's bullet to find any of his soldiers. If he were trying to attack the place, Zachary thought, he would try to fix the two forward platoons with a base of fire, then descend from the mountains, through the valley by the airstrip, and sweep the built-up area, using the Quonset huts for protection.

He was primarily concerned with his own ammunition situation. Each man had just one 30-round magazine of 5.56mm ammunition. Each squad's automatic weapon had one box of 300 rounds, and each M203 grenade launcher had only two high-explosive rounds and five white-phosphorous smoke rounds.

Arriving back at the CP Quonset hut, he stood outside and looked over at the men faithfully protecting the ammunition, not walking a standard to-and-from guard rotation, but from the prone or one knee, observing with night-vision goggles. They were nearly 200 meters away, but he could see their images burned black in his own goggles.

Zachary sat on his rucksack and removed his goggles. The perimeter was good, but something still gnawed at the back of his mind.

What am I missing? he wondered.

Three explosions answered his question. They seemed farther off than they really were. The sound came from the east, and Private First Class Teller, a backup radio operator from Kurtz's platoon, was immediately taking a phone report from Lieutenant Taylor that their positions were taking mortar fire.

"Sitrep?" Zachary said into his radio handset.

"Sir, we've got mortar rounds coming down all around us!"

"Anybody hurt?"

"Negative."

"See any enemy coming at you?" Zachary hated to use the word "enemy" because he could not define it. What was he expecting Taylor to see? They had received no intelligence from the Embassy.

"Nothing, sir. Just sheaths of three mortars coming—"

Zachary heard a solitary loud bang near the hut. The phone line was dead. Either Taylor had been hit or a mortar round had impacted directly on the underground cable, severing it. Hoping for the latter, he reached for the FM radio handset. Looking at Slick, he said, "Call our friend at the Embassy and tell him we're receiving mortar fire."

Hundreds of thoughts were tumbling through his mind. He needed to sort them and remain calm. It could just be a scare tactic. After all, Taylor said the rounds were not hurting his position.

Another stray landed just to the north of the CP. A spray of dirt, gravel, and shrapnel pinged against the thin steel wall of the hut.

"Net call, over," he said into the black microphone. His three lieutenants responded immediately by acknowledging they were listening.

"This is Bravo six. Red element is receiving mortar fire. I want every man in a foxhole and behind a weapon. Assume a ground assault will follow. Take full defensive measures to protect your men. I'm moving to Red Six's position now, over," Zachary said. Taylor's platoon was First Platoon, and their call sign was "red." Kurtz was second, "white." Barker was third, "blue."

Zach's voice had an edge to it, yet he managed to sound confident and collected. Jogging out of the Quonset hut, he looked for Slick, his primary radio operator, saw him working the SCAMP, and instead told Teller, the back up radio guy, to strap the radio onto his back and follow him. Teller gladly accepted the mission, grabbing the radio and his M4. Zachary first ran over to Kurtz, who was only 30 meters away, having had his men spread out and move into the prone position. The lieutenant had acted exactly as he had trained him.

"Mike, I want you to take your men and move about 200 meters to the west. Have them put their goggles on and watch that area from Barker's left flank to the tit," he said, pointing at the volcanic shape to the rear of their position.

"Array your men any way you want. I would prefer some depth, but you're still my reaction force, and you'll need to have a tight string on your guys in case I need you."

"Yes, sir," Kurtz said, a big wad of chewing tobacco stuffed in the side of his mouth looking like a large tumor beneath his cheek. He spit a mass of half saliva and half tobacco onto the ground. His face was ragged with stubble growth. He had rolled his combat uniform sleeves a quarter of the way up each arm, so his huge, bulking forearms strained the material.

He looked at Zachary with steely gray eyes and said, "No sweat."

Juan Ayala

Ayala's men moved swiftly through the night. They scampered single file along one of the ravines cut into the side of the old volcano. The men wore a variety of uniforms, mostly whatever they had worn to their lousy jobs the day before. Most of them had cinched red bandannas around their foreheads and carried old Chinese assault rifles or Japanese-manufactured M16s from the Mindanao plant. They were grateful to the Japanese for giving them the opportunity to achieve victory.

On the minds of every soldier were the oppressive Americans and how their own actions that night would allow them to form an Islamic nation and also grant them freedom from imperialism, feudalism, and capitalism. Although they weren't quite sure what that meant, it sure made a good rallying cry.

They ran in synch as if someone were calling cadence. At the front was Ayala directing his men with hand and arm signals. The mortars continued a slow but steady harassment of the eastern flank. Ayala knew that he and his men would soon exhaust their entire allotment for the operation. Resources were scarce and the Japanese had told them they did not have the capability to develop mortar rounds for them, having been out of the arms-production business for over 50 years.

Pouring from the ravine, they could see the lights around the Americans' command area. About 100 meters toward the water, he could see the large ammunition pile waiting for him and his soldiers. *Once again, the Americans have underestimated us,* he said to himself.

Suddenly, the lights went out, causing Ayala a momentary blackout. He had been focusing on the yellow-and-white haze, and his pupils were too constricted to gather enough of the surrounding starlight to let him see. Seconds later, the world came into focus again, as if someone had turned on an old television set.

After a brief pause, he motioned his men forward through the high scrub. Reaching the fence that surrounded the base, they quickly cut through it in five locations, using large bolt cutters. The men scurried beneath the fence, some ripping their clothes. One band of men broke off to the south to move along the pier and approach the ammunition from that direction. Another band moved toward the position where the lights had shone only minutes ago.

Ayala lowered his head and sprinted toward the American positions.

Zachary Garrett

Captain Garrett reached Taylor's platoon about the time the mortar firing slowed, finally grinding to a halt.

"Sitrep?" Zachary asked, lying behind Taylor's fighting position, looking down into the bunker beneath the plywood and sandbags that were the overhead cover. He could hear one soldier screaming loudly and saw through his night-vision goggles the blackened figures of two soldiers running to the wounded soldier's fighting position.

"That's Sergeant Cartwright, sir. He received a direct hit on his bunker. I've checked him. Pretty bad leg wound. The medic's with him right now. Do we have any kind of medevac support?" Taylor said in a hurried and nervous voice.

"Slick is calling the Embassy right now. We'll get a medevac here ASAP. You stay here and command your platoon while I go check on Cartwright."

"Yes, sir," Taylor said, his eyes darting back and forth in the darkness nervously.

Zachary told Teller to call back to Slick and have him contact the Embassy and order a dust-off, or medical evacuation, immediately. One of the few morsels Lieutenant Colonel Fraley had thrown Zachary's way was medical support.

He then high-crawled to Sergeant Cartwright's position. The screaming served as an audible beacon in the darkness. The fighting position had been reduced to rubble, splintered plywood, and dirt. The medic had pulled the squad leader from his foxhole and placed a dressing over his upper thigh.

"You gonna be all right, man," he heard the medic saying, confidently. "Nothin' but a little cut. Doc here fix you right up." The screaming continued into an otherwise silent night as the mortars failed to repeat their previously voluminous fire.

"Hey, Wheels," Zachary said, to the patient, who was one of Zachary's best squad leaders. Sergeant Cartwright was exceptionally fast, hence the nickname "Wheels," having made it to the last cut for the Washington Redskins and losing out to another wide receiver. Captain Garrett laid a hand on his soldier's knee and could feel it trembling. Zachary looked at the medic, whose face he could see in the moonlight. The medic looked at the captain with reassuring eyes, indicating that Cartwright really would be fine with some proper medical attention, that his words to Cartwright were not just shock prevention.

"That you, sir?" Cartwright said, comforted by the sound of his commander's voice. Cartwright's voice was raspy, punctuated by rapid breathing. Sometimes all a soldier needed to hear was the calm and reassuring voice of his commander. Surely the commander knew things that he did not, and if the captain was in control, then the situation must be under control.

"Yeah, Wheels, it's me. Doc says you'll be fine," he said, glad that Cartwright had recognized him. It was a good sign that he was not going into shock. Still, it was unnerving for Zachary to see one of his own soldiers writhing on the hard-packed dirt.

"You believe him, sir?" Cartwright asked, half-joking, looking at the commander with white eyes illuminated by the contrast to his black skin.

"Yeah, Doc gave me a behind-the-scenes thumbs-up. Only a scratch," he said, personally inspecting the bandage and acknowledging the fact that everyone knew the game. The medics were trained to reassure the wounded no matter what their condition. "I'm gonna check on the rest of the company. We've called the Embassy for a medevac and they should be here shortly. Doc, stay with him until the helicopter gets here." The medic nodded.

"Sir," Cartwright said before Zachary could stand up, "thanks for being here." Zachary slapped Cartwright on the shoulder, noticing the medic starting to elevate the leg to slow the blood flow, and ran back to Taylor's foxhole. When he updated Taylor on Cartwright's condition, the lieutenant stared blankly and nodded with a glazed look in his eyes.

Zachary wanted to talk to him, but did not have time as he heard the first gunshots ring out in the western part of his sector.

I know those sounds too well. He grabbed Teller by the shirt collar the way a football coach snags a player's facemask before sending him into the game, and they ran toward the fight.

Juan Ayala

Ayala had never seen anything like it. A withering crossfire had decimated his force heading directly toward the white buildings. Luckily, at the last moment he had joined the smaller group moving along the pier.

It now seemed to be clear sailing as they less than quietly padded along wooden ties next to the choppy bay. His plan had worked, as the

Americans had been so fixated on his larger force that they had neglected the obscure pier. Looking to his south, he saw Subic Bay, a mixing bowl of windswept water perhaps reflective of the murderous activities ashore. To his left was a five-and-a-half-meter iron retaining wall supported by I-beams that abutted the pier. The top of the wall was even with the ground, allowing him to view the outline of the ammunition stockpile about 200 meters away—until an explosion propelled him into the water.

As he flipped into the water, he was aware of the hail of bullets that cut them down three and four at a time. Tracers screamed at them like lighted arrows, too often finding their targets. The muzzle flashes came from behind the I-beams along the retaining wall, the bullets ripping open the attackers' flesh. There was no place for them to hide, as they were advancing along a bowling alley into a curtain of steel. Their determination was solid, though, like that of a weary marathoner nearing the finish line but about to collapse. Suddenly the night carried nothing but the reverberating echo of gunshots and the howling of dying men.

Ayala floated beneath the surface of the water, then bobbed back up, conscious, coughing, and wheezing for air. His rifle had dropped like a rock into the deep expanse of the bay. It was all he could do to stay afloat, as he was a non-swimmer fighting against the saturated weight of his clothes and backpack. Flailing his arms, reaching for anything that would support his weight, he found purchase beneath the pier on a long pipe that carried water to several points along the dock. Grasping the five-centimeter-wide tubing, he rested. After catching his breath, he listened to the diminishing battle above. From his position it had a distant quality, the sound dampened by the wood and steel pier above him. He could see through the slats in the wood, catching a glimpse of an American tracer etching an orange trail in strobe-like fashion as it flew above the pier. He lifted one hand to the strap of his backpack, which met his touch with the reassuring knowledge of his Shansi pistol tucked securely inside. Then he pressed on, shuffling hand over hand along the water pipe, his buoyancy in the water making the process remarkably easy.

The shooting ceased and distant echoes galloped through the low valleys to the west and north. However, he told himself, his plan had not failed. He was still alive and could take the Americans himself. He had 32 rounds of ammunition and he vowed to kill that many with his pistol. The rest would surrender, he was sure. He struggled beneath the pier, observed by huge rats pecking and scratching along the concrete to his left. He had seen them before. For a child growing up in the slums of Olongapo, rats were like pets.

Hand over hand he shuffled along in the water, making progress until he could hear the voices of Americans talking quietly. Perspiration beading on his forehead, he slowed so that his wake was an unnoticeable ripple, passing the voices above him. Making his way to the end of the pier, he located a steel cable hanging from the concrete wall that marked the end of the dock. Grabbing it, he pulled himself out of the water before realizing that his weight plus that of his drenched clothing outside the water were heavier than he'd expected, and he momentarily lost his grip. He quickly tightened his fist around the cable, grabbing into some frayed wires that dug deeply into the bone of his right hand. He wanted to scream but refused. He bit his lower lip with force, causing streams of warm, red blood to trickle down his chin and drop into the water like drips from a leaking faucet.

Pushing on, he laid an arm on the pier, his hand pulsing with pain. Putting pressure against his elbow, he flung his right leg on the pier and rolled onto the level surface. Quickly, he looked and saw a ladder that led to ground level.

He would continue his attack.

The entire engagement had taken only 20 minutes since the first mortars landed. At 0520 hours, it would be another 20 minutes until the sun provided enough daylight for them to assess accurately what they had accomplished. What would have been a beautiful sunrise amidst the pleasant music of the adjacent jungle was transformed into a barbaric scene of death, accompanied by the howls of wounded men.

"Red Three, status?"

"This is Red Three. We're counting bodies right now. We do need a medic. Say again, we need a medic!"

"Roger, he's on the way with a two-man security team," Kurtz said, motioning to his platoon medic and two members of the fire team that Quinones had sent to Kurtz's location.

"We've got all our personnel, but one has been hit in the neck. Say again, one hit in the neck! Currently holding position with four enemy prisoners of war. We are low on ammo but are redistributing right now."

"Roger. Good job. I'm sending your other three men to pick up those EPWs now. Continue to consolidate and redistribute," Kurtz said. Captain Garrett and Mike Kurtz sat, mentally exhausted, leaning against the pile of tires. Their exhaustion was paradoxical. Zachary felt the high and low of adrenaline rush and dump, coupled with the realization that he had a man wounded. Zachary had initially felt foolish running back and forth between positions, but he had reminded himself that he had to be at the critical point of the battle.

He had managed to change positions as needed. Plus, it was his plan that had earned what seemed like a victory for his company. Zachary knew in his heart that it was the hard training that had allowed them to survive this first battle. Both he and Kurtz had watched as tracers bounced wildly over the bay like some macabre fireworks display. Zachary had watched

Kurtz, wide-eyed and alert, like a wildcat waiting for the next intruder into his den.

"We will hold in position for now," Zachary said.

Zachary conducted a communications check with all of his platoons. The only real casualty was Sergeant Cartwright with the gash in his leg. The soldier in Quinones's squad had merely burned his face firing left-handed from behind an I-beam on the pier. The M4 was designed for right-handed shooters with the casing ejector port on the right side of the weapon. A white-hot metal casing had flown from the port, smacking the soldier in the face and searing his neck as it came to rest beneath the collar of his body armor. In the excitement of the moment, he had thought he was hit. Zachary was thankful and had personally inspected Quinones as well.

He had told his platoons to conduct ammunition redistribution and accountability of personnel. No one was missing, but Kurtz's platoon was critically short on ammunition. Zachary had Taylor send a squad with some of his platoon's ammunition to the tire stack, where he gave it to Sergeant First Class McDonell, Kurtz's platoon sergeant, to redistribute the ammunition. All of the platoons held their positions and watched into the surreal green world of the night-vision goggles.

The Embassy had radioed with good news and some bad news. The good news was that the medical evacuation helicopter was on its way to pick up Sergeant Cartwright. The bad news was that the attack on Subic was just a small part of an island-wide Abu Sayyaf attempt to seize power. They had a doctor in the Embassy who could examine Cartwright, but they believed that the Embassy itself was in imminent danger of being attacked. Zach told Fraley simply to get the helicopter to him ASAP, that he had a man dying.

The sun had risen far enough above the horizon across the island of Luzon to scatter the darkness, casting a gray shade on their position. When Kurtz took off his goggles he could see dark humps lying on the hardstand about 200 meters from the tire pile, where first and second squads had executed a perfect L-shaped ambush. Some of the bodies were moving, some were crying out in anguish, yelping as much in their mortal pain as they were bemoaning their complete defeat. The thick smell of spent powder hung in the air like a fog, waiting for the sun to burn it away with the memories of the horrible night. Zachary walked toward the ammunition pile, faithfully guarded by Quinones's squad, then looked over the bulkhead down onto the pier, where he saw Quinones and his men still oriented to the west, ever vigilant. The darkened lumps of bodies were scattered across the width of the pier.

Zachary returned to the tire pile, the de facto command post, with ever-growing numbers of soldiers gathering there. Some of the headquarters troops, who had remained in the barracks to monitor radios and react to emergencies, came out, looking in amazement at their company's baptism of fire. The platoon leaders had arrived and were kneeling next to each other, comparing notes. As Zachary approached, he made it a point to look at Taylor's eyes, looking for any sign of weakness. He saw none. They all stood as the commander and the tethered Teller approached. Taylor returned Zach's gaze with a reassuring confirmation that he had the mettle for this business and that he had matured immensely in the last hour.

Taylor was the tallest of the lieutenants but Kurtz's sheer breadth beside him made him seem larger. Barker was a rather short and slight officer, but large in heart. *He performed well,* Zachary thought. *He did not overreact and secured the flank.* Barker's red hair and boyish looks stood in stark contrast to Kurtz's partially unshaven face and Taylor's ruggedness. The three lieutenants stood next to each other, waiting for the commander.

"Take a knee guys," Zachary said. The lieutenants obeyed, forming a semicircle around the captain, who was still standing.

Teller, Slick's backup on the radio, looked up at the UH-60 helicopter, its rotor blades beating against the sky like drumsticks. The noise caused everyone except Kurtz to look skyward at the Black Hawk helicopter with the big Red Cross symbol painted on its side. It was the medevac for Cartwright.

Juan Ayala

Always shoot the two men nearest the radio, Ayala said to himself. His hand was bleeding profusely despite the white dirt caking inside his palm. His black hair hung in strands over his forehead. He had taken his bandanna and wrapped it around his wounded hand so that he could begin to eliminate the Americans, one by one.

Ayala low-crawled along the barracks adjacent to the command post and edged his scarred face around the corner. It was just light enough for him to see the ammunition pile about 50 meters to his left and a grouping of Americans kneeling around some old tires. He heard the helicopter fly overhead and used the cover of its roar as an opportunity to extract the Shansi pistol from his backpack. He checked the shoulder stock and fed one 10-round clip into the box magazine. He saw them looking up at the black helicopter and decided the movement could wait no longer. He painfully clutched his pistol, seated it in his shoulder, and began to rise. Moving first to a crouch, then to a low duckwalk, he began walking faster and faster in their direction, completely undetected.

Get the radio men first, Ayala thought again. He was only 30 meters away. He stopped as he saw one of the men begin to rise. His world moved in slow motion as he aimed the front inverted V and V-notched tangent rear sites at the American with the radio. He squeezed the trigger and actually saw the large .45 caliber bullet fly from the barrel, striking the American in the back of the neck, causing his head to jerk violently backward and his arms to outstretch as if to break his fall. The second round bored through the radio, scattering shrapnel in all directions.

The third shot must hit the man standing next to the radio. One down, 31 to go, Ayala thought, walking, then stopping to fire, then walking again. Success once again, as the third bullet tore the skull off its victim. Then he saw another American rolling to his left with a weapon. *The fourth bullet is for him,* Ayala said to himself. He aimed and felt his own blood pump from his chest as his shot flew silently but wildly into the air. "Yes," he whispered, "they must take many shots to kill me." He felt shots impacting on his body like small-fisted punches in a street fight. He watched his world collect before him and gather into a twisting cloud. Faintly, he could hear his deflating lungs wetly sucking for wind.

Ayala's last image in this life was that of the Americans loading their apparently dead commander onto the helicopter.

CHAPTER 18
Manila International Airport, Philippines
Matt Garrett

Matt felt the Gulfstream make a bumpy landing along the concrete run-way of Manila International Airport. He looked at the stiff windsock, which was pointing directly at the landing strip, indicating strong cross-winds from Manila Bay.

Jack Sturgeon, the pilot, rolled the craft to a stop on the tarmac. Before the flight, Sturgeon had briefly come back and introduced himself to Matt and Rathburn, having them both sign a logbook that he kept for his daughter and wife in California. Matt simply inscribed, "I know you're proud of your dad—Matt."

Matt felt Sturgeon pull the airplane to a stop. He looked through the oval window and saw that the morning was still a dark gray. The flashing red and orange wing lights pumped like strobes.

Grabbing his rucksack and Sig Sauer rifle, Matt followed Rathburn and Sturgeon down the steps, awkwardly lifting the ruck with his good arm. He was surprised at how much better he felt after nearly two days of rest. The Percocet and antibiotics were doing their jobs.

"Leave that here until we get past the formalities," Rathburn directed, pointing at the rifle.

"I'm never more than an arm's length away from my weapon, sir," Matt countered.

"I don't want it visible, so hide it in your ruck. We're not at war here, for God's sakes."

"Excuse me. We just had an American soldier killed in a shoot-down of two C-130s."

"That was an accident. Now do as I say," Rathburn demanded.

Matt looked at Rathburn for a long moment and stuffed the weapon into his ruck. They deplaned and walked toward the terminal building.

Matt's shoulder was beginning to bite and he wanted Percocet, but opted for a Motrin to keep his senses sharp. He walked into the latrine of the terminal and cupped some water into his hand to swallow the horse pill.

The advisory committee remained on the airplane for the moment, and Rathburn seemed a bit miffed that there was no delegation to meet him. He wandered around the empty terminal, looking for the red carpet, Matt presumed. Meanwhile, Matt knew that Sturgeon needed to file a flight plan for the next leg of his trip to Okinawa.

The three men gathered and all looked curiously at one another, thinking they heard the soft, but rapid, sound of distant gunfire.

Growing concerned with the rising noise of gunfire toward the inner city, Rathburn picked up a phone to call the Embassy. Matt extracted his weapon from his rucksack as the three men stood near a service entrance that led through two glass doors onto the airport tarmac. A long, dark hallway went in the opposite direction, toward the baggage-handling area.

"What do you make of the gunfire?" Rathburn asked Matt.

"Sounds like a combat zone," Matt said, stating the obvious as he stepped outside with his weapon at the ready.

"Just past the fence I saw Army trucks going everywhere. Green and orange tracers too."

The staccato sounds of small-arms fire continued, growing louder. Suddenly Matt thought about the women on the airplane. He should probably have them join the men in the terminal to keep everyone together.

As Matt jogged back onto the runway, he watched as a colorful truck with several hood ornaments drove along the runway and stopped less than 50 meters from their airplane. Three men poured from the back of the red truck and set up RPG launchers on their shoulders, aiming them at the Gulfstream.

Standing on the tarmac, Matt screamed. "No!" He leveled his weapon on the gunners as three rocket-propelled grenades left smoking vapor trails flying from their launchers and impacted into a wing and the side of the airplane.

The fuel tank in the wing exploded with a bright orange fury that immediately spewed flames and black smoke skyward. On either side of the wing, the rocket propelled missiles pierced the thin sheet metal and exploded beyond their impact points inside the passenger cabin. Matt knelt as he fired into the attackers, his accurate shots too late to save the women on the plane. The heat from the fireballs that erupted pushed him back and, as he turned, he thought he could see the women running desperately down the aisle. Their movement was visible through the elongated series of windows as they tried to escape a blazing inferno. Moments later, the aircraft exploded, billowing black smoke.

Matt sensed someone behind him, spun to his left, and swept his rearward attacker's feet off the ground. In a swift movement, he punched the small man in the stomach hard while grabbing the pistol with another hand. He noticed a knife moving to his side as he turned the pistol into the face of his initial attacker and shot him point-blank.

Sidestepping the lame thrust of a second attacker, Matt spun the now-dead rebel who had been holding the pistol into the path of the next insurgent.

"Hey, Joe, put down the pistol, no?"

"No," Matt said, then stopped when he realized what had occurred.

Two insurgents were holding Rathburn and Sturgeon by the neck, with knives pressing into their carotid arteries.

"Drop the gun, or we kill these Joes."

Matt sized up his predicament. He could care less about Rathburn, a Beltway lightweight, but he presumed the man had a family and was a patriot. Sturgeon did have a family and actually seemed like a decent guy. Matt eyed a total of four Filipinos, Abu Sayyaf, he assumed. Two were holding Rathburn and Sturgeon. One was talking to him from the same vicinity near the door to the terminal, and one was standing near him with a knife and pistol aimed at him.

Really, he thought, *I could make quick work of these clowns if they didn't have knives ready to slice through Rathburn's and Sturgeon's necks.*

"Let them go and I'll drop the weapon," Matt directed.

"You think we stupid, Joe?"

"My name's not Joe, dipshit, now let them go," Matt ordered again.

"Okay, watch this, Joe," the man holding Sturgeon commanded as he removed the knife from Sturgeon's neck and lifted it high.

Before he brought it down, Matt fired a single bullet into the man's head. Sturgeon quickly lifted the arm of the man holding Rathburn, using the surprise that Matt had created to their advantage. Another shot, and Matt had killed the insurgent who had been holding Rathburn.

As he turned toward the attacker closest to him, a shot rang out from the distance, felling the man. Quickly, though, Matt realized that the bullet had been intended for him as two truckloads of wild-eyed rebels poured from the backs of Jeepneys.

Matt lifted his hands, as did Rathburn and Sturgeon when they saw the M4s and AK-47s aimed at them. Soon, several insurgents were upon them, pushing them onto the concrete and taping their eyes and mouths shut and tying kite string around their hands and feet.

"How's this, Joe?" the Filipino said just before ramming the sharp toe of a boot into Matt's rib cage. He heard an audible pop and felt a deep pain in his ribs. Immediately he knew he had at least two broken ribs and possibly a bruised lung. Another kick in the same location made him sure about the lung; he could only pray it was not punctured. People were walking quickly all around him. He heard many loud shouts on the tarmac, men whom he presumed were celebrating their wily destruction of an airplane and the deaths of some American women.

The kicking had stopped but the concrete ground pressed against his bruised side, making his breathing difficult. When he tried to roll over to his left side, his shoulder screamed with pain and a hand grabbed a clump of his hair as a foot slammed down on his neck. Feeling the steel of a weapon against his temple, Matt heard a voice say, "I kill you, Joe."

The man seemed happy that he was in control. Matt knew intuitively that it was the voice of an Abu Sayyaf rebel. When they spoke Tagalog among one another, he was certain of it.

"What do we do with the Yankees? Kill them?"

"Magsaysay. Kill one by one. Get information, put on television. Use reporter's equipment."

Matt listened to this exchange. He knew Fort Magsaysay was in the central highlands of Luzon Province, about a four-hour drive from Manila, on a good day.

The rebels walked the men toward the airplane. Matt could feel the heat licking his face, making him sweat in the already-boiling morning. Their captors forced them to lie down in the bed of a truck, which Matt surmised was the truck that had escorted the rebels who had attacked the airplane.

The searing pain in Matt's shoulder increased as he began calculating how he was going to kill his captors.

The one time I hang out with a bureaucrat and this happens, Matt steamed. He closed his eyes and endured the long, bumpy ride.

CHAPTER 19
Mindanao, Philippines
Major Chuck Ramsey

Chuck Ramsey and his Special Forces team had been on the run for four days. The steep, jagged mountains had proved both a blessing and an enemy. Even these hardened men were having problems sustaining the rate of march necessary to elude Villanueva's Abu Sayyaf cell.

Ramsey stopped and looked down into a steep ravine. *Can we make it?* A few days ago, he would not have doubted it. Today, his men standing in single file behind him, panting, he was unsure.

"Take five, men," Ramsey told them. Despite their exhaustion, they moved to either side of their route and turned outward, each man taking a knee. They pulled their canteens out of their pouches and drank heavily. Every man was dehydrated. The heat had intensified during the last four days and the only respite was a gully washer, as Ramsey had called it. The near-monsoon-level rains had drenched his team and the Japanese man for hours, making them cold and miserable through the night. But the next day had brought forth the same burning, searing sun, and soon they were longing for the cool rain again.

Ramsey knew he had to find a river for his men to refill their canteens. They still had plenty of water purification tablets to make the river water acceptable. More importantly, though, they needed to find a way to establish communications. He felt like he was carrying a deep secret that the world needed to know. He had the key to something, he was not quite sure what. While he had grown to tolerate Abe, he seriously doubted the man's story. Although it was plausible that the United States would be rearming the Armed Forces of the Philippines, he doubted that they would fund Japanese factories to do so. He had to make contact with somebody who could relay the message.

Anybody!

Kneeling on both knees, he leaned back, stretching his weary back muscles. His 60-pound ruck was beginning to feel like an appendage to his body. He didn't bother to take it off. To put the weight back on again would somehow be demoralizing.

He gazed over some scrub, looking again into the ravine, which was about a 60-degree drop with no trails. High tropical trees gave way to dense undergrowth and rocks. The terrain pitched deep into a narrow bottom that ran east toward the ocean.

Ramsey grabbed his two-quart canteen and took a long pull. The water was warm. *Must be 100 degrees out here.* As he drank, he could feel his body rehydrate. Immediately his pores spewed forth sweat in an attempt to cool his scorching skin, only to have the beaming sun lick the moisture away.

Looking over his shoulder, he saw Benson turning his canteen up to the Japanese man's mouth. Water spilled over the edges of his dry, chapped lips as he gulped. Earlier, he'd had his men remove the tape from Abe's eyes and mouth. It only made sense. He was a healthy but gentle man. He would do them no harm and would not last a day in the jungle if he escaped.

Abe's story was unbelievable. Ramsey asked him repeatedly if they really were manufacturing tanks and helicopters in the plant. He always responded that they were indeed. Abe insisted that the American government was footing the bill, as they had done for Japan's defense needs for so many years.

But the rub, according to Abe—an obviously bright man—was that America was doing this because they needed help in the Global War on

Terror and wanted Japan to maintain stronger defenses. To Ramsey, it made no sense. Tanks and helicopters were not the best tools of the trade in fighting an idea such as radical Islam. *Why would the Japanese be building and stockpiling weapons on Mindanao?* Ramsey wondered. *In the Philippines?*

Ramsey looked at Abe, who was kneeling in the thick jungle vines, looking exhausted with his eyes fixed on the ground at his feet. He had kind eyes and a smooth face. His hands were not the hands of a warrior. Rather, they were soft and delicate like those of a lawyer or executive, or the engineer he professed to be. Ramsey had made him burn the orange jump suit and had given him one of his own extra uniforms. It was a bit large, but served the purpose. Abe had proven to be in excellent condition and could keep up with the group.

From the rear of the patrol, Benson came weaving through the elephant grass, a concerned look in his eyes.

"Sir, we've got movement to our rear," he said. Immediately the team fanned into an L-shaped ambush, with Ramsey at the corner so he could control any engagement. Crouching low in the two-meter-high elephant grass, he could still see nearly 100 meters along the path they had bored through the dense rain forest.

He saw it. There was movement toward them, following the trail they had inadvertently made. Of his own men, Ramsey could see no one but Eddie, the Filipino ranger who had captured the engineer and who was now kneeling and watching next to him. He peered through his binoculars, seeing only the undergrowth move. As his rising adrenaline level made his stomach twist into a knot, he felt a dry copper taste in the back of his mouth. He was tired. He was hungry. Perversely, he thought of all of the Vietnam movies he had seen in which soldiers shot at water buffalo thinking they were enemy. While he did not expect any water buffalo that high in the rain forest, nothing could really have surprised him.

Eddie motioned to him for the binoculars. Ramsey could see that he had grown quite confident and comfortable with the group. He wanted to make a contribution and had done so on many occasions. While he still painfully mourned the loss of his best friend, Ron Peterson, Ramsey was glad that Eddie had happened along. He handed the glasses to Eddie, who placed them to his eyes.

The standard plan for a hasty ambush was first to try to avoid detection. Ramsey figured they would use silenced weapons to the fullest extent possible to avoid further detection. His least preferred option was a conventional, loud ambush. For sure, the patrol would be lethally compromised.

He handled his father's Navy SEAL "hush puppy" with ease, rolling it back in forth in his hand to vent some nervous tension. The Smith and Wesson Model 39 pistol was modified with a noise suppressor. Used by the SEALs in Vietnam to kill sentries and guard dogs, the weapon's range was limited to 100 meters, but it was quiet.

The back of Ramsey's throat was dusty. *Is it the Abu Sayyaf? They've been following us for days. Must be them. How many?* Silently, he wished for a water buffalo instead of what he thought was coming.

"Mamanua," Eddie whispered, looking through the binos. Ramsey gave him a puzzled look. "Here," he said, leaning over and pointing nearly 80 meters from their position. They were directly in the middle of the ambush cross fire, whoever they were. Moving his pistol to his left hand, Ramsey lifted the binos to his camouflaged face.

"What the—"

"Mamanua," Eddie whispered again, covering Ramsey's mouth. Three Mamanua tribal natives were stalking through the rain forest hunting wild pigs or monkeys. They were dark-skinned and wore colorful beaded skirts and necklaces. Each held a spear at shoulder level, ready to release on his prey. The natives were Negritos, what the locals called black people, had immigrated from Malay to the Philippine Islands centuries ago, the first inhabitants of the archipelago. The Philippine government designated land, primarily rain forests not targeted for clear cutting, in which the tribal groups could operate with impunity. Such jungle woodlands were enclaves in time where technological progress had made no inroads.

The black tribesmen stalked carefully, one foot over the next, sensing something. He was 50 meters away. Could his men hold their fire? Ramsey looked at Eddie, who shook his head as if to say, "They are best left alone." Then, the lead Mamanuan looked through the bushes at Ramsey and raised his spear, preparing to hurl it forward. The others watched, lowering their spears.

He rifled the spear into the bush, not 20 meters from Ramsey's crouched position. Ramsey closed his eyes, fearing that they had gotten one of his men. He heard a high-pitched yelping sound and saw the spear dancing in the tall grass. The natives hurried forward. Ramsey raised his pistol, prepared to engage. He felt Eddie lay his small, brown hand on his arm, holding him back.

The short black men, skin dry and whitish from the dust and heat, leaned over their prey, a wild boar, and quickly tied its feet together with hemp. They carried the black pig in the opposite direction, slung over their shoulders on a spear. As they were leaving, the lead native stopped, turned his head, and stared directly into the bushes at Eddie and Ramsey. He saw them, held the eye contact for a brief moment, and disappeared into the lush jungle.

Ramsey lowered his pistol, comprehending that two cultures had just passed in the yellow-white Philippine sun. They had no interest in him, nor he they. Each had stared at the other, seeing a warrior of a different era. They were but mild curiosities to one another, each like a snake, harmless if unprovoked. He saw in the man's black face a sense of satisfaction and contentment. It was something more than just capturing dinner for his tribesmen. The look was the clear countenance of a simple life. Removed from the trials of government and international concerns, the Negrito seemed content with his lot.

Deciding he would contemplate the significance of his visual interchange with the Mamanuan tribesman later, he turned to more immediate problems.

In six more hours the helicopters would come, Ramsey told himself. They could survive that long, for sure. He had to maneuver his team to the north of Cateel City, where the beach was wide and uninhabited. All around him, the sheer cliffs either dropped sharply into the water or gave way to beaches. The mountains reminded him of the Na Pali coast off the island of Kauai in Hawaii.

With a pump of his clenched fist, he motioned to his men to get moving.

Looking to the east, he saw the ocean. Near the shore, the water was a tropical turquoise shade. Farther out, he could see a coral reef where waves tumbled harmlessly. Beyond the reef, the sea turned a deep, mystic blue. He knew the Philippine Trough was out there, reaching almost thirty-four thousand feet into the core of the earth. *What a world,* he thought. Primitive tribesmen, deep oceans, tropical rain forests. The beach was as white as sugar, like those he remembered from visits to the Florida panhandle.

He flipped his compass open, aiming it toward the small village nearly six kilometers away and seemingly another atmosphere below.

That's got to be Cateel!

He looked grimly again at the difficult terrain that lay ahead through the ravine. He knew that Villanueva's men were only about an hour behind them. Every time his team moved, the Filipinos seemed to pick up on the scent. Only when they went into hiding did it seem as though they were secure. More than once, they had doubled back on their trail, setting up ambushes but not executing them once they saw their pursuers. They were clearly outnumbered.

He snapped his wrist, closing the compass lid, and placed it in its pouch. Another drink of water and he would be ready. He sucked from the canteen, draining it, then stood.

From his vantage, everything was downhill. It was just a matter of how steep. Taking the point on this patrol, unusual for a team leader, he inched his way down the ravine. His footing was tenuous as he slipped on the damp deadfall and rocky dirt. The rainy season had not officially begun yet, but enough precipitation had fallen to make the rain forest dense with high timber, wild coffee bushes, rubber plants, and an assortment of other tropical shrubs. Huge leaves from elephant plants slapped him in the face as he let the weight of his ruck force him down as his men followed. Frequently he would turn his back to protect his face, holding on to plant roots above his head, a tactic he had been taught to avoid in Ranger school. But, thankfully the sadistic Ranger instructors had not yet thought of including a brigade of Abu Sayyaf rebels as a motivational tool in Ranger training.

The tactical satellite radio was another issue that he could not shake from his mind. *What was wrong with it?* They had checked repeatedly to make sure that they had the proper angle to the satellite. He even had Ralph Jones, the best communications sergeant in the Army, take the service panel off the radio to see if anything looked awry. Nothing did. They had no other radio or batteries to test the radio against and Major Ramsey had never been as frustrated as he was right now.

He had little time to think of such matters, however, as he reached an impasse. He had led the group nearly all of the way down the ravine. But the last 55 meters were comprised of sheer rock cliffs that dropped directly into a swiftly moving mountain stream. The sloping terrain had forced him continuously to the east, off his azimuth, trapping his team on an outcropping of rocks. To double back might lead him into his pursuers. To walk the ledge south would be too dangerous. To climb the rocks to the north would be suicide. There was only one option.

Ramsey halted the patrol. They took a knee, each facing outward again, except the last man, who faced to the rear. He whipped out his smokeless tobacco, smacked the can, and placed a wad in his mouth. He pulled a one hundred and twenty foot nylon military rope from his ruck-sack. Benson moved forward as all good assistant patrol leaders do when the patrol halts. He dropped his ruck as well, snatched a similar coiled rope from his pack, and began backward-feeding it to the ground, check-ing it for frays. Benson passed the word back to his men to begin secur-ing their "Swiss seats" and snap links. Each man carried a four-meter sling rope that he wrapped around his waist and ran through his crotch to form a seat. Placing a snap link through the point where the two ropes met near the belt buckle, the soldier had a seat by which he could rappel down a rope.

"Major," Benson said after a few minutes. Ramsey turned and saw that Benson had found a thick mahogany tree and was hugging it, lifting his feet off the ground and leaning back toward the rock cliff. The tree was sturdy, with green leaves and healthy bark. It would suffice as an anchor point. He tied a round turn knot with two half hitches, snugging the hitches tight against the tree. Using only one rope, he placed the other in his pack. Benson grabbed a third rope, which Randy Tuttle had carried, and stuffed it into his pack. If the first rope did not reach all the way down, then Benson could hammer some pitons into the rock facing and make another anchor point. Ramsey knelt and placed two burlap sacks between the rope and the rock ledge to prevent fraying. Benson would go first and Ramsey would go last. He gave an extra sling rope to Eddie, who as a Ranger knew how to rappel. Abe was another issue.

Each man was already carrying roughly 70 pounds apiece and could not afford to add another 160 pounds of Abe. Ramsey tied the seat around him and gave Abe a quick class on the techniques, all of them knowing full well that he would falter.

But there was no time for real instruction. Ramsey acted as rappel master, hooking in all of the soldiers and having Abe watch them lean singly over the cliff with their hands in their backs, braking their movement. As soon as each solider felt comfortable, he would extend his right hand at a 45-degree angle from his side, locking the right elbow while simultaneously pushing off the rock face. The green berets bounded their way quickly to the bottom of the ravine. The significant stretch factor in the rope allowed each soldier's weight to land him gently in the waist-deep stream, and releasing the rope would cause it to bounce crazily back to several meters above the water. The soldiers then moved slowly down the stream, filling their canteens and conducting reconnaissance while those remaining atop the cliff provided watch from above, as they would do until the last man slid over the cliff.

Eddie flew down the rope, showing off the fact that he was a prestigious Filipino Scout Ranger. Admittedly, he was an expert in jungle and mountain warfare techniques, and after a brief period of suspicion, the team had grown fond of him.

Eddie slid down the rope, jumped into the water, and took up the number eight position in the patrol. Two more of the team bounced down the rock face, and it was Abe's turn.

"You can do this," Ramsey said with conviction. He knelt before Abe, pulled the rope toward the anchor point, and looped it twice through Abe's snap link so the extra friction would slow his descent. Ramsey placed his gloved hand on the running end of the rope, then slammed it in Abe's back.

"That stays there until I tell you different." He then placed Abe in a good position from which to rappel and slowly pushed him over the rock ledge. Abe's eyes were wide with fear. Leaning back over a 55-meter cliff was as unnerving experience as any non-climber could have. He went to one knee shaking his head. Rocks slid from under his feet, almost causing him to slide down the rope.

"No. No." Abe said, looking down. He was ashamed. Ramsey had an idea. He quickly took the second rope out of his ruck and tied it in similar fashion around another tree less than two meters above the first anchor point. He would go down the rope next to Abe, coaching him all the way. Abe was reassured, but still not confident.

He said, "If you do not do this, you will die." The grim look on Ramsey's face told Abe that he had better collect the courage to back over the ledge. With his eyes closed, he inched backward.

"Look at me," Ramsey said, already forming an L with his body hanging over the cliff. The rope was taut, scraping bark from the tree as he wiggled his body into position. He leaned and rocked against the rope, giving Abe confidence. Abe slid over the edge, his knees scraping the face of the cliff. Exasperated, he looked at the brave major. Realizing he had made it over the cliff without falling, he smiled weakly. He could do it. Finally, he inched his way down, walking backward while Ramsey led the way. They reached the bottom, slid into the refreshing mountain stream, and rejoiced that they had made it safely. Abe bowed respectfully to Ramsey, standing waist deep in rushing water. Ramsey inclined his bearded face downward, accepting the compliment.

Standing in the cool water, Ramsey realized there was nothing he could do about the ropes. He would have to leave them as a major clue for the Abu Sayyaf. He just hoped that he and his men would not be swinging from them anytime soon. On that thought, he motioned to Abe to walk east and join the rear of the patrol, which had already started moving and clearing.

They had all filled their canteens and soaked their overheated bodies in the stream, which led to the northeast of Cateel City and eventually gave way to a flat area almost 75 meters above sea level with an excellent view of the landing zone for the helicopters. *Only two more hours*, Ramsey thought. *Two hours.*

CHAPTER 20

Major Ramsey's men climbed out of the stream and formed a tight perimeter, sensing that they might get out of this situation after all. They drank heavily from their canteens again and again to steer them away from days of dehydration in the high mountain air. Their new base camp was in a stand of tall mountain pines. The underbrush was relatively sparse.

Give the old tacsat radio one more try, Ramsey thought.

Jones, their radio man, took a knee in the middle of the patrol base beneath some tall pines. Ramsey and Abe watched as he dropped his ruck and flipped a switch on the radio. He popped the radial antenna out of his pocket and spread its arms so that it looked like the skeleton of an umbrella. He set an azimuth on his compass and found the direction to "bird 65," the satellite they had been told to use. It hovered somewhere between the Philippines and Hawaii. All he needed was to aim the antenna in the proper direction, and the radio should work.

Still nothing. Ramsey looked skyward in frustration to see the hot wind blow through the tall pines. He could hear the peaceful lap of waves on the coral reef some 600 meters away. His frustration was mounting. Normally he could control himself, but he was fighting to stay in control today.

Ramsey furrowed his brow, wanting to kick somebody or something, when Abe said, "May I see?"

Abe moved to one knee and looked at the radio stuffed into the rucksack for carrying purposes.

"Can we take out?" Abe asked Jones, motioning with his hands.

"You get take-out at Chinese restaurants, man. You can't fix that thing—" Jones said, just as frustrated as his commander.

"Let him look," Ramsey interrupted. Jones pulled the radio out of his ruck, a chore in itself. Laying it on the ground, he said, "Here," and walked away.

"Have any, uh—" He did not know the word. He was motioning with his hand, turning it left and right.

"Screwdriver? You want a freaking screwdriver so you can rip my shit apart?" Jones said, angrily pulling his flop hat off and slapping his thigh with it. "No way, sir," he said, looking at the major. Jones was protective of his radio, embarrassed enough that it, and he, had failed them.

"Do it, Jonesy," Ramsey ordered, spitting into the ground, resting his arms on his ammunition pouches. Begrudgingly, Jones obeyed his commander and handed Abe a jeweler's screwdriver set.

Abe proceeded to dismantle the radio confidently, as if had seen many like it.

"This have line of sight and satellite?" Abe asked, almost impossible to understand.

"Yes, it does," Ramsey said, walking over to where Abe was seated and had essentially disassembled the radio into several pieces. Worried, he sat in front of Abe and watched. Looking at the circuit board, Abe began nodding. He looked back at the front panel of the radio, which had a variety of switches: the frequency dials, voice and data receivers, satellite offset switch, volume and squelch dials, antenna nodes, and the encrypting port. In the bottom left-hand corner of the front panel, he played with the switch that read "off-sat-los." As he turned the switch back and forth, he watched the transistor gate on the circuit board. Nothing was happening.

"I find problem," Abe said, flatly.

"What?" Jones screamed, scampering back to where Abe was sitting.

"Show me," Ramsey said.

"This switch. Control megahertz. You not get enough megahertz. When I move switch, transistor gate stay on line of sight. Not go to satellite."

"I'll be damned," Jones said. "He's right. You need 25 megs to get satellite communications, and you only get four megs with the line-of-sight mode. I was on line-of-sight to keep comms with you guys when you found *him*," he said, looking at Ramsey and pointing at Abe. "Then my shit caught the impact when he fell on me that night. I'll be damned," Jones said, unsure now how to treat Abe. "Now it's frozen in place?"

"Think that's what he saying. Can you fix it?" Ramsey asked Abe.

"Maybe," Abe said. He would need a thin piece of wire, some solder, and something that would burn hot.

"Where's McGyver when you need him?" Jones asked.

Ramsey collected a small propane tank, which the medic Jones used it to heat his instruments. Jones carried both wire and solder in his communications repair kit. Ramsey watched as Abe worked on the radio for about 30 minutes. The propane tank made him sweat profusely. The noonday sun baked him and the rest of the team.

"I put into satellite position only," Abe said. "No way to fix for both."

"That's fine," Ramsey said, anxious to give it a try. Abe pieced the radio together with skill. No small bits were left when he was finished.

Ramsey saw Abe absently pat the pocket in his uniform where he had seen him put a photograph when changing from the orange running suit to the borrowed Army attire. Ramsey assumed it was his wife and children, as he'd made a habit of patting it often as there was little privacy to take it out and gaze at it. With quiet aplomb Abe stood, holding his hands out toward the radio, then softly patting his thighs and walking to where he could see the ocean, framed by two coconut trees. Ramsey let him go, seeing him pull the photo out of his pocket. Ramsey knew he likely felt no differently than his own men, longing to go home. The man looked thin, wiry, and small against the clear waters of Cateel Bay framing him and his photo. He may have just saved their lives in re-establishing radio communications for Ramsey and his men, and Ramsey believed he deserved to get home safely as much as they did.

"We're getting a signal," Jones said, excitedly. He had reloaded the encryption variable, turned on the power, aimed the antenna, and seen the red light indicate that he was reaching the satellite.

Ramsey saw Jones pick up the black microphone, eager to establish contact with their rescuers. Looking at his watch, Ramsey saw there was only one hour until the helicopters were to arrive. He hoped they would be there.

Commander Villanueva

Commander Villanueva moved to the front of the column. They had followed the rugged trail blazed by the enemy. He initially figured them to be the elite Filipino Scout Rangers. They were certainly the best that he had ever dealt with. But now he was uncertain.

He inspected the two ropes, which dropped over a steep cliff into the Cateel River. He knew the area very well. The Japanese manufacturing plant was nearby, and his men had patrolled the entire area during the rapid construction of the facility. Additionally, he was to link up with Takishi in less than a day in Cateel Bay to fly to Manila and assume control of the entire operation. As it stood, his handheld satellite communications had been sufficient to monitor activities that his years of preparation and rehearsal had allowed to occur with precision. There were other insurgent groups, such as the New People's Army (NPA), that were vying for control, and Villanueva chose to ally with Takishi, keep a low profile, then emerge as the conquering leader of the entire country with Takishi's backing.

Still, a part of him simply loved the hunt, and so here he was.

He was close. He could smell them. One chewed tobacco, he knew. At several vacant base camps he'd found bits of smokeless tobacco, decidedly not a Filipino habit. Some Filipinos use smokeless tobacco, but it was more of a—yes—an American habit.

Villanueva thought, kneeling next to the ropes.

Could it be? Good, new ropes. A fresh tin of good smokeless tobacco. Could it be Americans? Could it be Garrett?

Takishi had told him to kill Matt Garrett, but he had seen no sign of the man. Perhaps he was so good that he was never seen. Maybe there was an American or Australian advisor to the Scout Rangers. The sight of blood some 50 meters behind the ropes in the high grass confused him. Had one of the Rangers been hurt? Was it food they had killed? He couldn't be sure.

There were only two places they could have been going, either to the beach or to the top of the mountain. The terrain to the north was much too severe, and he knew they were tired as he had kept them on the run. They would not have rappelled down the ropes if they had wanted to go up the mountains. They had followed the stream east, toward the beach.

"Come, men. There is an easy way," he said. He had one of his men untie the ropes and coil them. The cause needed all of the material it could get. Doubling back and breaking bush for nearly 200 meters, Villanueva led his men to a path that followed the spine of a ridge down into Cateel City. "We will move along the ridge and find them on either side, waiting for something. They came here with a purpose."

Pulling off his bush hat, he ran a long-fingered hand through his sweaty, greasy hair. Villanueva was tall for a Filipino, nearly six feet. He was a strong man with a probing intellect. In another country, perhaps he would have been a doctor or college professor. But this was his destiny. His people needed him. Three hundred men followed single file as they walked the southern spine of the ridge that led toward

Cateel City. Mostly animals used the path to wander down from the rain forest and gain access to the river below.

Villanueva stopped and looked upon the ocean. He was nearly 750 meters above sea level and five kilometers away from the city. Looking skyward, he caught the image of a Philippine eagle silhouetted by the sun, wings spread, casting a large X onto the trail. In its talons, the eagle had a dead monkey it had just captured. Villanueva smiled, watching the "monkey eater" flap, then soar, heading for its nest. To his left was the huge ravine that Ramsey's team had rappelled. To his right was a dense rain forest. As the trees thinned, the elephant grass took over.

Villanueva reorganized his men, warning them to prepare for an ambush. The enemy was near. He had one company in the lead, walking softly but not soundlessly. The remaining two companies followed him down the path, which widened as the rain forest gave way to grass.

Villanueva followed a young fighter not a day over fifteen. As they walked in the sweltering morning heat, he recalled his earlier days with the movement. He yearned for the day when the children of the Philippines could lay down their weapons and pick up schoolbooks to learn. He had read hundreds of books during his lifetime: the Koran, the Bible, Weber, Marx, Rousseau, Jefferson, Mao Zedong, Sun Tzu, and many others hoping to understand the world beyond. He knew there were points of view other than his. He also knew that the Philippines would never prosper so long as the imperialistic powers maintained control of the country. They had to achieve their independence. In the early nineties, the Islamic movement seemed to gain traction, providing an opening. Abu Sayyaf had splintered from the bungling New People's Army, and Villanueva had seen an opportunity.

Like the Muslims in the Balkans, Villanueva had chosen to adopt a practical, almost Clausewitzian approach to warfare, meaning it was simply a furtherance of political endeavors. Villanueva's fight was not for Bin Laden, but for his people as a means to an end.

Walking down the path in his sweat-stained khaki-brown uniform, Villanueva wiped the moisture from his dark forehead. *So much hatred and violence. So many children dying. We can be free. We can have a better life.*

CHAPTER 21
U.S. Embassy, Manila
Zachary Garrett

"What's your name, son?" the voice asked. This was another dream, he was sure. He was inside of a dirty Coke bottle, trying to look out beyond the dusty glass. There were people standing above him, but their faces were large, then small, then large again as he rolled inside the bottle. Voices. He heard voices trying to talk to him. It was his brother Matt, calling his name. He could not see him, though, only hear his voice. The voice again, calling, pleading for him to come. Then he saw Kurtz rising from his crouch, yelling at him, grabbing his arm and pulling. He heard the voice again, calling a name. The voice. He must remember the voice. If he could only hang on, he could pull himself out of the bottle and find the troubled voice.

"What's your name?"

The doctor broke an ampoule of ammonia inhalant open beneath Zachary Garrett's nose, causing his face to wrinkle. Zach noticed his troops' eyes widen at his movement, an apparent good sign. The doctor had taken off the bandage and handed it to Sergeant Spencer, revealing a long, jagged wound that ran a six inch course above Zachary's left ear. The wound was more ugly than severe, and the doctor had concluded that the impact of the helmet being ripped from his head must have knocked him unconscious. *Must have been one hell of a big bullet!*

As Colonel Mosconi poked and prodded Captain Garrett, the overweight lieutenant colonel who had visited them yesterday morning in the helicopter, Fraley, came rambling down the dimly lit hall, rays of sunlight jumping from each office doorway and highlighting Fraley's cumbersome gait. Rockingham spotted him and angrily moved to meet Fraley in the hallway.

"You fat son of a bitch!" Rockingham screamed at Fraley, whose eyes bulged wide as Rockingham grabbed him by the lapels and slammed him against the porcelain tile wall in the corridor.

"Get your hands off me, Lieutenant!" Fraley snapped back, his voice muffled by the shirt gathered around his mouth.

"You listen to me," Zachary saw Rockingham say. He wanted to stop his lieutenant but knew he had no chance in his condition. Rockingham grabbed Fraley with one hand and in the other hand he was holding the blood-stained dressing from Sergeant Spencer, who looked on in amazement.

"You're gonna fry for this, Lieutenant, you hear me," Fraley said.

"You see this," he said, holding the bloody dressing up to Fraley's face, "you did this." He had lowered his voice, sounding calmer. Although Fraley was large, he was no match for Rockingham's powerful frame as Rock lowered the man to the floor.

"I want you to have our blood on your face," he said, wiping the bloodstained bandage across Fraley's cheeks, "because you've already got it on your hands."

Fraley quickly picked himself off the floor, brushing his green jungle fatigues, and screamed, "MPs!" Then he added, "Listen here, I'm calling your division commander to tell him to throw your ass in the brig at Pearl Harbor."

"Like hell you are," Sergeant Spencer said, moving in front of Rockingham. Spencer, taller than Rockingham, looked like an aboriginal warrior beside him.

"Stay out of this, Spence," Rockingham said, "this is between me and Fraley." Spencer moved out of the way, giving Rockingham a supportive glance. Fraley attempted to move past the men.

"You've got to get past me first," Rockingham said.

"Back off, sir," Spencer said, placing a hand on Rockingham's chest. "This guy ain't shit. He's already pissed his pants. Let him go do whatever he's got to do. We've got four eyewitnesses here that heard him threaten you and say you had a black ass. Now, really, what's he gonna do?"

Rockingham backed off, glaring at Fraley with catlike eyes. True to Spencer's prediction, Fraley turned and walked toward the back door, in the direction of his quarters.

"Zachary Garrett. My name's Zachary Garrett," Zachary said, trying to get Rockingham to focus on him instead of Fraley.

The troops snapped their heads back, watching as their commander awoke.

"Zachary," the doctor said, "how old are you?"

"Thirty-six," Garrett said, weakly, eyes trying to open, but mostly fluttering.

"Good. What is your job?"

"Commander. Commander of the best troops in the Army."

With the last comment, the soldiers knew their commander was going to be fine. They let out a collective "hooah" and gathered around him, where he still lay on the plywood.

"Not so fast, guys," the doctor said. "Zachary, I'm taking off your boot and socks, can you feel anything?"

The pregnant pause seemed eternal, casting a dreadful silence over the room. "Zachary?" the doctor asked again, this time pricking his foot with the top of his pen.

"I feel something, Doc," Zachary said hazily, "but I'm not sure." The doctor loosened the strap around Zachary's leg that had been securing him to the plywood. "Maybe this will help," the doctor said, massaging his leg, then returning to the chore of stabbing his foot.

"Oh yeah," Zachary said, to a collective sigh of relief.

"The combination of a pinched nerve and the tight strap deadened your senses down there. I think basically all we've got here is a decent head wound that'll heal nicely and a concussion that we can't do any-thing about except keep you awake for the next few hours."

No problem, Zachary thought, *I've got a ton of stuff to do.*

"Hey, XO, good to see you," Zachary said at the first sight of Rocking-ham since he had left with Fraley. "Sure could have used you this morn-ing." Then he realized his comment was like salt in an open wound for the XO.

"Don't remind me, sir," Rockingham said, looking at the floor.

"Don't feel bad. Your lieutenants did great. So did the rest of the com-pany. You should have seen Quinones and Kurtz," Zachary said, shaking his head in disbelief, then stopping at the pain. Perhaps it could be conso-lation to Rockingham that his lieutenants had performed well. Being the senior lieutenant in the company, he had taken the three "newbies" under his wing and personally guided them through the nuances of junior officership. But still, Zach suspected he still felt remorse for not being at his commander's side during the attack.

The doctor shaved and cleaned the left side of Zachary's head before cleaning and dressing the wound. "Might as well get the other side while you're at it," Zachary joked to the doctor, who laughed and complied. After that, he worked on Sergeant Cartwright's leg, a more complicated wound than Zach had originally thought. Nonetheless, he thoroughly cleaned the deep cut, put in a few stitches, and properly bandaged it. Digging through a cabinet full of pharmaceuticals, Zach received his and Cartwright's antibiotics.

After about an hour, Zachary, Rockingham, Sergeant Spencer, Ser-geant Cartwright, and the other three soldiers collected their personal gear and weapons and began to make their way up the stairs to the heli-copter. They straggled, with the healthy soldiers helping the wounded, all with thankful expressions on their faces. It could have been a scene out of the *Red Badge of Courage,* the wounded men limping slowly, arms wrapped around the healthy ones, their uniforms ripped and shredded in places, bloodstained.

They heard a commotion toward the front of the building, followed by several shots fired. Having had their fill for the day, they continued up the stairs, finally reaching the roof, where the medevac helicopter started its engine with the high-pitched whine of the turbines, blades turning slowly and awkwardly at first, then beating and chopping to full speed. The body of the aircraft fought the tremendous torque and bounced on its wheels.

As they left the air-conditioned building, the Philippine sun blasted Zachary's face with moist heat.

The gunshots grew louder. Automatic-weapons fire. The helicopter pilot was waving his arm at him, beckoning them forward. As the intensity of firing grew, three men and two women came spilling out of the stairwell toward the helicopter from the roof of the Embassy side of the compound.

The fleeing men and women were dressed in business suits and dresses that did not facilitate a rapid escape. The door swung open wide again, this time spewing Filipino rebels with blue and red bandannas. They knelt to fire at the fleeing American diplomats without noticing him and his soldiers.

"Spence, you go left, I'll go right," Zachary heard Rockingham said. His executive officer grabbed one soldier, leaving the other two for Sergeant Spencer, who moved rapidly around the hovering aircraft. Zachary saw the pilot look nervously at the armed Filipinos. Zachary knew the pilot had a moral decision to make. Did he save his own hide, or did he try to save them all? He saw the pilot's hand start to pull back on the cyclic and collective controls as if to take off, but the helicopter remained in place.

Zachary saw that the five American civilians were running toward Sergeant Spencer's team near the rear of the aircraft. Spencer waved his arms rapidly at the group, most of whom were too scared to notice the whirring, invisible tail rotor of the UH-60. They could not hear Spencer's cries of warning above the gunfire and chopping of the helicopter.

"Get down! Watch out!" Spencer yelled as he watched a young blond sprint toward them, eyes wide and hair tumbling across her face just enough to distort the fact that she was headed directly into the path of the tail rotor.

The ambassador realized his secretary's mistake and reached toward her, straining to grasp her as a hail of bullets chewed the cement behind him. He could not reach her. Spencer watched as the young woman's face splattered against the aircraft and parts of her arms and torso were tossed about the landing pad, looking like some grisly artwork display.

The ambassador rolled underneath the blades and the rest of his team avoided them as well. The ambassador and two civilians joined Sergeant Spencer's team of three soldiers as they rounded the aircraft. Spencer told the civilians to get down on the cement when he heard the XO's rifle open fire on five approaching insurgents, who were caught by surprise, reeling under the withering fire brought forth by the XO's two-man team and Sergeant Spencer's team from the opposite side of the helicopter.

Meanwhile, Zachary helped Sergeant Cartwright onto the helicopter then pulled out his 9mm Beretta. Noticing the civilians, he hurried them inside, next to Cartwright. He turned around and see the door open from the JUSMAG section of the compound. It was Fraley.

"They got Doc and Hewit!" Fraley screamed above the roar of the UH-60 blades as he ran from the Embassy roof door. Zachary, his back to the helicopter, saw three rebels spring from the doorway, chasing Fraley. It was Zachary now who had the moral decision.

He was a decent man so there was no real hesitation. He crouched in a good firing position and fired past Fraley's wide eyes at the three insurgents. Fraley rambled past Zachary and joined the increasing population on the helicopter. Zachary continued to fire, first selecting a target, then squeezing the trigger. He killed the rebels, who, like their countrymen across the heliport, were surprised by the armed opposition on the roof.

The soldiers quickly boarded the helicopter, their weight exceeding the load limit of the aircraft. The pilot gingerly adjusted the controls so the aircraft slowly lifted off the heliport, straining under the excessive weight. He pitched the nose forward and climbed slowly into the air.

Suddenly the door from the JUSMAG flew opened, and Colonel Mosconi, the Air Force doctor, fell forward onto the hot cement. He was bleeding badly from his left shoulder and held a pistol in his right hand. He crawled on all fours, craning his neck to see the helicopter. The cement burned his hands and the pistol smashed his fingers each time he slapped his hand forward to move another centimeter toward the helicopter.

"Cover me!" Rockingham yelled, jumping from the barely airborne aircraft.

Fraley reached across the aircraft, grabbing Rockingham, and screamed, "No! Leave him, or we'll never make it!"

Rockingham punched Fraley in the face, smashing his nose and knocking him out.

Zachary watched Rockingham sprint to Mosconi and slide under him to lift him into a fireman's carry, Mosconi's blood oozing down his back. He took long, heavy steps back toward the aircraft, as more rebels began spilling onto the rooftop. Flipping Mosconi into the aircraft and onto his lap, Rockingham winced as the Black Hawk pulled away. He held on to a metal tube that served as a seat frame, his legs hanging out of the aircraft.

Zachary had both arms around Mosconi, who lay unconscious and maybe dead. With one hand, he grabbed Rockingham's arm to give him support.

Rockingham looked at him with the blank eyes of a wounded deer. Zachary knew then that the XO had been hit in the back with a bullet. Bullets zipped past and into the frame of the laboring aircraft.

Sergeant Spencer grabbed Rockingham's other arm. Soon, both arms went limp, and Rockingham's eyes retreated into a world where there would be no pain. His body became deadweight against the pull of Zachary and Spencer.

With sudden alarm and shock, they realized their friend was dead. Hanging on, Spencer and Zachary looked at each other, trying to hold back their emotions. But they were only human.

The pilot banked the machine hard to the left, diving below the level of the building, Zach presumed to avoid the fire, and sped low along Roxas Boulevard with too much weight and too little time. They headed to the only relatively safe place for an American in the Philippines—Garrett's Gulch.

CHAPTER 22
Mindanao Island, Philippines
Major Chuck Ramsey

"**Any station, this** is Bushmaster Six, over," Major Ramsey said into the black microphone. He waited and still got no response. He had been trying for more than 15 minutes to contact either the Embassy or his group in Okinawa. He was sure the radio was working. Where could they be? He had Jones check the encrypting codes. The frequencies were correct and he was using the proper call signs. In the past, he had been able to reach Okinawa but was getting no response from there either.

"Which bird are we using, Jonesy?"

"Bird 65," Jones responded, looking at the sky as if he could read a bumper number on the satellite.

"How about bird 64, can we try that?" Ramsey asked.

"We can try anything," Jones said, picking up the small antenna dish and aiming its skeletal frame to the southeast toward New Guinea. "If we get anybody, it won't be our headquarters. Bird 64 can't reach Okinawa. Something about the horizon. It might be able to redirect our signal to another satellite, but I don't know how we could do that." Satellite 64 covered the Indonesia, Australia, and New Zealand area, lying somewhat low on the horizon. Its farthest reach north without retransmission was the Philippines. In a southerly direction it transmitted to the Antarctic teams that were stationed there doing ecological work.

"Well, I just want to get our message to somebody in authority in our government. Japanese making tanks in the Philippines would make a stir somewhere, I'm sure," Ramsey said.

Jones chuckled. "Yeah, especially the Philippines. Okay. Try it now."

"Any station this net, this is Bushmaster Six, over." He paused. Nothing.

"Any station this net, this is Bushmaster Six, over." Again nothing.

"Bushmaster six, this is Bravo Six Romeo, over," a voice responded. Ramsey scrambled to his knees, grabbing the handset. Jones pumped his fist next to his ribs in silent hope that it was someone who could help them.

"This is Bushmaster Six, who are you and what is your location?"

"Stand by. Authenticate Alpha Mike, over." That was a good sign, Ramsey thought, as Jones spooled up his digital encryption device. The two letters A and M had a corresponding response that only someone using the handheld encryption device could locate. They had to be Americans.

"I authenticate Delta, break," Ramsey said as Jones had indicated. "Authenticate Foxtrot Lima, over." It was customary to authenticate in both directions of the conversation so that each party could be reasonably assured that they were speaking with an authorized user. A brief pause ensued. Ramsey was hopeful, though. *Finally, wherever these guys are, I'm giving them the scoop.* He could unload his burden. He had felt a bit like the Navy lieutenant commander that had seen the radar images of the Japanese fleet bearing down on Hawaii from the north on that dreadful day in December 1941. He had the answer but could get it to nobody. And now Ramsey had the answer—though to what, he was unsure.

"I authenticate Sierra, over."

"This is Bushmaster Six. What is your unit and location?" Ramsey asked, doubtful that the young RTO would give him the information.

"Look at the bravo designator in your encrypting device." Jones was listening and promptly scrolled through his digital display and found the letter B, which for that day indicated a company from the 25th Infantry Division. Whoever these guys are, he thought, their radio guys go by the book. *That's good. I'm in touch with a squared-away unit.*

Jones showed him the 25th Infantry Division codes in their encryption device. "We're talking to Hawaii?" Jones asked incredulously. "If we can talk to them, we can reach Okinawa, can't we?" Ramsey thought for a moment, rubbing what was now becoming a beard on his chin. *Think, Chuck, think.*

"No. These guys are that ammo detail at Subic. Remember my bud, Zach Garrett, that I mentioned?" Ramsey said. He remembered walking out of the Embassy before what was to be a short, painless recon mission to Mindanao and seeing a calendar that showed one company arriving to guard some ammo that was being transferred to another ship. The manifest had listed Captain Zach Garrett as the leader.

"Okay, I've got your unit and I think I know your location. I am friendly. Look at Bushmaster in your device. That's me. I need to talk to your commander. I have some important information, over," Ramsey said.

The voice came back. "Wait, over."

Ramsey waited among the tall trees and elephant grass. The stream that had been their path was 50 meters to his south. He could see his ten men plus Eddie and Abe, one about every 50 meters, in a circular perimeter, constantly vigilant but very tired. Their worn senses were not as keen as they should be. He could feel the anticipation of the helicopters surge through him, washing away the dikes of caution that normally prevented emotions from interfering with the mission at hand. They had been peaking for four days, constantly on the run, never a restful moment. It was time, the body was saying. It had to be immediately. *I can't go much farther without rest and sleep and good food.* But they had to wait. Special Forces soldiers were always waiting for support from someone else who probably did not understand their precarious situation.

"Bushmaster Six, this is Bravo Six, over."

The voice was crisp with authority and impatience…and familiar.

"This is Bushmaster Six," Ramsey blurted, anxious. "Listen, we know each other. You are the unit that came here for ammo detail. You don't have to answer, but you know who I am, classmate. We are on another island and are supposed to have helicopters pick us up in about 20 minutes. But we lost contact with everybody because of a radio glitch and now we can't seem to get anybody but you. I have some important information. Prepare to copy, over," Ramsey said, rapidly.

"This is Bravo Six. You're right about who we are. I know the voice but give me a minute. You're not going to get anybody else on the radio. The Abu Sayyaf launched a major attack today across the Philippines. I've already had my XO and another soldier killed in action. The Abu Sayyaf took the Embassy and it looked like they had the Presidential Palace when we flew over it. We're stranded ourselves. I've got some Embassy pukes and a colonel in my base camp. We've called back to our headquarters and they're working on the situation. Plus, I doubt you'll get any helicopters. The enemy is everywhere. Send your message, over," said the voice Ramsey believed to be Captain Zach Garrett.

Ramsey leaned back on the heels of his green and black jungle boots and tried to comprehend what his classmate had just told him. Two dead. That makes three American soldiers killed in the Philippines in the past week. *What the hell is going on? The war is in the Middle East, Afghanistan and probably soon to be Iraq.* No helicopters were coming. He momentarily forgot his message and asked, "Do you have any transportation?"

"Roger. We've got one Black Hawk with a quarter tank of fuel. I doubt he can reach you, over."

"I know he can't. Can you get fuel from anywhere?" Ramsey knew the Black Hawk to have a range of over 950 kilometers. Their position was roughly 725 kilometers from Subic Bay. The helicopter could pick them up, but it would not make it all the way back without refueling somewhere.

"We'll try. What's your location?"

"Mindanao. We're near a place called Cateel City. If he can just fly above the shore north of Cateel City, we'll guide him to our location."

"I'll talk to the pilot. Christ, what are you doing in Mindanao?" Zachary asked.

"Zach, this is Chuck," Ramsey said, hesitating before he played the card and violated operational security over the radio. He wouldn't have time to regret it.

Ramsey saw Jones get hit before he heard the gunshot. The first bullet hit Jones in the right shoulder, knocking him back against a tall pine. The second pierced his neck, spraying red blood onto the bark. He stood for a second, wide-eyed, then said in his Boston accent, "Bastards." Sliding down the tree, Jones died.

Soon his team was returning fire. Enemy fire was coming from across the ravine. Ramsey's battle-hardened mind went into gear. *At least they have to cross the river to maneuver against me. That may save us.*

Then he remembered. *The message. Zachary Garrett was still waiting for a response. I've got to get the message to Bravo six.* He knew he was carrying the glass slipper. These rebels would not have been hot on his trail if the Japanese man had not been right about what he had said.

A bullet blew the bark off the tree next to his head, spraying chips of wood into his eyes. Temporarily blinded, he crouched lower. He had to be alive to send the message, and he needed Jones's radio equipment to do it. He reached for the radio and antenna from underneath Jones's leg, and he moved behind a tree. The enemy was obviously trying to knock out his communications equipment as the concentration of fire seemed greatest near him. Then again, it always seemed that way in a firefight. He grabbed his ruck and stuffed the radio and antenna inside. He had eaten all of his chow and had plenty of room for the comms equipment. Another bullet stuck in the wood next to his ear. They seemed to be everywhere.

He could see Benson and Eddie returning fire with vigor. Abe lay frozen with fear next to him. The other men had coalesced into groups that could conduct maneuver against the enemy.

He grabbed Abe, laid him next to his rucksack, and told him not to move. The volume of fire was unlike any he had ever heard before. Grabbing his M4, he moved north and linked up with his security man and backup medic Sid Bullings. They moved along the ravine, out of the hail of bullets. He could see enemy soldiers across the river, looking as if they were going to cross at any moment. It would be a long process on their part, getting down the steep bank and back up the far side. Looking back at his men, he saw Benson and Lonnie White running down the line, doing something he could not quite identify.

He flipped his M4 selector switch to semi-automatic. He had eight 30-round magazines. Ramsey looked through his telescopic sight and could see his weapon's noise suppressor with his open left eye. They took cover behind a rock, and Ramsey began to fire single shots that silently left the muzzle of his weapon and violently struck their targets.

He watched as one of his subsonic rounds struck an unsuspecting enemy, tumbling through his body like a bowling pin and ripping his insides to shreds, he imagined. The lower-than-usual velocity gave the round a chance for more destruction once it struck its target. He picked another target, then a third.

Suddenly, the enemy rose en masse. There were more than two hundred. At least there must have been before Ramsey's men had started shooting. His team was holding them off momentarily. But they stood like some confederate charge in the American Civil War, screaming and climbing down the near side of the ravine. Hand over hand, they scaled down the rocks and would have to do the same coming up the other side.

Ramsey continued to fire, killing every man he shot.

He looked along the ravine. The enemy fell into the waters below, which soon became a deep red. Benson had ignited a series of claymore mines, killing at least 60 who had tried to enter the ravine. Ramsey saw a man with an Australian bush hat running up and down the line, screaming loudly. He laid the sight on the man's head but he kept moving through the elephant grass, never presenting a stationary target.

Ramsey fired. Missed.

Villanueva turned and looked, but he did not see who had shot at him, feeling only the jet wash of the errant shot and listening as the bullet whacked its way through the jungle canopy. He was now certain that it was either Australians or Americans his men were fighting. He hoped they were Americans. *We will be like Vietnam*, Villanueva thought. *We will have started a war with the Americans but this time will destroy the most powerful army in the world!*

But first he had to get the confusion under control. He had ordered his men to open fire once they made contact. His point man had misunderstood the directive and fired when he saw the enemy across the ravine. Villanueva would have preferred to get past the ravine before circling around and coming at them from the north, driving them back into the ravine to their deaths.

He had issued instructions to kill the Japanese man as well. Takishi had told him that Abe might inform the world that the Japanese were making weapons for Abu Sayyaf's use, and that would effectively cut off their supply. He could not have that. Running through the elephant grass and avoiding the bullets that whizzed around him, he began to get control of his men. He pulled them back, ordering them to ceasefire or at least cover their retreat. They would stop and move into Cateel City, then move north of the river, swinging wide, and slam into the enemy.

The firing at his team stopped, but Ramsey continued to pick off retreating soldiers with deadly accuracy. The team kept up its volume of fire into the elephant grass until they could see no more enemy soldiers. Each man knew that the Abu Sayyaf would come again and that they would need their ammunition. They were equally aware that there were no helicopters coming to save them.

He organized his team quickly. Moving back to his rucksack, he looked down at Abe, who was shivering. He had pissed his pants and probably defecated, or so it smelled. Snatching Abe by the arm, Ramsey rallied his team and they moved. Benson slung Jones's body over his rucksack, adding another 150 pounds to his load. They could switch carriers often, but it would slow their move considerably. When they found a safe place, Ramsey decided, they could bury his body, write down the grid coordinates, discreetly mark the location, and return another day for their fallen comrade.

Ramsey walked hurriedly through the dense jungle. He looked over his shoulder and saw Benson struggling with Jones. His mind filled with rage. First Peterson killed, and now Jones. He took both deaths personally. When they come again, they will come from the northeast. *We will be ready to kill every last son of a bitch.*

Like a zephyr, Major Ramsey and his beleaguered A-Team vanished to the northwest.

Subic Bay, Luzon Island, Philippines
Captain Zachary Garrett

Ramsey. That was *Chuck Ramsey.* Captain Zachary Garrett knelt next to the ammunition stockpile, crates stacked to the sky, and looked at the microphone. He had heard a shot and knew immediately that his classmate and his soldiers were in trouble.

But so was he.

As night fell on this incredible day, he rallied his men just as Chuck Ramsey must have gathered his. The division commander in Hawaii, General Zater, had personally spoken to him on the radio, telling him that they were sending assistance immediately. He gave Zachary the authority to do whatever he felt necessary to further protect the lives of his men. When Zachary tried to brief him on the plan, the general cut him off, saying, "I have confidence in you. Don't risk compromising your plan. We've been watching CNN all day and we know you're the one who's been squeezing the trigger." The general's confidence in him had made him feel good, but only momentarily. The weight of his burden then sank in even further.

However, he had passed on his intelligence report to the General, who he assumed would pass it along to the appropriate channels.

The Navy supply ship was not due in until tomorrow, but he was not going to wait for it. Another night in the same location would make his company an even easier target. They could be attacked from practically all directions and they had little cover from indirect fire. Sure, their ticket to safety would be the ship, but waiting for it might only get them home in body bags. Zachary had his men pilfer the ammunition stockpile, then had his forklift driver dump the rest off the pier and into the water to keep it out of enemy hands. He would be damned if he was going to let American ammunition kill his men. They gathered claymore mines, JAVELIN medium anti-armor missiles, all of the 5.56mm ammunition they could carry, smoke grenades, high-explosive grenades, tear gas, star clusters, parachute flares, trip wires, anti-tank weapons and 60mm mortar rounds, even though they had not deployed with any mortars.

After gathering the ammunition and waiting for nightfall, his platoons spread into a large formation of successive Vs with the point of the Vs aiming westward, toward the high ground that bordered the ocean. That would give him at least one secure flank. Each man wore night-vision goggles and they walked slowly at first, then more steadily as they once again became familiar with moving at night.

Zachary had placed the bodies of Teller and Rockingham in body bags, one of those items in the supply room he'd never planned on using. Then he had Sergeant Spencer's squad load the bodies on the helicopter. He gave grid coordinates to the helicopter pilot and told him to meet his company there after doing some false insertions in other places. They were only moving about five kilometers, but the destination terrain was eminently more defensible than the valley where the naval base was situated. Zachary had his men lock their duffel bags in one of the Quonset huts, expecting they would never see the clothes or *Playboy* magazines again.

He made the civilians walk, despite much protest, thinking that any base would be safer than trekking through the jungle. Fraley and the ambassador had argued, but Zachary was in no mood for their bullshit. Zachary sat the ambassador down and reminded him that he was the commander of the unit, and if the ambassador didn't like it he was more than welcome to stay there.

"You guys hosed me over, and you hosed over Chuck Ramsey, who is fighting for his life, I'm sure," Zach had said.

He wanted nothing to do with the ambassador, the other civilians, and especially Fraley, who in just twenty-four hours had demonstrated not only his arrogance and short-sightedness but his selfish cowardice as well.

"Either you let me make the decisions," Zachary said, "or you can walk in another direction. The way I see it, if you couldn't help Ramsey, you can't help me. And that makes you useless." With that, he walked out of the white Quonset hut near the tire pile, threw his ruck on, and led his men into the jungle that rose above Subic Bay. *We will be safer there.*

As they walked, a sliver of the moon smiled wickedly at them from above.

CHAPTER 23
Pentagon, Washington, DC
Secretary of Defense Robert Stone

"What seems to be the problem, Lionel?" Stone asked his assistant. Colonel Lionel Thompson was a "fast mover" in the Army and had been assigned as an aide to Secretary of Defense Stone. He had just run from the National Military Command Center to see his boss.

"Sir, we've just gotten word from General Zater in Hawaii that there's been a revolution in the Philippines."

"Come in," he said, putting his arm around Lionel. "What are you telling me? Wait just a second." He picked up his phone, buzzed Fox, and said, "You might want to get in here."

In less than a minute, both media pundit Dick Diamond and Deputy Secretary of Defense Saul Fox appeared from a side door into Stone's office. Wordless, they sat in the two leather high-backed chairs as if they were spectators at the theater.

"Sir. Gentlemen," Thompson said, looking at Stone, then at Fox and Diamond. "The Abu Sayyaf rose up across the islands to overthrow the government. It appears they were successful. They have control of the Presidential Palace and the television and radio stations. President Cordero is now in jail. The news on our side is worse, however." Stone's eyes cut sharply upward.

"Sir. First off, Assistant Secretary Rathburn and a CIA paramilitary operative, Matt Garrett, have been taken hostage, along with one of the pilots."

"Christ," Stone said, sliding into his chair and placing his face in his hands. He was sitting at his desk and looked out the window. "What else?"

"It gets worse, sir. A stinger missile or some rocket-propelled grenades hit the DC Guard Gulfstream. It blew up, with…"—he hesitated, almost unable to say it—"with the DACOWITS committee on it."

Stone looked at Thompson. Stone had known almost every one of the women on the committee. All of them were women who had fought the barriers of discrimination and had been representing their country on a mission to help improve the lot of women in the military. Their loss was unfathomable to him. And then he realized that he was experiencing the law of unintended consequences.

"Say what?"

"Yes, sir. There's more." Thompson looked down at his Army trousers, hanging perfectly atop his shoes. His light green shirt conformed to his muscular frame. His eyes searched Stone's, hesitating. Stone knew it was never easy being the messenger, who usually got shot, but he continued to meet his eye, waiting.

"The U.S. Embassy has been overrun. Abu Sayyaf insurgents killed five of our people there, four military, to include Lieutenant Colonel Fraley, the senior officer there, and one civilian."

Stone grimaced. "Berryman?"

"Sir, Ambassador Berryman flew to safety on the medical evacuation helicopter with four other embassy personnel and two officers from the embassy. We have an infantry rifle company at Subic doing an ammunition guard mission, and apparently they had some men at the Embassy being treated for wounds from the attack on their position this morning."

"What?" Fox said loudly from behind Thompson.

"Yes, sir. About 80 insurgents stormed the ammunition location. The company performed well, killing 70 and taking 10 prisoners. We, um…" Thompson trailed off again, obviously pained.

"Go on," said Fox.

"We lost two soldiers in the fight. One enlisted man was killed at Subic, and a lieutenant was killed at the Embassy. He jumped off the helicopter and saved the Embassy doctor. When he was getting back on, he was shot in the back."

"What the hell are you telling me, Lionel?" Stone screamed, standing up. "Just what in the hell is going on? We're fighting in Afghanistan and getting ready to fight in Iraq, and there can't be a war in the Philippines! This isn't part of the plan!" He picked up a glass paperweight with a picture of a bear inside, a gift from a Korean diplomat, and chucked it at the wall.

"Sir," Thompson said, now calm, "there's one more item of information you need."

"What's that, the Abu Sayyaf now has Chinese nukes aimed at us?" he said angrily, firing another shot at the messenger.

"No sir. Ambassador Berryman sent a Special Forces team into Mindanao a few days ago. Some Filipino helicopters were supposed to pick them up today, but obviously they did not. No one has heard from the team for four days."

"How did all of this happen, Lionel? Tell me. How did we let this happen?"

"Sir. I just got off the phone with the Pacific Command intelligence guys. They said that a week ago they got the order from us to collect intelligence in the East China Sea. They've been focused like a laser beam on China and Taiwan. Something about a naval attack from Taiwan into Chinese waters."

Stone looked at him with a dumbfounded expression. He remembered his promise to the Japanese ambassador. And he remembered thinking, *Yeah, that should work.*

"Get me the Chairman of the Joint Chiefs of Staff, Sewell," Stone said flatly, reaching for his phone. He dialed and told his wife that he was going to be working late. Waiting for the chairman, he thought to himself: *Bobby old boy, you deserve an Oscar. Your buddies would be proud. You started your very own insurgency and it looks like it's going to slow this bullet train to Iraq.*

Fox and Diamond began to shift uncomfortably in their chairs. Fox was dressed in a dark blue suit with a gray silk shirt, while Diamond was wearing a dark gray suit with a blue silk shirt. *Photonegatives,* Stone thought.

"Who authorized all those troop movements to the Philippines?" Fox asked, standing in front of Stone's desk.

"That is depleting our focus on Iraq. Jeopardizing the mission," Diamond said.

"Exactly," Fox added.

"This is a one-hand-doesn't-know-what-the-other-is-doing thing. I can guarantee it," Stone said angrily.

"We need to get both hands out front where we can see them," Fox said. He held his hands in front of him to emphasize his point.

"Both hands," Diamond added, doing the same as Fox.

To Stone, both men looked like mimes pressing their hands against invisible walls. "Don't worry, guys, it's under control. I've got Central Command bringing me the plan this week."

"We might have to go this spring. Just do it," Fox said. "Get in front of this developing Pacific thing."

"We can't get there from here. We don't have the munitions," Stone said.

"What we lack in armament we will more than compensate for by surprise," Diamond countered.

"Why are we arguing about this? We all agree on the strategy," Stone said.

"Do we, Bob?" Fox asked.

Stone assessed the two men, still sitting in their chairs. How could they be so willfully ignorant? They had just heard that American lives had been lost in the Philippines and they knew damn well that the fight in Afghanistan was a slow-motion strategic nightmare.

While the soldiers on the ground were performing magnificently, Stone knew that the strategic window to crush Al Qaeda had slammed shut as the enemy senior leaders escaped through the rugged Hindu Kush. Stone's position all along had been now that 9-11 had occurred, the United States should use the event as a rallying cry to attack Islamic fundamentalism everywhere. Hence, the gambit in the Philippines. It had everything to do with putting pressure on the global extremist network. The threat was so obvious to Stone, who wondered how Fox and Diamond could blindly sit there and ignore the evidence that Iraq, while important, needed to wait.

"We do," Stone replied. "Now if you'll excuse me, I've work to do."

Diamond and Fox followed one another out and Stone shut the door behind them.

Walking to his desk, Stone picked up his phone, thinking, the plan was underway but they were not in control, like a glider buffeted about by the winds. *Let's pray for a soft landing.* He dialed Rathburn's number and frowned when he didn't receive an answer. He was certain the hostage thing was an elaborate plan that Rathburn had hatched to further draw attention away from the Iraq mission. An improvisation, for sure, but a smart one nonetheless.

Matt Garrett, our number one operator, is a hostage!

Stone left a message: "Good move, my friend. Call me when you get a chance."

CHAPTER 24
Greene County, Virginia
Karen Garrett

Karen Garrett, Matt and Zachary's sister, had been calling the Department of Defense, the Central Intelligence Agency, and her congressman for the last 24 hours, but she had only run into the usual bureaucratic nightmare. Nobody could tell her the location of either of her brothers, not only because they did not know, but also because everything was "classified."

Angry and frustrated, she had not slept for almost two days. Their mother had passed away and the funeral was scheduled for that day. They could not put it off any longer. She had reported to her father, almost shamefully, that nobody could locate his two sons. Her father had looked away, sad. "Bring the boys home," was all he had said before walking away.

Karen turned her coffee cup in her hand, looking out the window, recalling the events of the past few days. She had not cried, thanks to some help from bourbon, but her eyes remained moist, ready to gush whenever the switch flipped. She watched curiously as a sedan slowly approached the house, pitching and rocking. She could see some writing on the door of the car: U.S. GOVERNMENT.

Usually, uninvited, official looking visitors around here did not bring good news. The car parked in the gravel lot to the front of the wooden porch and stopped. Karen watched a blond woman step out of the driver's seat. She was wearing a nice blue dress with high heels. Karen checked her own visage in the hallway mirror as she stood. Trademark ponytail yanked into a knot revealing a fresh, sans-makeup look.

The funeral was not for another two hours. Who was she and what could she be doing here? She let the woman knock on the door. What bad news would this woman bring now? Where she got her strength, she did not know. But she would have to trust it would come from somewhere. Opening the door, she stared at the mountains behind the woman's pale hair.

"Hi. I'm Meredith," the woman said. "You must be Karen."

"That's right," Karen said, blankly, not making a connection. She held the door open with one hand, her body blocking the entrance to the wooden foyer.

"Karen, may I come in for a second? I've driven down from DC."

"Let's sit on the porch," she said, closing the door behind her as if to protect what remained of her family from the intruder. The porch was a typical farmhouse addition. The roof hung over a high wooden structure that had old metal chairs that would rock if one leaned back in them hard enough. The red bricks from the house were stained with red clay. She let the screen door slam behind her and walked over to a metal chair, taking a seat.

"I'm sorry, Meredith, did you say?" She cupped her hands on her knees. "The funeral's not for another two hours—"

"I'm so sorry for the loss of your mother," Meredith responded. She had been traveling for the past two days on her return from Palau. A secretary had told her that Matt's mother had died and that his sister was trying to get in touch with him for the funeral.

Her first stop, though, had been at the home of Chief Warrant Officer Ron Peterson outside of Seattle, Washington. She accompanied the casualty-assistance team on their grim notification duties and passed Ron's identification tags to his wife, as she had promised Matt. After then arriving on the East Coast, Meredith was exhausted but had decided to travel to the farm, two hours away, immediately, and inform the Garrett family of the situation.

"Karen. I have some information on Matt and Zachary," Meredith started.

"Yes," Karen said, eyes darting up quickly, "tell me."

"Both of your brothers are in the Philippines. We have communications with Zachary, who is in the jungle with his company. They have been fighting, but he is fine. Matt," she sighed, "Matt..." She hesitated again.

"What's happened to him?" Karen said, hearing her pitch rise as she stood and approached Meredith.

"Karen, Matt's been taken hostage by some Filipino rebels," she said, finally.

"Oh my God. Oh my God," she screamed. "My family. What's happening to my family?" Meredith stood and hugged her, dropping her purse on the wooden porch. Karen pushed away from the bearer of bad news. Meredith's clutch was too tight, though, and they both were crying.

"We'll get him back. He's special, I know." Karen then hugged Meredith back, more from lack of strength than for any other reason. The dam of stoicism burst under the relentless pressure and even the bourbon couldn't stop it. She felt isolated, with nowhere to turn, so she held on to Meredith for no particular reason. She could not show her father such emotions. She had to be strong for him.

But her father had heard her scream. Her head leaning against Meredith's shoulder, Karen saw her father out in the field. He dropped his hoe, took a knee, and grabbed a fistful of dirt, squeezing tightly.

She heard him cry, "Bring the boys home," loudly and with passion. "Bring the boys home!" he screamed at the heavens, arms stretched high reaching toward the God he knew and loved.

Karen pulled herself away from Meredith, squared her shoulders and went out to retrieve her father. They moved inside to the parlor, as they still called it in the Garrett house. Karen had started to fix coffee, but

Meredith quickly took over, floating around the kitchen as if she had lived there forever. Soon she came out with a tray of coffee and hot tea. She and her father drank silently, absorbing some of the shock before Meredith repeated the story, this time with less emotion on both sides. She said that the Departments of State and Defense were doing everything they could to get a handle on the situation. Meredith tried to be positive, talking up the actions of Zachary's company. Word had gotten back to the Department of Defense that he and his soldiers had acted bravely, she told them.

"I expected nothing less," Mr. Garrett said, proudly.

Then Meredith told them about the airplane and how lucky Matt was to be alive. Karen was glad that Meredith stayed with the family, attending the funeral and meeting many of the fine people of Stanardsville, who had always relied so heavily on Karen and the rest of the Garrett family. She said they reminded her so much of her own family and friends from her part of Virginia. It seemed that everyone from town came to the funeral. The Reverend Early arrived beforehand and consoled Karen and her father. He delivered a warm and powerful eulogy, describing their mother as a woman of the soil. Recalling her family tradition throughout the county, he quoted from Romans 11: "If the root is holy, so are the branches."

They attended church that afternoon, as well. It was a small brick structure. They sat in a row and prayed for Zachary and Matt and all of the other soldiers in the Philippines as well as those deployed in Kuwait and Afghanistan. It was hard, but they all held onto their faith. Then Meredith helped cook for all of the well-wishers who had stayed after the funeral and visited with the family. Many people stayed late into the evening, and she enjoyed the company, but the pall of Matt's and Zachary's absences hung over the room like a deadly fog. No one could concentrate.

After the mourners departed, there were cups and dishes everywhere, and Karen looked at Meredith, who had changed into a pair of sandals and was clearing the tables.

"Thanks, Meredith. You don't have to do all of this."

"Why don't you just go to bed," Meredith said, holding an armful of plates.

"No. Just leave it. I'll get it later. I think I'm gonna go sit on the porch for a while," Karen, exhausted voice.

"It's no problem," Meredith said. Karen looked at her and smiled for the first time in days. There seemed to be nothing self-serving about Meredith. Karen walked up the stairs, then came back down holding a pair of blue jeans and an old flannel shirt.

"Here," she said, tossing Meredith the clothes. "You'll be more comfortable in these."

"Thank you, Lord," Meredith said, looking skyward. The two women gave a hint of a smile, but it was a fleeting moment, gone like a rabbit into the bush. Karen walked onto the porch and sat on the steps in the cool mountain air, while Meredith changed her clothes and cleaned the rest of the dishes. Soon Karen heard the screen door slam behind her against the door frame as Meredith came out to join her. Karen looked up.

"Sorry," Meredith said.

"No bother. Daddy's a sound sleeper," Karen replied. Meredith sat on the steps next to Karen. They stared at the lights in the small town of Stanardsville about a mile to the south.

"What are you thinking about?" Meredith asked.

"I want my brothers back," Karen said softly, her voice floating into the night. Crickets chimed rhythmically. Two bullfrogs barked at each other in the pond.

"I want them back too," Meredith said, quietly.

Karen watched the stars blink at them from the heavens and hoped that God would be good to them. She believed in so many things. She had faith in God, believed in her country, and believed that people were basically good. She got the sense Meredith was the same way.

"Thanks for all your help today. You really helped," Karen said. After a pause, she said, "You see that light just beneath the moon?"

Meredith looked and said, "I think so."

"It's blinking, sort of."

"Yeah. I see it," Meredith said, leaning over to gain Karen's perspective, her hair falling across Karen's shoulder.

"I read somewhere, can't remember now, that you could see satellites in the sky. I never believed it, but that doesn't look like a star, and it sure isn't an airplane," Karen said. Meredith didn't respond. She just watched the dark sky flutter with millions of lights. She looked at Karen, still fixed on the bright moving object. "You shouldn't drive back tonight," Karen said. "You can sleep in Matt's old room. His old twin bed is still in there."

"Thanks. That's sweet," Meredith said.

"You, okay?" Karen asked.

"Just thinking of Matt," Meredith said.

"He's like that, Matt is. Whatever you do, don't get hooked on him. He's trouble."

Meredith smiled. "Yes, I could tell, but there was something he said in Palau that keeps coming back to me."

Karen perked up. "What? Something that could help us find him?"

"Probably not." Meredith's face fell. She said, "I'm sorry, I shouldn't have said anything. I wish I had something helpful to say but I would just be rambling." She rested her hand on Karen's shoulder.

"That's okay," Karen said. "I'm sure you'd let us know if you came up with something important."

"I would," Meredith said, standing up. You must be exhausted. I won't keep you up any longer. Thanks for the clothes." Karen followed her and they walked up the stairs, hugging once before retiring to their separate rooms. Meredith seemed lost in her thoughts and Karen just needed to sleep.

Meredith Morris

Sitting on Matt's old bed, Meredith studied the room. Half of it had an angled ceiling from the A-frame. The other half was flat. Pictures of Zachary and Matt hung on the knotty pine wall. Other than the bed with cowboy-and-Indian sheets, there were three boxes in the room. They stood stacked on the tongue-in-groove floor. She stood and looked in the top box, pulling back the cardboard flap. She saw a manila folder inside, labeled: WHAT IS GOING ON?!

She took the folder and sat back on the bed, opening it. Several pages of yellow legal paper were folded so they would fit in the undersized folder. Beneath them was a stapled packet of about 15 pages, once again labeled: WHAT IS GOING ON, this time without a question mark or exclamation point. "Huh," she said to herself as she began reading.

Iraq and Afghanistan ... I just don't understand. We had just commandeered several mules from a local farmer and took the path just north of Torkum gate. We knew we were in Pakistan, but we had a solid lead on two specific persons of interest. Then I've got the shot. Then someone is screaming at me denying my kill chain. Next thing we know a JDAM bomb lands closer to us than to the AQ and we get the call on sat phone ordering us to turn around and come back. Less than two days later my team is in Iraq and I'm on my way to the U.S. for a makeover to chase some phantom Predators in China. What the hell is going on?

These political appointees have their heads so far up their asses they can't see straight. The one time the nation has asked for a head on a platter and we can't deliver. Bin Laden and his cronies dealt us a sucker punch and we must destroy them.

Where will this lead? There's no question about the rightness of killing Saddam. Hell, give me the mission and I'll go do it. But it's a tougher problem than anyone can imagine. There is no question that a democratic Iraq may be game-changing in the Middle East. Who wouldn't want that? But is it feasible? They should take a look at the Balkans and all the warring factions there to see what might be in store for a fractured Iraq. They should look at Post–Cold War Yugoslavia, but Iraq will be far more kinetic. One thing is for certain: we are treating Afghanistan and Al Qaeda as a secondary mission. Maybe the right thing to do, but I can't see how.

Even more, what happens if we get locked into major combat in Iraq and another country becomes a sudden threat? We will be caught flat-footed. Take a look at any of the regional contingencies: China-Taiwan; North Korea-South Korea; Iran-any neighbor; Russia-Ukraine or any of its breakaway republics and there are other possibilities. The world is short on resources and long on demand. Water and oil will drive the next decade's social and economic policies. What happens if a nation decides it must act only for its own survival despite the impact on economies around its region or around the globe?

Take Japan for instance. We think of it as a friendly neighbor but they are headed for the worst economic crisis they've face since World War II. With over 50 nuclear power plants, they are vulnerable to natural disasters and terrorist attacks. Mostly, they need the raw materials and agricultural base to balance their booming manufacturing sector. Japan is a country we need to watch carefully as we also focus on Afghanistan, Iraq, Iran and North Korea.

Meredith dropped the paper in her lap and put her fingers to her temples. *My God, what is he saying?*

She read on. Matt delineated several Pacific Rim regional threats but drifted back to Islamic radicalism. He highlighted the Abu Sayyaf insurgent factions that were struggling for help, ripe for outside support. While philosophically aligned with Bin Laden, the Abu Sayyaf's need for resources outstripped Al Qaeda's ability to provide, Matt argued.

She felt close to Matt reading his paper. Obvious to her, these were just thoughts typed into a computer through stream of consciousness. She closed the folder and sat still, looking through the window into the night. She turned off the light, still thinking, and let the darkness settle over her like a blanket.

As she drifted off to sleep, in her mind a hawk circled, looking for prey. As her brain wound down, there it was. Its talons clutched the rabbit, and her last thought before drifting off:

It cannot be possible.

CHAPTER 25

The following morning, Meredith ate the eggs and toast that Karen made for her, after which she printed out a MapQuest set of directions to the University of Virginia library. She sped down Route 29 into the heart of Charlottesville and found the library after a few wrong turns.

Once she was parked and in range of a decent cell tower, Meredith powered up her Blackberry, read her messages, and stared at the library for a minute. Then, energized, she barged in, showing the monitor her Department of Defense badge and asking if there was an office with a fax machine. Getting a good look at the blond official, the student manager gladly let her use the librarian's office. Meredith threw off her coat, still wearing Karen's jeans and flannel shirt. She then walked quickly to the reference and periodical sections, spending nearly 30 minutes collecting country reports and studies on Japan and the Philippines. Then she did a Google search and found the British "Economist Intelligence Unit" country reports to be the most insightful and comprehensive.

She spun the mouse until the Japanese trade figures appeared. When she had read the contents of Matt's folder in his room, she had not thought of the Philippines as an actor but as a target. It was resource rich but infrastructure poor. It was a rabbit with no hole to hide.

And Japan was a potential hawk. Circling, starving, resource-poor Japan; its wings spread high into the stratosphere of advanced nations, yet it had little bounty within its own territory.

She studied the figures, which showed that trade was declining with Europe and the United States. Next, she looked at the demographics.

There would be a manpower shortage in Japan in a couple of years. She looked at the energy reports. Japan's coal production had fallen and its alternative sources program had reached the point of diminishing returns. Gas prices were already exorbitant across the country. She read the EIU report that asserted that Prime Minister Mizuzawa was tiring of American claims of unfair play. She searched the documents, looking for a link between Japan and the Philippines. She also knew that about two years ago, the Abu Sayyaf had announced their alignment with Al Qaeda, hoping to reach into Bin Laden's deep pockets. She turned away from the computer and reached under the stack of books and papers, grabbing country reports from two years back. Tucking her hair behind both ears, she dug in. She read agricultural reports, manufacturing reports, trade figures, imports, exports. Nothing seemed unusual.

Then she saw it.

Buried in a "Recent Developments" paragraph of the two-year-old EIU report, she found the sentence, "Surprisingly, Japan has invested in construction on the island of Mindanao in the Philippines. That the Japanese would construct mines and mineral-gathering facilities on the island, which is riddled with Al Qaeda sympathizers, demonstrates the desperate lengths to which they will go to secure resources for their economy."

That was the link, but what did it mean? Maybe they were just getting resources like timber and minerals. *Think, Meredith, think.* She stared at the wall, searching her mind for a clue. How would they transport the stuff? On ships. What kind of ships?

She picked up the phone and called her office in the Pentagon. Mark Russell, a young intern, answered the phone. Perfect.

"Mark. Listen. I want you to go to the guys at the Philippine desk and get reports for all shipping activity out of Mindanao. I need you to fax it to me in 10 minutes," Meredith demanded. She gave him the number.

"Okay. But they're pretty busy with this current sit—"

"Listen!" she said loudly, "this current situation may be bigger than we think. Now do it. And tell them that Stone wants it."

"Yes, ma'am." She hung up the phone. It was not a total lie. If she could prove a link between Japan and the Philippines, she would try to brief Stone that afternoon. The implications of fighting an insurgency, if that was what her country was going to do, would be vastly different if Japan was supporting the rebels for their own possibly sinister purposes. How else would Japan get the new weapons other than manufacturing them secretly in Mindanao? How had they grown so fast in the past two years? Five minutes later, the fax machine jumped to life and began to spit out pages with the past year's shipping data from Davao City and Polomoloc, the two major port cities on Mindanao. She stacked them on the desk, which was cluttered with open books turned upside down to mark pages.

It was monotonous, looking at the figures of ships and their names and the cargo that they hauled. The only Japanese ships she could identify that went into either port were some taking in consumer goods, several ships carrying timber back to Japan, and 10 oil tankers. Oil tankers? She checked the oil export figures for the Philippines. *They don't export oil to Japan!*

She called Mark back and asked him for some tracking data on the ten Japanese oil tankers that had left Davao City in the past six months. Once again the fax machine whirred to life.

Those ships never off-loaded any cargo in Japan! They entered Davao City empty and left with their hulls deep in the water, the reports read. It looked like a routine oil pickup, but it had to be something other than oil. While there might be oil reserves in Mindanao, the Philippine government had not invested any infrastructure in either finding or pumping it.

By a process of elimination, she came to the conclusion that there were ten, possibly eleven, Japanese ships somewhere in the Pacific with something other than oil as cargo. She also surmised that whatever the Japanese had constructed, they were not gathering minerals. The mineral export-and-import data remained the same after the Japanese did the construction in Mindanao.

She also noticed that the EIU reported that Japanese defense spending remained the same as a percentage of gross national product. But, she noticed that overall government spending had increased without accounting for the rise anywhere in any other line item.

Convinced she had found an unthinkable clue, she gathered her faxes, purse, and coat, and sped out the door.

CHAPTER 26
Pentagon, Washington, DC
Secretary of Defense Robert Stone

Secretary Stone pulled a rumpled pack of Camels from his top desk drawer and shook it until two cigarettes revealed their crushed filters. He had been smoking since the beginning of the crisis. Grabbing one butt with his large, fleshy fingers, Stone stuffed the white stick in his mouth and lit it with a shaky hand.

Coughing smoke, he said, "It's a different world, this post-9-11 thing, you know?"

"Yes, I know," said Kaitachi, the Japanese Ambassador to the United States. "But we need your help. Not only with the Philippines and the China situation, as you might suspect, but with Korea as well—"

"What the hell does Korea have to do with this?" Stone retorted, the cigarette jumping wildly in his mouth.

"The North is playing with nuclear weapons and, we believe, is trafficking nuclear materials. How would it look for North Korea to be passing nuclear weapons to our enemies? And with Islamic fundamentalism threatening our sea-lanes, we now have threats on all of our borders," Kaitachi said. "And they are part of your Axis of Evil."

Stone looked at the third man, Taiku Takishi. *This should be interesting.*

"Mister Secretary, on behalf of Prime Minister Mizuzawa, I must also convey our deep concerns over the situation in Korea and China. He believes, rightfully so, that both countries on the Korean peninsula pose a significant threat to Japan," Takishi said.

"What are you talking about?" Stone responded. "We're all part of the United Nations. We won't let that happen anymore. Even with everything going on in Iraq and Afghanistan, we won't let it happen, I'm telling you." As Stone spoke, Kaitachi and Takishi looked at each other with reassuring eyes.

"One final thought over Korea—" Takishi began.

"Why the hell are you so concerned about Korea all of a sudden?" Stone demanded, his chin rattling around his neck and growing red where his shirt collar chafed. He looked at Diamond and Fox and shook his head. "Can you believe these guys?"

"It is not a new concern, and we have reason to believe China may be orchestrating the events in Korea," Takishi said. He crossed his long legs as he spoke and used his hands to animate his point. "The Japanese people are beginning to feel increasingly threatened and confined. Almost surrounded, you might say. Without your help, we feel our region may grow unstable," Takishi continued. Stone knew he was doing nothing more than creating white noise for Fox and Diamond and perhaps his Ambassador. While this wasn't part of the plan Stone, Rathburn, Takishi, and "Ronnie Wood" had hatched, he could go along if Takishi need this kind of support to please his ambassador.

Stone lit another cigarette and thought for a moment, then said, "Look, we've got hostages to get out of the Philippines, then we're off to Iraq. We can maybe help you after that."

"We'll see. You do know we can help with your hostage situation," Takishi said. "We have established contact with Commander Villanueva, the senior Abu Sayyaf commander, and can arrange for all Western and freedom-seeking peoples to depart the country by way of Subic Bay Naval Base."

Stone leaned forward, acting almost jubilant, as if the albatross that had nested on his neck had flown out of the window and across the brown waters of the Potomac.

"Why the hell didn't you mention that first?" Stone asked, smiling.

"This would be huge," Fox said, entering the conversation for the first time.

"Timely," Diamond concurred.

"Wait," Stone said, sitting back in his leather chair. "What's it going to cost us? What's the trade-off?"

"Villanueva simply wants a guarantee of no American intervention in their political quarrels with the Filipino government, to include the departure of any U.S. troops immediately, in exchange for allowing any Westerners who want to leave the country. He sees this as a domestic situation and claims there is no threat to United States' interests. Of course, we have tacked on our interest in the shipping lanes to the negotiations," Takishi said.

"Of course you have. That still sounds too easy," Stone said. He was really thinking: *That's not part of the script. American intervention is the entire purpose, you moron, Takisihi.*

"It may be. We are still highly concerned about our shipping lanes, and as I mentioned earlier, all of the other threats we perceive," Takishi said.

"Yeah, okay," Stone responded, confused. "One thing at a time." *Is Takishi double-crossing me?*

"Of course," Takishi said. "We need to close the deal with Villanueva secretly. Give us a day, then you will need to start sending airplanes into Subic Bay and arranging for the withdrawal of your people. Villanueva has indicated he will give you two days."

"Two days!" Stone shouted.

"Better two days than none. Villanueva will not reconsider," Takishi said flatly.

Kaitachi and Takishi stood, straightened their pants and coats, and bowed slightly toward Stone, who crushed a smoking butt into the ashtray and followed the two men to the door.

"At a later time, we will discuss our concerns about Korea, China, and our shipping lanes," Kaitachi said as the two men walked past the administrative assistant and a disheveled-looking blond clutching a stack of papers and books to her breast.

"Let's work the hostages first. Then we can go from there," Stone said, looking at Takishi.

"Good plan," Takishi replied.

The two men departed, and Stone reentered his office as Fox commented, "I think we can see our way through this, Mr. Secretary We get the hostages back and evacuate the Philippines, then we continue to steam toward Iraq. We can't let Saddam think that we are weak. Plus, Villanueva's demand gets us off the hook. We'd love to send in more troops to fight the terrorist problem in the Philippines, but hey, we can't." Fox mocked himself, shrugging his shoulders as if he were helpless.

Stone looked at the diminutive man and said, "You know, Saul, I think you're right. I just hope this thing in the Philippines doesn't get any worse."

Diamond leveled his judgmental eyes upon Stone and asked, "Are we protesting too much, Bob?"

"Why are you saying this to me?"

"We just believe that this situation in the Philippines seems a bit, how shall we say…" Diamond said, looking at Fox, who finished the sentence for him, "…contrived."

"Well, call whoever contrived it and tell him to turn it off so I can get some sleep at night," Stone retorted angrily.

Diamond and Fox stood in unison and turned to exit through the side door into Fox's office. Diamond stopped, turned around, and said, "What is it that gathers no moss?"

Stone watched the two men depart and stood there dumbfounded.

Had he been compromised? Was Fox possibly warning him?

His intercom buzzed and his secretary said, "Sir, I think you'll want to see Miss Morris."

Meredith Morris

The secretary of defense's administrative assistant, whom Meredith knew, looked at her with a raised eyebrow as the two Japanese men exited. Meredith was holding her materials in one hand, her coat and purse in the other. She looked quite the country bumpkin, she knew, in the blue jeans and flannel shirt. She looked up and saw Stone open his office door.

Two Japanese men stepped out, smiled, and gave her an awkward glance. The three men shook hands, and the two Japanese men departed. One of the men looked at Meredith lustfully, his eyes undressing her with the look of a hyena sensing carrion.

"Sir, I just need a couple of minutes about Secretary Rathburn," she said.

He held up a hand and closed his door behind him. She turned to Latisha White, the secretary, and mouthed the word, "Please."

"You come dressed like that, it must be important," Latisha said. She buzzed the secretary, and a few minutes later he reappeared, asking, "You are?"

"I'm Mr. Rathburn's assistant, Meredith Morris. I need to talk to you." Stone must have been persuaded by the urgency in her voice as he gave her a standing audience just inside his closed door. "Sir, I think we've got a concern over this entire revolution—" she was nervous. Her words were not working.

"Of course we're concerned. Now if you'll let me get on with the business of resolving this crisis—"

"No. Please. I've done some research. I think Japan is behind this whole thing. They're providing weapons—"

"What!" Stone screamed. "I'll have you know that the Japanese ambassador just came in here and offered to solve the entire affair for us in the next two days without firing a shot."

She was confused. There had to be a motive. They would never offer to do such a thing. It was unprecedented.

"It's a trick," she said, holding up her hand.

"A trick?" Stone asked. "How do you mean?"

She could see she had his attention now.

He walked over to the intercom and said to Latisha, "I'll be receiving a briefing from Ms. Morris for the next 15 minutes. Please hold all calls and readjust my schedule accordingly. He looked at Meredith and said, "Okay you've got 15 minutes. That's more than I give the Chairman usually."

"Sir, I put Secretary Rathburn on the Gulfstream in Palau hours before they landed in Manila. I should have been on that plane but the DACOWITS group trumped me." Her voice trailed off as she considered the possibility that she could have been killed in Manila.

"So, we don't know for sure that he's captured," Stone said.

"I think that's established, sir. The rebels have contacted us with demands. We've seen grainy photos taken with cell phones."

She watched Stone consider her comments and nod, indicating she should continue. She proceeded to give Stone her analysis and the reasoning behind it. Stone appeared confused as he had when escorting the visiting Japanese men from his office.

"There certainly seem to be some inconsistencies, but why would they offer to resolve the issue for us?" he asked.

"How did he say he was going to do it?" she countered.

"He said they could work through Commander Villanueva and get our people out of there. If he can do it, I don't care what he's got up his sleeve," Stone said, flatly.

"Unless it's nuclear weapons," she replied. He stared at her. "These shipping logs here show that ten ships left Davao City significantly deeper than when they arrived. Loaded at night and departed at night. It's either weapons or nukes or both."

"I doubt that," he said. "As you know, Japan's constitution prevents any production of nuclear or offensive weapons, and I don't think they'd want to invite the consequences of violating their agreement with us. I'm sure it's a snafu in the shipping log."

Frustrated, Meredith dropped her head on his conference table and stretched her fingers out as if to choke somebody.

"Do we know for a fact what's on those ships?" she asked.

"I don't need to know. The Japanese have been a good and faithful ally for almost 60 years," he said.

"Because they needed us," she replied. "Before that, Americans were dying because they bombed the hell out of Pearl Harbor with no warning. Can't you see it?"

She slammed her fist into his conference table.

"It's the perfect crime. They start the revolution. Then they ask us to back down while they handle it. Next thing you know, they own the Philippines." She had not come to that conclusion until then. It was so obvious, though. Especially after reading Matt's paper, it all made sense.

"That's preposterous," Stone said. But his face said, *Holy shit.*

"Sir, you okay?"

"Anything else, Meredith?" Stone asked without emotion.

"No, sir," she said, looking away and grabbing her materials. She walked out of the office and passed Latisha, whom she thanked.

Meredith trudged to her office, where she thanked Mark for his quick response earlier that afternoon. The office was a zoo, with everybody working hard on the crisis. She guessed it was good news if the Japanese ambassador could get the Americans out of the Philippines. Then the U.S. could wash its hands of the entire ordeal.

But she knew nothing was ever that simple.

CHAPTER 27

Meredith walked into Rathburn's office and sat down at his desk. There was the usual assortment of photos of the political appointee with various administration dignitaries as well as foreign leaders.

She picked up one framed picture of Rathburn with his wife and two boys. They were leaning together, all dressed in white, with the chrome stanchion of a sailboat behind them. The waters reflected in the picture made her think the photo had probably been taken while they were sailing on the Chesapeake Bay.

She sighed and twirled around in the chair, looking through the yellowish tinted window.

She thought about Japan, the Philippines, Iraq, and Afghanistan. What did they all have in common?

Nothing. *So separate them,* she thought to herself. *First came Afghanistan, and now this weird, almost myopic drive to get into Iraq. The country wants to kick some ass and Iraq look primed for a good ass kicking,* she thought. *Not enough juice to squeeze out of Afghanistan to satiate the appetite.*

"Enough for what?" she whispered.

And now there is this Abu Sayyef problem in the Philippines. Where had that come from? Had our intelligence seen this coming?

She remembered her discussion with Matt and everything he had told her about Japanese soldiers on the island of Mindanao. She coupled that information with her newfound intelligence about the ten missing ships.

Something was out there floating around, and she thought she had it nailed. Japan was going to be the aggressor somewhere, and the Philippines made sense to her.

But why would they start a war just so they could fight it? How could they be that confident that America would not intervene in a significant way?

Unless they had assurances.

She tapped her finger against her lip, thinking. Chess moves. Everything was choreographed, orchestrated, she determined.

But who was doing it?

Everyone knew that that troll Fox and self-aggrandizing Diamond were poking and prodding their way to get everyone hooked into Iraq. There was no question about their intentions.

But was there a countermovement? Were there people in the U.S. government who believed that going into Iraq was *off the mark*?

She knew that Stone had neoconservative leanings but was very much his own man when it came to decision making. Meredith also wouldn't pretend to know the Byzantine machinations of decision making within the Pentagon or even the White House. Yet she did understand that sometimes frenzy and momentum became currents too swift to fight lest you drown trying to swim against the tide. *And so perhaps,* she thought, tapping her lip, *just perhaps there were some folks trying to do what they considered to be a good deed. Stop a war in Iraq by starting one in the Philippines.*

The more she thought about it, the more sense it made.

Meredith waited until everyone had departed for the day, walked through the outer cubicles and offices one time, then reentered Rathburn's office.

Dead men tell no lies, she thought. Meredith immediately scolded herself. *He's not dead. Yet.*

She tried to stop herself, but she couldn't prevent the sinking feeling that her boss was either dead or about to be killed.

She wandered around Rathburn's E-ring lair, where he had worked for the past three months as the newly appointed assistant secretary of defense for international affairs. Typically an impotent position, Rathburn had seemed unusually powerful and connected in his early days with the Department of Defense.

What were his connections? She knew he had been a professor at Georgetown University's National Security Studies Program and was woven tightly with the party leadership that had risen to power. But what gave him that link?

Meredith, just over 30, had always wondered how powerful men achieved their status. There were worlds that she could simply not imagine, and even the idea of taking a simple trip to Palau with Rathburn had excited her beyond belief. Did powerful men likewise think they could wave their hands over the wafting fumes of power, inhaling them, and experience the sensation themselves? Achieve the status? Maybe Rathburn had also somehow drunk the elixir and one morning found himself in position to influence world events via his connection to the secretary of defense.

She picked up a football signed by all of the Washington Redskins. Next to it was a large machete given to him by a Gurkha soldier in Nepal. Other mementoes were scattered on several bookshelves and display tables.

She studied the diplomas on the wall for the first time as she spun the football in her hands the way a wide receiver might as he shot the breeze with the quarterback. She had seen the diplomas before, of course, but she had never really read them. Rathburn had earned a Harvard undergraduate degree with a major in economics; a Harvard MBA; and a Princeton Ph.D. in political economy. *Interesting,* she thought. *Mostly a finance background.*

I guess that's what makes the world turn, she mused.

She sat at his computer and contemplated what she was about to do. Meredith had thought at length after her meeting with Stone. She pulled out the three-by-five card she'd had the computer technician give her months ago. Rathburn was always forgetting his password and finally the overworked 22 year-old had jotted on the card the secret and regular computer code words for access to Rathburn's computer for her.

"Don't tell anyone," he had said, winking at her. "I'll deny it." Now, just as they had when Rathburn had called her for help after forgetting his passwords, the passwords worked. She was into both his unclassified and classified hard drives.

She checked his Internet browser cache to see and saw that he had used a variety of search engines, and she was interested to see that Rathburn had never cleared his history file. She was able to view his activity from three months before, when he had assumed the job. She spent some time perusing the search engines that he had visited. He apparently had a G-mail account and a Yahoo! e-mail account.

She tried to find the user names of those accounts, but everything came up with the blank sign-in screen. If he had been logged in, the browser had ultimately logged him out for inactivity. She then opened his Outlook work e-mail account, scanned through those, and again saw nothing that would raise a red flag.

She clicked on "My Pictures" and saw nothing, then clicked on "Trash Bin" and found one deleted photo.

It was a photo of four men, one of whom she presumed was Rathburn, all standing with arms laced around their buddies' shoulders. She did a double-take as each man was wearing a Halloween mask. She immediately recognized Mick Jagger and thought she could tell which one was Keith Richards with his wrinkled face and long hair, but she wasn't enough of a *Rolling Stones* enthusiast to remember the other two members of the band. There was a big tongue and lips superimposed on the photo, and she remembered that to be the logo on one of the *Stones'* albums. *Sticky Fingers* maybe? Maybe not.

Huh, she thought.

She switched the Cybex Switchview box to the classified computer, which could not access the Internet but could access a Secret domain. There wasn't much there, only some routine e-mails on Outlook.

She closed the dialogue boxes and opened the "My Computer" icon. She saw the common O: drive where they shared office files and such, which she opened. They held nothing she either hadn't seen or hadn't put in there herself during her duties as his special assistant.

She closed the O: drive and studied the "My Computer" box and looked at all of the network drives. Again, nothing out of the ordinary. Just the one photo, but what did that mean?

Frustrated and beginning to feel foolish, she stood, grabbed the football she had initially picked up, and began to put it back in the orange placekicker's tee from which she had lifted the pigskin.

Her eye caught something in the center of the tee. She studied it more closely and saw that there was a small tear in the middle where the ball would rest on its pointed end. She touched it and determined that the tear was actually a tab, like a battery compartment cover. Meredith pulled at the tab and peeled back the soft orange material.

In the bottom of the well of the tee was a small thumb drive.

Huh, she thought.

Meredith flipped over the tee and a SanDisk 1-gig removable drive tumbled onto the desk. She sat back down and picked up the drive.

She removed the plastic tip and inserted it into the computer. A moment later a dialogue box appeared asking her if she wanted to open a file.

"Of course," she whispered.

She clicked on the box and a series of tan manila folders appeared on the screen. They were, in order:

PRED-CHINA
AIG
MICK JAGGER
CHARLIE WATTS
RONNIE WOOD

None of the folders would open though, as they were all password-protected.

Fearing locking the drive from errant attempts to enter a password, she closed all the dialogue boxes, clicked on the icon to eject the thumb drive, and removed the device from the computer. Meredith pocketed the drive, pushed the orange plastic back into the tee, replaced the football on the tee, and dusted off everything she had touched.

After shutting down both computers, she walked out of the office. Stepping through the darkened halls of the E-ring after most of the Pentagon work force had already departed, Meredith stopped and turned. What had she heard?

There was a noise coming from directly across Rathburn's office. Then she saw it. A stairwell door closed just as she looked farther down the hallway.

Creepy, she thought, and quickened her pace.

As she finally reached the dark South Pentagon Parking Lot, she shook off the creepiness and wondered: *Why wasn't Keith Richards, the second most famous Rolling Stone of them all, on that list?*

But then she remembered. She picked up her pace, looking over her shoulder as she unlocked her car. If she was right, now that she'd spilled her knowledge to Stone she could have a few enemies. She wasn't worrying just about Matt and Zachary's lives anymore.

Now she had to protect her own.

CHAPTER 28
Mindanao Island, Philippines
Commander Villanueva

"We had a deal," Takishi said. "We produce the weapons for you, and you do not kill Americans." Takishi spoke from the luxurious confines of a Japanese government Gulfstream executive jet settling into its final approach into Tokyo where he would shift venues to his Shin Meiwa. He needed to give Bob Stone the personal reassurance so that he did not deviate from their plan. He believed he had succeeded. The 48-hour diversion had set him back, yet the information gained had been invaluable, and useful. This was the tricky part for Takishi, transitioning from able co-conspirator with the Americans to Machiavellian statesman for his country.

"No. The deal was that you make us weapons, and you get the free extraction of the many minerals in my Mindanao countryside," Villanueva replied.

"Why did you have to attack the Americans," Takishi said, an edge in his voice.

"This is my country, Takishi. Don't tell me what I can and cannot do. We have suffered for nearly a century from the imperialism of the United States and your country as well. So don't tell me how to run a revolution," Villanueva said. Takishi assumed he was talking into the satellite phone he had provided Villanueva.

"Consider me, then," Takishi said, changing strategy like a chameleon, "an emissary from Japan. On behalf of the Japanese prime minister, I respectfully request that you set up a release point for all of the American soldiers and citizens, to include the government officials your men have taken hostage."

"What's your interest in this?" Villanueva asked.

Takishi knew that Villanueva needed to establish his presence on Luzon before the New People's Army beat him to the seat of government. Though the Islamic Jihad recommended small cells fighting under a unified commander's intent, Villanueva had bigger aspirations and could not afford to leave a power vacuum in Manila

"We have an interest in maintaining strong ties with the United States for trading purposes, as you will need as well if you ever want to be anything other than a fourth-world country," Takishi said. "You are so close to victory, Commander. Can't you see that?"

"We have already achieved victory!" Villanueva replied. "We have overrun the U.S. embassy. We own the Presidential Palace. No problems."

"You idiot, you have bitten the tail of a snake. Right now you have a Marine brigade coming down from Okinawa and carrier groups steaming from the Indian Ocean and Hawaii. Their infantry division in Hawaii is scheduled to fly to Guam tomorrow to establish an intermediate staging base. The head of the snake, my fine Filipino friend," he said sarcastically, "is about to give you a fatal strike."

"How do you know all of this?"

"My ambassador was given their entire deployment plan. They're prepared to throw everything they've got at you unless you cough up every American on these islands."

"Then they will leave us alone?"

"Then they will leave you alone."

Of course, Takishi was completely bullshitting Villanueva, but that didn't matter. It *could* be true, soon enough.

Villanueva cast his gaze upon Cateel Bay a kilometer and a half below him, its water sparkling like so many diamonds. They had achieved total strategic, operational, and tactical surprise in their attack. Of course, it would not have been possible without the Japanese-produced weapons. Villanueva firmly believed, though, that they did not owe the Japanese anything. He knew that the Luzon cell planned to kill, or had already killed, one of the American hostages and was about done with the others. He felt he was making good progress in chasing down the invaders in Mindanao and had issued instructions to the Luzon cell to kill the American soldiers at Subic Bay.

You told me to kill Matt Garrett, he wanted to say, but didn't. He sensed that Garrett was at the core of the illusory nature of the men he had been chasing. And so he remained on the front lines, determined to protect his people of Mindanao and to kill the American spy before relocating to command all of the Philippines.

Villanueva felt an adrenaline rush, then sighed. Their struggle had always been difficult. They had often taken two steps back for every step forward. As much as he wanted to take revenge on the Americans, he decided that Takishi's advice was solid. The cause must come before revenge. He would not let his petty emotions stand in the way of freedom for his people. He had to start thinking like a strategic leader, a president, as opposed to an operational military commander.

"Okay, Takishi. I will inform my men that Subic Bay Naval Base is off-limits. The Americans have 48 hours to depart. But tell them that I only want non-combat aircraft to come get their people. I am doing this in an exchange for our right to determine our own form of government. If we want to be part of Bin Laden's caliphate, so be it. If I see combat troops or planes, we will shoot them from the sky."

"Of course," Takishi said. "I will pass on the message for you. My plane should be arriving shortly in Cateel to escort you to Manila so that you can assume the presidency."

"Thank you," Villanueva said.

"And Villanueva, you should talk to your men at Fort Magsaysay. They have succeeded where you failed."

"How's that?"

"They've got Matt Garrett locked in a cell."

CHAPTER 29
Kanishi Abe

Abe was glad that Major Ramsey's team had finally eluded the insurgents. It was dark, and they had been on the move for a full night and an entire day, each man taking a turn carrying Jones's body. Abe was glad to contribute and demonstrate strength and character by carrying the dead man once, albeit briefly.

Abe felt compassion for the American men. They were strong and rugged, but he knew they must have families as he did. They were only doing what their country had asked them to do. He watched their stark faces as they faded into and out of his sight in the moonlit night, silently stalking through the high-mountain rain forest. Their painted faces, streaked with black and green camouflage, reminded him of the Indian warriors he had read about in American history. The men stepped lightly, seeming never to touch the ground. Large green leaves would brush against their faces, leaving the moisture from the dew and rain across their brows. Each man held a weapon, pointed outward. He was impressed at their professionalism and quietly yearned for their, and his, safety. One day he would write a poem about the contrast in their compassion and their duty.

He could sense that the men were scared, but they dared not focus on fear. He was reassured by their compassion for one another and the fact that their leader, Major Ramsey, had brought him into the fold. He sensed that they still did not entirely believe his story about the weapons. To them, it did not compute. To him, it made perfect sense.

Over the past five days he had become drawn to Major Ramsey. Abe found himself respecting the commander's authority and command presence. In his society, it was natural to be drawn to the source of power and obey. He had noticed in Ramsey an ability to remain calm even in the most dangerous situations. To Abe, the more confusing the situation, the more stressful, the more dynamic, the more the major would retreat into his inner sanctum and draw from a deep reservoir of knowledge and power and control.

Like adding ballast to a listing ship/the man in green/leads his men/they the arrow/and he the tip.

He patted his empty pockets for a pen to jot down the thought, then hoped he could remember it.

In the growing darkness, Abe looked down at his jungle fatigues with the crazy black, green, and brown patterns interwoven in the fabric. He was beginning to like them, he thought. As they walked, he carefully chose his steps through the dense underbrush to avoid the dreaded black palm plants and any poisonous snakes that might be lurking. He stepped first with his heel, rolled his foot gently to the side away from the arch, then pushed quietly with his toes.

He still did not carry a weapon but could taste the excitement as they moved like an invisibly connected team through the jungle. He saw that each man knew where the other was, like a sports team. They were always looking in a full circle, turning slowly halfway around, then back again, lifting an arm to quietly push a branch aside. He was learning the discipline of martial arts that he had eschewed as a young man in Japan. So many of his friends had trained in the jujitsu and karate skills, but he had chosen piano lessons and engineering at an early age.

That night, as he moved in sync with the soldiers through the lush green highlands, he felt something instinctual that had never been there before. He wanted to be a part of the team. His mouth was dry and tasted like copper. His heart beat fast, but in control.

He watched as Major Ramsey halted the patrol in the darkness. They had doubled back on their trail and were about six and a half kilometers northwest of Cateel. Their initial path had been 200 meters below the slope they now occupied, and a rare clearing in the forest connected their current position to the previously traveled path. Abe watched as Ramsey gave instructions to Benson, who quickly went about the business of implementing them. Ramsey then slipped his rucksack off his shoulders, grimacing as he did so because of its weight, and set up the tactical satellite radio.

Abe listened to the conversation.

Major Chuck Ramsey

"Bravo six, this is Bushmaster Six, over," Ramsey whispered into the radio. The sun had fallen behind the mountains to his rear. He faced east, peering between two mahogany trees into the clearing. Slipping on his night-vision goggles, he saw Benson directing his men into different positions and tacking what looked like fishing line ankle high to trees near the other side of the clearing. They worked quickly and professionally, knowing exactly what to do despite their hunger and fatigue. Three days ago they had officially run out of food. Most of the men had conserved their combat rations however. They had lasted up until that point only through Eddie's expert foraging.

"Bushmaster six, this is Bravo Six Romeo, over," a voice responded. Ramsey sighed with relief. His connection to civilization was intact.

"This is Bushmaster Six, get me your zero-six, over."

"This is Bravo Six," Captain Garrett's voice came back, "good to hear from you. We've been trying to contact you."

"This is Bushmaster Six. Yeah. We have some enemy hot on our trail We lost another man," Ramsey said.

"Christ. Chuck, this is Zachary," he responded. They were emotionally connected, Garrett and Ramsey, two West Point classmates finally recognizing they were in the midst of an impossible situation. It was only natural that they forgo proper radio procedures and share a moment of friendship. It *was* lonely at the top and sometimes leaders needed reassurance.

"I know. I'm glad it's you up there. Any luck with that helicopter?" Ramsey asked, hopefully.

"He's on the way. He departed our area about an hour ago and will try to island hop and steal gas until he can reach you. We've moved. Like I said before, this whole place is under attack by Abu Sayyaf. We can still hear fighting down in Olongapo. I know you're sucking, man," Zachary said.

"Okay," Ramsey said, hopeful. "Any way to predict when he'll be here?"

"Couple of days at the worst. If he's lucky, about 24 hours."

"Okay. I think we can hold out. Zachary …"

"Yeah."

"If I don't have a chance later … thanks. I know you could use that Black Hawk. You didn't have to send it."

"I'll see you in a couple of days and we'll drink a San Miguel and go chase bar girls," Zachary said.

"Listen, I've got some important intelligence that you need to get to your higher. I can't seem to get bird 65 right now, so you have to relay this information, over."

"Send it," Zachary said.

"We have captured a Japanese engineer who has been working in a weapons-production plant on the island of Mindanao for the past six months, break," Ramsey said, taking a moment to spit some smokeless tobacco from his bearded lips. "Says he's an automotive engineer. Builds cars, normally. We found him jogging in an orange running suit. He said that there are four production facilities on Mindanao. Three produce tanks and helicopters and the other produces small arms and ammunition, over."

A long moment of silence ensued. He assumed the commander was copying.

"You gotta be shittin' me," Zachary responded.

"I kid you not. What I need to know is, were there any tanks or helicopters in the Abu Sayyaf attack this morning?"

"None that I saw. We captured about 10 enemy and they all had new M4s and M16s. Hell, we just got those M4s a couple of years ago ourselves," Zachary responded.

"Yeah. I know what you're talking about. Listen, I've got about a battalion of insurgents hot on my ass. Just get that information to your higher headquarters. Then we won't have died in vain over here. Gotta run, out," Ramsey said without emotion.

Subic Bay, Luzon Island, Philippines
Zachary Garrett

Zachary dropped the hand holding the radio handset into his lap and stared into the darkness. His company position was facing west on the slope of the rain forest just north of Subic Bay. The hopelessness of Ramsey's situation perversely gave him optimism. His father had always told him never to feel sorry for himself, because somewhere somebody had it worse than he did.

Immediately, Zachary called the 25th Infantry Division headquarters in Schofield Barracks, Hawaii. He had Slick angle the small SCAMP dish between a saddle in the mountains behind them. He had positive contact with bird 65.

He contacted the headquarters and passed the message to a tired young lieutenant pulling shift duty in the early-morning hours. The International Date Line separated Hawaii and the Philippines, but in reality the time difference was only six hours. For Zachary in the Philippines it was 2200 hours, yet for the lieutenant in the division operations center, a rather monotonous duty, it was 0400 hours of the same day. The old joke was that someone could fly from Manila to Hawaii and get there before they left.

The lieutenant assured Zachary that he had the message, including the bit about the Japanese auto executive in the jungle. Zach had asked him to repeat the message, but the lieutenant would not respond. Zachary hoped that he had raced to the division commander with the information.

Zachary was not encouraged that his report would be handled properly. Then he heard Slick on the radio.

"Pitts, is that you?" Slick said. His given name was John Cane, Zachary knew. They called him Slick, though, because he considered himself such a ladies' man.

"Pitts?"

"Slick?"

"It is you!" Slick responded. He had been monitoring the radio and could hear Pitts as if he were only a kilometer away.

"Hey. Got your message," Pitts said.

"Hey is that Pitts from headquarters in Hawaii," Zach asked, perking up.

"Yes, sir," Slick said, grinning. "My best bud."

"Yeah. Some pretty wild shit, isn't it? Scary—"

"Get off the net! Changing frequencies now," a voice boomed over the improper radio conversation.

The two privates gave a "Roger, out," but Zachary grabbed the handset and continued to try to reach the headquarters.

"Try to find what channel they've switched to," he ordered to Slick. "They are probably thinking we found some old World War Two stuff."

Zachary said those last words with a sudden belief that was exactly what had transpired.

Mindanao Island, Philippines
Major Chuck Ramsey

Major Ramsey saw the first man enter the engagement area slowly. He was glad to see them pursuing them at night. It meant that they still did not know they were fighting Americans for certain. Or if they did, they were stupid. The insurgents, to his knowledge, had no night-vision goggles. Chuck Ramsey's team did. All except Abe. Ramsey had given Jones's goggles to Eddie, who had become an indispensable member of the team. Eddie held down the pivot position in the L-shaped ambush. He would be firing diagonally across the engagement area.

Looking through his goggles, Ramsey saw three infrared chemical lights glowing softly. Benson had tacked the three lights to tall bushes along the main trail cutting across the open field to be used as fire-control measures. The lights were positioned perpendicular to Eddie's line of fire, invisible to the naked eye but clearly evident through the goggles. When the lead member of the enemy patrol reached the last light, Ramsey would initiate the ambush with a claymore. The other two lights helped divide the engagement area into sectors of fire to avoid redundancy of killing. The five men positioned along the top portion of the L, facing downhill, would fire between the two lights farthest away, almost directly down the hill. The other six men would fire along the slope of the hill, directly across the frontage of Ramsey's position. That would produce an effective crossfire that might, once and for all, get this particular enemy off his ass.

By then a four-man patrol was at the second light, directly in the middle of the engagement area. Ramsey could see a man feeling his way with one hand in the darkness, ensuring no branches or twigs caught his eye. He looked like a blind man groping his way through an unfamiliar room. *Soon, he* would *be blind*, Ramsey thought to himself.

Nearly 30 Abu Sayyaf were stacked single file behind the lead team, wandering aimlessly into their sights.

As a precaution, Ramsey had sent Abe nearly 50 meters to his north to serve as a listening post on the left flank. He had tied their remaining rope around Abe's waist so that he did not get lost and to serve as a communications device. Two tugs from Abe meant enemy soldiers were coming from that direction. Abe had readily accepted the mission, glad he could help. Ramsey, desperately short of personnel, placed confidence and faith in him.

Villanueva struggled up the mountain, still reeling from his conversation with Takishi and the fact that the Luzon faction had Garrett. He had unsuccessfully tried to contact the Fort Magsaysay team that captured Matt Garrett and vowed to try again in the morning.

Rocks slipped beneath his feet. Branches whipped into his face, unintentionally launched by the man to his front. They had found a trail, which made movement easier and faster. With Takishi's report that Matt Garrett was detained in Luzon, Villanueva's frustration mounted. He found himself thinking less of the enemy and more of a way simply to get to Cateel so he could fly to Manila and become President.

His men had slowed, reaching what seemed like a clearing. The lead company, whittled to only 40 rebels, noisily passed back the word to the other two companies of equal size that they would slowly move across the clearing. Villanueva was impatient, frustrated at the elusiveness of the soldiers he was pursuing. Prior to this week, he had caught them easily. He had known all of their tactics. They were particularly careless at night, bunching into tight clusters with little to no security. Now, they were slippery and he wanted a quick victory. His brothers in arms had seized control of the government and he could not even catch a 10-man patrol.

As his first men crossed the clearing, he heard the second element move along the trail. He had positioned himself at the lead of the second unit and felt the commander brush past him quietly as he watched dark figures drift silently through the night. His frustration was mitigated by the exhilaration of watching his men perform. He had read all of the American manuals on patrolling and conventional combat and watched his men execute what he believed to be a perfect danger-area clearing. He thought it was good, too, that his other two battalions had remained north of Davao City. Having too many people in the jungle would be difficult to control. His men slid past him in silence as they followed the trail. He was close. He could feel it.

Ramsey had watched the four-man team barely clear the danger area. They had not checked the far side. Looking through his goggles, he saw the lead man of the patrol walk past the third infrared chemical light.

He squeezed the electrical blasting machine, a small, handheld device that generated an electrical pulse via the rapid pumping of a handle that turned a small motor, sending an electrical signal along the wire to ignite the claymore mines.

Nothing happened. He squeezed again. No response. Groping in the dark, he found the firing wires. Somehow one of the wires had come loose from the post. He awkwardly reinserted the wire, pressing down on the post as if he were inserting a stereo wire into a speaker. The blasting machine tumbled clumsily out of his hands as he watched five men move past the last infrared light. His hand dug into the dirt, snatching the small device. He pumped the blasting machine with two hands cupped around it, forcing it into his chest.

A bright light flashed into the darkness like a single strobe. He had forgotten to look away from the blast, and the sudden whiteness burned out the batteries in his goggles. He was as blind as the rebels, and with the deafening blast he could barely hear.

Nonetheless, his team began firing. All of them had PAQ-4C infrared strobes mounted on their weapons to augment their goggles. Their fire control was rough at first. The men on the right flank started by shooting the lead five men then turned their rifles on the predetermined sectors. Tracers rocketed downhill and side hill, most finding their way into the warm bodies of Filipino rebels. Screams of pain sang out in the night, interrupted by the now-cadenced fire of M4s, M203 grenade launchers, shotguns, and sniper rifles.

Because he had lost his night vision, Ramsey could only direct his fire toward the tracers in a default fire-control technique. He hoped that whoever was firing the tracers could see what he was shooting. But he felt stupid pulling the trigger with no target. Being so low on ammunition, he stopped, deciding wisely to conserve. The withering fire stymied the Filipinos, nonetheless. He could hear men drop and had yet to see a single shot returned.

Villanueva registered shock as he watched his first company get raked by a screaming hail of bullets. Half of the second company was trapped as well. He had jumped back into the first cut of trees at the sound of the explosion. Popping his head above a rock, he could see the fire outlining the enemy's positions. The tracers were coming from directly up the hill and immediately to their right about 150 meters away.

We can flank them. He tightened down his hat and grabbed a shaking soldier, telling him to get the rest of his company and to follow him.

"Sir, there are only five men left in my company," the soldier said, smelling of urine.

"Then get them!" Villanueva yelled beneath the sound of the raging American rifles.

He had the trail company lay down a base of fire to imply that they were not moving. Swiftly, he took his five-man team to the north, moving through the rain forest with unexpected ease. *This is brilliant,* he told himself. As they moved, they were clearly out of any danger from the ambush. The firing grew more distant as he led his team behind the enemy's north flank. It seemed surreal, the tracers diving into the ground, sometimes arcing eastward toward the ocean. The soft pop of the weapons belied their destructive nature. He and his men made the turn and were moving parallel to the ridge. Villanueva could not believe his good fortune. He was behind the enemy, unimpeded. They moved to set up a position from which to kill them. They would attack silently, he decided, using knives to kill each man individually.

Abe watched with amazement the execution of the ambush. If only he could play a role. He felt his hands reaching for a weapon, pulling an invisible trigger, and delighting in the kill. *What kind of transformation am I experiencing? Is this some part of me I hadn't known was there?*

Suddenly, he heard footsteps in the darkness. The major had told him that no one friendly would be moving unless he saw a green star cluster. None had been fired. Without hesitation, he pulled the rope twice, watching five bodies pass him on either side, moving toward Ramsey and his men. One stopped, cocking his head to one side like an alert deer, then proceeded. Abe watched them move toward the young Filipino Ranger, Eddie. He wanted to cry out to the man, but feared giving away their position. He watched in horror as the enemy circled Eddie from behind and one man slid a knife into his back.

Ramsey felt the tug and turned in Abe's direction. He could see dark outlines moving quietly through the trees, as if the enemy were still guessing and searching for their location. They passed him. He had not been firing. They had not noticed a muzzle flash from his direction. Then he saw a dark figure stop only three meters away, turning his head slowly in Ramsey's direction.

Ramsey leveled his hush-puppy pistol in the man's direction, hoping it was not Abe, and pumped a single, silent shot into the chest of the man, who fell backward into the bushes.

He sensed the others stop and turn. They came back to the shot man and Ramsey fired another bullet at a rebel who was bending over to check on the first. Then he sensed at least two had moved to his left, on his downhill side. His position was between two trees. Quickly, he backed away, and the three enemy soldiers converged on one another. One screamed in pain, apparently at a knife wound, as they inflicted friendly fire upon one another. The other two leapt directly at him, knocking his pistol to the ground.

Ramsey grabbed his K-Bar knife out of its sheath as he felt the hot steel of an enemy knife pierce his left arm. He screamed in agony, thrusting his knife into the innards of one of the men on top of him, turning the blade back and forth like a fork collecting spaghetti. Pushing away, he saw a man, older than he, wearing a bush hat poised above him ready to end his life.

"Americans," the voice said.

"Die, scumbag," Ramsey said, trying to throw the man off him with no success. The man held down Ramsey's good arm while his wounded arm lay helpless at his side.

"No, my friend. This is a great victory for my people. We will parade your stinking bodies down Roxas Boulevard. Bin Laden will give us money. America will suffer," he said, smiling.

Ramsey spit tobacco in his face. His attacker, who was wearing an Australian bush hat, raised his right arm, the knife silhouetted against the dark sky.

Three shots from the hush-puppy knocked him off Ramsey. Bursts of machine-gun fire suddenly erupted around the two men. The tracers and muzzle flashes lit the night sky like strobes. Gaining visual acuity was difficult, and Ramsey sensed that the enemy combatant was no longer next to him. Staying low to avoid elevating into the cross fire, Ramsey low-crawled through the elephant grass.

The bush hat man was gone. Grasping at the grass to his left and right, Ramsey touched a foot, then a leg.

The fire abated and Ramsey rose to one knee as Abe helped him to his feet. Looking up, Ramsey saw Abe's face highlighted by the weak moon. He looked at Abe's hand, holding the hush-puppy pistol. He'd obviously picked it up when he saw Major Ramsey drop it. With a calm demeanor, Abe looked down at the weapon, then at Ramsey.

"Why this thing make no noise?"

The moment was almost comical. Then Abe moved to one knee and lifted an Australian bush hat from the grass. He held it in his hand without commenting as he stood again.

"That man, with the hat, where did he go?" Ramsey asked.

With Ramsey's night-vision goggles busted by the first blast, Abe and Ramsey were both without night-vision goggles and had lost their advantage in the darkness.

"Ran. Like the wind. Not find. Need to get you a medic."

The ambush had slowed in intensity, producing an occasional pop from a friendly weapon. No tracers burned in the sky. There was only the collective moan of wounded bodies. Ramsey stood eye to eye with Abe, grabbed his pistol, and said, "Thank you." But then he had to kneel again, suspecting his wounds were worse than he had initially believed.

He still had a fight to command, however, and people to protect. He found his rucksack, which was riddled with bullets. He cringed when he found the radio shattered inside. The green star cluster was still serviceable, though, and he promptly sent it screaming into the air, giving the signal to move to the next rally point. He handed Abe his rucksack, and said, "Please."

Abe seemed happy to help. Ramsey watched Abe flip his rucksack onto his back, fitted the Australian bush hat onto his head and started up the mountain.

CHAPTER 30
Near Fort Magsaysay, Luzon Island, Philippines
Matt Garrett

Matt was squatting on his haunches in the corner of a dank cellar with adobe walls and a thin green slime of mildew and mold along the dirt floor. So far he had killed one snake and four rats. He should have just let the snake live, he thought; maybe it would have eaten the rats. He looked across the cell at Bart Rathburn, the high level defense department appointee, and Jack Sturgeon, the pilot of the airplane they had flown to Manila. Both were slumped against the far wall, avoiding the filth as much as possible. He was thankful that he was practiced enough that he had brought no identification materials and truly looked like a security guard. To his knowledge, none of the rank-and-file insurgents had connected that they had a CIA operative in captivity. They were focused on Rathburn with all of his important-looking badges. *Sucks to be him,* Matt thought. So far, Matt had not been questioned and no apparent leader had presented himself.

Rathburn and Sturgeon appeared visibly shaken, though the pilot seemed like he could handle himself better than Rathburn could. The guy was coming unglued, Matt realized. Sturgeon was leaning against one shoulder in the far corner as if he might be twirling a toothpick in his mouth at the local soda fountain. Rathburn was pacing back and forth looking at the floor and muttering to himself like Rain Man.

Their Filipino captors had stripped them of their weapons, rifles, pistols, and knives, and dumped them unceremoniously into this basement.

When they removed their blindfolds and restraints, Matt noticed that there was another man with them; he looked Native-American and sat in the muck along the other wall. The man opened his half-lidded eyes when the three of them had appeared in his previously solitary cell. Just as quickly he closed them, as if retreating back into some sanctuary.

"Gotta call Mick Jagger," said Rathburn. "If he can't help, Ronnie Wood is the man. *The man*, you know what I'm saying? This is Mick's doing, I know. You know? If not Mick, then for sure Ronnie. You know what I'm saying?"

Matt walked across the slimy surface and stopped Rathburn by placing a hand on his shoulder. Rathburn spun wildly, which caused Matt to snatch his wrist and hold it.

"Actually, no. I don't know what you're saying," Matt said. He looked at Rathburn's eyes, which were wild with fright. *Flight-or-fight*, Matt thought. *This bureaucrat has no fight in him, for sure.*

"Jagger must have screwed up somehow. This wasn't part of the plan," he said, as if Matt should understand exactly what he was saying.

"They took my iPod. I had some Stones," Sturgeon said, providing a bit of levity to the scenario.

"The Stones, man. We are the Rolling Stones, and this thing happened too soon," Rathburn said.

Matt noticed that the political appointee had the thousand-yard stare of a man who knew he was going to die soon. His crazed look indicated a man whose eyes were searching for reason but coming up empty. Imagining the worst and trying to find a scenario to escape the end that awaited him, Rathburn was spiraling out of control.

"What the hell are you talking about? You knew about this?" Matt growled.

Rathburn stopped his pacing and stared at Matt, perhaps through him.

"I'm Keith Richards, don't you understand?"

"You're a whack job," Matt replied.

"Hey, Keith, either gimme shelter or shut the hell up," the large man in the corner said.

Matt turned to the man who had been silent to that point, looked at him, and watched him stand. He was enormous, probably pushing seven feet, Matt guessed.

"What's your name?" Matt asked, still holding Rathburn's trembling shoulder.

"Rod Stewart," the man said, breaking into a wide grin. Matt noticed his teeth were white and straight, at odds with his disheveled appearance. "Let's have a jam session."

"Don't mock me, asshole," Rathburn said, trying to point but unable to because Matt was restraining him.

"I don't know you, but I will kill you," the stranger said to Rathburn. "But I would be doing you a favor, so I think I'll let the guys running the show do it."

As if on cue, four Abu Sayyaf guards barreled down the steps and opened the door, splashing a rectangular spotlight of sunshine across the floor.

"Hey, Joe. You die," one man said as three gathered up Rathburn and took him up the stairs.

"We're going to see Jagger, right?" Rathburn shouted. "This is all a ruse. Make it real. No propagandists. It's all real." Then he pointed at Matt, and shouted, "He's the one you're supposed to take! That's Matt Garrett. He's who you're looking for!"

They listened at the incoherent ramblings as the guards escorted Rathburn out of earshot.

"What the hell was that?" the big man asked.

Matt watched the men drag Rathburn up the dusty concrete steps and said in a low whisper, "What the hell was that all about?"

"Sounds like you were supposed to be set up," Sturgeon said.

Matt remained silent, then turned to the large Native American.

"Name?"

"I told you…"

"Don't mess with me," Matt said approaching the larger man. He leveled his jade laser like eyes into the man's bloodshot brown pupils.

"You don't scare me," the man replied, shrugging his shoulders. "But just so you know, Johnny Barefoot's the name."

"American?"

"Yeah. Was here on assignment."

"You work for CNN, right?" Jack Sturgeon asked, moving toward the conversation.

"That's me. I was supposed to cover some deployment of an infantry company from Hawaii to here. CNN was getting all kinds of static from the Department of Defense as to why there were no embeds in the Philippines covering this 'war.'" He made quotation marks around the term "war."

"So they sent one dude?"

"That's right. Not even my thing, you know. I do American West, Native-American issues, casinos, corruption, that kind of thing."

Huh, Matt thought. He turned away and walked toward the door, which he checked. It was secured, as he'd expected. Matt's mind spun. *I get pulled out of Pakistan when I'm about to kill Al Qaeda senior leadership. My team is broken up, and I'm sent to China and the Philippines pursuing teaser leads on Predators. I'm told to jump into a plane wreck only to find an American body I wasn't told about. I find Japanese tanks on Mindanao and a Japanese man flying in a float plane to Palau, where, coincidentally, perhaps not, Rathburn is cooling his heels. Then I run across a second-tier journalist who was sent to "embed" with a 100 soldier rifle company in the Philippines, where a Muslim uprising has suddenly taken root. And Rathburn is giving up my name to Abu Suyyaf.*

None of the threads made sense separately, but there were some he could see that created a fabric. With Barefoot standing there, he was reminded of a Bev Doolittle painting *The Haunted Ground.* At first glance, the painting was simply a cowboy atop his steed looking over his shoulder as he fled through an aspen forest pulling his galloping supply horse. When he stared at it long enough, the knotty trees dissolved into an image of three Native-American faces and an eagle watching the intruder.

What was he seeing when he stepped away from the individual threads and put the mosaic together?

As his mind spun to wide field of view, he stopped, a gear catching.

"Who were you supposed to interview?"

"That's the thing. The company was in a hell of a fight, a couple of guys were killed, and they bugged out to the jungle."

"Who?" Matt asked, approaching Barefoot.

"Some company commander named Captain Zachary Garrett."

CHAPTER 31
Pentagon, Washington, DC
Secretary of Defense Robert Stone

Stone placed the secure phone in the cradle and leaned back in his leather chair.

Some captain had just called in a Japanese weapons stockpile in Mindanao.

The weapons are supposed to be distributed already. What else could there be unless it is the armored vehicles? But really, how could Japan build tanks in Mindanao? No, this is good, he thought. *We're definitely going to have to commit some resources to the Philippines. But what do the Japanese have up their sleeves? Ten ships Rathburn's assistant mentioned. Four to six, not one, weapons-manufacturing plants on Mindanao. Bart Rathburn is possibly dead. What kinds of chess moves is Takishi making?*

Fox and Diamond entered the room via the side door. Each man had removed his suit coat and had the sleeves on their respective Egyptian cotton shirts rolled up just below the forearm. *We are working hard,* their appearances screamed.

"This is out of control," Fox said.

"Exactly," Diamond reiterated.

"I'm busy, guys. You *just* may be right," Stone agreed.

"We are getting off track here," Fox said.

"And we have some ideas to get back on course," Diamond said.

"I'm thinking we'll have to wait until next year to do Iraq," Stone said.

"That's unacceptable. The window of opportunity is now. The American people want to kick some ass," Fox said.

"*Now*," Diamond seconded.

Stone, tiring of the tag-team duo, said, "Well, how about we kick some Filipino ass?"

"Not enough targets. We need more targets," Fox said.

"More ass," Diamond added. "The more targets, the more ass we can kick. Who wants to kill a bunch of zipperheads?"

Stone looked at Diamond and gave him a disapproving look for using the derogatory term.

"We don't go to war with the theories we wish we had; we go to war with the theories we've got," Stone said. *That ought to clear it up for these twits.*

Fox and Diamond stopped, looked at one another, and seemed to ponder this pearl of wisdom.

"Yes, but what the hell is in the Philippines?" Fox continued. "I've got CENTCOM's troop list right here. If we keep pouring troops into the Philippines, we won't have enough troops for the invasion of Iraq!" Fox shook a thick stack of papers at Stone.

The two men were machine-gunning Stone as if sensing they needed to close him the way a real-estate agent gets a skittish buyer to sign the contract.

"Democracy in the Middle East is important, but can't we wait a year? Develop a plan, maybe?"

"CIA says it's a slam dunk. We need to go," Fox said.

"What *is* a slam dunk is that Al Qaeda is still on the loose. We've captured or killed a few mid-level functionaries, but the big fish have just changed streams," Stone said.

"Al Qaeda is incapacitated," Fox said.

"Out of commission," Diamond reiterated.

"Is this how you really feel?" Fox asked Stone.

Stone sighed. Where were his true friends when he needed them? One might be dead; another was half a world away. Maybe Ronnie Wood would come to his rescue. He was really the most powerful of them all but had asked for the Wood pseudonym to further disguise his participation. If Wood was ever found out, the whole thing would come tumbling down. That left Stone to carry the weight of this Philippine effort on his own shoulders.

"You guys are killing me," Stone said, ignoring the question. "I've just ordered a Navy SEAL team to check out the ships the Japanese have supposedly loaded with tanks and helicopters."

"All conventional weapons. Iraq's got nukes," Diamond said. "And, we'll need the SEALS to get into Basra and other port areas immediately."

"Yellow cake, aluminum tubes, and rockets," Fox sang.

Stone thought he might hear Fox mutter an "Oh my" à la *The Wizard of Oz*. He turned away and looked out of his window. He could see the Washington Monument standing erect in the middle of the Mall.

Yes, as soon as he could shake his leg loose from these two terriers, he would call Ronnie Wood and talk things through.

Stone watched Diamond and Fox depart, then ordered Meredith to report to his office immediately. He was going to see Ronnie Wood, and she could come in handy.

As the last person to see Rathburn alive, Meredith could be valuable, Stone figured. He didn't know what, if anything, she knew about the Rolling Stones, but she could provide some clues to Rathburn's situation.

Once she'd arrived and he'd conjured up an excuse about needing her help, they made the quick trip to the Old Executive Office Building adjacent to the White House. It was an overly ornate structure, almost a medieval eyesore amidst the modern office buildings. There they met Vice President Hellerman, who deemed it necessary for Stone and Meredith to give the briefing personally to President Davis. He ordered the National Command Authority to convene in the White House Situation Room, a small room with a cherry conference table where the president sits behind a white phone.

Eventually, the service chiefs of staff, the CJCS, SecDef, vice president, Central Intelligence Agency director, and Meredith all huddled around the table. The secretary of state was already on his way to Japan to discuss regional security issues and possible economic sanctions against the Philippines.

Meredith Morris

Meredith was dumbstruck. In her inexpensive dress instead of a power suit, and with a stack of papers and books tucked in her arms, she felt like a schoolgirl, much younger than every other person in the room.

They all stood when the president entered, then sat quickly when he waved his hand at the group. The chief executive sat at the head of the table with the vice president on his right and the national security advisor on his left. Stone was next to the vice president and across from Sewell, the CJCS, and Frank Lantini, the CIA director. The chiefs of staff filled the other seats, with Meredith awkwardly positioned at the other end of the table, providing a weak counterbalance to the president, who was opposite her.

"I know almost everybody," President Davis said in his smooth Southern drawl, looking at Hellerman, who smiled and stood.

"This is Ms. Meredith Morris. She's an analyst, is it, with Bart Rathburn's group?"

Meredith stood, trying to appear more confident than she felt.

"No, sir. I'm his special assistant. I handle a broad range of issues for Mr. Rathburn."

"Okay. Let's proceed," the president continued. "The situation, as my national security advisor has advised me, is this: The Abu Sayyaf has taken control of the Philippines, President Cordero is in jail, Secretary Rathburn and two others are hostages." The president went down the checklist as if he were grocery shopping.

Meredith winced when she heard Matt's name fall into the "others" category. The president continued. "And, we have a Special Forces team on Mindanao and an infantry company on Luzon. We lost 15 women, some military and some civilian, on an airplane at the Manila International Airport. The Japanese have arranged for us to use Subic Bay Naval Base for the next two days as an airport of debarkation only. No ships, is that correct?"

"Yes, sir," Sewell responded. "That's a good summary. It's also important to let you know that we have developed a joint task force under the command of Admiral Dave Jennings with Pacific Command. Right now he's got the majority of a light infantry brigade and division headquarters in Guam, a Marine expeditionary force moving south from Okinawa through the East China Sea, and a naval carrier group steaming from the Indian Ocean. They should be in the South China Sea in two days. We've got the fighter and bomber wings at Guam on alert. And, of course, portions of the Ranger regiment are waiting on the airstrip in Guam."

"Okay, but we plan on a simple extraction of our personnel, correct? I mean, we just start flying airplanes in and taking our troops out. Right?" the president asked. "I can see no reason for becoming militarily involved in the Philippines, unless we can't get all of our people out. I still want to focus on Iraq and Afghanistan as the main front in the Global War on Terror. I don't want anything to divert our attention there."

Meredith was convinced that he passionately believed what he was saying.

"We want democracy and market systems in the world, but not at the expense of American lives. Communism is no longer our enemy, and last time I checked, these rebels were really communists just trying to hook on to the Muslim thing. It's like Cuba suddenly saying, 'Hey, me too.' So, if these communists cum Islamists want to have it, then let's find a way to contain it and get after the real threat." The president looked around the room and continued, "We will be able to use other forms of power to influence whatever regime is in control of the Philippines. We should let the Philippines go through the growing pains of revolution, assisting them in ensuring human rights and economic prosperity if possible."

Communism? Meredith was certain everyone in the room was having the same thought. *Where is he getting that? Sure, they were communists 20 years ago, but Islamic fundamentalism has always been an issue in the Philippines.* Meredith leaned back in her chair as if blown away in slow motion. *And what about the Japan angle? Hasn't anyone mentioned that to the president? If not, I wouldn't want that ass-chewing afterward.*

Sewell looked at Stone, motioning for him to take charge. There was something in the exchange that piqued Meredith's curiosity. *What was it? A knowing look? A familiarity?* After all, they were counterparts. Davis also saw the interchange and asked the secretary of defense to respond.

"Sir, there has been a development that warrants our discussion. It significantly muddies the waters if our intelligence turns out to be true," Stone explained, looking at Lantini, the CIA Director. Lantini was a wiry man with a lean face. He had deep set black eyes and brown hair that was groomed just above his ears. Meredith knew he was an enigma. A career CIA man, he had been a paramilitary operative, just like Matt Garrett, before ascending to the highest position in the Agency. She well knew that Lantini had a gravitas that few in the room possessed. Rathburn had mentioned to her once out of frustration that Lantini listened well and rarely spoke in a group, which frustrated him to no end.

"Go ahead," President Davis said, kicking back in his chair with his hands behind his head and briefly resting against the nearby wall that made the room so cramped.

"We just received an intelligence report from the Special Forces team in Mindanao that they captured a Japanese auto executive jogging."

The group chuckled.

"This executive, it appears, had been in Mindanao for six months"—Stone paused, looking at the rest of the group—"operating a massive assembly line making tanks, armored personnel carriers, helicopters, small arms, and ammunition. The whole operation has been going on nearly two years." Stone stopped, then added, "According to the report."

"What!" McNulty, the Air Force chief of staff responded. "That's bullshit!" Meredith knew he had served as the commander of the 35th Fighter Wing at Misawa Air Base in Japan and apparently couldn't believe what he was hearing.

"All we know is that we got the spot report through about 10 different parties," Stone said, "but I brought Meredith here to discuss some of the background and implications."

"Really, Bob, a secretary? I've heard of sleeping your way to the top but this is ridiculous," McNulty retorted.

"I resent that," Meredith said, angrily. She stood amidst the all-male gathering, tucked her hair behind her ears, and glared at the general, who turned red. She did not need his harassment, and she was certainly not there for the prestige or to get a job. She had the answer and she knew it. President Davis was about to speak, but Meredith began by slapping her notes onto the table.

"Pardon me, Mr. President," she said, the president motioning for her to continue, smiling at her confidence. "But that little spot report confirms what our intelligence has been missing for the past two years."

Lantini glared at her as she picked up a stack of papers stapled together and passed them around. "It's bad enough you got your jockstraps handed to you on 9-11, but it's about to happen again. In these packets, you'll see copies of newspaper articles that discuss Japanese mining activities in Mindanao. The next page shows Japanese mining imports remaining the same over the period of alleged activity. The next page shows Japanese oil-tanker activity in the Davao City port. And the last page is a newspaper article concerning an oil find on Palawan Island, Republic of the Philippines."

She tossed another stack at McNulty. "These papers show Japanese economic statistics. Declining population plus declining trade plus declining resources equals declining economy."

With dramatic effect, she said, "When your entire security environment revolves around your economy and your ability and need to buy protection from others—primarily the United States–then a U. S. shift toward the Middle East and a reduction in economic growth combine to form a severe threat to Japan's national security." She paused for a breath and let the men thumb through the packets. When the president finished reading, she continued.

"So what the Japanese have done is to exploit the Abu Sayyaf revolution. They produced weapons for them, giving them more of a chance to overthrow the government—"

"Well then, why didn't they just attack the Philippines if that's what they want?" McNulty whined.

"General, I'm sure you've read Sun Tzu, so you know that the ultimate form of strategy is to win without fighting," she said. "So why not arm the rebels, stage a show of force in the East China Sea, ask the U.S. to watch the pending conflict between China and Taiwan so we wouldn't be looking at the Philippines as the rebels take their assault positions, let the coup happen, then step in with tanks and helicopters to subdue the country?"

Stone thought to himself, *Holy shit. Has she been talking to the Rolling Stones? Everything up to Japan stepping in with tanks was our plan! How much else does she know?*

"Sounds a bit far-fetched to me," Lantini said, looking at Stone. Meredith knew that as CIA Director, Lantini, who during his heyday had been an impressive college linebacker at Boston College, would feel upstaged by an assistant putting all that together based upon simple open source research.

"I don't know," Rolfing, the Marine commandant, replied, "let's hear her out."

"Well, everything I said is verifiable up to my theory of what happens after the coup. How else do you explain the Japanese tanks and helicopters?"

"Why would they let Americans be killed? Wouldn't that jeopardize this plan of yours?" McNulty commented dismissively.

"It's not my plan, sir. The Abu Sayyaf, like Al Qaeda, are decentralized. They probably didn't get the word or just didn't care about hurting Americans. I mean, how many of you knew we had an infantry company in Subic guarding ammo, or a Special Forces team in Mindanao?" Meredith asked.

Stone wanted to scream: *Know! Hell I sent them there. You're carrying my water and doing great. Keep going!* He glanced at Ronnie Wood, who had a pensive look on his face, and winked.

"You've got a lot to learn about talking to superiors, Miss Morris," the Air Force general said.

"With all due respect sir, you've got a lot to learn about listening to the evidence," Meredith responded, fully expecting to be asked to leave the room. Davis saved her.

"She might be right, you know," the president said, taking control. "We need a way to verify this."

Stone picked up on the cue quickly. "Sir, we've located the ships that Meredith identified as going into the Davao City port and supposedly leaving with oil or minerals. They all are suspiciously anchored just off the Luzon Strait. Talking with Bill here, I thought we'd send some SEALs to board one of the ships and inspect them."

"Good idea," Davis responded. "What if Japan really is trying to pull a fast one on us? What do we do? What's our new strategy? How does this compare to the threat of Islamic terrorism and its potential nexus with weapons of mass destruction?"

Meredith leaned forward, thinking President Davis asked a good question. Had the 9-11 attacks opened other seams for Machiavellian statecraft, seams for which they may not be prepared? Meredith believed it all came back to the economics, resources, and culture, issues that had all been exacerbated previously by communism and currently by the threat of Islamic fundamentalism. In the Global War on Terror, allied relationships were shifting, like the earth's tectonic plates, bound to create a rumble, or God forbid, a full-blown quake.

Only the strategic landscape was not so clear, Meredith knew. Officers and statesmen trained in the Cold War era were unsure of how to proceed. She wondered if they could set aside preconceived notions to deal with the obvious, though sudden, threat? It was sounding to her as if Davis was guiding his foreign policy staff in the proper direction.

And what about Afghanistan, where it all began? That had been Matt's issue all along, she remembered. They had called him off the shot. Why? To preserve strategic flexibility? If bin Laden was dead would that deaden the excitement of a headlong rush to Iraq?

Secretary Robert Stone

Secretary Stone had been watching. He looked directly at the president, who was seated next to Vice President Hellerman and CIA Director Frank Lantini, with Saul Fox and Dick Diamond behind him. Chairman Sewell was next to Lantini and in Stone's line of sight. As Stone looked at each of the men, when he finally locked eyes with Ronnie Wood the man returned his gaze.

What is he thinking? Stone wondered.

The entire premise had been that the actions in the Philippines had to occur in order to create enough military movement to make rushing into Iraq logistically impossible. While the president was not yet on board, the Rolling Stones had released the glider and it was flying strong, creating the effect. Many were beginning to question the drive to Iraq and whether the United States needed to forestall the massive military buildup against Saddam Hussein and focus more on the global transnational threat of Al Qaeda.

If the China-Taiwan tension gained more traction, and if the Philippine situation was not resolved in the next couple of days, then the Rolling Stones would have a chance at presenting a *fait accompli* to the neoconservatives without losing their power base, while appearing entirely logical and practical to the American people. The president would then follow.

It would be a win-win for everyone. That was always the Rolling Stones' goal. Their secretly sponsored Philippine insurgency would restore a patriotic fervor, crush Islamic fundamentalism, keep balance of power in the Middle East, and deliver the endgame: a stable, secure, and prosperous America.

So the question was, how could they now keep the Philippine insurgency to a manageable level—a containable insurgency–given all that had occurred? With the deal Takishi had cut, the urgency would likely subside in a couple of days, as American troops would get out freely. That wouldn't be enough to divert attention away from Iraq. Plus, if Takishi was indeed planning some kind of imperialistic grab at their Pre-WWII power, they would have a whole new problem on their hands. He looked at Dick Diamond and Saul Fox, who were sitting next to each other whispering and trading notes. Like puppeteers, they always sat closest to the key decision makers in the room, so their presence could be felt.

He flipped his notebook on the table, wishing for a cigarette and gaining a bothered look from President Davis, his friend. So he stopped and looked down. As he stared at his black notebook, he saw a yellow sticker protruding from one of the pages. He opened the book slowly, half-listening to the conversation. His pencil scratching from the ambassador's visit yesterday looked up at him. The big let-ters "KOREA" leapt off the page. Yes, he thought. Takishi was sending him a signal that the Rolling Stones needed more fodder to enhance the illusion of chaos in the Pacific. Stone looked up, smiled inwardly, and said, "Korea."

Amazed, everyone turned in Stone's direction.

"Korea. That's it. Korea," he said, shaking his head with the appear-ance that he had figured it all out.

"How's that?" Sewell asked.

"The ambassador, you know, Kai," he said, looking at the president, "came over yesterday with an envoy from Mizuzawa."

Lantini shifted in his chair and glared at Stone. He looked panicked. "Why didn't they ask to see me?" Davis interrupted.

"I don't know," Stone said. "They probably did not want to bother you and were asking for our assistance in the Philippines and Korea. They're worried about China and Taiwan, and now they're getting rumblings from North Korea."

"They really presented that to you as an issue?" the president asked.

"Yes, sir. It makes sense. North Korea keeps shooting missiles over Japan, and China is always testing in Mongolia or somewhere. So I'm thinking the Japanese government developed these weapons to protect themselves from the growing Chinese and North Korean threats. My guess is that they felt like they had to do it in the Philippines to get around their constitution. You know, article seven—"

"Nine," Meredith interrupted and then sat back quickly as if regretting the correction. McNulty, the Air Force Chief of Staff, cut a mean gaze her way. Stone purposefully looked confused.

"Anyway. My reasoning," Stone continued, "is that these ships are sort of a floating weapons storage site, you know, prepositioned stuff ready to react to threats. Post-9-11, it might not be such a bad idea. They've got security challenges all around them with China, North Korea, and now this situation in the Philippines. I mean can we really do it all?" It was a risky strategy, and Fox predictably pounced on the unprotected pawn in the debate.

"Perhaps the flotilla of tanks could be used as a balance of power in the Pacific so that we don't have to commit sizable U.S. forces there, allowing us to proceed with our levelheaded strategy of removing Saddam Hussein and his weapons of mass destruction from Iraq," Fox explained.

"Now that makes sense," McNulty said, finally finding something he wanted to believe.

"So the choice is to deal with the Pacific or invade Iraq? What happened to grand strategy? Why can't we make it an all-inclusive strategy?" Diamond asked. "We should take a look at the Islamic terror threat as a multinational threat, much the way we viewed communism, and develop the equivalent of a containment, or destruction, doctrine that informs our decisions," Diamond continued, then looked at Stone.

Now that made sense, Meredith thought.

"If the choice is between the two," Fox said from his back-row seat, "then there is no question that Iraq, with nuclear potential, must be handled promptly."

Stone saw that *Ronnie Wood* was staring at him, wanting him to take the lead and counter Fox. *He never says anything anyway*, Stone thought.

"Think about how many nukes are in China and North Korea. There's as much of a terror nexus there as we might find in Iraq," Stone said, picking up the ball for Wood.

"But what we are really talking about is some minor revolution in the Philippines. The China and North Korea arguments just don't hold water," Fox replied.

Everyone looked at President Davis, who said, "Let's give it 24 hours and see how this plays out."

Fox slammed back in his chair, his feet dangling above the floor like a child's.

Still dodging the bullet, Stone thought. *Our glider is still hanging in the air, buffeted about a bit, but still hanging, flying, creating events. Real events.*

"Mr. President, I recommend that we keep this all tightly under wraps, which will of course preserve our strategic flexibility," CIA Director Lantini said.

About time you said something! Stone thought.

"Of course," Davis replied, smiling at his old friend Bob Stone.

Stone rode back to the Pentagon with Meredith at his side, their legs almost touching in the back of the Town Car. He wondered about her personal life. He glanced at her crossed legs, his mind defaulting to his testosterone-driven instinct to worship all things beautiful. Silky panty hose covered her slender thighs. She was beautiful sitting there looking out the window, watching DC glide by. Maybe she would be drawn to his power. Yes, maybe that would work, he thought, ogling the naked skin above her neckline.

Besides, he was tired of his buddies getting all the chicks.

CHAPTER 32
Tokyo, Japan
Taiku Takishi

Takishi raised his glass to Mizuzawa's. The expensive crystal chimed like a bell signaling a new era.

"Wonderful job in Washington," Prime Minister Mizuzawa said, complimenting Takishi on his joint performance with Kaitachi.

"Thank you, sir," Takishi said, feeling vindicated for losing Abe and the Americans. Now the plan was proceeding nicely.

"As we anticipated," General Nugama said, also holding a glass of champagne in his hand, "phase one is going smoothly now that we have arranged for the departure of the Americans. Fine job, Takishi." It was a rare compliment from Nugama, the Japanese Chief of Staff. Nugama was Mizuzawa's age, almost 70, but appeared fit. His bearing was as impeccable as his creased uniform. They had strategically fooled the Americans. The demonstration in the East China Sea had worked.

The three men stood and talked in Mizuzawa's private garden behind his office. Normally he did not allow visitors in the area, but it was a special day.

The resurgence of Japan to her rightful place in history had begun. The result of their actions would be no more reliance on the United States for security and no more kowtowing to the American people. The Philippines would provide ample resources for future Japanese domination.

The first order of business was to finish the job in the Philippines. Next would be to bring Taiwan home. What could the Americans do?

Economic sanctions would be unrealistic. They would effectively be shutting down one-third of their economy. They would have to continue trading with Japan. No, this was Japan's moment in the sun. She would rise from the seas like King Neptune, pitchfork in hand, almighty and all-powerful.

It was a good plan that Stone had bought totally. *First the business about the Chinese and Taiwan. Now we have them thinking about Korea,* Mizuzawa thought to himself.

"Hopefully," Mizuzawa said, smiling, "they will 'turn another satellite' for us." He did his best Robert Stone impersonation. "That was a good one, Takishi!" They laughed heartily. Deep and guttural. It was a sinister laugh, low-pitched, and evil.

Their conversation ran in sharp contrast to the peaceful surroundings of the garden, where a pagoda and bridge rose above them as they stood next to the dark water of the goldfish pond.

"Yes, maybe we can tell them 'we need you to change your constitution,'" Takishi said. More laughter.

Then they stopped, noticing Mizuzawa's eyes, fixated and burning red-hot. His eyelids wrinkled together, like knife slits in his skin. Takishi watched the hatred and emotion well inside him. He knew he remembered Nagasaki and Hiroshima, MacArthur and his constitution. He knew he'd been there for almost 60 years of American domination and control.

"No more!" he yelled, shocking Takishi and Nugama, causing them to step back. "We shall prevail!" he said in a husky voice. He raised his champagne glass high into the air, framed by the bridge and pagoda. Then he crushed it with his bare hand, squeezing the glass to tiny pieces, gashing his skin. Blood ran down his thick arm as the Prime Minister stared at him.

"We shall prevail!" Takishi barked, following suit.

"We shall prevail!" General Nugama yelled, caught up in the emotion of the moment. The two men raised their glasses, crushing them, and grinding the glass into their hands as blood streamed down their arms.

"We shall prevail!" The words echoed in the garden enclave as the three men stared at one another, blood dripping from their hands, shards of glass stinging Takishi's hand.

CHAPTER 33
Japanese Imperial Palace
Prime Minister Mizuzawa

Mizuzawa stood and walked slowly to his office. After washing and picking the glass from his hands, he walked across a courtyard to the ornate Imperial Palace, the residence of the Japanese emperor.

He knocked on the door and opened it without waiting. The emperor stood in the foyer wearing a robe the color of a rusty mauve. It symbolized the rising sun.

Mizuzawa bowed slowly. The emperor returned his bow with a slight nod.

The one concession the United States had made to Japan at the conclusion of the Great Pacific War was to allow the emperor to remain as the head of the Japanese state. Truman had done it from a purely practical standpoint. He had seen the emperor as the one figure most revered in Japanese society and the one person who could pass the message of utter defeat to the Japanese people. It had worked.

But the emperor also served as the single thread to the era of the Japanese warlords. Most other aspects of Japanese culture and society had blended with the dominant Western society, but he was a man of direct lineage from some of the most barbaric and courageous warriors in Japanese history, and theirs was a bloodline of savagery. The Imperial Palace was uniquely Japanese, as was the emperor. Mizuzawa was unsure what the emperor knew about his plans for the future of Japan…and he had to do something about that.

The emperor, an aging man in his early seventies, wore a peaceful look of contentment and solitude. His wife, the empress, had passed away recently, and he was lonely. But he served in his figurehead position well. He held state dinners and entertained guests, a Western tradition, Mizuzawa thought with disgust.

"Greetings, Prime Minister," he said.

"Good afternoon, Your Majesty," Mizuzawa said in response.

The two men walked into the palace along a dark koa wood foyer decorated with paintings of the former emperors. Mizuzawa recognized them all. He noticed with pride the paintings of Prince Ninigi, the grandson of the Sun Goddess Amaterasu Omikami, and Emperor Jimmu, Ninigi's grandson. The oil paintings were cracking with age and in desperate need of restoration.

As is my empire, Mizuzawa thought.

They walked into a small room. It was the emperor's private room for discussing matters of importance. Japanese pine framed a large trophy case that had been built into the wall. Behind the Plexiglas cover to the trophy case were three items. On either side of the trophy case were paintings of the eight gods of heaven and earth, who were viewed by the Japanese as the guarantors of their security.

Mizuzawa and the emperor stood in front of the case, looking at the three sacred treasures, the Mirror, the Jewels, and the Sword.

"What is this matter of importance you bring to me tonight, Prime Minister?" the emperor asked. His wrinkled eyes were drawn and set, as if he were ready to die. His pallid face was in sharp contrast to the rose-colored beauty of his flowing robe.

"Your Majesty," Mizuzawa said, looking at the sad, pale figure, "may I have access to the sacred treasures of Ninigi?"

"Why do you desire this access?" the emperor asked without suspicion.

"Your Majesty, I have embarked on a long and arduous journey as prime minister. I need to feel the strength of the sword in my hands; I need to fondle the beauty of the jewels against my skin; I need to see the vision of my actions in the mirror," Mizuzawa said poetically.

"What is this journey?" the emperor asked, sliding open the glass, revealing the three sacred Japanese treasures.

Mizuzawa looked at the items lying harmlessly in the open case. The jewels were curved jade beads nestled against a black velvet bag. The mirror was simple, yet old. Black and brown spots dotted the glass. Its frame was black lacquer.

But the sword. The sword was wide. Its ivory handle gave way to a pristine, curling blade. It was the Kusanagi sword of Japanese legend. Mizuzawa fixated on it, knowing what must be done.

"Your Majesty, I have taken your Japan on a course that will provide for her security for many generations to come," Mizuzawa said, kneeling at the case and running his hand lightly over the jewels. His thick hand brushed the delicate velvet, causing it to wrinkle.

"That is good, Prime Minister. Tell me more."

Mizuzawa shifted his gaze to the mirror. His face looked distorted reflecting back at him from the antique glass.

"We have begun to build the military again, your Majesty. We will soon attack to regain Formosa," Mizuzawa said. His words hung in the air like smog, polluting the Imperial Palace.

"But for what purposes would you do such a thing?" the emperor asked, slowly. "We are protected by the eight gods of heaven and earth. They shall provide for us."

Fool, Mizuzawa thought.

"Your Majesty," Mizuzawa said, turning his lusting eyes to the huge saber, "we have many concerns." *None of which I expect you to understand.* "Our economy cannot sustain itself forever. Our military is not adequate to defend the homeland against the Korean Peninsula or Chinese nuclear weapons."

"But the United States—"

Fool. Just as I thought. The last tie to our true heritage has been tainted with Western lies.

"—has guaranteed our security. They will come to our aid if it is necessary. I cannot allow your plan," the emperor said, sternly, vestiges of the old warrior bubbling forth in his words.

"Your Majesty," Mizuzawa said, taking his handkerchief out of his pocket and placing it on the pearl handle of the sword, "we must pursue this course. We have no other choice."

"You are wrong—" The emperor's eyes grew wide, bulging outward as the sword sliced through his abdomen.

Mizuzawa had lifted the sword and turned slowly to the emperor, who had been only two steps behind him. He slid the sacred sword into the emperor with a well-trained thrust.

He grabbed the emperor's hands and placed them on the saber's handle, as if he were performing *seppuku*, or *hari-kari*, suicide. He guided the old man onto his knees, ensuring he avoided the gathering pool of blood on the floor. He watched as the blood gushed onto the emperor's robe, casting a dark image onto the rust-colored hue that once represented the morning glow of the rising sun.

Its image had changed to something far graver. It was the unsettling darkness of a cold and eerie night, spreading across the robe, engulfing the fabric.

Mizuzawa turned the sword in the emperor's hands. The emperor looked at him and gasped, "Thank you," said the old man. "Now it is your responsibility." He sucked one last gurgling breath and closed his eyes.

The emperor's body toppled to the floor, his hands still holding the sacred sword as he died.

Mizuzawa stood above the man. "That's right, old man. It *is* my responsibility. And my reward."

I didn't think you had the stomach for it.

The president sat at his desk in the Oval Office. The camera's huge eye blinked at him as it came to life. He stared into the TelePrompTer and read.

Today I speak to you concerning Operation Enduring Freedom in the Philippines. American lives have been lost as they were caught in the cross fire of a revolution in that tormented country. Our nation's heart goes out to the family members of the 22 brave individuals who were killed.

Likewise, Filipino terrorists are still holding three Americans hostage. Thankfully, our gracious allies, the Japanese, have worked with us to secure the release of the hostages and all other Americans and coalition partners who wish to depart the country.

We are conducting an evacuation of all U.S. personnel who wish to depart from the Philippines. Tonight, as I speak to you, American aircraft are soaring to a designated point in the Philippines to pick up our beloved countrymen.

We will not tolerate attacks against Americans, and we will respond to countries that willingly harbor terrorists acting against Americans. While I firmly believe in the Filipino people's right to determine their own form of government independent from colonial or superpower influence, we will not stand by while Islamic fundamentalism imposes an oppressive form of government on freedom-loving peoples.

As an initial step in countering the Philippine insurgency, I intend to impose economic sanctions on the country until the insurgents allow the elected government of the Philippines to return to power. I know sanctions at this time are no consolation to the family members of those Americans lost in combat, but it is a moral policy that allows us to continue to focus on the United States' vital interests and national security.

God bless our fighting men and women and God bless America.

The camera eye closed. Davis cast a glance to Stone, Lantini, and Sewell, who were standing in the opposite corner of the office. They gave him a thumbs-up sign, approving of his performance. The men shook the president's hand as the camera crew packed up its equipment.

"That should do the trick," Sewell said.

"I hope so," replied Davis, who looked at Stone and shrugged.

On his way out, Sewell pulled his satellite Blackberry from his breast pocket and frowned as he scrolled through his messages.

The Japanese Emperor committed suicide?

CHAPTER 34
Subic Bay, Luzon Island, Philippines
Captain Zachary Garrett

Zachary Garrett watched airplane after airplane land, load civilians, and take off into the sky from the very runway that they had used to enter the Philippines. The white Quonset huts were occupied with kitchen facilities and administrative personnel who seemed to be orchestrating the evacuation of Americans.

Resting his binoculars against the strap around his neck, he pondered why he had earlier received instructions to move to Subic Bay to board an aircraft for Hawaii, only to have that decision overturned by a message from his division headquarters to freeze in place. Moments later, another message from division informed him to move all civilian, wounded, and deceased personnel to the airfield that evening. He was to do this under the cover of darkness and conduct link-up with a CIA operative named X-Ray, whoever that was, at a specific grid-coordinate location northwest of the airfield just outside the naval base fence. X-Ray would have an infrared strobe light flashing and would use proper bona fides to identify himself.

How refreshing, Zachary thought. X-Ray was to escort the personnel onto the airfield, load them on an aircraft, and send them home. His security platoon, however, was to retreat to his base camp and await further orders.

The flaming sun hung low over the western horizon, large and distorted, sinking into the ocean. With it, the heat simmered. It was like turning an oven dial from broil to bake but it made a difference. Zachary watched the sun dip below the horizon on the sea.

In the musty jungle darkness, he listened to his men prepare for the mission. Stan Barker's platoon would escort to the airplane the ambassador, his four civilian support staff, the wounded Sergeant Cartwright, Lieutenant Colonel Fraley, and the Air Force doctor who had been severely wounded. Doc Gore, the young enlisted medic who had so expertly patched Captain Garrett, had also performed field surgery on the doctor, removing a bullet from his shoulder using a hot knife and tweezers before rinsing the wound with Betadine. But it was the ample supply of penicillin that Gore had given Zachary and Sergeant Cartwright that held the fever and infection in check. Zachary was ambulatory and that was all he cared about regarding himself. His wound also had begun to heal nicely. A long scab had formed on the left side of his head, making it uncomfortable to wear his helmet, but other than that, he was fine.

Barker's men had enough of a problem carrying the bodies of Lieutenant Rockingham and Private Teller the three kilometers to the airfield. The platoon members had constructed two stretchers using rain ponchos and mahogany branches. By snapping two ponchos together, then folding them, they slid the sturdy branches through either side. But it was not so much the physical aspect of carrying their deceased comrades away that caused the bigger problem, but the mental vision of two of their own, brutally slaughtered in a war they had not expected. Surprised, shaken, and unnerved, his men had handled themselves exceptionally well. He feared though that their adrenaline had been blocking their emotions, and soon fear and unrest might set in. He would need to be ready to counter that if it occurred.

He watched as Barker slipped past him in the twilight, moving his men and the dead bodies to a rally point. Zachary saw him coordinate with Kurtz, whose lines he would be passing through. Kurtz had marked a single passage lane and designated his best squad leader to serve as the guide through that lane. Each man in Barker's platoon had popped an infrared chemical light and placed it in the camouflage band of his Kevlar.

Barker's platoon moved quietly through the center of the patrol base. The other men watched as they saw the civilians, Fraley, Mosconi, and Sergeant Cartwright hobble past. Cartwright made one last plea to the commander to stay, but Garrett told him no. His fever had risen in the last 24 hours, and hot dust always found its way to the most remote parts of the body where it could cause infection. He was not going to be responsible for Cartwright losing a leg.

Zachary handed Sergeant Cartwright two envelopes and told him to get them to the addressees. Cartwright limped back into the growing mob near Kurtz's position, where soldiers casually hugged and encouraged him about the next time they would see him.

Then Lieutenant Colonel Fraley came forward in the darkness, moving close enough to Zachary to whisper. Zachary could make out his rotund outline carved against the crazy array of the jungle.

"I just want to apologize," Fraley said, his head hanging low. It must have finally occurred to him that he was dealing with a professional combat unit. They had saved his life despite his poor treatment of them. During the night in the jungle, alone, apart from his world of Filipino concubines and whiskey, Fraley had got some religion, Zach surmised. *Tough shit*, Zachary thought. *That won't bring back Teller or Rockingham.* There was always a soldier out there somewhere, on the ground, holding a weapon, looking through the sight, wondering, waiting, hoping, and praying that someone above him had made the correct call, that someone cared. Zachary could not respect men like Fraley, who promptly forgot that once they made it to higher positions of command. Zachary looked over Fraley's shoulder as Barker's platoon hoisted the bodies of Rockingham and Teller past him, carrying them into the darkness like a medieval funeral procession. Out of the corner of his eye he heard Slick mutter, "*Son of a bitch*," and saw him turn away.

"Don't tell me," Zachary said, staring into Fraley's eyes. Fraley looked away, down toward the ground. "Tell the families of those two men." Zachary walked away and spit into the ground. No way was he going to ease Fraley's conscience. The whole fiasco might have been avoided had Fraley done his job. But it was too late to dwell on that now. Zachary still had a job to do.

After an hour, Zachary received word that Barker had conducted link up with the guide, who had provided some good news.

Upon hearing this report on the radio, Zachary immediately had Taylor and the first sergeant move to the command-post area beside a huge mahogany tree. Slick had set up the SCAMP and aimed its antenna to the northeast. Other communications gear surrounded the tree in a scattered fashion. In the darkness, only the white casing of the SCAMP stood out.

Zachary sat in the dirt facing his three lieutenants and first sergeant. Slick and a couple of the other headquarters platoon soldiers acted like they had something to do near the meeting and listened intently. There was a certain amount of pride associated with hearing the fresh scoop from the commander before anyone else did. Later, they would be able to take the inevitable rumors back down to ground zero and assert that they "were there."

"Guys, we've lost two of our own. I know nothing will ever bring back Rock or Teller. I was closer to both of those guys than any of you can know," Zachary began.

A monkey screamed in agreement from high in a tree off in the distance, adding an eerie quality to Zachary's gathering. He noticed the dark outline of Slick's head turn in the direction of the noise, which was followed by another. It sounded like a wounded banshee, lost in the dense jungle.

"It hurt me bad to watch Stan's guys haul their bodies away. The envelopes I gave Sergeant Cartwright were letters of sympathy. I handwrote them today as soon as I knew he was going back. One was to Pat Teller, and the other to Glenda Rockingham." The lieutenants knew both of the wives. Glenda was a major force in the company, organizing events, and Pat had seemed eager to contribute to platoon events even though she was new and pregnant.

"I have to tell you, it's the hardest thing I've ever done." It was important for Zachary to share that moment with his men, who needed to understand that he felt the loss. They needed to know that if one of them was killed, he would handle the situation with the same compassion.

"We held off a large, unexpected attack with minimal loss of life. We safely evacuated the frigging ambassador and his staff from an Embassy under attack. And now we have successfully put those people plus Cartwright and Rock and Teller onto an airplane to fly home.

"We performed those missions well. In fact, Stan's contact gave us a message from the president that I want you all to convey to your soldiers. I want you to do it personally, walking from position to position.

"The president said, and I quote from Stan, that we 'did a kick-ass job.' We're a good company, probably the best I've ever seen," he said, intentionally mixing his feelings with the president's quote. "But we've got more missions, probably tough ones. There is a reason we did not fly out on those planes tonight, I guarantee you that.

"Now I want you to go talk to your men. Comfort them, but keep them alert. The fat lady ain't singing, yet. That's all."

The men departed and did as their commander said. After an hour, Zachary had heard the word in the company was that the president of the United States had personally called the commander over the tacsat radio and told him that they kicked serious ass, had absolutely the best unit in the Army, and would receive the Presidential Unit Citation when they returned. The United States infantryman was the undisputed master of creating rumors and talking bullshit.

Zachary smiled in the darkness when Slick informed him with a grin of the transformation of "the word," as soldiers commonly referred to commanders' edicts.

He sat near the mahogany tree looking west into the ocean 550 meters below their position, pitching his K-Bar knife into the dirt and pulling it out only to toss it down again. He shook his head. Only two weeks ago, he had been looking at a similar sight in the Kahuku training area after his platoon leaders had botched a night raid, and now his men were being commended by the president. *They've come a long way. No better test than the real thing.* But he knew with due modesty that it was his training that had prepared the lieutenants.

Zachary thought about Glenda Rockingham and Pat Teller. They would be crushed. On the thought, he pounded the knife into the ground, venting some anger. He wondered if he had failed. Could he have done something different? What if he had not gathered his men on that first morning? What if he had carried his own radio? Then maybe Teller would still be alive.

But then he would be the dead one, and where would that have left his men? He reconciled his doubts, thinking about his daughter Amanda, whom he barely knew anymore. Would she ever get to know him outside the image of him created for her by others? What if he were killed? She'd live the rest of her life thinking he had abandoned her. On that note, he decided that he would not die there in the Philippines. Exhausted, he lay back in the tall grass and closed his eyes.

His rest was short. Barker reappeared from the darkness. "Sir, I have another piece of information I didn't want to share over the radio," Barker said.

"What's that?" Zachary responded, wiping his face before he sat up. *Good thing it's dark.*

"X-Ray said that they had extracted all of the Americans except three hostages. Seems the Abu Sayyaf blew up an American plane, but three had already gotten off and were taken."

"Oh yeah. Maybe that's our follow-on mission," Zachary said, thinking aloud.

"I never thought of that, sir, but he said they were three Defense guys."

"Department of Defense," Zachary said.

"Some guy named Rathburn and two of his assistants."

"More bureaucrats to save," Zachary grunted. Slick's voice interrupted, "Sir! First Platoon says they've got enemy in the wire!" Slick exclaimed, holding the telephone to his ear.

What?" Zachary grabbed his radio handset. *No way, this shit has gone too far.*

Taylor's voice was on the other end, finishing a sentence. "—four to five personnel, over."

"Andy, what's happening?"

"Sir," Taylor said, "I've got five personnel to my front signaling my forward observation post with an IR flashlight. My guys challenged them, and they came back with the proper response. But I told my men not to let them pass. So they're just lying there in the grass."

Zachary's mind raced quickly, making the quantum leap from familial worry to steadfast concern for the men the president had entrusted to him. Had his company's encryption codes been compromised? Had they lost a radio? No, the first sergeant had done a sensitive-items check earlier. Did he have any patrols out? No. The next patrol didn't go out until midnight. Who could they be? He thought back to his call from the division operations officer. He gave him an exact grid coordinate of his unit's location. Had that transmission been intercepted?

The Embassy! The embassy had been taken over by Abu Sayyaf. They had all the call signs and secure-encryption variables. He had Slick call the other two platoons using the field phone. Then he decided to inspect the situation personally.

"Get back to your platoon, go to 100 percent security," he told Barker, who split like a scared rabbit.

Zachary hurried down the hill the 100 meters to Taylor's position using his night-vision goggles. In the darkness he passed the clear-cut area where the Black Hawk helicopter had once sat idle. Moving beyond it, he saw the lieutenant and his platoon sergeant kneeling next to the platoon CP area. They were wearing their goggles as well.

"Where are they?"

"Down there, sir," Taylor said, pointing to the northwest. Zachary looked and decided to move forward. He walked, high-stepping the roots and bushes that made for tough going. Taylor followed and the platoon sergeant stayed at the CP. Approaching the two soldiers, he noticed they were nervous. One had his night-vision laser sight trained on the individuals lying in the grass only 10 meters away. The other soldier was scanning for more intruders.

"Sitrep?" Zachary asked, assuming the prone position next to the private.

"Sir, these guys got our codes. They know our shit," he responded, continuing to look through his weapon's sight. Zachary pulled his Beretta pistol out of its holster and went to one knee.

"Carnival!" Zachary yelled across to the group lying in the grass. His goggles picked up five bodies with rucksacks lying side by side.

"Saloon!" a Boston accent responded with the proper password.

Zachary listened carefully to the voice. It was American, he was sure. Not only that, he recognized it.

"McAllister?" Zachary asked.

"Garrett?" the voice responded.

It was too good to be true. Bob McAllister was the A company commander from his battalion.

Bob McAllister, the dateless wonder?"

"Not the case since you left, my friend. Riley and her sister say hello," McAllister said, not moving.

"Ease off, guys," Zachary said to the young privates. They did so warily. Their wires were strung tightly. They kept trained eyes on the five men as they passed. Then they saw their commander and Captain McAllister hug each other.

"Never in my wildest dreams did I think I would be glad to see your ugly ass here," Zachary said.

"Well, you've got a lot more than my ass to deal with. The whole stinkin' battalion just landed about 12 clicks northwest of here. Pave Lows flew us in from an aircraft carrier. I'm the lead. Got any hot chow?" McAllister said.

"Yeah, right. Take out the 'hot' part and you'd have a good question," Zachary strained.

"Yeah, that's what we've heard. You guys kicked ass, though, man. Whole division's talking about you like you're Rambo or some shit," McAllister said.

McAllister was an ROTC officer, commissioned from the University of Massachusetts. He was cocky but always backed up his bullshit with proper action. He had knotty red hair that sometimes looked too long and freckles splashed across his face in asymmetrical disarray. He was about six feet tall and looked like a ruffian, which he was.

"I'd love to stay and bullshit, but we've got to call back to the Buckster and let him know we found you weenies," McAllister said, kneeling and grabbing his radio microphone from his radio operator He radioed the battalion commander and informed him that he had affected link-up with Zachary and his men. Buck seemed beside himself in his response, as if he'd never expected it to happen. He delivered an order to proceed as planned and McAllister handed the handset back to his radio operator.

"The Buckster, you gotta love him," he said, shaking his head with a huge grin. "Hey," McAllister said, "did you know Riley and her sister each has a mole underneath her left breast? Talk about genetic symmetry—"

"Not a good time for sex jokes, McAllister. This is the real thing, dickhead so move out before we get fired up," Zachary said, half-joking, half-serious.

"Hey, just trying to lighten you up a little. You're gonna need it when you find out our next mission. Here," McAllister said, handing him a stack of letters, adding, "She sends her love and misses you." Zachary rifled through the stack; though glad to have love letters from Riley, there was nothing from Amanda.

McAllister patted Zachary on the back, grabbed his radio operator, and moved out.

The news of their next mission traveled through the company like a lit fuse. After talking with Buck on the radio, Zachary went back to his command post lay down, and went to sleep. Buck would have a meeting in the morning with the commanders to discuss the plan.

Looking at the letters from Riley, oddly enough, he thought of his brother, Matt, wondering where he could be. *Sure would be nice to get him in here to help us out,* Zach thought to himself.

Where can he be?

The thought slipped away from him as he spiraled into a much-needed sleep.

CHAPTER 35
Near Fort Magsaysay, Luzon Island, Philippines
Matt Garrett

It had been 24 hours since Rathburn had been snatched from their cell, and Matt wondered if he would ever see the man again. Maybe whoever he was calling Mick Jagger had saved him, who could tell?

"You're sure you never saw Zachary?" Matt said, stepping toward Barefoot.

"Yes, for the 10th time. I got there and the place was vacant. Looked like a hell of a firefight had taken place though. Spent ammo everywhere. Bloodstains. No bodies. It was weird. I started snooping around the barracks and got waylaid by a bunch of angry rebels," Barefoot said.

"Roger," Matt replied, dismayed. For 24 hours they had tried breaking the door, picking the lock, and screaming to get a guard, but it appeared they were all alone.

"Wait, I hear something," Barefoot said, holding up his hand.

The outer lock rattled and the door opened, casting a bright yellow sunlit square across the green slime on the floor. Rathburn's body fell with a thud, his head smacking the wet concrete.

Matt slipped behind the door while Barefoot stood in the middle of the small cell. Sturgeon was reaching into his boot for a Velcro-pocketed knife that his captors had overlooked as he squatted in the other corner. They had been over this as many times as Matt had asked Barefoot about Zachary.

"You all go next, Joe. Let's go," a Filipino voice said.

Matt moved closer to the door, which began to open slowly, casting a brighter spotlight onto Rathburn's body like some eerie floor show.

"Hey, Joe! Time to go!" the voice called out again. Matt saw one shadow fall atop Rathburn's body, then another. They both appeared to have something in their hands.

The first guard stuck his head around the corner of the door, unable to see in the darkness.

"Hey, Joe!" he screamed. "Where Matt Garrett go? You number one customer today!"

Matt stood slowly and rapidly wrapped his belt around the short Filipino's neck, pulling the ends in opposite directions.

An errant shot escaped from the man's pistol, ricocheting off the wall and leaving a spark in its trail. The second guard responded immediately, pulling at Matt's arm.

Matt punched the guard in the face and heard the clank of pistol metal striking the floor. On cue, Sturgeon stood from his crouched position.

Matt snapped the neck of the first guard as Sturgeon leapt across the splash of light that separated him from the fight and drove the knife into the back of the second guard.

The guard, shorter than Matt, turned toward him as Matt pulled the pistol from the man he had just strangled, placed it against the advancing guard's neck, and fired two bullets.

"Let's haul ass," Matt said, looking at the two dead Filipinos lying next to Rathburn's body in the box of light that framed the bodies like a large coffin. He stripped the Filipinos of weapons, handed Jack a Chinese Type 67 pistol, and said, "C'mon" to Barefoot, who followed.

Matt saw daylight for the first time in days as they exited the structure. They had been in the basement of a small adobe building. Leaving the cell, they found themselves surrounded by a high wall and a dirt ceiling, as if the cell had been cut into the ground. They were facing a stairwell carved into the dirt that led to the open skies. Matt carefully ascended the steps, then hesitated as the full brightness of the morning sun entered his dilated pupils.

He looked back at Jack Sturgeon, who was holding his own hand, almost doubled over in pain. Matt pulled a rag from his pocket and wrapped it around Sturgeion's hand.

"I don't see anyone, but it's full daylight so we have to run. There's a truck," Matt said, pointing to the right to a pick-up truck about 20 meters away. "It's running for some reason. Our best bet is to get in that mother and go."

Matt stopped as they were nearing the truck and said, "Rathburn. Never leave a fallen comrade." He ran back down the stairwell and reemerged moments later with Rathburn's body slung over his back in a fireman's carry.

"Let's go," Matt said. The three men ran across the hardstand to the drab olive pick-up truck. Matt flipped Rathburn's body into the back as Sturgeon opened the passenger door for Barefoot, who slid across the torn cloth bench seat. Matt quickly slammed the automatic gear level into DRIVE and sped along the only road he could see.

The sun was to their backs, so he knew they were heading west if it was morning. To his front was flat or rolling countryside. He passed a series of buildings and saw a sign that read FORT MAGSAYSAY. He sped past a gate onto a cement road that led off the gentle slopes onto a plain. It was an area of rice paddies, some terraced into the hills behind them and others lying low beneath the flat, flooded ground.

"What's all that shit bouncing around in the back of the truck?" Matt asked, looking in the mirror. Barefoot turned and looked.

"That's my film and commo gear. Remember, I was supposed to do a satellite link-up and conduct a live interview of your brother? They stole it and must have been carrying it around."

"Zachary," Matt whispered. "We've got to find my brother."

Matt maneuvered around the patches of drying rice that farmers had laid on the cement road. There had been a noose around his neck since landing in Manila, and he felt it slacken just a bit.

His new mission: *find Zachary.* Then they could join forces to fight their way out of there.

CHAPTER 36
Manila, Luzon Island, Philippines
Taiku Takishi

Takishi rode atop the bridge of the lead ship as it approached the port of Manila. He watched in the darkness as the captain adroitly maneuvered the large commercial tanker alongside the international port just south of the Pasig River delta. The pier they approached was 150 meters wide and 450 meters long.

Looking over his shoulder, he saw the huge rock outcropping of Corregidor Island, which guarded the mouth of Manila Bay. His countrymen had fought valiantly there. There would be no such fight again. American airborne forces would not come descending from the sky as they had almost 60 years ago to secure the mouth of the bay. He saw the second ship steaming past Corregidor and made a mental note that the other two should be docking at Subic about then. He wondered in amazement how his countrymen had not only developed such an awesome supertanker, but had actually converted 10 of them to roll-on-roll-off military transport ships and an 11th to—well, he did not want to think about the *Shimpu*, a different matter altogether.

Nuclear weapons loaded on an automobile merchant vessel headed for the port of Los Angeles would provide the great leverage and bargaining power. As soon as the Americans learned of the Japanese invasion of the Philippines, Takishi will have checkmated the Americans with the Shimpu sitting in Los Angeles harbor.

Mizuzawa had given Takishi the order to launch the ships, each carrying a thousand-man Japanese combined arms division consisting of tank, infantry, and attack helicopter maneuver battalions. He had planned to introduce force into the island of Luzon at some point in time, mostly for control purposes, but he believed that the situation could get out of hand rapidly if Villanueva turned on them. Control of the Philippines was absolutely vital to the remainder of Takishi's plan.

Yesterday, Takishi had flown in his Shin Meiwa to Mindanao to find Commander Villanueva in a small thatch hut in Cateel, recovering from wounds received in combat. He had been shot and nearly fatally wounded.

"When you told me about Garrett being in Magsaysay prison, I ordered them all executed," Villanueva had told him. Only his familiarity with the Cateel area had allowed Villanueva to get to the beach, where some of the peasants had provided medical care and escorted him to Takishi's airplane.

Takishi's medical team had patched up Villanueva during the flight, and Takishi had a security team take Villanueva to the Presidential Palace, placing him "in charge." It was a fine line Takishi had to walk with Villanueva. The insurgency needed to have enough traction to be credible before he killed Villanueva.

"You will respond to my every order, do you understand?" Takishi demanded.

Villanueva had given Takishi a long look and nodded.

"I thought I was close to your Matt Garrett until you told me where he was," Villanueva said.

Takishi had looked at the weakened warrior and said, "Slippery son of a bitch." Stone had contacted Takishi too late to save Rathburn, or to kill Matt Garrett. Takishi shook his head at the irony. There were minute degrees between life and death. If only he had gotten the word a day or two earlier, he could have saved his friend, Rathburn, and eliminated an unpredictable variable he didn't need, Matt Garrett. For the first time a jolt of sadness coursed through him as he realized his Harvard classmate, Bart, was dead...because of him.

After dropping Villanueva in Manila, he had flown to the location of the oil tankers that doubled as troop and equipment carriers north of Luzon in the Philippine Sea, landing his seaplane amidst the collection of ships. There he'd boarded the command and control ship, *Ozawa*, and radioed the prime minister with the news about the death of Rathburn.

Takishi felt the ship nudge the side of the cement pier. There was no activity in the large port area. The fighting had served to halt most of the commercial shipping. What was in the docks at the time of the revolution, the peasants had pilfered. The insurgents had not yet organized the Philippine naval vessels, though they had sunk several of the ships during the revolt. A few Corvette attack boats were still operational, yet were of no use until Villanueva could train some men how to operate them.

It was all coming together smoothly Takishi thought, and he sent the U.S. Secretary of Defense, who called himself Mick Jagger, a text message:

Things are getting interesting.

He heard the captain tell him they were prepared to unload the ship. He stepped down from the bridge and heard the first Model 90 tank roar to life.

This will be easy.

CHAPTER 37
Pentagon, Washington, DC
Meredith Morris

It was a close call, letting the Japanese move ships into the harbor, Meredith thought.

She was sitting next to Stone when his phone buzzed with a text. He looked at it and frowned then put his phone away.

Meredith was distraught, fighting the notion that Matt might be dead and that she might have sent him to his death in that airplane. They sat in the National Military Command Center. CNN played on a large screen to their front. The Joint Chiefs of Staff flanked them.

CIA Director Frank Lantini was updating them from his office in Langley, Virginia, over video teleconference.

Lantini's voice boomed over the video conference speaker. "Two Japanese oil tankers have passed Corregidor and are currently unloading tanks, infantry fighting vehicles, attack helicopters, trucks, jeeps, and large numbers of personnel. There appears to be a crew for every weapon system. Two others have entered Subic Bay Naval Base and are conducting similar unloading activities. More are on the way."

"Frank, how did we miss hundreds, if not thousands, of Japanese soldiers getting on these ships in Japan?" Stone asked Lantini.

Lantini stared at the video camera a moment and then said, "Turns out they loaded in Suruga Bay at night. There's a Japanese training area just north of there called Gotenba in the Shizuoka Prefecture. They supposedly had some big exercise there, Yama Sakura, something like that, in January and just kept mobilizing troops in the wake of 9-11 under the guise of anti-terror training. We've got information that during that time they infiltrated from the training area onto troop transports that took them out to these ships." He paused a moment, then volleyed back to Stone. "We missed it because we were watching Taiwan and China."

Meredith watched Stone shake his head, finding the exchange curious.

"We've got two SEAL teams checking those ships out," General Sewell said, bringing the discussion back to the point. "Both are using SCUBA gear, swimming freely around the ships, inspecting hull dimensions and giving us spot reports on the unloading operations. They're ready to act when we are. The Rangers are ready as well."

Marine Commandant General Rolfing said, "Our Marine expeditionary force is now three full brigades and is positioned to the south of Manila Bay, well offshore. They're ready now also."

General McNulty's 90th Fighter Squadron from Guam was on standby alert with F-15s, A-10s, and F-16s. The B-52s from Diego Garcia were also ready.

"Andersen Air Force Base is so packed with aircraft and people, you couldn't land a glider, so let's be reasonable here," McNulty said. "I don't think we can fit any more troops in this corner of the world."

Army Chief of Staff General Wilson, said, "The lead battalion of the rapid deployment brigade from the 25th Infantry Division has landed safely and undetected, we believe, on the island of Luzon, thanks to some Air Force Pave Low helicopters and MC-130 Combat Talons. They have linked up with the company commander there and are prepared to continue operations."

"We're all relieved that the young commander is no longer alone, but what about the absence of the Special Forces team in Mindanao? Any word?" Stone asked.

"No change," Sewell said. "They have not communicated for over two days."

"What kind of force are we showing near Korea, Admiral?" Stone asked Chief of Naval Operations Admiral Simmons.

"Sir, we've got an entire carrier battle group steaming there now."

"Good. The president has a meeting with the Japanese ambassador in an hour. I'll give him the information."

"What did he say about the hostages?" Lantini asked. Meredith lifted her head.

"We've checked the 3000 names over and over. Rathburn and the other two aren't on any of the manifests for outgoing planes."

"Could they have used other names?" Meredith asked.

"They could, but probably not. Someone would have recognized them," Stone said. "Okay. The evacuation procedures have gone well. No other non-combatant Americans who wanted to leave the islands are there except the hostages that we know of. Let's monitor and advise as appropriate. I'm going home. Everyone stood when Stone left the room.

Stone walked with Meredith the short distance back to his office and closed the door behind them.

"Meredith," he began, "I know you're worried about Bart and your friend, Mark—"

"Matt, sir."

"Yes, of course, Matt. Anyway, I've got a meeting tonight at my home in McLean. I need you to come over and assist me with this thing if you're free," Stone said, looking out of his window.

"Well, sure, I guess," said Meredith.

"But first we've got to stop by the White House."

Thrust into the heady atmosphere of political power, Meredith could only follow.

"Sure," she said, looking down at her dress. She had bought two new dresses since she started reporting to the secretary of defense every day as a special assistant. Her official title was still as Rathburn's assistant, but Stone had elevated her status temporarily for the crisis.

They showed their credentials at the west gate and walked into the national security advisor's office, where President Davis was waiting with Yves Gerald, the National Security Advisor and Frank Lantini, who had just made the trip from Langley where he had been on video conference.

"The way I see it, we've got to make them show some force. We can't just sink the ships in the ocean," Gerald said..

"Why *can't* we just sink the ships, Yves?" Davis asked.

"Well, sir," Gerald answered, "The Japanese could claim that they were going to use those weapons, if they ever admitted to owning them, for defensive purposes. They could claim that they were building storage sites. It would make us look bad."

"Maybe, but we can't let a war happen if we can avoid it," the president said, concerned. "We'll lose too many American lives. Hell we've already lost over 20, and maybe the hostages."

"Sir," Meredith interrupted, "I have a friend who's one of the hostages, and—"

"I'm so sorry," Davis said.

Meredith looked at the president. Okay, friend might have been a stretch, but she did feel close to Matt, and she was inexplicably worried about him.

"Thank you, the point I want to make is that I believe force is necessary. Think of how many lives it will cost if we don't stop the Japanese. What happens if they seize the Philippines? What kind of message does it send the world if we don't respond?" she said, still appearing uncomfortable asking the president questions. She continued, "The real issue may be, how much do we let the world know about?"

"What do you mean?"

Gerald chimed in when Meredith didn't respond. "I think she means that if we can sink the other six ships and blockade Japan from doing much else with their rather large 'self-defense force,' then we might just be able to show the world a still somewhat weak Japan that went crazy with four divisions. But if the world, especially China and Korea, find out that they have 10 divisions floating in the water with three or four manufacturing plants in Mindanao still cranking tanks out every day, we've got a regional conflict beyond anything we could imagine. So the issue is letting them look like the aggressor but limiting what they can fight with."

"I agree," said Lantini.

"Is there any way to negotiate our way out of this?" Davis asked.

"Sir, we've already been out-negotiated. If they've got four divisions' worth of equipment moving into Manila Bay, in my opinion they've already attacked. They did this whole thing behind our backs, lying to us every step of the way," Gerald said.

"Still, why can't we just call up the prime minister and tell him not to attack?" the president asked.

"Once again, sir, the Japanese do not appear to be concerned with our response. Mizuzawa wouldn't even see me when I flew out there, so I came straight back. I think they truly believe we will not respond—"

"Then we must make them continue to believe it," Meredith said.

"Right," said Gerald, appearing unsure of how to treat Meredith. "If we're gonna fight this thing, we need to make up our minds. I'll go negotiate, but they've been bullshittin' us for a couple of years, and as far as I'm concerned that constitutes breaking diplomatic relations. In effect, sir, they declared war on us when they developed this plan of theirs."

"This thing has the potential to get way out of hand," the president said. "They need to know that I will do whatever is right for the American people, even if that means waiting to deal with Iraq. Okay? That's the plan then. We wait for their attack on the Philippines to commence, then we sink the six ships in the water as we launch our forces. I assume we've still got the carrier group moving to Korea?"

"Yes, sir," Stone responded. "I've got a team working up an assessment of the impact this will have on the Iraq time line also."

"That's fine, but if we get locked down here, I want to do it right," Davis said.

A military aide stuck his head in the door and said, "Sir, the Japanese ambassador is here to see you. He's waiting outside the Oval Office."

President Davis looked at the gathering and declared, "Showtime."

CHAPTER 38
White House, Washington, DC
President Davis

Japanese Ambassador to the United States Kaitachi was waiting for the president in the anteroom to the Oval Office. The president shook hands with the Japanese diplomat and placed an arm around him as they walked in.

"Good afternoon, Mr. Ambassador," the president said.

"Good afternoon, Mr. President," Kaitachi responded with a bow.

They walked into the Oval Office and a military aide closed the doors behind them. The president walked to a window and looked at the Washington Monument. The cherry blossoms were in full splendor around the tidal basin. It was a beautiful, tranquil sight. *The trees were a gift in 1912 from the Japanese ambassador's wife,* Davis recalled. *What other gifts are they bearing today?*

"I've considered your plea for a response from us," the president said.

"Oh?" Kaitachi said, sounding surprised.

The president shot his eyes to the side, measuring the inflection in the ambassador's voice.

"Yes," he said, turning and looking at the old man. "We will send a carrier battle group off the coast of Korea and warn them against any aggression."

"That is not necessary," Kaitachi said, backtracking. "We were only hoping for satellite assistance in observing the region."

"Well, why didn't you say so? Now I've moved an entire carrier group over there."

"You are free to call them back, sir. My intentions were not to have you send forces, simply provide us intelligence in keeping with the spirit of our alliance," Kaitachi said.

I bet that's all you wanted. He's smooth. Very smooth.

"Whatever you say, but it may take some time to get them turned around. How do you guys feel about this situation in the Philippines?" he asked. The president grabbed a handful of peanuts from a bowl on his desk and popped them into his mouth.

"We are still concerned, but now believe that we can handle the threat regionally," Kaitachi said.

"What do you mean?" Davis asked, interested. *Could this be it? Are they finally going to come clean?*

"Through statecraft, we can ensure our sea-lanes are not intercepted. We do not believe the Muslim insurgents, the Abu Sayyaf, will be a large threat to the region as Bin Laden is to the world, though we will watch. If it is more of an internal revolution that may, in the long run, improve the condition of the average Filipino, then, naturally we support such improvement. But the primary reason I am here is to relay to you that my prime minister is very satisfied with your leadership in this crisis."

I'll bet, you sneaky son of a bitch.

"Well, thank you. Send my regards to Prime Minister Mizuzawa."

"I shall."

"Oh, by the way, my condolences on the death of your emperor. He was a good man," the president said sincerely. He had known Emperor Shigazawa to be a kind and caring person.

"Thank you. I will pass your remarks on to the prime minister."

President Davis watched Ambassador Kaitachi leave his office, knowing full well that the diplomat was lying. He wanted to stop him and tell him that they knew everything, but that would have been a mistake.

Davis felt confident for the first time in days. He finally had the upper hand.

Sitting at his desk, the president wondered if they might be able to let Japan attack the Philippines, then counter with American force, eschewing the United Nations initially. They then could petition the UN for a peacekeeping force and mandatory trade concessions that would regulate trade imbalances. The key was making it clear Japan was in the "Hitler" aggressor role as America had rightly made clear with Saddam Hussein. *Considering their recent actions, that shouldn't be too hard,* the president thought.

President Davis jotted a note on White House stationery, then called his press aide and instructed him on packaging his speech to the American people, the one that would inform the world of impending American action in the Philippines.

Not against the Islamic insurgents, but against Japan.

He picked up a remote and turned on the television, flipping through the channels quickly before stopping and backing up. He recognized someone. There it was.

Kaitachi was on television. The president noticed the small C-SPAN symbol in the corner of the screen. Kaitachi was briefing the General Assembly of the United Nations. He raised the volume and listened as the interpreter spoke after Kaitachi talked in his native tongue. The ambassador must have taken the Japanese diplomatic jet to LaGuardia. Door to door from DC to the UN was less than two hours with the efficient transportation that a head of state or ambassador typically commanded.

"I have just received word from Prime Minister Mizuzawa that I am to address the body today concerning the revolution in the Philippines. Also, I briefed the president of the United States this morning on my remarks today."

What the hell is he talking about? The president sat forward in his chair, pressed an intercom button, and screamed into the receiver, "Yves, get in here, now!" National Security Advisor Gerald came running into the oval office and saw the president watching C-SPAN.

"Look at this shit!"

They watched as Kaitachi spoke.

"Today, we have joined alliances with the United States in a dramatic way in this Global War on Terror. The Japanese military has landed on the Philippine Island of Luzon with a small show of force in an effort to ensure that our critical sea-lanes remain open. As you all know, we orchestrated the release of American and freedom-seeking peoples from the Philippines. Regrettably, further negotiations with Commander Villanueva, the so-called Abu Sayyaf leader, have led to his refusal to cooperate with U.S.-Japan efforts and resulted in a serious threat to Japanese sea-lanes and freedom-seeking peoples in the country.

"The barbaric acts of this Islamic ideologue must not go unchecked. His actions threaten the nascent democracies in the region. We have had several discussions with President Davis and his secretary of defense, who have requested assistance regarding this vital matter. I will provide transcripts of these conversations for the media. Our partners, the United States, asked us to handle the situation ourselves, and so we have.

"We promise to attempt to crush Islamic fundamentalism, restore the democratic process to the Philippines, and ensure that our vital sea-lanes remain open. In addition to stemming the spread of Islamic fundamentalism in our own region to protect our national security, our goal is to alleviate the burden and pain of the Filipinos, who will surely suffer under the rule of Sharia law.

"Rest assured, we have no designs beyond protecting the fine people of the Philippines and our vital interests. We want to thank our great allies, the United States, for their advice and assistance in this matter."

Kaitachi finished and walked away from the podium, leaving behind a speechless delegation, U.S. president, and world viewers.

Gerald snatched the remote and flipped to CNN, which was scrambling with the news. A CNN correspondent was sticking a microphone in his ear, looking at his notes, ready to provide some cursory analysis.

Gerald shut off the television.

The President and National Security Advisor looked at one another for a few brief seconds. Japan had surrounded them with bishops, knights, and rooks. The president felt frozen in place. *Was America facing a potential checkmate? No, that wasn't possible,* he thought.

It occurred to him, as it might have occurred to Napoleon that Wellington was indeed on the reverse slope of the hill as his forces impaled themselves on the British lances, that they had been at least one step behind Japan at every juncture.

"Why do I feel like we're standing here holding our jockstraps, Yves?"

Gerald looked uncomfortably at the floor, then leveled his eyes on the president.

"Because we are, sir."

CHAPTER 39
McLean, Virginia
Meredith Morris

Meredith had raced to her condo five minutes away in Pentagon City, where she was pulling her nylons over her legs and had a hairbrush clutched between her teeth doing the "Superman change," as she called it. It was nearing seven o'clock and Latisha had called to remind her that Stone was expecting her to arrive at his home for some planning. Latisha had mentioned that they might return to the Pentagon after the secretary had his dinner, depending on developments in the Philippines. Meredith was not thrilled about having to fight DC rush-hour traffic from her Arlington apartment to his McLean mansion.

The television was blasting FoxNews in the background as she stood, yanking the hose up around her waist, then letting her cocktail dress fall to her knees. She stepped to the mirror, sighed, and said, "This will have to do."

She slipped Rathburn's thumb drive into her purse, disappointed that she'd not had much time to truly consider what its contents might be or portend.

"Ambassador Kaitachi has just announced that Japan intends to join forces with the United States in the Global War on Terror to, and I quote, 'crush Islamic fundamentalism' in the Philippines…"

She was brushing her hair, then in slow motion she stopped the smooth stroke against her blond locks, staring at the image of the television in the mirror.

"Oh my God," she said.

Her mind raced and locked onto the big picture. Just as the Third Reich had begun with the embarrassment and constraining loss of territory from World War I's Treaty of Versailles, Japan was still smarting from World War II's post conflict occupation and dominance by the Americans. Like an ill patient who has sweat through the sheets shedding a virus, Japan had suffered the alien imposition of Western culture only to come back to their native heritage.

Hitler had started with the Night of the Long Knives, where key German leaders had been murdered in order to allow for consolidation of power. *The Japanese Emperor had just committed suicide,* she thought.

Then Hitler got around the German constitution limiting their Army to 100,000 soldiers by merging the Army and the Sturmabteilung, the assault force. *Japan is circumventing their constitution by building tanks and helicopters in the Philippines.*

In 1938, Hitler compelled Austrian Chancellor Kurt von Schuschnigg to capitulate in a bloodless invasion. Then followed Sudetenland, or Czechoslovakia, then Poland and…

"Oh my God," she said again.

Japan is starting with the Philippines, then going to Taiwan!
How did we miss this?

She jumped into her old Honda Prelude and took the George Washington Parkway from her Pentagon Row apartment onto Dolley Madison and into McLean. She found the address and debated a few minutes whether to pull into the long driveway or park on the street. She looked around and determined that her piece of junk might get towed if she left it on the street. As she pulled into the long driveway, she noticed that it arced in front of the huge colonial mansion. She followed the curve and stopped just beyond the hedgerow that abutted the asphalt.

She stood, grabbed her briefcase and purse, and walked up the steps.

Secretary of Defense Robert Stone

Stone swirled his Scotch in his glass and thought about the day. He had met with the joint chiefs once again to discuss the Japanese ambassador's announcement at the United Nations. The media frenzy was predictable but unnerving. They had plenty of questions. War in Afghanistan was raging, and now the Philippines? How were Abu Sayyaf and Al Qaeda linked? Did the Philippines add a Pacific Rim dimension to the Global War on Terror? Did it scuttle the plan for Iraq? How much joint and combined planning had the United States done with the Japanese?

All good questions.

He had given a brief press conference, not wanting to say anything of significance before the president's speech. They had worked hard through the day, and there was little else he could do tonight other than monitor the situation from home. Besides, he had Meredith coming over for dinner shortly, and with his wife out of town, he thought he might digress from the rapid pace of events for a while. *It's officially a meeting*, he thought to himself.

Stone muddied his mind with prurient thoughts of Meredith. He sat in his leather recliner in the study of his McLean mansion, which had cost well over $2,000,000. The house was beautiful. It was a large, red-brick Colonial design with far too many rooms for two people. Stone even had a servant who lived in separate quarters.

He heard the doorbell ring and listened to the footsteps of Andre, his butler for all practical purposes. He heard the banter of small talk and smiled when he heard Meredith's voice sing sweetly in the large foyer, drifting through the expansive hallways and echoing into the abyss of his mind. *She wants me. Otherwise, she would not have shown.* He had changed into a shirt and sweater with khaki pants, figuring that the collegiate look might attract her. The sweater could not hide his protruding gut though, and the khaki pants did not make him look any taller. In fact,

Meredith was a good two inches taller than he was. It made him uncomfortable, and therefore he had to conquer her.

"Hello, sir," Meredith said in a cheery voice. She was dressed in a simple blue cocktail dress that plunged moderately low into her décolletage.

White pearls lay softly against her bare neck. Her hair was its usual blond splendor, only frozen into place with hair spray. The dress cut a few inches above her knees and angled slightly up on the left side, teasing him. A faint smell of perfume circled him, accelerating his lust.

Her innocent smile and wide blue eyes greeted him, comforting him in his own knowledge that indeed she did want him. *She dressed up just for me.*

"Meredith, you look beautiful. I'm sorry I underdressed. I thought we were just going to go over a few notes. I can go change if you'd like," he said, standing from the chair. *Good move. Make her the aggressor.*

Stone watched Andre had float back to the kitchen with a shit-eating grin on his face. After catching sight of Meredith, Andre would be knuckle punching him later tonight.

"No, no," she said. "Actually I wasn't sure what was appropriate and figured overdressing is better than looking the slob. I've got the briefcase right here. And after hearing Kaitachi today, I think we've got plenty to work on."

"I was just going to have some dinner with Mrs. Stone, but she got called away. Would you like her plate?" Stone said.

"I'm so sorry," Meredith said, "I didn't mean to interrupt your dinner." She brushed his arm as she walked by, and he wanted to reach out and satisfy her on the spot. She obviously wanted him. The dress, the hair, the perfume, the pearls, the face, the smile, the high heels, the touching. Yes, there was no doubt it was for him.

"Drinks?" Andre asked, returning from the kitchen. He wore a white butler coat and shirt with black pants and a black bow tie.

"Meredith?" Stone said, smiling, knowing what bounty lay ahead for him. He would savor the moment.

"Whatever you're having, sir," she said, her voice oozing over him, causing his heart to flutter. He blushed.

"Two glasses of champagne, please Andre," he said. "And bring the bottle." Yes, they would drink, loosen inhibitions, and maybe even skip dinner. *I knew it. She's wanted me since day one.*

They sat on the leather sofa and drank champagne. At some point Meredith grabbed the remote control and flipped the television to CNN, muting the volume so they could talk. She had one eye on the television though. Soon the president would be on.

Andre had served dinner and cleaned up, retiring for the evening to his quarters after bringing a second bottle of champagne. Stone had drunk most of the first bottle, distorting his perception of the evening. Meredith had successfully nursed two glasses but looked like she was feeling the effects of the alcohol. "Ready to get to work, Meredith?" Stone said. He stood and stumbled.

"Don't you want to wait for the president's speech, sir?" Meredith asked seriously.

"No, I've seen a copy. Let's go to the study."

Stone stood, hovering over Meredith as she stared at the television.

Meredith Morris

For the first time in the evening, Meredith was uncomfortable. She saw a glint in Stone's eyes that sparkled of a hidden agenda. She looked nervously at her attire and suddenly felt guilty for the way she was dressed.

"C'mon. Let's head to the study, there's a TV in there," he said. She began wondering how she could have been so stupid. Had she led him on? No, maybe his motives were pure. She had done much for him, and indeed the country, in a behind-the-scenes sort of way over the past week. Perhaps this was Stone's way of saying thank you, by letting her, some of the help, into a small part of his life. She wanted to believe that.

"I haven't read the speech though. I'd like to see it, sir."

"Hell, you wrote part of it," he said. "I gave your report to Gerald. He said there was no use reinventing the wheel and that he'd embellish your comments and give them to the president."

"Well, now I really want to see it," she said, forcing a smile. Yes, she could do this. Delay until he got tired. He was an old man and would probably get sleepy soon.

She turned up the volume of the television as the camera panned the face of the president. He looked worried and tired.

Stone turned on the stereo, put a CD in the disc changer, and soon the Rolling Stones' "Wild Horses" was belting out of the speakers, nearly overriding the television. Stone played a bit of air guitar, grabbed a mock microphone, and said, "Mick Jagger!"

WTF!

Then he moved behind the sofa and rested his hands on the leather to either side of Meredith's shoulders. She could feel his hot breath blowing into her hair. "I'm a rock star," he whispered in her ear.

Gross.

"Good evening, my fellow Americans," the president said. "Tonight I speak to you, the nation, and to the entire world concerning the rapidly unfolding events in the Philippines.

"As you all know, earlier today Japan announced her intentions to intervene militarily in the affairs of the Republic of the Philippines. Specifically, Ambassador Kaitachi stated that Japan wished to restore democracy to the freedom-loving people of the Philippines. Such a move is consistent with our desire to maintain democratic governments around the world, yet it competes with the emerging international con- sensus of guaranteeing the right to self-determination of individual countries." Meredith forced a smile. It was her line. Stone had not lied, at least not about using her words for the president's speech. He hadn't let up on the heavy breathing, though, sounding like a stalker on an obscene phone call.

"However, we will begin dialogue with the Japanese government to discuss alternatives to the physical military occupation of the Philippines. We believe there are other methods of securing Japan's lines of communication through the South China and Celebes Seas. I ask the international community to be patient with us and with Japan. We will find a solution through statecraft.

"My message to the American people is, there is no reason to be alarmed. The situation is well under control. My message to the people of the Philippines is that we will work to ensure your country is not beholden to the dark vision of Islamic extremism. My message to the world is that we have the lead in this action. Our Japanese allies will work independently, yet we will closely monitor their military action. All freedom-seeking people wish to stem the flow of Islamic fundamentalism and the sinister future it harbors.

"Thank you and God bless America and all freedom-loving people."

Short and way off the point, Meredith surmised. *But he had to say something to reinforce the Japanese belief that the Americans would not respond,* as she had suggested. *Now how the hell do I escape from here?*

It said so little, but meant so much. The world would interpret it as meaning Japan's actions were intended to fight Islamic extremism, saving a bit of face for the president and perhaps calming the fears of China, Russia, and Korea. Those nations, at least in the near term, would be reluctant to take any kind of action against Japan. She had agreed that it was crucial to portray Japan as an ally, thereby negating a knee-jerk response from any one country, lest they have to contend with the American nuclear and conventional arsenal.

"I told you, dearie," Stone said. Meredith looked down and instinctively pulled her skirt toward her knees.

Stone had dimmed the lights during the short speech. It was clear he had not listened. She looked at the second bottle of champagne. He had nearly sucked it dry, and she cringed at the thought of what would come next. She had eluded several college men in similar circumstances, but never did she imagine she would have to pull the plug on the sexual batteries of the secretary of defense.

"The study, darling, or would you prefer to use—stay on the couch?" Stone said.

He was clearly on testosterone override. The alcohol had flipped a switch in his brain, sending an electrical current to his penis, thereby relinquishing all control to the lower appendage for the time being.

She looked at her watch and said, lamely, "Sir, I must really be going. You know what they say about wearing out—"

"The sofa?" Stone said, moving around to her front, intercepting her before she could escape. He grabbed her arm and sat next to her. He stared wildly at her breasts, which she instinctively covered.

"Sir!" Meredith said, weakly.

"Don't you want to make love to one of the most powerful men in the world, Meredith?" Stone asked, sounding a bit like he was trying an impersonation of Jack Nicholson. His fingers pressed into the flesh of her slender arm. His breath was sour with the musty odor of the champagne fermenting in his belly.

"Sir, really. This is inappropriate," she said, pushing him away and snatching her arm back.

"You want me, don't you? You've wanted me since you showed up in my office. Now let's get down to business, Meredith. Let's cut to the chase. I'm Mick Jagger," Stone said, hungrily. He pulled at her dress and a naked breast popped out of the fabric.

"Yes, that's more like it. I knew you wanted me."

He grabbed her arms and lay on top of her, hiking her dress all the way up to her waist. He looked down at her hose and pulled at them with his fingers, wanting to secure his prize. He deserved it, he figured. It had been a hard week at the office.

Meredith, do something! He's raping you! she thought.

Meredith used all of her strength to push Stone's drunken body off her and onto the floor. She stood, stepping over him.

"Oh, you want to get on top, huh? I should have guessed," Stone said.

She pulled her hose up, grabbed her purse, and tried to run. Stone grabbed at her legs, causing her to fall and strike her forehead on the oak coffee table, leaving a huge gash, which gushed blood onto her face.

"You son of a bitch!" Meredith screamed, standing up and running from the study. She bumped into Andre, who had awakened to the commotion, splattering blood onto his white T-shirt.

"He tried to rape me!" she said, running from the house and getting into her car. She fumbled with the keys, trying to find the ignition.

Suddenly Stone's face was at the driver's side window. She locked the doors and finally cranked the engine. She floored the gas pedal, flooding the engine. It cranked, pouring white smoke from the exhaust. She sped away, purposely veering the car into Stone and knocking him on his rear.

Stone was frustrated, sitting there on his ass. *She's just playing hard to get. Mick Jagger never gets rejected.* He picked himself up, ascended the steps on his porch, and saw a small metal object in the dim light. Wobbling, he bent over and picked up the small device.

"What's this?" he asked himself, his words slurring a bit as he pocketed an object about the size of his thumb.

As she pulled onto the George Washington Parkway heading toward Pentagon City, Meredith noticed a car following her closely.

Whoever was chasing her was now less than five car lengths behind her. She figured it might be the Secretary of Defense's personal security. The person flashed his bright lights at her.

She floored the accelerator, fearful that she would not escape Stone or whoever it was if they caught her. Her pursuer pulled up directly behind her as she was approaching 100 mph on the narrow, winding road. The tall trees lining either side of the road made her feel as though she was driving through a dark tunnel.

She accelerated into the turn and the Prelude left the road.

She felt the car fail to negotiate the curve and flip onto its side. The low roof crumpled near her head and sparks were flying everywhere, then the vehicle skidded off the road, falling 30 feet below into a ditch just before the bridge.

Then everything went black.

CHAPTER 40
Island of Luzon, Philippines
Taiku Taikishi

The attack had been successful. Takishi sat atop the turret of a new Japanese Type 90 tank with its 120 millimeter smoothbore gun.

It seemed they could not miss. They had secured the Presidential Palace early in the operation. He had flown in the Mistubishi AH-X attack helicopter, still in its experimental phase. It had performed beautifully. Hellfire missiles reduced the thin-skinned rebel vehicles to burning hulks in seconds. The captured Scorpion tanks and old American M-113 Armored Personnel Carriers were no match for the new and improved version of the Japanese Imperial Army.

The rebels, believing that the Japanese were there to help them, as they had provided them weapons, were that much easier to kill.

Once in the compound, they had completely destroyed the radio and television stations. A holdover from the Marcos Era was the fact that the government controlled the only two means of real-time communication to the people. Takishi had them destroyed immediately, preventing incoming or outgoing television or radio reports. Villanueva had appeared shocked to see Takishi enter the presidential grounds with nearly 200 Japanese infantrymen trotting beside him carrying American M16 rifles. Takishi was wielding his New Nambu revolver, waving it and smiling at Villanueva.

"Let's go, my friend. It is time to move on to another life," Takishi said, pointing the revolver in Villanueva's face.

"What are you doing, you fool?" Villanueva screamed.

"You are the fool, letting us build weapons in your own backyard." Takishi laughed.

Villanueva's eyes sank to the ground.

"I guess everything does come full cycle," Villanueva said softly, looking at Takishi. "First the Spanish, then the Americans, then your ancestors, then the Americans again, and now the Japanese again."

Takishi smiled and nodded, watching as his forces rolled through the streets of Manila amidst an angry mob of people.

Lifting his pearl handled revolver to Villanueva's head, Takishi pulled the trigger from point blank. Villanueva's lifeless body slumped at the front gate of the Presidential Palace. As if to celebrate, the Japanese soldiers shot into the crowd, killing some and quickly dispersing the group that had assembled to protest. The Japanese army had gathered almost 2000 members of Villanueva's Abu Sayyaf and were marching them north past the airport, into the countryside in the direction of Cabanatuan.

The tank treads creaked forward slowly, as if to nudge the stragglers in the group of rebels. Some women and children had accompanied their husbands and fathers for the march north to wherever. Those still walking away from Manila were the fortunate ones, Takishi conceded, as thousands lay dead behind them.

The insurgents had put up a valiant fight but were no match for Takishi's sophisticated weaponry. His Japanese army fought from the technological comfort of their machines, mowing down the rebels, who would foolishly stand and fire small-arms weapons at them. The insurgents had used most of their anti-tank and anti-aircraft weapons during the initial assault. In fact, they had gotten downright careless with the ammunition, thinking and hoping they would no longer need it.

They had been wrong.

Takishi's plan was to drive the Abu Sayyaf north to Fort Magsaysay where they would either lock them in prison facilities or shoot them, whichever Prime Minister Mizuzawa decided.

The crowd neared 3000 as the Japanese soldiers stormed a hamlet of thatch huts and added the residents to the group. The prisoners walked with bare feet along the white cement road, past their neighbors and friends, some of whom watched the procession, others joining out of defiance. The Filipinos were a proud people, regardless of political orientation. Takishi guessed that they were tired of foreign domination of their country and would remain defiant to the end. So be it.

But the large mob was getting hard to control. Takishi's soldiers formed a cordon on either side of the tired, hungry group, walking much faster than the heat of the day allowed for. The pavement was piping hot, burning hardened bare feet at the touch. Pregnant women passed out along the way, dropping to the side, only to be nudged with the pointed tip of a soldier's bayonet. Some lost their babies and others simply did not continue.

None of the group had enough time to secure any food or water for the march, many dropping from heat exhaustion. They traveled over 20 miles in less than six hours, a brutal pace. Fort Magsaysay was 50 miles north of Manila.

They were almost halfway there. Takishi would make sure they made it by nightfall.

CHAPTER 41
Matt Garrett

"Piece of shit," Matt yelled, kicking the truck, which had died on them. No idiot light came on. No gauge needle pegged out. The truck just crapped out. They had traveled just five miles from their captivity then camped out for the night.

"Where the hell are we?" Sturgeon asked, not really expecting an answer.

"We're just outside Cabanatuan. Used to be an Abu Sayyaf stronghold. Still is, I guess," Barefoot told them.

The morning sun bore down on them like an 18-wheeler with high beams. At least they had made it past the sunken rice paddy area. The sun was rising and Matt knew they needed to find concealment. Now they were standing amidst a desolate expanse of hardpan covered in white dirt with isolated patches of grass shooting through.

Matt spied a small wooded area to the west and said, "We need to do something about Rathburn's body. We need to bury him and somehow mark the spot so one day we can come back for him."

"Yeah, you're right," Sturgeon said.

"There," Matt pointed. There was a small hill with a tight cluster of hardwoods about 300 meters to their west. The terrain feature contrasted sharply against the indistinct hardpan upon which they stood and the soggy rice paddies behind them. The town of Cabanatuan was less than a mile to the west, interrupted by the clump of trees on a small hill.

"That looks good," Sturgeon said.

"Good," Matt said. "Barefoot, is there any way we could get the place on film, in case, you know"—he paused—"something should happen to us? At least there would be a record of where we buried him."

"Why don't I do a story on this if my batteries work?" Barefoot asked, pointing to his camera with tripod and remote, a satellite antenna, and the four-port uplink that linked the antenna to the camera and processed the information digitally over the computer.

"Yeah, let's do that," Matt said. "Tell the world where we are. Why didn't you tell us your stuff worked?"

"It will only record. I'm sure the rebels pilfered it," Barefoot said. "I'll check it once we get where we're going."

Two of the men carried the media equipment while Matt carried Rathburn's stiff, putrid body across the dusty surface.

They entered the comforting shade of the wooded knoll and disappeared amidst the trees. The mahoganies were tall and dark, blocking the searing, penetrating rays of the sun. Each man had a canteen of water they had found in the back of the truck, curiously, and drank.

Arriving at what felt like the right spot, Matt dumped Rathburn's body on the ground. The dirt around the trees was darker and softer than the crusted hardpan they had traversed. The woods were larger than they had initially appeared, running a couple of hundred meters to the west, toward Cabanatuan. He found a tree branch, snapped the twigs away, and whittled the end into a spade with Sturgeon's knife. He tossed the knife to its owner, who did the same.

The two men dug a shallow grave in nearly an hour. They worked feverishly for some unknown reason—they had all the time in the world, but their sense was that Rathburn had been violated and by planting his body in the ground, somehow it would begin the healing process. Perhaps then, his soul could escape the horror of the past few days and ascend to the heavens.

Meanwhile, Matt noticed Barefoot set up his equipment, testing and checking. Matt was surprised when Barefoot mentioned everything was in working order. Done digging, Matt joined Barefoot as he pointed the satellite dish toward the sky until he got a red signal indicator showing that he had link-up with the CNN satellite. Then the signal faded.

"CNN's satellite," Barefoot said, "It is geostationary, so either we lost the signal or my batteries are weak."

"Press on," Matt said, turning back to the grave they had dug.

Matt and Sturgeon lifted Rathburn's body into the grave and began the burial process. Barefoot popped a blank tape into his camera and began filming. When Rathburn was covered with dirt, Matt took the two field-expedient spades and drove them deep into the ground with a rock, marking the head and foot of the grave. When the June rains came and all the ground seemed the same, the two branches should still be protruding a foot or so from the earth's surface.

"I would just like to say a few words," Matt said, unaffected by the camera. He stood with the mound of dirt behind him, framed by the two branches. To his rear, the trees thinned, giving way to the hardpan below and the city of Cabanatuan to the west. The cement road was visible in the background as it emerged from some tiny shacks on the edge of the town only 200 meters from their location.

Sturgeon took a knee in his salt-lined flight suit. He had sweat completely through it digging the grave. As Matt spoke he noticed the red light from the satellite transponder; it had come back on. They were transmitting somewhere. Maybe someone was watching?

Matt was a continuing contrast, like a photo-negative. His khaki shirt was now gray from dirt stains collecting on the wetness of his sweat. His cargo pants were nearly white from the dusty hardpan. Sweat had washed away the film of dirt from his unshaven face, revealing his drawn, hardened features. He had not eaten for two full days and was weak. His hair was matted and unclean. His voice was solid, though, as he spoke.

"Today we mark the death of Mr. Bart Rathburn, the assistant secretary of defense for international security affairs. Two days ago rebels from the Abu Sayyaf kidnapped Mr. Rathburn, the pilot of the destroyed Department of Defense airplane Jack Sturgeon, and myself, Matt Garrett. We are fortunate enough to have the company of Johnny Barefoot, a CNN correspondent whom the rebels mistook for a spy. The rebels attacked and took us hostage, and for two days we sat in a rat-infested jail cell at a place called Fort Magsaysay near a small town on the island of Luzon called Cabanatuan.

"It is a sad day. Bart Rathburn gave his life in the service of his country. He died before his time. He had resisted his captors in the spirit of the American fighting soldier, but in the end the Abu Sayyaf tortured and killed him.

"I did not know Bart Rathburn well, but his assistant, Meredith Morris, described him as a dedicated family man with a beautiful wife and two boys. We are making this documentary to record the location of his burial in case we do not escape from this conflict."

Curiously, as Matt talked, he could see beyond the camera a group of people walking on the road and thought he heard a faint, high-pitched squeak of machinery. Momentarily, Barefoot cut the camera to the side of Matt's face. Matt turned and saw about 20 Filipinos dragging in the dirt. Behind them were soldiers wearing dark green, olive drab uniforms, holding weapons and sometimes prodding the stragglers.

Matt spoke as Barefoot continue to film the death march. He could now see Japanese soldiers poking and prodding the emerging masses along the road.

"Are you getting this, Barefoot?" Matt asked.

"If everything's working I am," Barefoot said.

Matt thought that the images Barefoot taped, perhaps even transmitted to a satellite, were images of another era. *This is not possible today,* he thought. He saw soldiers herding young children onto the hot pavement in the afternoon sun. He saw muzzle flashes of random gunfire that some-how seemed too accurate. He saw tanks and mechanized fighting vehicles rolling slowly, setting the pace of the march from the rear. But there was no rear. The procession was an endless line of downtrodden Filipinos. Mothers and fathers carrying their children. Some shot through the backs if they could not keep up.

He watched in horror and zoomed to a full body view as a young Filipino male shouted angrily at a Japanese soldier, who leveled a pistol at the young man's head and squeezed the trigger. Through the camera, the execution seemed to have a higher resolution. The faces of the two men. One angry, the other cold and expressionless, simply doing a duty. Asian faces, one soft, almost European, the other harsh, brutally so. Their bodies. One brownish, the other yellow, one lean and malnour-ished, the other strong and stocky like a barrel. Their weapons: one only his courage, the other a Japanese 9mm officer's pistol.

Matt and Sturgeon snapped their heads when they heard the gunshot that sounded so close. They had become accustomed to the random, dis-tant firing of weapons but knew this to be something else.

"Look between the trees," Barefoot said, pointing.

Matt saw the procession and then said, "If there are any viewers out there, what you are witnessing seems from antoher time, but it is happen-ing now, in real time. The Japanese Army appears to be detaining and marching Filipinos to an uncertain destination."

The young woman was unsure if she was watching HBO, reality TV, or a broadcaster's transmission. She was just a young college intern in Atlanta, Georgia, but was watching the scene transmitted to the Syncom 3 satellite, an old coaxial slotted array communication satellite positioned 1900 kilo-meters north of Fiji. Almost 40 years ago, American television companies had used the same satellite to transmit the Olympics from Tokyo, she had been told. Thinking she had better check it out, this being her first day on the job, she asked the Headline News production manager, Lewis Silver, to take a look at what was on her screen. Carrying a cup of coffee into the room with a bank of television sets, all transmitting different images, he sat down and looked as she pointed. It was early in Georgia, only five o'clock, and Americans were not awake yet. At least most were not.

President Davis looked away from the television screen and at Gerald.

"There it is," Gerald said.

"I agree," Stone said, working off his champagne hangover. Thankfully, Fox and Diamond hadn't been called into the early-morning meeting in the White House.

"There are other options," Lantini protested mildly, drawing a curious stare from Stone.

"We've got to do it," Sewell said, then looked at Stone.

Three to one, Davis thought, then said, "Pull the trigger."

CHAPTER 42
Island of Luzon, Philippines
Captain Zachary Garrett

Through the greenish hue of his night-vision goggles, Captain Zachary Garrett could see about 30 tanks from where he was sprawled in the prone position atop a jagged ridge to the west of the airfield—the same direction from which the first attack had come. The early-morning air was relatively cool and damp with dew, but Zach knew that the steaming heat would arrive with the sun.

The unsuspecting Japanese forces had not secured their rear area very well. The tanks he saw were lining up to move out in single file, practically in an administrative mode. He could see short men running about wildly waving their arms as if they were reacting to an emergency. The tanks were only 500 meters away, and his Javelin tank-killing missiles should destroy them with ease. His company had procured 20 sights and over 60 missiles from the ammunition stockpile. There were more, but his men had not been able to carry all of them.

Still, with his original nine sights from Hawaii, that gave him almost one weapons device per tank. Looking to his left, he saw Barker's platoon lined up along the ridge, his men peering through the thermal sights, waiting for the signal. Taylor's platoon was to the south, beneath the ridge, while Kurtz's men were opposite him on the other side of Barker.

The other three companies from the battalion were prepared to assault from the North, across the airstrip, toward the pier. Garrett's company was providing supporting fire for the attack. He was glad that he had a support-by-fire mission for a change. His men would welcome the relative safety of covered and concealed fighting positions as opposed to advancing on the enemy again.

Morale had risen significantly when the rest of the battalion had arrived from the aircraft carrier following the link up with McAllister's company. The men ate the extra rations that had been dumped by helicopter into their position the following morning. Their stomachs full and their minds rested, Zach knew his men relished the thought of avenging the losses of Teller and Rockingham.

And then there was Matt, his brother. They had received word of the three hostages and Zach had heard that Matt was one of the detainees. The thought of Matt as a hostage had worn on him, sapping his strength and diverting his attention. But something had transpired in him, temporarily at least, to allow him to command his soldiers. Partly, Zach knew that if anyone could survive in the Philippines, it was his brother. And partly, despite the pain, worry, anxiety, and frustration, he could feel the hand of God inside him, hammering the molten ore of his character and dipping a hot rod of support into the reservoir of his strength and pulling it out, steaming and rigid, once again allowing him to be the commander he had to be.

The radio crackled with a whispering voice making a net call. Zachary acknowledged. He nodded when he heard McAllister's distinctive Boston accent and was comforted by his friend's confident cadence. One night over a few beers at the Schofield Barracks O-Club, he and McAllister had waxed philosophical, something most infantry officers avoided. But out of deep respect for one another, they had tried to reach out in a masculine way. Each had wanted the other to know he trusted the other with his life. "If we ever get on the two-way rifle range, old boy," McAllister had said, eyes glassy from alcohol, "I hope to hear your voice come crackling over the radio."

Zachary had looked at McAllister, feeling the same way and sorry he had not used the line first. "Same here, bud. I want you on my flank."

The two warriors had stared at each other in a moment of martial kinship, an intangible combat multiplier understood by few.

And there it was. McAllister would not let him down. He knew that much if he knew nothing else. It was a good feeling.

"Cardinal, over," Zachary said into his radio.

Cardinal was the code word for commencing the attack. Zachary was to initiate the fires with the Javelin anti-tank weapons, then lay down a base of small-arms fire to mask the battalion's movement across an open field. Zachary had recommended against going across the airfield, but Buck, the battalion commander, believed it to be the best route.

As Zachary was about to signal his unit, he heard the unique sound of an M4 weapon falling to the ground. It rattled loudly off the lava rock with the distinctive sounds of plastic and metal crunching. It was a foolish mistake, one of the small, uncontrollable things that happen when there are 115 young men gathered together. Everybody makes mistakes.

Zachary felt his stomach tighten as he saw a Japanese soldier guarding the fence only 100 meters to his front look-up, ready with his weapon. *Too late*, Zachary said to himself, radioing his platoons to commence firing. The word spread quickly to the Javelin anti-tank gunners, who squeezed the triggers of their command launch units, sending 29 bright flashes arching through the night toward their pre-planned targets. Zachary had identified 10 tanks for each platoon to destroy to avoid overkill.

The platoon leaders had then divided the tanks by squad for the same reason. The squad leaders had done likewise.

Zachary grabbed his M4 and leveled it at the Japanese guard who had reacted to the falling weapon. Looking through his goggles and following the infrared aiming light onto the man's chest, he squeezed the trigger three times and watched the guard kick backward with each impact. It made Zachary feel good, but thinking of his brother, he wanted more.

Seconds later, many of the tanks exploded into bright fireballs, some with turrets tipping loose. In the confusion it was difficult to determine how many they had destroyed, but they suddenly found themselves under fire from somewhere. Large-caliber bullets were impacting all around them.

The sound of helicopter blades in the distance sent a chill up Zachary's spine. That was no Abu Sayyaf unit with rented small arms. Japanese attack helicopters were engaging them at night. The very technology that the United States had developed and employed in their state-of-the-art equipment had been cloned by the Japanese, who were at the moment using it to kill American soldiers.

"Net call, get your men down, engage all helicopters if you can acquire," Zachary said into the company radio net. Then he switched to the battalion net. "Knight Six, this is Bravo Six," he said loudly into the radio handset. Bullets were raining down on his position with heightened ferocity, streaming from behind the white huts with precision.

"This is Knight six," Buck's nervous voice came back over the radio.

"Roger," said Zachary. "We have destroyed over 20 enemy vehicles but are receiving helicopter fire from the barracks vicinity, over."

"Roger, good job, over," Buck said.

Dirt kicked into Zachary's eyes as a 30mm chain-gun round impacted less than two feet away.

Zachary, crouching low in a ravine, looked at his microphone and rolled his eyes. He was not looking for praise but wanted to warn the battalion commander that they needed to wait until he could engage the helicopters and the rest of the tanks before he moved the battalion.

Too late.

Through his goggles, the green landscape showed hundreds of small black dots moving rapidly on foot across the airfield.

The suppressive fires lessened on Zachary's position, and to his disgust, he saw orange tracers, enemy orange tracers, raking the airfield, causing the black dots to fall to the ground.

"Engage all helicopters!" Zachary screamed into the microphone, reissuing his earlier order.

On that order, he saw no less than 15 missiles soar through the air, resulting in a fireball at the end of each smoke-filled path. The trails of spent gunpowder etched white lines in the darkness of the night, crisscrossing and merging like some crazy traffic pattern.

Then Zachary heard helicopters behind him.

They're everywhere!

He turned and saw four to his right flank and noticed his anti-tank gunners whipping around to engage them.

He could make out two hellfire missile racks on either side and its two Hydra 70 rocket pods balancing the stubbed wings. Beneath the belly of the ship was the 30mm chain gun, hanging low. He watched as a hellfire missile let loose from its rack and scorched a hot path into an enemy tank that had turned on his position. The two turbines rode high in the back near the tail rotor, making the craft look like a hovering wasp.

They're friendlies!

Too late.

He watched in horror as a young private first class gunner followed his commander's orders to "engage all helicopters."

"Cease fire! Cease fire!" Zachary yelled into the radio to no avail.

The Javelin missile screamed upward in a flash and impacted with a silent thud into the Apache helicopter, jarring it from its aerial fighting position. The helicopter shuddered once, then began to lose altitude rapidly. He heard the engines quit and watched as the pilot turned his head frantically to see what had hit him.

Fortunately, the gunner that had fired was within the 65-meter arm-ing zone for the missile. Outside of 65 meters, the missile would have armed and exploded into the helicopter, vaporizing the two-man crew.

The pilot auto-rotated the main blade and achieved what his aviator buddies called a "hard landing." The tail boom split in two, sending the tail rotor whipping through the Japanese positions like a circular saw blade. Eventually the fuselage of the helicopter stopped spinning and Zachary sent a squad from Kurtz's platoon—SSG Quinones, who had acted so brilliantly during the defense of the pier—to gather up the cop-ter crew, if they survived, and reel them back to safety.

"Bravo Six, this is Alpha Six, over!" came McAllister's voice.

"This is Bravo Six, go, over," Zachary replied.

"The old man's gone to yellow brick. I'm in charge of the maneuver element now until I can talk to his second-in-command."

Buck's dead? The battalion commander? This can't be happening!

Zachary had no great affection for Buck, but he was a nice guy. The man had a wife and four sons. *Now what?*

"This is Knight Five," the voice continued. "Copied last message, moving into position now."

Knight Five was the battalion executive officer, who was second-in-command during the maneuver phase. The battalion operations officer was positioned with Zachary's unit and was responsible for controlling the supporting fires. With Buck dead, Major Kooseman had taken charge as best he could.

Zachary watched through his goggles as the remainder of the battalion performed fire and maneuver across the airfield, through the high brush and into the Quonset hut area, where his company had defended only days earlier. He thought he could see McAllister with three radio opera-tors hovering around him and wanted to tell him to be careful, that someone might come surging from the water with a pistol in hand trying to kill him. He rubbed the clotted scar above his left ear as he gave the order for his men to lift their fires.

The bulk of the Japanese helicopter force had reacted to the Marine landings on either side of Manila Bay, allowing Buck's battalion to seize the critical airfield at Subic Bay. They needed to secure the area quickly, call the C-17s circling in the sky, and prepare to defend against a heavy counterattack.

As quickly as it had begun, the battalion's first battle had tapered off. Casualties had been heavy on the airfield as Japanese AH-X 30mm chain guns had formed a curtain of steel, killing Buck and at least 30 others. The infantrymen had to contend with the 40 wounded first, though.

With Buck dead, a young major fresh out of the Army Command and General Staff College was commanding the battalion. He spoke to the attack helicopter battalion commander, asking him to expand the security zone to the south so that the circling C-17s could land and discharge the combat troops waiting at the back ramps, rifles in hand, faces painted, adrenaline pumping, ready to go at it and kill the bastards that had once again forced them to fight and try to steady the tumbling play blocks of world power.

The C-17s came screaming in from above, landing almost atop one another. They received some small-arms fire from isolated pockets of Japanese soldiers not yet quelled. The Apaches fired Hydra rockets and let loose with 30mm chain guns on the enemy, driving them from Subic Bay Naval Base.

Two U.S. F-117 stealth bombers flew low across the water, like bats hunting insects, and dropped precision-guided munitions into each of the cargo ships that had off-loaded the Japanese weapons. Black smoke billowed high into the night, black on black, dimming the Manila City lights from Zachary's vantage point.

His troops watched the display of combined arms warfare in awe. Naval gunfire began to pound the remaining Japanese vehicles positioned along the pier where the ammunition had been stacked—and from where the first attack had originated.

"I guess this is what they meant when they said we were the main effort, huh, sir?" asked Slick.

Zachary didn't answer. He watched as he saw an F-16 explode in the sky with a bright fury that momentarily lit the entire engagement area to include the ever-resilient white Quonset huts. Like a star cluster, pieces of the jet sprinkled down, seeming lighter and less dangerous than they really were, and fizzled in the water just off the pier.

Was it theirs or ours?

Who knew? Only the pilots fighting in the skies and the radar airplane reading squawk signals and directing traffic.

Curiously, it occurred to Zachary that it was his company that had made all of this possible. Without his guys, America's course would have been much different. Then of course, there was Chuck Ramsey and his team to think about. And his brother, Matt.

Must get them both. Matt, where can you be? Are you safe? Chuck, has the Black Hawk found you?

CHAPTER 43

The next morning, Zachary watched as Major Kooseman briefed the operations order to the assembled officers sitting in the dirt. Kooseman had done well for being thrust into command during a raging battle. The tall major spoke nonchalantly about their next mission in a sharp contrast to the befuddlement of Colonel Buck, Zachary believed. Then he realized Buck was dead and squelched the thought.

"Right now, guys," Kooseman said, "we've got two Ranger battalions hiding in the jungle, pinned down by an armored division. Over 200 tanks."

The battle still raged on the perimeter. U.S. Navy gunfire popped in the offing, American M1 tanks fired as if they were making headway, U.S. Air Force jets screamed overhead, U.S. Army helicopters came and went continuously, and, of course, the supply planes landed through it all.

They sat on the crusty, dried lava from Mount Pinatubo amidst all the noise, just to the north of the white Quonset huts. The battalion was arrayed in the center as the brigade reserve, with the other two battalions securing the main avenues of approach into the naval base. Planes were landing every five minutes with support troops and supplies, trying to develop sufficient combat power to sustain extended operations.

Water was desperately needed, and it came rolling off the C-17s by the truckload. The heat had soared to over 115 degrees and the intelligence officer, Chip McCranum, had briefed that the heat was here to stay, with no relief in sight.

Kooseman stood again, rising from the white dust and brushing his Army combat uniform. Wisps of white dirt exploded off his pants. He squinted as the sun tried to reach inside his eyelids and fry his pupils.

"Tomorrow morning at 0400, we attack to seize the prison at Cabanatuan," he said, making circling motions with his hands on the map that was positioned on an easel. "Our actions will be in concert with the Rangers, who will move from the jungles in the east as a feint to make contact with the enemy, draw their fire, allowing us to attack from the west."

He continued to describe the mission and Zachary's ears perked up when he heard his company mentioned.

"B Company will attack to secure the road that joins Cabanatuan and Fort Magsaysay," he said, pointing to a small line on the map that represented the three-mile road. "Zachary, Bravo Company will establish blocking positions preventing enemy reinforcement either way."

"Got it," Zachary said, making a note to get with Kooseman later. He hated when other commanders interrupted the order with their parochial questions, and he had vowed never to do it.

"Alpha Company and Charlie Company, you'll be coming with me into the prison of Cabanatuan. We will attack to seize the prison from enemy control, then our mission will revert to one of protecting the Filipinos. Delta Company, you'll be in reserve, but I want you right behind us as we land and move in to attack the prison. Once we land, I expect that the Japanese will divert some forces from Magsaysay, where they have two battalions, and try to counterattack into Cabanatuan. Zachary, you've got to stop those guys."

"Got it."

Three battalions of tanks against a light infantry brigade. Zachary shook his head. *Those zoomies better get out of the O-Club and fly then, dammit.*

A hot wind blew across the hardstand, circling into a miniature funnel, picking up twigs and grass and disappearing. Zachary looked skyward, thinking that the entire operation depended on aircraft. They were using helicopters to air-assault into the objective area, and they needed attack helicopters and Air Force fighters to destroy the tanks.

Zachary squinted into the noonday sun, wondering if the air support would be able to do anything more than get them there.

Matt Garrett

"Japanese Defense Forces, can you believe it?" Sturgeon said to Matt and Barefoot, crouched low in the dirt behind a cluster of thick mahogany trees. The consensus was no, they could not believe it. With Japanese soldiers swarming around them, they had little time to discuss the matter. *Are they friendly or enemy? Should we give ourselves up? Is this a joint operation with the United States and Japan trying to put down the rebellion?* Even though Matt had theorized on that very occurrence, he was shocked at its reality.

But his brief stay in Mindanao was beginning to make some sense. World War I was to Germany's rise as World War II was to Japan's emergence today.

They had spent the first night lying silently on the reverse slope of the wooded knoll. Barefoot had packed his satellite gear and stashed it for fear of emitting a signal that the Japanese could detect. They were out of water and food, but the continuous procession of Japanese tanks and infantry fighting vehicles made any move impossible. It seemed that the three-mile road between Cabanatuan and Fort Magsaysay was a main supply route for the Japanese.

A small Japanese patrol had wandered aimlessly into the tree line less than 100 meters from their hide position. The squad of seven sat in the shade, drank from their canteens, and joked in their native language. Matt could see that one was carrying a Shin Chuo Kogyo submachine gun, normally a tanker's weapon. Another had a Type 62 machine gun slung across his shoulder with two belts of 7.62mm ammunition wrapped around his body. The weapon had a small telescopic sight perched atop the rear sight assembly. The others were carrying M16A2 rifles.

They sat upon the grave, unsuspecting, and departed without incident when one of the members, probably the leader, stood and began to walk back to the west, toward Cabanatuan.

Earlier, they had witnessed the spectacular airdrop of hundreds of paratroopers at two in the morning. Barefoot had been on watch, and he awoke the others as he had spied the C-130s flying about 500 meters above the ground discharging soldiers. Immediately orange tracers were seeking out the elite soldiers as they fluttered to the ground. Who was friendly and who was enemy?

They could still hear gunfire as the curtain closed on a second day on the knoll. Were those American soldiers jumping in the middle of the night, or Filipinos? It had been too dark to tell. The Armed Forces of the Philippines certainly had C-130 airplanes capable of dropping soldiers. Had the insurgents pirated the airplanes and were now fighting Japanese forces?

"We need to link up with those paratroopers," Matt said. "Provided they're friendly."

"I'm game for anything," Barefoot added, his dark skin white from the dust.

"Okay, about two in the morning, we'll run along the ridge to the west," Matt said, pointing to his left. "We also need to find some water, so as we move, let's see if we can't find a well or something. After that, maybe we can steal a truck and haul ass."

It was risky, it was loose-knit, and it was desperate. But they had no alternatives.

Matt shook Jack Sturgeon and Barefoot until they both wakened.

"Time to go?" Sturgeon asked in a groggy voice.

"Yeah. It's a little bit before two. The shooting's stopped some. Figured it would be a good time to bolt," Matt said, adrenaline pumping through his body. He held his pistol in his hand, popped the magazine out, and counted bullets. Six. He had seven shots including the round in the chamber.

"Good, let's book," Jack said.

"Okay, I'm taking my gear, too. Just FYI." Barefoot said, patting his satellite gear.

"No, leave it here, but bring the tape of Rathburn's burial. If we have time, we'll circle back and get the equipment. But more than likely, we'll just have to scrap it," Matt said.

"No. I need to document this. It's my load. My gear. I'll carry it."

"Okay," Matt said. "Your load. Gets too heavy, you drop it."

They stood and moved in single file beneath the towering mahogany trees, stepping lightly over the high roots to follow a trail that led the mile to Cabanatuan. Jack and Matt carried their pistols in hand, poised for self-defense. Matt knew that they were hungry, thirsty, and tired but slipped through the woods quietly. They were acting on instinct. It was a simple calculation. Either get up and move or die from heat exhaustion and hunger.

Lacking energy but full of adrenaline, somehow they managed to wind their way through the hills and find a perch from which they could survey the half-lit town of Cabanatuan. In the prone, they lay next to each other and watched as green Army trucks ambled back and forth along the white cement road less than 75 meters away. The trucks coughed and spit diesel into the air, masking the trio's movement down to the back of a thatch hut.

One of the drivers turned on his lights, making the small village visible. Matt noticed and said, "Come, this way."

Sturgeon and Barefoot followed as they ran behind a series of thatch huts. Matt saw Barefoot was carrying the camera gear with ease, as if it wasn't any weight at all.

"Over there," Matt said, pointing. "It's a school. They always have wells at their schools."

They ran, crouched low, heading toward a wooden building that contrasted with the thatch huts. Oddly, they crossed over a dirt court with two baskets at the other end. *These guys play basketball?* Matt wondered. Reaching the building, they huddled against the wall as headlights traced a line above their heads, finally turning away.

"Must be on the other side," Matt said.

"Let's go."

They ran to the back of the school building, which was a modest, one-room affair that looked more like an old country church without the steeple.

There it was. Matt saw it. The pump handle was cocked high in the air above the open-lipped spout. The area beneath the spout was muddy, a good indicator that the pump was functional.

The three men scampered to the device, pulling their canteens off their belts. Matt grabbed the handle and pumped hard, letting the others drink from the spout, then fill their canteens. When they were done, Matt stooped low, knelt in the mud, and drank. He drank some more. Then he gulped down more, letting it spill across his face. Finally, he opened his mouth again, letting the force of the liquid push open his throat and race down, nearly causing him to choke.

He felt his body rehydrate. Glistening beads of sweat formed on his dusty arms beneath his torn sleeves. He filled his canteen, letting the water spill on his arms, then he stuck his head beneath the rushing water. That was why he did not hear the first shot.

As he turned, Matt saw a bullet catch Sturgeon in the top of the thigh. Then the gunfire came pouring forth, kicking dirt into the air. White puffs of dust rose into the blackness of the night.

Barefoot pulled Matt from under the pump, then flipped Sturgeon over his shoulders with acrobatic ease and ran back toward the woods. Matt yanked his pistol from the waist of his pants and began searching for muzzle flashes, back-pedaling as he followed Barefoot.

As they rounded the school, they saw ten Japanese soldiers coming from the other corner. They had an opening, however small. If they could only race back behind the thatch huts and get in the woods, they would stand a chance.

Barefoot ran with large steps, his gait like that of a show horse. His powerful frame seemed none the worse from the weight of Jack and his camera gear. Matt saw Sturgeon's face grimace in pain as his blood drained onto Barefoot's shirt.

From behind the row of thatch huts jumped an aggressive Japanese soldier, holding a Kogyo submachine gun with folding stock. He yelled something indiscernible to Matt and raised his weapon to fire.

Matt stopped, crouched, and fired one round into the soldier's forehead, 10 meters away. The enemy soldier stood still as if there were something he could do about his mortal wound, then fell backward to the ground, dead.

As they passed the dead man, Matt saw that his face was covered in blood. He stooped and stole the man's weapon without breaking stride.

Matt felt a hot, stinging sensation in his lower right leg, like a snakebite. He looked down and saw that his trousers were shredded along his right calf. Other bullets punched into the ground around him. *Only a graze*, he thought and continued his sprint.

They crested the rise and entered the wooded area, then hurriedly followed the trail, winding through the trees as if racing down a ski slalom.

"Go back to the equipment," Matt said. "I'll meet you there." Barefoot nodded and continued to run. Matt pulled off the path and circled back. He quickly checked his new weapon. He did not know what it was but figured if he pulled the trigger, it would shoot.

The path to Zachary is through these bastards, Matt thought as he waited behind a small stand of deadfall on a wooded knoll near the village.

Zachary Garrett

They darted into a clearing, then pulled away like a ride at the local carnival. Zachary peered out of the open door, the wind beating the back of his head, and saw at least 30 other UH-60 Black Hawks performing similar maneuvers into the false insertion area.

Two minutes out, Zachary thought. He looked at his watch, then cut a gaze at Slick, who gave him a thumbs-up. The trusty radio operator. In many respects, there was no better friend to a commander. Not only was it tough humping the 30 pounds of radio gear, living with the commander took a special breed. Confidant, friend, lackey, supporter, idea man, humorist, the radio man was always there, always ready, always prepared. Slick was typical, with his wry sense of humor and devastating ability to make the commander laugh when he least expected it.

In addition to the battalion radio system Slick carried, Zachary carried a radio in his own rucksack that could communicate with his platoon leaders. He saw no need to suck another soldier away from the platoons when he was stronger than most in the company. Slick would monitor Major Kooseman and the other company commanders on battalion net, and Zachary would maneuver the company through the platoon leaders on the company net. The platoon leaders would then maneuver their squads on platoon nets.

Oh shit, Zachary thought when he looked up. Orange tracers rocketed skyward at the helicopters as they came in for a hot landing between Cabanatuan and Fort Magsaysay. The helicopters banked hard and low, pushing the envelope trying to gain cover. They touched down for a brief moment behind a large wooded knoll, discharged their passengers, and pulled away, turning toward the west to make another lift.

Zachary took a knee and watched the beauty of the battalion air assault. In training, they had never had the opportunity to perform entire battalion lifts, and the sight of the helicopters pulling away like a swarm of wasps impressed him. He watched and listened to the battalion radio net as McAllister's company took the lead for the assault into Cabanatuan.

McAllister's voice gave him comfort again. He was among friends. No longer was his company isolated, the world surrounding them.

"Let's move to checkpoint three-one, over," he said into his company net.

Taylor, Kurtz, and Barker acknowledged. Zachary and his platoon leaders gathered their men, formed into a series of wedges, and headed toward the wooded knoll.

Matt had decided to use the pistol first. He waited until the lead soldier was less than 30 meters away, then pulled the trigger. He needed to buy Sturgeon and Barefoot some time.

As he watched the lead man drop, he grabbed the submachine gun and fired into the confused mass. The weapon jumped wildly in his hands, but he was hitting his targets. He saw three others fall to the ground.

As he started receiving fire, he pulled back into the forest, ran across the trail, then doubled back to gain the flank.

It worked. The Japanese soldiers, under new direction, charged headlong into the woods where Matt had originally entered. As they melted into the sparse forest, Matt held the Kogyo tightly and sighted into the backs of the Japanese.

His aim with the unfamiliar weapon was far more effective this time, killing at least 15 soldiers who had bunched in their confusion. They turned on him, coming at him like a Rebel charge through the Devil's Den at Gettysburg. The enemy soldiers were screaming and firing weapons, the orange tracers blowing through the leaves, cracking branches, and temporarily painting the night sky like some wicked airbrush.

He swallowed dry spit as he felt the hammer fall on an empty chamber. He saw the barrel steaming and smoking directly in front of him when he realized he had fired all of the ammunition. There was nothing left for him to do except to move back through the woods with judicious use of his pistol.

He scurried along the reverse slope of the hill, hot lead chasing him only a step behind. He heard the helicopters come and go and assumed that they were surrounded.

A twig dug deep into his cheek, just beneath his eye, and snapped. His head turned and as he looked back toward his front, he tumbled over a large root, snapping his ankle as he fell.

In no time, three enemy soldiers were upon him, frothing at the mouth like rabid pit bulls ready to complete the kill. Using the pistol, he shot one through the lower abdomen, then fired a shot into the face of the man to his left.

The bayonet came arching downward, piercing Matt's abdomen. The Asian man smiled, and with the bayonet holding him in place, Matt heard a gunshot.

Fury swirled around him. He felt pain before pieces of his world began wafting back and forth in his mind as if on a pendulum. First he saw the leering Japanese soldier, delighting in the kill, then he heard the faint sound of helicopters chopping behind him. Then he thought of Sturgeon and Barefoot, and seconds later he saw Rathburn. The pendulum swung toward Meredith's face, then back again to the farm and his family. Then something about the Rolling Stones, but only briefly. Then the farm, rolling hills, the Blue Ridge, Karen, father, mother, Zachary. *Yes, Zachary. My best friend.* Fishing in the stream together. Catching trout. Then Meredith, blond hair, soft skin, sitting by the pool, telling secrets, connecting.

Then Zachary's voice.

Then nothing.

"**Bravo Six, this** is White six," Kurtz said into the company radio net.

"Send it," Zachary said, recognizing the voice.

"We've got enemy contact to our left flank. Say again. Gunfire you hear is enemy contact, over."

"Roger. I want you to move to the west, through the woods, and try to develop the situation. I'll maneuver the other elements after you make contact."

"Roger."

Zachary moved quickly and fell into the flow behind Kurtz and his men.

"Contact," came Quinones's voice over the platoon radio net, followed by a brief exchange of fire.

"Roger," Kurtz said, moving to the squad leader's position. Zachary was about fifty meters behind Kurtz and saw that the point man had killed a single Japanese soldier.

Zachary listened to Kurtz' radio spot report that crackled above the relentless rifle fire.

"Sir, we've made contact. Killed three enemy soldiers and have found one civilian, looks like it anyway, with severe wounds to the abdomen. Doc says this guy's not much longer for this world. Continuing mission, over."

"Roger. I'm moving to your location now. Red Six is moving to your right flank. Blue Six is in reserve." Taylor was Red and Barker was Blue.

Again, there was another brief interchange of fire at the point of Kurtz's platoon. "Three more enemy dead," came the report.

"Okay, Mike," Zachary said to Kurtz as he came running forward. "We're gonna move two squads abreast along this ridge and pop these guys like a zit. When they spill into the open, the rest of the battalion can have them, or we play turkey shoot."

"Got it, sir."

Zachary and Kurtz were kneeling next to the wounded civilian, talking. It was dark, especially in the forest with the mahoganies blocking what little moonlight was available, and their robust outlines etched against the black sky. They had taken off their night-vision goggles to talk, allowing their eyes to adjust to the night. Doc Gore worked feverishly on the civilian less than a meter away from them.

Something landed on Zachary's knee. At first, he thought it was a bug and brushed at it, but then he noticed the hand. He had no time to deal with some civilian right now. His guys were fighting. He quickly scanned the dark, shredded cargo pants, khaki shirt matted and stained with blood, and the disheveled hair of the civilian. Shrouded in darkness, the dying man was unrecognizable to Zachary. *Poor guy*, he thought. Like a penny dropped into a shallow cone, a thought or instinct spun around his mind, circling wide before arcing more rapidly until it dropped and Zachary had the distinct feeling that something was dreadfully wrong. Not with the mission. Hell, he could not even concentrate on that at the moment. No, the feeling increased as he looked back at the wounded figure, moving his face closer to the dying man's face. The sounds of gunfire continued but faded in Zachary's mind as he downshifted from the world of battle to some other cognitive level.

He did not truly recognize his brother's face, the green eyes or the signature square jaw, but he realized with sudden and complete devastation that it was Matt reaching out to him, somehow recognizing him, almost magnetically pulled to him, grabbing his kneecap, trying to say something. He looked away in disbelief, then back, and once again saw his brother Matt lying on the ground next to him, his stomach gurgling, the pool of blood growing, the medic poised over him as if he were giving him last rites instead of applying medical aid.

A voice whispered, "Kill those bastards, Zachary."

Then it registered.

Christ Almighty!

Zachary scrambled to Matt's side.

"Oh Jesus Christ," he cried. "Please, Jesus, please, no."

"Medevac, get a medevac!"

He ripped off his helmet, then snatched the first-aid dressing from his pouch and began to press onto the bleeding area, but there was blood everywhere.

"Sir, that thing ain't gonna do much good on him. Hole's bigger in the back than in the front," Doc Gore said, matter-of-factly.

"Shut up, Gore. This is my brother and—and—this is my brother. This is my only brother," he said, his voice reaching a crescendo, then tapering rapidly as his throat knotted and the tears gushed. "This—is—my—brother!"

"Shit," Kurtz said, under his breath. "Break, Break," he said, grabbing the battalion net handset from Slick. "Request immediate dust-off at checkpoint three-one. We have a man dying. Need dust-off now," Kurtz said, authoritatively.

"Roger, loitering behind checkpoint three-one now. Mark with strobe." The medical evacuation pilot spoke with calm precision. Fortunately, the plan had anticipated casualties and had called for pre-positioning of the medical teams.

Zach barely noticed Kurtz pop the strobe from his pouch. He nudged Zachary to one side and lifted Matt's body onto his wide shoulders, blood draining down Kurtz's uniform.

The troops stared at Zachary for direction. Slick, Quinones, and the others. But Zachary simply watched as Kurtz hauled his brother away into the clearing behind the knoll. The company was receiving heavy fire, tracers dancing out toward Kurtz and the helicopter. Zachary saw Kurtz turn a steely gaze in the direction of the back-fire as if to will it away. He saw the intermittent flashing of the strobe, then watched as the helicopter darted upward. Kurtz's large shadow re-emerged into the forest. He picked up the company radio and told Taylor and Barker to continue the mission, then turned to SSG Quinones and told him to monitor the platoon net.

"Sir, sir," Kurtz said, shaking the commander. Zachary was trying to regain his composure. "We've got to get moving. He's on the medevac. They'll take care of him."

Zachary looked at Kurtz from below and grabbed the outstretched hand. He had been there for his lieutenants so many times that it never occurred to him that they might one day be able to return the favor.

About the time he pulled himself to his feet and snatched his helmet from the ground, he heard the high-pitched squeak of mechanized vehicles moving to the east. The recognition of a large enemy presence served as a catalyst to force him to gather himself. The world shifted into focus like a camera zooming in, then out.

"Thanks, Mike," he said to Kurtz while snapping his Kevlar.

"No sweat, sir. I'll light a candle tonight, after we kill these bastards," Kurtz said.

Zachary took notice, then grabbed Slick by the shirt collar, pulling him toward him so he could command his company.

"Sir, just want you to know how sorry—" Slick began.

"Give me the mike," he said, cutting off Slick. There was no time for sympathy. He had already wasted valuable seconds with his little display. *Unprofessional*, he thought to himself, hardening his nerves into steel rebar. First, Teller, then Rock, then his brother. The circle of death tightened around him as he wondered if he was next. *Who cares?* he thought. There it was again, the hand of God, hammering and forging and striking the anvil, dunking the piping-hot ore of his soul into the shallow pool of faith. *Please God, save him.*

"Net call, enemy moving vicinity checkpoint three-zero. Blue, I want you to move to the eastern tip of the woods and set up an anti-armor ambush now, break," he said, releasing the push-to-talk button to avoid enemy direction-finding capabilities. "Red, link up on Blue's left flank, you have the first ten vehicles, Blue has the next ten. I'll move with White. We'll maneuver onto the enemy if necessary. Acknowledge."

Barker and Taylor acknowledged, but then Barker's voice came crackling back through the handset.

"Bravo Six, this is Blue Six, I'm fighting about 20 enemy on the west side of the knoll! I can't break contact!" Barker screamed, the sound of machine gun fire amplified by the microphone.

"Blue six, call a fire mission to help you break contact. Make it high-explosive and white phosphorous. Keep fighting those guys while we set up for the ambush. Let me know when you link up with Red's left flank, over," Zachary said into his radio handset.

"Roger!" Barker sounded confused and anxious.

Zachary was placing a great burden on Barker to fight an essentially even-ratio battle, guard the company's left flank, and join the anti-armor ambush. It was too much, but he had no other choice.

Zachary moved with Kurtz along the back side of the wooded ridge. He found Taylor and told him he was in charge of the over-watch element, that he and Kurtz were going to move about 300 meters to the east and try to extend the company's position. Taylor was already sighting his anti-tank weapons. Each man carried an AT-4, the successor to the light anti-tank weapon, and his platoon had 15 Javelin missiles for six command launch units.

Zachary pulled Kurtz and Slick with him as they jogged down the back side of the hill. At the bottom he stopped, put on his goggles, and turned on the bright green world.

"Holy shit," Zachary said, sighting at least 30 tanks moving in single file along the road nearly two miles away. The low, flat ground made for excellent observation. In the darkness, though, the hulking beasts traveled slowly, as if they feared something.

"C'mon, follow me," Zachary said. Kurtz and his men jogged behind the commander as he raced across the level hardstand into the clearing They ran with increasing speed, sounding like a small herd of buffalo trampling across the great open plains.

Zachary had run almost six hundred meters when he suddenly fell, his head jerking backward, and landed in a shallow pool of warm, stinking water. Some of the other troops followed suit while others tried to stop, each man stumbling over the next like Keystone Kops.

"Rice paddies," Zachary said. "Perfect."

He could still hear Barker's platoon fighting off the enemy about a kilometer away, maybe more, as he called Taylor and changed the plan.

CHAPTER 44

Taiku Takishi

Takishi was through with the games. His forces had practically destroyed the paratroopers, who had so whimsically thought they could tangle with his armored division. *Fools. They are all fools. The Americans, the Filipinos, the Rolling Stones. The world.*

But then, a report from General Nugama in Manila had given him great cause for concern. Apparently the Marines were about to close on the Presidential Palace. Losses had been heavy on both sides in the street-to-street fighting of Manila. The Americans, Nugama had told him, were bringing more troops into Subic Bay by the minute, and he had no contact with any of the other ships north of the Luzon Strait to reinforce him. The only saving grace for the Japanese was that Takishi had a fresh division.

"Quit messing around with those infantry forces, let the bastards have the prisoners, and come to Manila," Nugama had told him. "I need you now!"

But that had been two hours ago. It had taken Takishi that long just to organize his units for movement at two in the morning. He had decided to leave the prisoners locked in the prison buildings to rot. There were nearly 6000 Filipinos wailing inside. He had a headache. He had slammed the door to the big building and locked it, drowning out the collective sounds of agony and pain.

Takishi spoke through the small microphone attached to his combat vehicle crewman's helmet and told his driver to lead the column to the east. They would button up their hatches and destroy the light infantry soldiers and blow down the road to Manila to defeat the Marines. *No problem.*

His tank creaked along the cement road, crushing week-old rice that had been laid out to dry in the searing sun. The sun would rise in an hour, meaning he needed to make as much ground as possible before then. Somehow he felt safer in the darkness.

He sat inside the buttoned-down hatch and watched the world pass through the high-definition thermal sight. Slewing the turret left and right with the commander's override, he made out low ground to either side of the road.

"Be careful," he said to Private Muriami, his young driver. The driver slowed, then Takishi said, "Not that careful," realizing he needed to make time and fight the American infantry, the least of his worries. He had an opportunity to deal the Americans a crushing blow.

He slewed the turret to the left as he passed through the Fort Magsaysay gate. He watched with pride as all 200 tanks lined up, crawling slowly along the dirt road that met with the main avenue. He had left behind two infantry battalions and 60 fighting vehicles to hold off the Rangers while the tanks moved toward Manila. He had given the brigade commander instructions to maintain light contact, like a feint, while they discreetly slipped away from the Rangers until they had cleared Cabanatuan. Then he could move his two battalions along the same route, eventually effecting link-up.

As he watched, he saw a group of AH-X helicopters lift slowly off the airfield and take up positions on both flanks of his column, hovering like drone bees around the queen. He told Muriami to pick up the pace, and like an arrow he slung the entire column to the east.

Captain Zachary Garrett

"**How many do** you count, Slick?" Zachary asked, as they crouched low in the water.

"From the first one I see about 50, then there's a bunch of hills, but it sounds like there's a helluva lot more," Slick said with a nervous edge on his voice. They could hear the tanks whining, their tracks squeaking on the cement.

"No shit." Then turning to Kurtz, Zach said, "Mike, spread your guys out along these dikes. Put your men with AT4s closer to the road, about 200 meters. Keep your other Javelin guys back about 600 meters—about where we are now. We'll let Taylor and the boys knock out about the first twenty tanks, then the whole column will be stuck right here with nowhere to go."

"Got it, sir," Kurtz said, anxious to enact the plan. The tanks were rapidly approaching and he would not have the time he needed to brief his men. He would only be able to tell his men where to go and when to shoot. Sometimes, that's all it took, Zachary knew.

Zachary had called Major Kooseman for back-up attack helicopter support, but received only a "wait, out" from the major, who was busy orchestrating the fight in Cabanatuan. "There may be no fight if you don't get me those birds," Zachary had said in response, "I've got tanks heading in your direction."

"Bravo Six, this is Red Six, over."

Zachary responded to Taylor's call.

"I've got two civilians in my AO. They're Americans. Might be two of the hostages we heard about. One's wounded pretty badly in the leg. What should I do with them?" Taylor asked.

So far, he had successfully put the issue of his brother on the back burner. Taylor's call had served to rotate the turnstile, as if his mind could only handle the array of events one at a time. First, the war, then his brother, next the war, then his brother. He envisioned an usher taking tickets as the thoughts strolled through the stile. Brother, war, brother, war, and so on.

Kneeling in the stinking mud and water, he called back to Taylor.

"I'll call a medevac for them. Have *two* troops move them to check-point three-one for pick up."

He imagined that there were two brothers back in the United States somewhere who were glad a medevac would come for the two men.

"You okay, sir?" Slick asked, sensing his commander disconnect from the increasingly pressing events.

Zachary turned and looked at the young soldier, patted him on the back, and said, "Let's kill some bad guys."

The tanks passed to his front, only 600 meters away. It was nerve-racking, watching them from such a short distance. Would one of his soldiers screw the plan and fire too soon, or too late? It was a distinct possibility given the haphazard pace of events.

"They look just like M1s, sir," Slick said. The American M1 tank was a formidable machine and anything resembling its characteristics would be a difficult kill.

"More like the German Leopard 2, Slick. Almost an exact copy," Zachary said, releasing some nervous tension. He rested his M4 on his dry knee as he lay back against a muddy dike.

He saw the first missile strike the second tank, causing a brief fireball that lit the immediate surroundings. Successive missiles scored hits as well, stopping the column so that roughly 30 tanks, two companies, were on Zachary's side of the rice paddies and heading their way.

That's too many, Zachary thought to himself. But he waited. Maybe they could still do it.

Takishi slewed the turret to the right, wishing his tank column would quickly get off the dike that was the road separating two large paddy fields. *This place will be good for factories one day*, he thought, as his tank finally passed beyond the rice paddies.

He turned back to the left, enjoying the ride. *Okay, where are these guys?* He had reports from his logistical units in Cabanatuan that they were under heavy fire from what seemed like a battalion of light infantry. *Are you kidding me? A battalion?*

"Muriami, let's go find these people and get to Manila," Takishi said as Muriami raced the jet engine, slamming Takishi's ribs into the steel seat back.

The other tank commanders followed suit, glad they were able to move faster, no longer impeded by the sudden drop on either side.

When he noticed some hot black spots burning in his thermal sight, he aimed the gun at them.

There they are!

"Gunner, high explosive, enemy personnel in the woods," Takishi said, mimicking the precision of a skilled soldier.

The loader slammed one round into the massive breech while the gunner took control and lased to the target. Takishi saw the signal come back quickly, indicating he was a mere four hundred meters away.

"Acquired," the young sergeant announced.

Takishi said, "Fire when ready," but then accidentally turned the turret when he saw the missiles screaming toward his column of tanks.

The gunner's shot flew errant, cutting a white hole into the black night, landing almost a mile away without doing any damage.

Zachary watched in disbelief as the first tank continued to roam free on the hardpan. Taylor's men had fired two volleys of Javelin missiles and three sets of AT4s. He thought he counted 15 enemy vehicles burning. They burned a brilliant orange hue that quickly mixed with the black smoke of melting rubber.

But that's only half of the tanks they had to fight. Zachary was growing increasingly concerned. He did not want Kurtz to shoot his wad on the thirty or so tanks lined up to his front if Taylor needed the help.

The Japanese tanks that could turn off the road raced for the wooded knoll, offering only frontal shots, the worst kind for Taylor's gunners, and randomly spitting machine-gun fire into the edge of the forest. It was almost too late for Zachary to have Kurtz's men do anything about the advance.

Zachary achieved a small measure of reassurance when he saw five tanks burning bumper-to-bumper at the junction in the road where the rice paddies gave way to hardstand.

No way they're getting around that.

"Bravo Six, this is Red Six, we're taking heavy fire, over!" came Taylor's nervous voice in a high pitch. Zachary thought he could hear the bullets whipping past Taylor over the microphone.

"Roger—"

"Break, break," Barker said, loudly, short-circuiting the commander. "This is Blue Six. I'm on your flank now. Engaging. Out."

Zachary watched as six missiles arced through the sky and found targets, stopping the tanks in their tracks.

That leaves nine of thirty.

Another volley, and this time AT4s disabled two more tanks.

Seven.

Zachary watched as some of the tanks stacked on the road tried to turn off and support the attack. They were unsuccessful, mostly dipping over the edge of the concrete road, then rolling into the deep mud and sticking, unable to move forward or back. One tank turned its tread until it chewed the concrete, made partial purchase in the mud, then flipped, pinning down and ultimately drowning the tank commander, who had opened his hatch to guide the effort.

Some of the other tanks, though, turned their turrets and began to support the attack with small-arms fire and main gun blasts. Finally, his tactical patience had reached its limit.

"White, this is Bravo. Do it."

"Roger," Kurtz responded.

Kurtz's men rose from the swampy bog like Francis Marion's American Revolution cavalry, water and mud and rice stems streaming and hanging off their bodies. They fired volley after volley of anti-tank weapons, nearly depleting the company's entire stock, including the plus-up from the ammunition pile at Subic.

The return fire was unexpectedly heavy, splashing into the mud and spraying water in all directions.

There they were again. Those damned helicopters, firing 30mm chain guns at his men.

Zachary radioed Major Kooseman and asked again about the attack helicopters, "We need support now, sir," he told him.

"Helos are five minutes out," Kooseman told him.

Five minutes? This thing'll be history in five minutes.

Zachary watched as another volley from Barker's platoon cut the attacking force down to three tanks.

"Bravo, this is Red, we're out of tank-killing systems, over," Taylor said.

"This is Blue. Likewise," Barker said, piggy-backing on Taylor's bad news.

Zachary dropped his hand into his lap after saying, "Roger, continue to fight, attack helicopters on the way."

He felt the first draft of the cool wind lift a matted hair off his forehead as he heard a helicopter in the background. Could it be? No, it was the medevac for the two civilians.

A raindrop touched his nose. At first he thought an enemy round had kicked water into his face. He looked skyward. Lifting his goggles from his face, he saw heavy clouds racing across the creeping grayness of the morning like a Yankee clipper cutting through stormy seas. Then he looked at the stack of enemy tanks, some burning, some firing, some cocked crazily over the lip of the road. *What a perfect target.*

Defenseless tanks were lined up single file on the road with only a few enemy helicopters swarming for protection. The beauty of it was that the Japanese self-propelled artillery was stacked on the road as well. For the moment they were safe from any indirect fire, but they were still in great danger from the enemy helicopters bobbing up and down behind the tree line near Fort Magsaysay.

The rain was sudden, cool and heavy, and the drops felt larger than normal. The wind blew sideways, making the rain feel like tiny darts against Zachary's face that felt hot and cold at the same time. Zachary prayed for the aberration to go away, hoping it was a simple thunderstorm. The wind gusted, defying his hope by spitting cold water in his face as if signaling that things were only going to get worse.

The intensity of the rain increased, pelting down in sheets.

CHAPTER 45
Greene County, Virginia
Meredith Morris

Other than being humiliated and having her car destroyed, Meredith's worst injury was the gash on her head from Stone's fireplace. She had crawled from the wreckage, running without looking back, fearing that either Stone was chasing her or that her car was about to catch fire and explode.

The car, while totaled, did not burn, and thankfully she had been wearing her seat belt. She had spent one night in the Georgetown hospital and rented a car so she could go to the one safe place she believed was still available to her.

She spoke to her assistant, Mark, over the phone from the Garrett house in Stanardsville. She told him that she'd had an accident and needed to recover, and that she would be reporting back to work in a few days.

"Yeah, the SecDef personally came to the office looking for you," Mark said.

I bet he did.

"Really, did he say anything?"

"Not really. Just said he was doing 'battlefield circulation,' otherwise known as management by walking around. He asked where you were, then split. He looked nervous."

"Thanks, Mark. I'll see you in a few days. And Mark, please don't mention you've talked to me or that you know where I am," Meredith said.

"Well, I don't know, so we're good there. You okay?"

"I'm okay. Talk later."

Karen joined her in the study, which was lined with pine paneling and had two bookshelves at the back. A smallish desk was covered with mail and books and a black-and-walnut UVA college chair with an orange and blue seat cushion was pulled away from the desk. A bench was underneath the window that opened onto the north part of the farm and offered a generous view of the mountains.

"Karen," Meredith asked, "Can I use that computer I asked you about last night?"

"Sure thing. I do all my business on it. I have my own server too, and it's pretty secure."

"Good," Meredith said. "You any good with security stuff?"

"I have a certificate in IT support and do the occasional house call for folks around here to fix their stuff, so I know a little. Why?" she asked, raising an eyebrow.

"I've got a thumb drive and I can see the folders on it, but I can't open them."

"You didn't try to open them did you? It must be password protected and you may get locked out."

"No, I figured that much out after I clicked on one and got the password dialogue box. I never tried a password."

"Good," Karen said. "Matt and I have played around with some algorithms for code breaking." She looked up at Meredith after she sat at the computer and said, "Given his line of work."

Meredith dug through her purse and said, "Well?"

"Problem?" Karen asked.

"I can't find my lipstick, but here's that thumb drive." It was the one conscious thought she had as she crawled from the wreckage. *Get the thumb drive.*

Karen took the device, plugged it into the USB port, and pulled open the dialogue box with the files. Then she opened another program from her Windows display and played around with it for a minute. A black screen came up and scrolled through hundreds of lines of code and stopped. Karen minimized that screen and said, "Interesting."

"What?" Meredith asked, hopeful.

"Did he have a problem memorizing passwords or something?"

"All the time," Meredith said, hopeful.

"Well, he used Firefox, and all you have to do is click on the Firefox icon here in his thumb drive and you get all the passwords," Karen explained. She performed the function and a series of boxes with asterisks in them popped up.

"They're still protected," Meredith said.

"Watch this." Karen clicked on JAVA SCRIPT. Suddenly the asterisks disappeared and the passwords appeared.

KeithRichards2002.

"He a Stones' fan?"

"You might say that." Meredith grimaced.

"Okay, I'm going to leave it with you. I never did this. And if I ever get a call about it, this computer will be in the fireplace before I hang up the phone."

"No worries. I promise. You're awesome, Karen. Thanks so much."

Karen left, and Meredith sat down to begin plowing through the files. The password worked for each folder, and what she found shocked her.

In the first file, the Pred-China folder, she read document after document that recorded financial transactions of U.S. technology sales to China totaling some $100 million. Meredith figured that at $5 million each, the Chinese had received about 20 Predators. The money, it seemed, was then funneled in two directions.

First, there was a clear chain of transactions to a man named Takishi, whom she presumed was the man she had seen leaving Stone's office and with the Japanese Ambassador.

What could Takishi be doing with $75 million?

Well, she thought, he could be building weapons plants on the island of Mindanao. Was this any different than selling anti-tank missiles to Iran, then funding the insurgency in Nicaragua? Instead of Iran-Contra, do we have China-Abu Sayyaf, she wondered? That would be a twist, fund the bad guys to start a war...for what?

Next, she opened a file labeled "AIG." American International Group was the world's largest insurance company. In this file she found stock-trading records for early September 2001, prior to September 11. They were a combination of short sales of AIG and United Airlines stock as well as option puts. In essence, whoever the account numbers belonged to had bet in early September that AIG and United stocks were going to go down big.

Bottom line: Rathburn and his friends knew about the coming attacks.

Was that where it ended? Did the Stones only know about the attacks and make money off of them, or did they not only know about but help plan them? Meredith had read all of the reports of the high-ranking CIA officials who were under investigation for placing short trades on airline and insurance stocks a few days prior to 9-11. For whatever reason, the story never got much play in the press.

But the evidence was staring her in the face. The Rolling Stones, or at least Keith Richards, aka Bart Rathburn, had either known of the short trades or had placed the short trades...or both. Rathburn, after all, was a finance major and had worked at a hedge fund before finding his way to academia and the Pentagon. Had the other $25 million gone to short trades? Or had it gone to helping the hijackers?

She remembered reading somewhere that 9-11 had cost Al Qaeda somewhere around a half million dollars. That was peanuts to these guys.

Or, had their cooperation, if there was cooperation, been more subtle, such as pushing aside a report on the flight training of insurgents, for example?

She shuddered. The bottom line, she assessed, was that the Rolling Stones at least had known that the 9-11 attacks were going to occur.

So, let's see who they are. She opened Mick Jagger's file and saw a complete dossier on Secretary of Defense Robert Stone. She scanned through the document and closed it.

Next she opened Charlie Watts' file and saw a Harvard Business School picture of Takishi, smiling and handsome. It seemed Takishi had been an HBS classmate of Bart Rathburn.

She had assumed that Rathburn was Keith Richards since there was no file on Richards and because Stone had once mistakenly called him Keith. So when she opened the Ronnie Wood file, she was not surprised because she didn't see Rathburn's face. Instead, she was shocked at the image staring back at her.

Dick Diamond?

CHAPTER 46
Island of Mindanao, Philippines

Major Chuck Ramsey could hear the helicopters circling in the distance near Cateel Bay. He saw one of the U.S. Air Force Pave Lows zipping low along the beach, then banking high into the air above the thatch huts, blowing the roof off one of them.

There was little he could do to effect link-up with this soaring, hovering angel above them, though, with no radio.

The helicopters were a welcome sign, as he had lost six more men besides Eddie in the last series of ambushes. The Abu Sayyaf was still out there chasing him. For the past week, they had walked, then fought, walked, then fought, like two boxers in the twelfth round, slinging wild punches, then moving away, circling, holding a lone fist outward to keep one another at bay, circling some more, then fighting. It was ceaseless.

Ramsey licked his dry lips and steadied his dizzy gaze as he peered through the gray-morning skies, searching for the Pave Low. A rainstorm looked to be moving to his north. He was weak from lack of water and food. The bodies of his Special Forces team littered the trail they had cut through this unspoiled rain forest on the Mindanao eastern shore. First, there had been Peterson, then Jones, then Eddie, then one here, two there, and suddenly only Ramsey, Lonnie White, Randy Tuttle, Ken Benson, and Abe were left.

Abe had survived it all and carried a rucksack and M4 rifle from one of the fallen soldiers. He had painted his face with a camouflage stick.

During the last small engagement, similar to the others where they had doubled back on their own trail as some Louis L'Amour scouts often do, Abe had surged forward, bayonet fixed on his rifle, rising out of the tall grass and charging the stunned and equally tired rebels. They had fled down the mountainside as Abe had impaled a 14 year-old boy toting a rifle on the end of his bayonet.

The Pave Low circled back, and Ramsey briefly saw it through the top layer of the thick triple-canopy jungle. There was a small window of sky above him. He angled the metal tube in his hand toward the opening and slapped it hard on the bottom, bruising his weak palm.

The star cluster rocketed skyward, making it through to the small hole before bursting green and sparkling back into the jungle nearly two hundred meters away.

The Pave Low reacted and tightened its search arc to about a one hundred meter area.

He pulled another star cluster from his ruck, his last, and repeated the procedure. Benson, White, Tuttle, and Abe all watched with hopeful eyes.

Ramsey turned on his strobe, holding it high in the sky, hoping that somehow it might help. The Pave Low passed the opening once, then circled back, tilting and trying to draw a bead on them.

The pilot hovered the aircraft over the opening as a steel cage called a jungle penetrator began to push its way toward them from seventy-five meters above the ground. Lowered by a hydraulic cable, the penetrator turned and twisted as it floated toward them.

Ramsey looked skyward, thankful, but still not convinced they were free. The adrenaline began to rush, though, giving him the strength to reach up and grab the metal basket. He felt a mild shock from the kinetic energy created by the massive torque of the whipping blades and transmitted along the steel cable.

Tuttle was first to go. He had been wounded in the leg and needed better medical attention than White could give him with his limited supplies.

The basket came down again, and White was next to take the ride.

Ramsey's hopes began to grow like a blooming flower in the spring, betting against the inevitable final frost of a winter not complete. Two of his men were safe aboard an Air Force helicopter. Its blades beat loudly above the jungle, which was why they did not hear the first salvo of AK-47 weapons fired their way.

A bright red spot suddenly appeared in Benson's forehead, growing rapidly as the blood gushed outward like a fountain. Benson kicked back, eyes open, and fell against the dangling basket, knocking it crazily to the side.

Abe crouched low and immediately returned fire.

"Get in cage," he told Ramsey, who looked briefly at Abe and took him up on his offer. He pulled Benson's limp body onto his lap as he climbed into the basket, charging his M4, and began to fire as he ascended into the heights of the jungle.

Beneath him he could see Abe shooting and moving, rolling from tree to tree, firing. He watched as Abe pulled out his bayonet and snapped it onto the front end of the rifle. Two Abu Sayyaf charged Abe with bayonets fixed as well. He felt the cage break through a tree branch, hanging momentarily on the stub before kicking free.

Abe parried the first slash by holding his rifle above his head, then kicking at the attacker with his foot, pushing him away. The second man ran into the powerful thrust of Abe's lunging bayonet, skewering himself. Abe pulled the trigger, exploding the man backward into a tree and freeing his weapon to fight the dead man's partner.

Is this what it has come down to, Abe and me against four enemy? Ramsey thought as he felt the cage strike metal. A large hand opened the top, and a voice said, "You're safe now, sir." Hands grabbed Benson's body, then him, pulling them into the aircraft.

"Send it back down," Ramsey said, weakly.

The crew chief lowered the basket as Ramsey peered over the ledge. He watched the basket twist and turn its way through the jungle.

Abe cocked his right arm and straightened it, stroking the butt of his rifle into the man's face only to have him lower his head and avoid it. Ramsey watched Able reach for the basket with his left arm, pulling it toward him, sliding his body into the seat.

The enemy bayonet poked at Abe, glancing off the metal basket, making a spark, then finding purchase in his rib cage. Abe kicked at the raging rebel, violently flailing his bayonet as he lifted into the sky.

Ramsey aimed his rifle as the rebel stopped, smiled, and looked down at his weapon, realizing Abe had no more ammunition.

The young rebel lifted his rifle bringing it to port arms, and like an executioner, measured his next move, leveling the sight on the swinging basket.

Ramsey lowered his weapon and sighted the rebel. Then Abe. Then the rebel. The penetrator was oscillating, preventing Ramsey from getting a good shot.

"Pull this thing up! Pull up!" Ramsey yelled to the crew chief.

"We'll lose him, sir. We've got to get him higher!" the crew chief screamed back.

Kanishi Abe

Abe looked down with fear as the basket pulled him away. On the ground, an instinct must have taken charge, making him a warrior, but now as he lifted through the fog of war, sensing perhaps that he was moving closer to perhaps his safety, he appeared fearful again. Abe pulled the picture of his wife and family from the breast pocket of his borrowed uniform, smiling at him from a photographer's studio in Tokyo.

The rebel looked away, then sighted again. He was having trouble with the wooden stock of his Chinese rifle, which was covered with mud and dirt, but he sighted again after wiping away the debris. He pulled the trigger as the basket reached the bottom of the helicopter, firing one shot, then another, then stopping, flipping the selector switch to automatic, then emptying his magazine into the cage like a magician sticking swords into a basket.

Abe felt the first bullet crush his kneecap. The second burned a hole in his hamstring, cracking his femur. Some bounced off the cage, leaving hot sparks in their place.

The hand reached in and pulled him away from the cage as a series of bullets bounced off its metal frame, some catching the reinforced belly of the helicopter, others digging their way into his flesh.

Chuck Ramsey

Ramsey grabbed one of Abe's arms and helped pull him into the aircraft, which banked away with the basket dangling below.

He watched a rebel who saw a special forces soldier's green beret lying on the ground, thrust his bayonet into it, then plucked it from the blade and placed it on his head.

He had won.

Ramsey looked at Abe's fading eyes. The man was dying, he was sure. Abe looked at him and grabbed his hand, rolling toward him as the helicopter banked over the ocean.

Pressing the picture of his family into Ramsey's palm, he said "Please call them and tell them I love them." He spoke with unusual clarity, his accent almost absent. Ramsey watched Abe's eyes flutter as he felt the hand close in on his, pressing the picture deeper into his palm.

"Thank you, my friend," Abe said.

Ramsey turned his head and his eyes caught the sight of five body bags stacked in the helicopter. Each had a name written in black marker on green tape.

He stared at one bag and the name written in bold letters: Peterson. *Ron Peterson, where it had begun. The jump into the central highlands.*

Ramsey turned away and looked through the open door of the helicopter. His sullen gaze fixed on nothing in particular as vivid images of his dead soldiers spun through his mind. He watched the medics work feverishly to save Abe as the helicopter blew past Cateel Bay and raced to the north, where the hospital ship was waiting.

CHAPTER 47
Island of Luzon, Philippines

Prime Minister Mizuzawa had boarded the Shin Meiwa aircraft, flown to the site where the oil tankers had originally been located, saw nothing, and landed in the mouth of the Pasig River near the Presidential Palace, using the rainstorm as his cover. The pilot had balked at Mizuzawa's insistence, but gladly agreed when a Japanese "New Nambu" .38-caliber revolver was pressed against his temple. The sheering winds pushed the aircraft down, then seemingly backward, releasing its force and allowing the plane to speed forward, almost tripping over itself.

If you want something done, you have to do it yourself, as the Americans say, Mizuzawa thought.

Dressed in combat fatigues, the prime minister and his security guards made their way through the streets of Manila, which were raging with block-to-block, street-to-street, and building-to-building fighting. The entire affair was confusing. He saw M1 tanks shoot at each other, mistakenly. Filipino civilians still roamed the less chaotic streets as if times were normal. Japanese soldiers were holding the Americans back from taking the Presidential Palace and the critical financial district as well.

Mizuzawa and his entourage entered the grounds of the palace practically unchallenged. The gate guard was huddled against the fence in a soaked poncho, the rain pelting against the porous fabric. Mizuzawa yanked his revolver from his holster, pulled back the hammer, leveled it alongside the temple of the shivering guard, then lifted it and fired a round. The blast might have made the young soldier permanently deaf in one ear, but it woke him up.

We have become too weak. It occurred to him as he strode into the palace that he was talking about himself. *I should have killed him.*

Several soldiers converged on Mizuzawa, recognizing him immediately. One summoned General Nugama, who came hustling down the steps, buckling his pants. His hair was disheveled, and the buttons to his uniform top were open. Mizuzawa could not determine if the man had been sleeping or taking liberties with a Filipina concubine.

"The spoils of war are not ours, yet, Nugama," Mizuzawa said, deciding on the latter.

"Yes, sir. Merely catching up on my sleep," Nugama said.

Mizuzawa caught a glimpse of a beautiful Eurasian woman peering around the banister from atop the stairs. *We are getting weak.*

They walked into the operations center, where several soldiers sat before radios, television screens, and computers. All the men were wearing headsets and talking. A huge map of the Philippines hung on the wall, with red and blue markings on it indicating the location of friendly and enemy forces.

"Where is Takishi?" Mizuzawa asked Nugama.

"Sir, he is in Cabanatuan. He started moving with his division, and was stopped by"—he paused as if he hated to say it—"by an infantry battalion."

"What! Fools. I didn't give him command of that division just so he could piss it away. I wanted him to be victorious. To know the smell of blood and death so that one day he could take my place as prime minister and understand necessary sacrifice." It was true. Mizuzawa wanted Takishi to return to Japan as a conquering hero. It was just another step in the mentoring process; but like all of the other steps, the mentor can only get the pupil the job. He can't ensure that he succeeds.

"Yes, sir," Nugama said.

"How bad is it?"

"He's only lost a battalion, but all the aircraft are grounded and he's got two brigades stuck on the road, trapped by rice paddies. He's still got two infantry battalions able to move, but they're fighting the Rangers in the jungles. Those Rangers didn't know what hit them," he said.

"What else is happening?" Mizuzawa asked, walking over to the map.

"We've got four divisions on the ground. Two are at about 50 percent but holding well in the city. We had enough time to establish a decent defensive perimeter. One division was holding Subic, but I moved it over here," he said, pointing at the northern outskirts of Manila, "to flank the enemy Marines. They got caught in a pretty heavy crossfire from enemy air, and their reserve got destroyed by some infantry to the west of Subic. Our intelligence was not very good," he said..

"So we've got three divisions at 50 percent or less, and Takishi's almost full strength," Mizuzawa said. "Where's the ship?"

"Yes, sir. The ship is halfway between Hawaii and Los Angeles. As you know, it was not like the others. Its top deck looks like any other Toyota merchant ship with new cars on top. But the hull is very different. Admiral Sazaku is piloting the *Shimpu* and is very trustworthy. He will perform either mission we ask of him. He can detonate the nuclear bomb in Los Angeles harbor or he can sit there as a queen checkmating their king," Nugama said.

"Good. This thing is still a potential win. Two of our divisions against two American divisions. He has more aircraft, but we have more tanks and soldiers on the ground," Mizuzawa said, studying the map. He walked over to a larger-scale map of the Pacific, and traced his finger to a point midway between the Big Island of Hawaii and the big city of Los Angeles. He ran his fingernail across the map, making an indentation, and scratched an X on Los Angeles. He popped the city with his finger and turned to Nugama.

"I want you in the field, General, where you can command your soldiers, not in here sleeping with women, understand?"

"Yes, sir," Nugama replied.

"Perhaps if you had been out there, our position would not be so precarious," Mizuzawa scolded.

A young private walked up to Nugama and handed him a sheet of paper, which he read aloud. "Latest spot report has Takishi back with the main body of his division. He's lost nearly 60 tanks. The road to Cabanatuan is blocked, and the rain is still coming down too hard for the Xs to fly," he said, referring to the AH-X attack helicopters.

Mizuzawa walked back to the map and pondered. Initially, his strategy had been to take the Philippines through political surprise. They had achieved that, but something had gone wrong. Villanueva had defected, or so he thought. Then he had directed the brilliant move with the ambassador's speech to the United Nations, effectively handcuffing the Americans. There was no way they could legitimately react. But then a lousy journalist had captured the death march on film. But still, he figured international opinion was split evenly between believing he had the right to restore the government of the Philippines and siding with the American response. The simple fact that they had gotten that far was a great achievement, but he was still far short of his goals.

He needed to adjust his strategy. His presence in the operations center was a bad sign in its own right. His goals remained to reassert Japanese military power in the region. Could he do that if he lost the fight? Maybe, maybe not. The conventional fight on the ground could go either way. Japanese soldiers had softened over the past sixty years. They had rarely trained and were not used to the rigors of combat.

Mizuzawa felt the palace shudder once, then a second time.

"Can they reach us down here?" he said to Nugama.

"No, sir. We are safely deep," Nugama said.

"Okay. Let's hold with what we've got in Manila," he said, pointing at the map. "We'll focus our efforts on getting Takishi's division out of Cabanatuan. If he can break free we pull back, deeper in the city, sucking the

Americans in with us. Then Takishi comes from the north, slamming into the enemy rear."

Mizuzawa had moved from the strategic plan to operational art in a matter of seconds. It was all a mind game. Technology and soldiers were important, but the only thing that could truly tip the balance was a superior mind. Why else would theorists such as Sun Tzu and Clausewitz still be relevant today?

He needed something to maneuver with, though, and he hoped his good friend Takishi would come through in the clutch.

CHAPTER 48
Zachary Garrett

Zachary moved Kurtz's platoon out of the rice paddy and sent them back to the wooded knoll near checkpoint three-one. They trudged through the pelting rain, unaware of any change in their condition, having just left the soggy rice paddy. The sky was battleship gray, vomiting rain, with a peripheral darkness that seemed prescient, like a dark circle closing in around them.

Upon approaching Taylor's position, he saw five bodies lying on the ground, covered in ponchos.

"They ours?" Zachary asked Taylor.

"Yes, sir." Taylor proceeded to list the name of each soldier and what had happened to them. Zachary noticed that Taylor talked with a hardened authority, as if something measurable had changed in him that morning.

One of the enemy tanks had fired multiple high-explosive rounds into Zachary's position. One soldier had caught a round in the chest, blowing a hole right through him. It impacted in the ground behind him, leaving his body still pretty much intact except for the big hole. Taylor spoke about it matter-of-factly, no edge in his voice.

"About four guys jumped from one tank we hit with an AT4. We killed two, I think, and one ran in your direction. I called you, but you were on battalion net. Slick took the message," Taylor said. Water dripped in a steady stream from the front lip of his helmet. He held a map covered in acetate in his right hand, the rain smacking it with steady drip.

"Yeah, he told me, but we never saw the guy. Bastard is probably back there right now pinpointing our position for the next attack."

Zachary walked over to Barker's position and saw three more bodies. They had been cut down during the initial action on the flank. Barker said, somewhat embarrassed, that he thought two of them were friendly-fire casualties. He had maneuvered his squads in a fashion so that they converged on each other in the darkness.

"It happens," Zachary said.

Kurtz was the lucky one so far. He had only lost Teller, who had been serving as a back-up radio operator to Zach, and that seemed like an eternity ago.

Zachary huddled with his platoon leaders around a stand of mahogany trees.

"We're moving," he said. The words were painful. Everyone knew they had to, but the logistics of moving in the rain with dead bodies and demoralized troops, were overwhelming.

"Your men have an hour to get ready. I'll let battalion know what we're up to."

He walked with Slick over to a secluded spot and knelt in a pool of water, into the thick mud beneath it.

"Sir, what're we gonna do?"

Ten dead, was all Zachary could think about. Then he gathered himself.

"We need to move, Slick. We stopped them for now. But they're pissed, and as soon as this weather clears, this entire hill's gonna be a free-fire zone. Arty, mortars, helicopters, tanks, you name it."

Slick gave the commander the handset and turned his back. Placing his hands on his knees and leaning over, he vomited into the mud. Zachary watched without emotion. *It happens.*

He called Kooseman and gave him the word he was moving to the north side of the road and closer to the fort. He would give him an exact grid coordinate of his command post later, when he found a decent location. Kooseman reported they had secured the prison and freed the 6000 captives. His voice sounded as though he thought he had made a mistake.

Instead of setting them free into the countryside, he explained, he had unlocked their cells keeping the gates to the prison locked to keep the refuges safe from combat. Most stayed inside the protective confines of the prison simply to stay out of the rain.

Zachary shrugged. Not his issue. He told Kooseman that he needed more anti-tank missiles. Kooseman obliged, gathering five Javelin missiles and ten AT4s from each company and sending them forward in a Filipino jeepney, trading the ammo for eight bodies. Zachary appreciated Kooseman's good sense.

The casualties gone and the wounded patched, Zachary had the battalion's 105mm artillery pieces fire continuous mixtures of smoke and high-explosive rounds into the enemy tank column. All of the tanks that could move had backed along the cement road until they were out of sight.

He hoped no one would see him move. With a grim look of determination, Zachary lifted his arm, palm stretched outward, then brought it forward, saying, "Follow me."

They slogged their way across the muddy field.

The sun never made an appearance. It was a full day of monsoon-force rains. His men waded through knee-deep mud, slipping and falling in the miserable muck. During the move, some forgot their overarching concerns of living through this war and cursed the rain and mud and weight they were carrying on their backs.

Some even cursed Captain Garrett for making them move. The wooded knoll was a perfectly good position. They had defended well from there. Zachary heard the men swearing but figured it might do them some good to get their minds off the previous battle, so he said nothing. By nightfall, they had found a good spot from which to defend. Zachary had purposely taken them on a circuitous route so that any Japanese intelligence collectors would have a hard time figuring their intentions. When they reached their new defensive position, indistinguishable from any other terrain in the area, he told his men to go to 75 percent security and get some rest. Most tried but few were able to.

Zachary looked into the sheets of water blowing horizontal with the wind. He had led them to the northeast of Fort Magsaysay along a small ridge covered with high grass. The jungle was only 300 meters to the rear and Fort Magsaysay about one and a half kilometers to the south. He called Kooseman and told him he was in position and gave him the grid.

Kooseman went ballistic.

"What the hell are you doing way over there?!" Kooseman screamed.

"They're coming this way next," Zachary said, without hesitation or emotion. He was not going to move, no matter what, and had decided before they moved from their previous site that he was going to ask forgiveness instead of permission, knowing he never would have received the latter.

"I need you to move back and guard my flank," Kooseman said. Zachary looked at the handset. Kooseman was a good guy, but he sounded too dry. He was in a building somewhere, Zachary was sure, as was the rest of the battalion, probably.

"Negative. Have McAllister move 600 meters north of my old position. That way we'll be able to catch them in a cross fire," Zachary countered, unflinching.

Kooseman paused. Zachary figured he was looking at a map or weighing Zach's insubordination. He didn't care. He wasn't moving. He knew he was right.

"Roger," Kooseman responded.

Zachary gave the radio handset back to Slick. Looking through his night-vision goggles, Zachary identified what appeared to be an airstrip, less than a mile to the southwest. He saw the faint black outlines of helicopters and had an idea.

"Think this shit'll ever stop?" Slick asked his captain, shivering in the dark night.

Zachary hardly noticed the question. He summoned Kurtz and SSG Quinones, who appeared moments later, faces painted black for the movement. He gave them instructions and told them to report back once they were prepared. The two men returned within the half-hour and Zach went over the plan again.

"It's 0200; let's go," he said.

The four of them moved through second platoon's leg of the triangular patrol base. Wearing the goggles felt good, keeping their faces dry for a change. Zachary led the men down the ridge, staying low. Zachary, Kurtz, and Quinones had emptied their rucksacks and loaded them with the company's supply of C4, detonation cord, and other demolitions equipment.

They moved silently through the loud rain. *Infantry weather.* Wading through a small stream, engorged probably to twice its size, Zachary pulled at a root on the far bank, which dislodged, causing him to fall back into the water. Kurtz and Quinones were behind him and lifted him out immediately. Finally clawing their way to the far side, they spied a weak roll of concertina barbed wire guarding 15 helicopters parked innocently on the cement runway.

Zachary designated five aircraft for each man. When they were done, they were to shine their IR flashlights three times in his direction. Slick's job was to watch for the signals.

There appeared to be no roving guard. Zachary could make out a small shack at the far end of the runway but could see no one. He low-crawled up to the wire and nudged it with his rifle, just to be sure, then took his wire cutters and snipped the strands of razor-sharp metal, cutting his hands as he did so. The pain was sharp and unnecessary; he should have been more careful.

The task complete, they slithered like snakes through the opening. Zachary had chosen the five aircraft farthest away. As he crawled on the cement, his body armor and outer tactical vest dug into his skin, and the pools of standing water stung his hands.

He gauged the aircraft through the driving rain. The helicopters looked like sleek, new-model Apaches.

He slid his rucksack off his shoulders and dug into its dryness, producing a standard M112 block of C4 that they had rigged with time fuses, blasting caps, and nonelectric firing devices.

He opened the door to the first helicopter, placing the explosive next to the control panel and leaving the door cracked slightly. He repeated the process for each of the other aircraft before flashing his Infrared light in Slick's direction. Slick flashed back that he acknowledged. Kurtz and Quinones did the same, and Slick flashed four times to the captain, indicating they were all ready.

Zachary knelt next to the helicopter farthest away from where they had entered the airstrip and closest to the small hut, which was less than 100 meters away.

That was why he saw the light come on. A huge spotlight followed, shining in their direction.

He pulled the first nonelectric firing device, listening for the hissing of burning time fuse. Running from helicopter to helicopter, Kurtz and Quinones followed suit. He reached his last aircraft and stooped to pick his rucksack off the wet pavement when he heard a bullet whiz by his ear like a closing zipper and ricochet off the helicopter. Looking back over his shoulder, he tripped, severely bruising his elbow.

The rate of fire increased as they scampered back through the wire. Quinones had gone through the hole in the wire first but was screaming and writhing on the ground as if he was hit.

"Medic! I need a medic!" His body was bouncing wildly on the ground. Zachary approached him, sliding off his goggles and keeping below the enemy fire.

After his eyes adjusted to the night, he saw a horrible sight. Quinones had apparently slipped as he ran through the wire and fallen. One of the razors from the concertina had snagged him just beneath his left eye and ripped open the socket.

Blood was everywhere and Zachary saw the eye, strung to Quinones's face by a thread of red membrane or muscle, nearly falling out of the socket.

"Help me, sir," Quinones whispered, watching the commander out of his remaining eye.

Zachary pulled out his first-aid dressing and wrapped it around Quinones's head, securing the eye in place. He didn't know; maybe they had the technology to fix it.

Kurtz slung Quinones over his shoulder and grabbed the man's weapon and went to one knee, saying, "Son of a bitch."

Zachary looked at Kurtz, who groaned and stood, blood pouring from his lower right leg. The Japanese soldiers were racing across the airfield, firing their weapons.

The first explosion knocked about seven of them back. The next blasts happened almost in unison, giving Zachary, Slick, Kurtz, and Quinones enough time to melt into the high grass to the east.

They fled into the jungle, clawing their way up the hills without regard for direction, turning to check for pursuers on occasion.

"Halt, who goes there?" came an American voice.

"We're Americans!" Zachary screamed.

"Advance forward to be recognized."

"Eagle."

"Viper."

"Welcome to Second Bat. What the hell are you guys doing?" the Ranger said from beneath his patrol cap, the sides of his shaved head glistening in the night.

Zachary turned and watched the Japanese try to extinguish the fires on the helicopters. It was no use. Every one of them was now destroyed.

It could make the difference.

CHAPTER 49

President Davis looked at his friend, Bob Stone, thinking, *He's not himself.*

"What's the matter, Bob?" he asked. "You seem nervous. You're not getting weak on me, are you?"

"No, sir, just a little tired," Stone said, his voice shaking in the confines of the diminutive Situation Room. They were waiting for Jim Fleagles, the Secretary of State, and Yves Gerald, the National Security Advisor. Sewell was sitting next to the president, staring at Stone, who was looking across the table at President Davis, then Frank Lantini.

"Looks like the rain'll stop soon," Lantini said, trying to change the subject.

"Is that good or bad?" the president asked.

"Both, depending on how you look at it," Lantini said.

Fleagles and Gerald walked in and sat down.

"Chairman," the president said.

"We were just discussing this rain that's slowed the action some. Looks like it'll lift soon," Sewell said.

"That's good, right?" Fleagles asked.

The President watched Sewell smirk. "Could be. But we've put the rest of the infantry division on a ship, which is taking them around the other side of Luzon," he said, standing and pointing at a map. "We've got almost two brigades ready to assault from hovercraft, walk the short distance over this ridge, and come in on the enemy's flank. We think that if we can take away this guy," he said, thumping a red square symbol with two Xs, indicating a Japanese tank division, at the top, then we win today. If not, then the fight goes on. And if we don't win in the next two days, I'm afraid the international scene could get out of control. It'll be another week before we can get enough tanks over there to make a difference."

"Thanks, Chairman. Impacts on Iraq?" the President asked, turning to Stone.

"Significant, but we think we can be on schedule for next winter or spring," Stone said.

"If that's the math, then okay. But we've got to watch the terrorist flow into Iraq. If they've got weapons of mass destruction, then we need to accelerate."

"This Pacific Rim thing has soaked up time and talent, sir," Sewell said, reinforcing Stone's position.

The president had begun to speak when a young Army captain, Stockton Ackers, stuck his head inside the room from the operations office and said, "Sir, pardon me, but we need you in here."

"Can it wait?" Davis asked.

"No, sir," Ackers responded, his serious eyes locked firmly with the president's.

The President led the entourage into the small operations cell, where computers thrummed with messages, phones constantly rang, maps hung on the wall crazily, and young military officers dressed in civilian clothes performed yeoman's work, often clocking in 18- to 20-hour days.

"Sir, we've got reports of Chinese nuclear weapons moving from the western border with Russia," Ackers said, pointing at a large map about where the Great Wall would be, "to the eastern area near Shanghai. They've never moved those missiles before. We think it's a response to the Philippine crisis."

"So we're tracking them with satellites?" the president asked.

"Sure, sir, but if they launch, they launch. Nothing we can do about it," Ackers responded to the simple question.

"Okay. I'll talk to President Jiang today. Anything else?"

"Yes, sir. About an hour ago a Korean destroyer sank a Japanese Kuang Hua VI attack boat. They were both in international waters, but the attack boat looked like it was trying to get inside Korean waters. We think it was the newest Japanese ship—"

"I guess I'll talk to President Park after Jiang," the president said, shaking his head, wondering what could happen next.

"Sir," Ackers said, hesitating. "Taiwan's pushed its navy out from Taipei and is poised just southwest of Okinawa, and we've still got the Chinese navy building forces in the East China Sea. This thing could blow any minute."

"Spare me the editorial, Captain," Davis snapped.

The president thought about the implications of Ackers's information. How should he respond to China, Korea, Russia, and Taiwan? Each felt threatened, he was sure. The era of the Japanese warlord had left an indelible imprint on the minds of many of the leaders of that region, like Hitler in Germany and Napoleon in France.

But they saw Japanese culture and society as more capable of producing the racist, demagogic warrior of the past. Perhaps Germany was beyond Hitler, and France, Napoleon, but its Asian counterparts might interpret Japan to be reemerging as a nationalistic threat off the east coast of the Asian continent, driven by warlords indistinguishable from the executive auto manufacturers.

Their economic expansion during the past 60 years was the 20th century's Trojan horse. The Japanese had funneled their historical penchant for war and aggression into highly productive endeavors such as industry, manufacturing, and other high-technology development, but sooner or later they had reached a point of diminishing returns. Like the once-successful merchant who fell on hard times, they could either fight back or file for bankruptcy. Japan wasn't about to go for Chapter Eleven.

The men retired to the Situation Room again burdened with new information. The President called the Chinese prime minister and had a brief conversation.

"We have to finish this thing in the next 24 hours," the president said, hanging up the phone with the Chinese prime minister.

"The Chinese say that if Japan is not defeated by midnight tomorrow they will take matters into their own hands."

The President stared at his team, realizing how right Meredith had been. She had picked up the horseshoe and tossed a perfect ringer, the metal surely clanking loudly through each man's ears today.

Their collective mind, though, was frozen by the news. At the strategic level, if they could not keep China and others out of the war, the United States would lose everything. The most dynamic free-market economy in Asia would wither, taking with it a large portion of the European and American markets and potentially launching the world into another depression.

China had the ability to annihilate Japan with nuclear weapons. The ultimate irony would be China's introduction into the war. The United States would have to side with Japan to stop an even-more-dangerous aggressor. The international community's economic interdependence had made the world economy a house of cards. To pull one away might very well bring the entire house down. Worse, at the foundation were the United States, Japan, and Europe, all mingled together like the wrong sized parts of the same machinery.

The President watched his team stare at each other, none appearing to know what to say.

Then he saw Sewell wink at Stone, who decided to break the ice.

"Let's just see how this thing pans out."

CHAPTER 50

"The move with Takishi was risky," Fox said to Diamond.

"Risky indeed," Diamond agreed.

The two men were sitting in Fox's office again, Fox in his throne and Diamond in the facing chair. Fox put his hand on the desk next to Diamond, his fingers spread casually toward his partner. Rezia's aria, "Ocean! thou mighty monster," from Carl Maria von Weber's *Oberon*, played quietly in the background.

Diamond pointed a well-manicured finger at Fox.

"But it was necessary to get China sufficiently concerned to put forth their ultimatum," Diamond said.

"Yes, that was a brilliant move. Now the 24-hour ultimatum is in effect. We will have to complete the destruction of the Japanese, or else China and North Korea will 'take matters into their own hands.'" He used his hands to make quotation marks around his sentence.

Fox leaned forward and ran his delicate hand through Diamond's sparse hair.

"So 9-11 opened the door for action in Iraq," Diamond said, eyeing Fox. "Then we retaliated against Al Qaeda and the Taliban sufficiently to get them out of Afghanistan, but not sufficiently to destroy them. Brilliant suggestion by the way, Saul. The lingering threat will continue to open so many opportunities. The possibilities are limitless."

"It *was* a good idea," Fox purred. "We haven't put more than a brigade in Afghanistan. And when that Matt Garrett crossed over and was about to get the mastermind, well, your quick action to blackmail Stone was genius. Using Stone's personal information to create an E*Trade account so that 'he' could short AIG and United Airlines was pure brilliance."

"Thank you." Diamond sighed. "It certainly got Stone to move Garrett far off the Al Qaeda trail quickly." The two men were becoming aroused, stimulated by their manipulations and grand strategy. "I hear Matt Garrett's dead now anyway."

"Good. Good. That was a loose end we didn't need," Fox said. "Not that he knew anything. But he was too aggressive, too good."

"That's right. Then, as we gathered the momentum on Iraq—we have to hand it to Stone, who worked faster than we thought he could—to get the Philippine situation to a sufficient level actually to be a diversion," Diamond said.

"But they had been working on that for two years." Fox chuckled. "The Japanese used him and outsmarted him."

"Well, we've been working on our project longer than that," Diamond said.

"Yes, we have," Fox said. "Which is why we had to intervene with Takishi to get him to ratchet up the force levels so that there was a credible threat to the region."

"So that China and North Korea would issue an ultimatum," Diamond whispered, blowing into Fox's ear.

"Which brings us full circle." Fox sighed. "We will wrap this up soon and begin large-scale deployments to Kuwait. I've already signed the deployment orders."

"I'm just thankful that you broke the Rolling Stones' code," Diamond said..

"Rather easy, Dick. Our friend Bart Rathburn, whom Stone calls Keith Richards is dead. Taiku Takishi, known as Charlie Watts, will be dead soon, and we will ruin that idiot Bob Stone, who calls himself Mick

Jagger. That only leaves the question of what to do with Ronnie Wood," Fox said.

"Problematic," Diamond agreed, kissing Fox's neck.

"We have to make sure the Philippine action is done quickly and leave Wood intact. He may not be much, but he's what we got," Fox said.

"He's our man," Diamond agreed.

CHAPTER 51
Island of Luzon, Philippines

Zachary watched the convoy move out and called Kooseman, the acting battalion commander.

"I've got about 120 tanks and a shitload of infantry fighting vehicles moving north toward Bongabon," Zachary said, peering above a rotted log. He lay in the prone position, holding a set of binoculars to his face and counting. He had slipped a knee pad over his swelling elbow so that he could hold the binos steady.

The Ranger medic had done all he could for SSG Quinones, the morphine shot being the most helpful. With the rain, a medevac was impossible.

"What I'd give for a few A-10s and some F-16s," Zachary said.

"Like you always say, sir, this is infantry weather. Them zoomies can't handle this shit," Slick said.

Zachary smiled, at his radio operator, even allowing himself to feel a sense of safety as the procession moved away from them to the northwest. It was a comforting feeling, as if he might never see them again.

"Yeah, but they'd make short work of this. I don't see a single air-defense weapon," Zachary said.

He was right. In Zachary's assessment the Japanese had gone into the conflict severely unprepared, despite their strategic and tactical surprise. They had some stinger gunners riding in the tanks and infantry fighting vehicles, but all they could do was react. There was no integrated system set up for early warning such as the Americans used.

Zachary and Slick lay against a rotted log, soft from the rain, waiting for the word from Kooseman. Zachary had played cowboy enough for one war and was growing apprehensive over his isolation from the rest of the unit. Once again, he and Slick were all alone, save for the Rangers to their left flank. It was, however, his fault. He had moved the company on his own initiative.

But something instinctual had governed him, almost forcing him to the new position, as if he was supposed to be there, and he trusted it.

They heard wet, muffled sounds of artillery rounds leaving their tubes and cutting a path through the driving rain and high clouds. The rounds popped in the distance. Through his binos Zachary saw timber crash and mud splash on the wooded knoll they had earlier defended. The Japanese self-propelled artillery pumped round after round into the infamous knoll before shifting its fire onto the town of Cabanatuan, indiscriminately spraying the area.

Zach could see thatch huts, the ones that had withstood the onslaught of the rain, disintegrate under the now-incessant bombardment. They had learned one lesson, Zachary figured, and that was to go nowhere without artillery support.

"Bravo six, this is Knight five, over," came Kooseman's voice over Slick's radio handset.

"This is Bravo six, over," Zachary said.

"Can you do anything about that artillery?" Kooseman asked, anger in his voice. "It's getting pretty bad over here."

Zachary's mind raged white-hot. *He's got a lot of balls.* Kooseman had chastised him for moving so far away but had the nerve to ask Zachary to attack the enemy formation and compromise his new position. Yesterday, he would have done it without fail, but today he had gained a better perspective. Some of the edge had dulled from his rage and his driving force to kill every Japanese soldier. He recognized that he had a larger responsibility to protect his company and complete the mission.

"What do you want me to do, sir? I've got about 15 missiles," Zachary said, hoping that would discourage Kooseman.

The artillery volleys increased and for the first time Zachary heard the impotent U.S artillery battalion 105mm rounds impacting near the Japanese 155mm self-propelled guns. They landed harmlessly around the armored hulks of the Japanese guns.

"Can you see their arty? How many guns do they have?" Kooseman asked.

Zachary didn't like the way the conversation was going; but then he thought of guys like McAllister and Glenn Bush, who were probably over there getting shelled.

"Roger. I count sixteen guns. Looks like two batteries. All are firing," Zachary said, knowing immediately what his new mission was going to be.

"You've got enough to take them out," Kooseman said, trying to make it sound like an order.

Water dripped steadily off the black handset that Zachary held to his ear and mouth. His elbow had busted a hole in the log and he saw some maggots crawling on his sleeve. As he brushed his elbow against the soggy wood, he wondered about Kooseman's mathematical capabilities. Sure, he could get most of the artillery, but then he would have to bear the brunt of nearly 200 armored vehicles turned against him.

It was suicide.

"I'm not so sure it's a smart move," Zachary said into the handset, realizing he was being insubordinate.

"I'm not asking your opinion, Garrett. Shoot the artillery. Do it now," Kooseman retorted. Zachary heard loud explosions amplified by the transmission. Looking through his binoculars as the gray shade of morning lightened ever so slightly, he watched as a shell tore a huge hole in the prison roof.

"What happens when these two brigades turn on my ass?" Zachary asked.

"We've got you covered. Have you shot the artillery, yet?"

"Roger. Happening now," Zachary said, tossing the handset to Slick. Zachary ordered his platoon leaders to his position and they rapidly arrived, Kurtz limping with a large bandage around his lower leg.

"We have been ordered to destroy that artillery," he said, pointing at the dark figures jumping backward each time they fired. They were nearly five hundred meters away, the perfect distance for Zachary's missile gunners. Zachary hated to use the passive voice regarding an order. Normally he took responsibility for everything, but he had a hard time justifying to his men that their company was supposed to attack a 200-strong armored vehicle convoy.

"Then what?" Taylor asked.

"Then we fight like good soldiers, Andy. We do our best. We've been given a mission and we're gonna do it."

Kurtz and Barker were silent as Zachary sketched out a new plan. It was simple: assign each gunner an artillery piece, everyone would fire simultaneously, then the company would move a kilometer to the rear, into the jungle.

He watched as his platoon leaders trod back to their platoons and could not help wondering about a similar night attack they had botched in training over two weeks ago.

Just don't screw the pooch here.

"Packers," he said into the radio after receiving word from the three platoon leaders that they were ready. *Packers* was the code word to commence firing of the missiles.

He looked over his shoulder and thought he saw something, something blue, but then watched as his anti-tank gunners once again scored strikes on the enemy armor.

Despite the pelting rain, thirteen of the sixteen Japanese artillery pieces were burning a bright orange hue, the color of the sun.

The sun, yes. Blue skies mean the sun will come out.

Zachary looked back over his shoulder and saw a blue patch of sky moving too slowly above a mountain peak.

Hurry up!

"Knight this is Bravo. Destroyed thirteen of sixteen and we're out of missiles," Zachary reported, ready to pack his bags and move into the jungle.

"I sent you some AT4 yesterday," Kooseman responded. "Get the other three. We're still taking arty." Zachary wanted to tell him to pack sand, but he obeyed.

"Roger, out," Zachary replied.

"You don't say out to me, Captain! You say, over, over."

Zachary threw the handset into the mud and stood. He could still hear Kooseman squawking, but he quit listening when he noticed…something was different.

It had stopped raining.

CHAPTER 52
Taiku Takishi

Takishi told Muriami to move out. They weren't going to wait for the rain to stop. Muriami gunned the jet engine, tossing Takishi's ribs into the padded rubber of the commander's hatch.

Takishi surveyed the wet, gray morning. The rain had continued through the night and Takishi had decided to move his tanks after the enemy had destroyed his helicopters.

He radioed his commanders and told them to follow him north. He positioned an infantry battalion on each side of his column of tanks. His soldiers, all soaked to the core, revved the diesel engines and began the muddy trek north toward Bongabon, only to cut south from there toward Manila.

"This time, we must make it," Takishi said to Muriami, as they splashed along the muddy road. The tank tread bogged down briefly, then got a grip, gaining purchase on firmer turf. Takishi looked ahead and saw that the road was strewn with chunks of asphalt. Without a decent surface, the road would be impassable.

After an hour of tough slogging, Takishi slewed his turret 180 degrees and ordered Muriami to stop the tank. The going had been slow anyway, and a brief halt would not make a big difference one way or the other.

Frustrated, he watched the American missiles chew into his artillery, then he saw about 30 men come charging downhill toward the pieces that were still firing. They set up shoulder-launched weapons and fired, setting the remainder of the artillery ablaze.

All he had left was direct-fire capability. He pressed the toggle switch on his crewman's helmet and ordered the right-flank infantry battalion commander to dismount and destroy, once and for all, the pesky light infantry.

Whether it was for glory or because of pure frustration, Takishi lifted his M4, a prize among all of his troops, and stepped out of the relative protection of the tank turret. He jogged into the fray behind hundreds of his infantry and saw a man running down the hill with a radio handset in his ear and a black coil stretching to another soldier, who was trying to keep up.

As he slogged through the mud, he thought about his Harvard Business School classmate, Bart Rathburn, who had brought him the initial idea of using Japanese manufacturing to make rifles for the insurgency. Sitting in a nondescript sedan parked in a secluded forest outside of Tokyo, they had agreed on the terms of the contract.

He had, of course, changed those terms and built tanks and helicopters faster than the one hundred per day that the Americans had built during World War II.

Now, he led those tanks and his infantry into the fray, having double crossed Stone and the others, which was the plan all along.

Zachary Garrett

Standing, Zachary predicted that the right-flank battalion would turn on his position. It did.

Soon, a 25mm chain gun was chewing the soggy ground to his front. Barker's platoon, having just destroyed the remainder of the artillery, was suddenly stranded by the advancing vehicles.

Like Army ants, Japanese infantry came pouring from the backs of the fighting vehicles, firing their American weapons at American soldiers.

With horror, Zachary watched as ten vehicles started driving at Barker's platoon of thirty men, who were caught in the open like a herd of mustangs surrounded by cowboys. Some of the troops had time to move, but many did not. The twenty-ton armored weapons crushed them, some pivoting atop the bodies.

Zachary saw Barker crouched low, firing his M4 at an oncoming tank, his bullets ricocheting wildly off its rolled steel. The tank impaled him on its front deck as the tank commander leaned over the turret and emptied a full magazine of submachine-gun ammunition into Barker's body, leaving it glued to the tank by streaming blood. Zachary saw Barker's head bouncing crazily as the tank stopped, then backed, forcing Barker's body to slide onto the ground. It pivot-steered to gain the proper angle, finally chewing the wet turf and Barker, mixing the mud with the blood and bones of the young lieutenant.

"I need artillery, air, and helicopters here now!" Zachary screamed into the battalion radio net.

"Hold on, Zach," came McAllister's voice, "I'm almost there."

McAllister's voice comforted him briefly, then the wave of at least 300 charging infantrymen flushed the thought from his mind. His remaining two platoons, positioned along the open ridge, began firing. The squad's automatic weapons sang through the morning air, thrumming lightly in contrast to the Japanese 7.62mm machine guns, which made loud, cracking sounds.

"Fix bayonets," Zachary said calmly into the company radio.

Some did, most already had.

The two lines of soldiers merged, one indistinguishable from the other. Zachary saw Slick's eyes grow wide with fear as he fumbled with his bayonet.

Too late. A small Japanese soldier drove the butt of his weapon into Slick's helmet, knocking him back. Zachary took his pistol and fired it almost point-blank at the man's face, leaving a mangled mass in its path.

Zachary stuffed the pistol in his belt and lifted his M4, firing it at the many targets. The scene reminded him of a Civil War painting he'd seen at Gettysburg, the Union and Confederate lines locked against each other in combat, brother against brother.

These were no brothers, though. He knew about brothers. The thought sent a hot, violent rage surging through his body.

He stood, let out a low, guttural moan, then screamed wildly and waded into the fray, flailing his weapon back and forth, stabbing some with the bayonet and shooting others who were far enough away. Japanese men clad in dark olive uniforms, their mouths contorted, were screaming words foreign to Zachary. As he parried bayonet thrusts, he had a sense that he was invincible, or that nothing else mattered. Perhaps it was the same.

A knife pierced his left shoulder from behind. He turned and saw the blackened face of a Japanese officer as the knife made a cracking sound cutting through his clavicle.

Zachary pulled the pistol from his holster with his right hand, dropping the empty M4, and bored a hole through his attacker's neck. Bright red blood sprayed in all directions.

He pulled the knife from his shoulder in time to thrust it into another enemy soldier coming at him with a bayonet. The forward momentum of the small man knocked Zachary onto his back as he slid through the mud, coming to rest at the feet of two men fighting.

He saw Kurtz wildly swinging his rifle, crushing a man's temple. Zachary stood and wheeled around as he pointed his pistol in Slick's face, pulling the trigger only milliseconds after realizing his error and moving the barrel to the side.

Slick grabbed the commander and pulled him from the mêlée.

The sound of gunfire and screaming men filled the air. It was a horrible noise, the decibels of death, rising into the fresh, cool morning.

"Sir, Captain McAllister just called. He's coming up the hill!" Slick said as if wanting to protect his commanding officer. They had developed a bond, a bond that intensified as soon as Zachary watched the bullet strike Slick in the gut, just beneath the outer tactical vest, causing blood to pump like a stuck water fountain.

"Medic!" Zachary screamed, realizing he would get no help. He pulled Slick's first-aid dressing, ripped open his uniform, and placed it on the wound, but blood was everywhere.

"Kill those bastards, sir," Slick said as he died, his hand holding the black handset that had practically become an appendage.

Bastards!

The circle of death, once again, tightened its noose around Zachary.

A bullet struck him in the back of his right shoulder, balancing the throbbing pain from the knife wound and knocking him onto the ground. He stared skyward, his mind fuzzy, and would have sworn he saw buzzards circling the sky.

Big black birds, hovering, and turning, high and low, their beaks closed tight, waiting for the kill. Some moved fast and others just circled, while others just hovered above the trees…and began to fire at the Japanese tanks.

Suddenly, AH-64 Apache helicopters and Air Force A-10s began swooping along the strung-out column and pumping 30mm depleted uranium sabot bullets into the backs of the enemy infantry climbing the ridge in order to complete the destruction of B Company.

Then he saw McAllister's men rise from the stream that bordered Fort Magsaysay and converge on the left-flank infantry battalion that had by then dismounted. Only 300 meters away, he saw McAllister leading the charge with an M4, bayonet fixed, his head turned, screaming something over his shoulder and pulling his arm forward with his palm open. He saw his lips form the words, "Follow me," as his troops came screaming from the riverbed and tangled with the Japanese infantry.

The Apaches and A-10s raked the Japanese column with relative impunity, concerned only with ensuring that they didn't shoot any American soldiers.

Zachary watched an A-10 swing low, spit its 30mm, and take a direct hit from a missile, knocking it sideways and forcing the airplane to tumble end over end through the enemy infantry.

At least he took a bunch with him.

Flaming tanks and infantry fighting vehicles burned a brilliant orange, emitting a black smoke that rose to the heavens like dusty souls escaping the dying.

Zachary stood and joined his company, still locked in hand-to-hand combat. He had lost his weapons and used his helmet to hold at bay a charging Japanese soldier, crushing the Kevlar into the man's face. His attacker flipped backward in the mud, the man's weapon firing errantly into the sky. Curiously, Zachary noticed that the downed man was no soldier; his attacker looked more like a civilian. Perhaps he was Japanese intelligence?

Zachary pulled his K-Bar from its sheath and drove it into the man's neck until he felt it penetrate into the mud below. It hung on the civilian's trachea as he pulled it out, forcing him to grab the neck and yank hard to retrieve his knife. The jagged edge of the knife caught Zachary's hand on the way out, cutting deep into the bone of his thumb.

He felt the crushing impact of wood on his mouth as he caught a glimpse of an enemy pant leg move toward him. Teeth bounced loose into his throat, almost choking him.

He grabbed the man's thrusting weapon, slicing open his hands on the bayonet but somehow gripping the muddy stock tightly before the pointed object could enter his body. It didn't matter, as the infantryman pulled back on the weapon, leering at him from above. Zachary held on firmly and rose as the man pulled the trigger.

Frozen in time, he saw the weapon emit a bright muzzle flash He felt something hot burn its way through his abdomen. Another muzzle flash and he fell backward, reaching out with his knife, trying to stab at the foot of his attacker.

He could barely sense the feel of the wet, cold steel against the back of his head.

There was no time to remember the flashing images of Amanda or Matt or Riley or Karen or Slick or Teller or Father or Mother.

He heard a shot…and suddenly was back at the farm with his shotgun. He saw a quail drop. He looked at his brother, Matt, and smiled. They both watched their dog Ranger bounce through the high weeds and cattails along the stream in search of the fallen game. They followed, bare-chested and laughing in the cool mountain air, each looking at the other, Matt's crooked smile prominent. Thorny vines scraped at their tattered jeans as they reached a high rock outcropping, which rose 60 feet above a deep pool in the South River. Turning their heads slowly, they looked back at the towering Blue Ridge, waved at each other, and leapt over the brink.

CHAPTER 53
Manila, Philippines
Prime Minister Mizuzawa

A large gold cross was perched atop the simple white building adjoined to the Malacanang Presidential Palace by a short catwalk. Beneath the cross was a stained-glass window depicting the Mother Mary holding Baby Jesus. The welcome sun shone upon the multicolored glass, diffusing its light like a prism and licking at the standing puddles of water.

Five hundred years ago, Mizuzawa reflected, when the Spanish first colonized the archipelago and named it after King Philip, they Christianized the natives by introducing them to the Catholic religion. Every leader of the country since that time has been a Catholic, in name at least, and after achieving independence in 1947, the chapel was erected as a monument to the religion and its important role in Philippine society. The Pope himself had visited the enclave and declared the fenced chapel the property of Vatican City.

That day, a week after the final battle at Fort Magsaysay, Mizuzawa used it for other purposes.

"Get me Sazaku," Mizuzawa said to General Nugama from the confines of the small chapel. Mizuzawa did not expect the Americans to wait much longer, but he hoped they would respect the sanctity of the Catholic Church long enough for him to make one last move.

The Marines had unhinged the northern edge of the Manila defensive line, rolled the flank with one brigade, and surrounded the Presidential Palace with another brigade, while the third brigade fixed the southern flank, preventing the Japanese from reinforcing the tenuous flank.

Takishi had made a frantic call only moments before Mizuzawa and Nugama had run into the chapel with as much radio gear as they could garner.

"I'm being destroyed!" Takishi had reported. The road from Fort Magsaysay to Bongabon was littered with burning Japanese tanks and infantry fighting vehicles, some ignited internally from stored ammunition.

"You're on your own," Mizuzawa responded to his friend, hearing the sound of exploding tanks in the background of Takishi's transmission.

Mizuzawa later learned from the Americans that Takishi had been found among the dead littered on the battlefield outside of Fort Magsaysay, a knife wound to the neck. Indeed, Mizuzawa was watching his plans for a new, more dominant Japanese Empire fade like the setting sun, melting into the western horizon.

But he had one more card to play. It was, after all, a game of high-stakes poker in which each country tried to read the other's bluff, raising the ante when appropriate. Mizuzawa reached into his shirtsleeve and yanked out the ace he had tucked away before he had set the deadly train of events in motion.

"Sazaku, my friend. It is time," Mizuzawa said into the satellite radio.

The transmission soared as a neat bundle of words through the atmosphere, bouncing off one satellite, then another before finally entering the receiver screwed to a metal frame inside the cabin of Admiral Sazaku's merchant marine car carrier: the *Shimpu.*

"Yes. Our mission. Our glory," Sazaku responded.

"How long until you will detonate?" Mizuzawa asked, an edge to his voice. He was anxious to deal the Americans a fatal blow, even if it was a solitary strike that might invite massive retaliation. A nuclear explosion in Los Angeles would be devastating to the Americans.

"I'm six hours out from the harbor. As soon as I touch the pier I will vanish in a blaze of glory for my country," Sazaku answered, reminiscent of the kamikaze pilots of World War II. Sazaku had carried on the

Japanese kamikaze tradition of writing a final poem before the splendid final moments of life, which he read to Mizuzawa.

"I am the final victor/my country proud/the ship I steer/finishing loud/I am not alone/friends by my side/others gathered/in the ebbing tide/in the end/my floating corpse/finding safe harbor/Banzai Japan, no remorse."

"Yes, good. Continue your mission," Mizuzawa ordered before placing the handset back in its receiver. He looked at Nugama, an old friend whom he trusted.

"Do you have misgivings?" Mizuzawa asked, hoping for an honest answer.

"We can still win, Prime Minister. We can have Sazaku enter the port. Then we can sue for peace on our terms," Nugama responded, his gray hair shining bright beneath the stained-glass window. They could hear the intermittent pop of small-arms fire and the horrifying noise of American jets slicing low above the Manila skyline.

CHAPTER 54
Greene County, Virginia

While she was recovering at the Garrett farm in Stanardsville, Meredith continued to pore over the thumb drive, finding little else of use. She stood and stretched, catlike in her angora sweater.

She went back to Matt's room, where she had been sleeping, and studied the computer notes he had typed, which gave her an idea.

"Karen," she shouted down the stairs. "Think Matt would mind if I looked at some files on his computer?"

"No, just stay away from all the Sports Illustrated swimsuit editions. He copies the pictures in Adobe PDF and saves them." Karen smiled.

"I always thought of him as a man who could judge quality swimwear," Meredith said, smiling. The two women were able to manage pockets of humor even though the situation they faced was a disaster.

Karen opened Matt's computer and was soon inside his storage files. She was missing something—something she couldn't remember, and Meredith believed it was substantial and may just be somewhere in front of her.

She scanned his personal e-mail. Lots of Viagra offers, announcements that his Bank of America account was going to be closed if he didn't provide all of his financial data, and personal emails from people who looked like stray friends, perhaps lovers.

She reprimanded herself for perusing a note from Kari Jackson. Apparently they had once been an item in college and Kari wanted to reconnect. With a career like Matt's, Meredith wished Kari good luck. Well, actually, she didn't. Not the way she had grown to feel.

As she stared at the screen, an unread e-mail sat at the top in the form of a text message, meaning it was most likely sent from a cell phone. She didn't recognize the phone number but did understand the message.

Check out *Shimpu*. Contact KIA. New location. Standing by.

That was it, Meredith remembered, the missing piece. The eleventh ship was out there floating in the Pacific as a wild card. Matt had mentioned this to her when they first met in Palau. His contact had been shot and killed and he had raced away and been given the mission to determine if there were any survivors from the Filipino Ranger paratroop operation.

She ran downstairs and kissed Karen on the cheek, then jumped in her Prelude to make the two-hour drive to DC along Route 29 and I-66. She called Mark, her assistant, to get her the proper parking clearances and to let them know she had urgent information. She fishtailed her small car into a parking space on the Ellipse less than 500 yards from the Washington Monument.

She could see the tall white structure pointing into the sky, and even at that urgent moment was amazed that there was nothing actually holding the granite blocks together but their sheer weight.

She ran to the southwest gate of the White House, flashing her credentials and passing through the metal detector. The guard recognized her from her few visits with Stone and allowed her to pass after phoning Yves Gerald, who told him to send her through.

Worry etched lines of concern across her soft face. Dressed in blue jeans and flannel shirt, she had driven as fast as possible from Stanardsville.

She jogged beneath the awning that led to the business portion of the White House in the West Wing, then bounced up the stairs into Gerald's corner office where Stone and Lantini were looking at a map on Gerald's desk. She steeled herself against Stone's presence and pro-jected a determined demeanor.

"You've got to find this ship," she demanded, slapping down a piece of paper on the desk with the word *Shimpu* scribbled in large, erratic script.

The three men looked at her, then the paper, and Gerald asked, "What's the big deal? We've won this thing. We've got the Presidential Palace and have defeated their operational reserve. They've got nothing left. All we've got to do is root Mizuzawa out of the Catholic chapel there and we can pack our bags." His matter-of-fact demeanor only served to ignite a simmering fire in Meredith.

"You don't understand. The ship has nukes on it and is roaming in the Pacific," she said, shaking. She tried to maintain her professionalism, fearing that Gerald might just mistake her for another woman with PMS. The barriers were still there. If she had been a man, she could have done or said whatever she wanted, but as a woman, if she got too irate, she was just another crazy bitch.

"What makes you so sure, Meredith?" Stone asked, apparently giving her the benefit of the doubt. After all, she had predicted with certainty the reaction of Japan's neighbors and in fact, the president's policy was based in large part on Meredith's analysis. Thankfully, the defeat of the Japanese ground forces had kept the Chinese and Koreans in check. The Russians and Taiwanese were merely extending their security zones and had never had any intention of provoking Japan beyond convincing her to put her toys back in her bag and go home.

"This is the eleventh ship. I don't know how I missed it, but remember there were 10 that pulled away from Davao City weeks ago. They were military sealift ships disguised as oil tankers. But look here," she said, flipping some pages to a shipping log, "the *Shimpu* docked at Zhoushan a month ago, spent one night, never off-loaded anything, then arrived in Davao City and departed port the day Matt Garrett's contact was killed on the pier. And Matt reported this."

Gerald took a minute to scan the log, a product of United States HUMINT, human intelligence, and passed it to Lantini, whose organization had originally provided the document. Routinely, operators around the world tracked foreign ships, particularly among high-risk nations.

"We know this ship docked in Zhoushan, loaded something, then left, then arrived in Davao, and left. Now we don't know where it is. Is that right?" Gerald said. He added before she could answer, "Christ, what happened to your head?" He saw the six stitches that the Georgetown doctor had put in her forehead near the right temple.

"Jogging accident," she said quickly, staring directly at Stone. "Why don't we just try to find the *Shimpu*? And then we can hazard a guess as to what it's doing."

"What evidence do you have that there are nukes on the ship?" Lantini asked.

Meredith said nothing.

"Well, why don't we worst-case it, then?" Sewell said, walking into the office. He wore his green Army uniform, bedecked with medals from conflicts in Vietnam, Grenada, Panama, and Iraq. Meredith smiled. Sewell returned the nonverbal greeting, shaking her hand.

"The president called me over to discuss his speech tonight, but I couldn't help overhearing your conversation as I walked by," Sewell said.

"Everything we've got right now is looking at the Pacific rim." Gerald said. "It's a big ocean out there to find one ship."

"Why don't we start looking at places like Guam, where we have most of our logistical support, Hawaii, God forbid, and even the West Coast. We can do it in that order. If it's Guam or Hawaii, we need to find it fast. Heck, depending on how long this cannon's been loose, it may already be docked somewhere," Sewell said.

"Why can't we just tell Mizuzawa to call off the dog or we'll level Japan?" Gerald said.

"Get real, Yves. He knows we would never destroy the Japanese economy. It would never work for us in the long run. Besides, he's probably already made up his mind," Sewell said, which made good sense to Meredith.

"That's right," Meredith said, "he's probably been holding that ship in reserve somewhere, keeping his options open."

"What does *Shimpu* mean, anyway?" Gerald asked.

"*Divine Wind*," Meredith responded, and added, "Back in the late 13th century, monsoons saved the Japanese from defeat at the hands of the Mongols twice. The Japanese saw it as divine intervention." Meredith shuddered once, then went on, "Then in homage to that, in World War II the Japanese pilots who flew their airplanes into our ships were known as the *Shimpu* force, not kamikazes. Kamikaze was an American term. Those men were supposedly divinely chosen to provide victory for Japan. Now I bet Mizuzawa thinks it is Providence that he can hold us hostage with a nuclear device on a ship."

They remained silent for a moment, letting the gravity of the situation settle over them, like a gray haze. There was nothing worse than good news followed by bad news. The Armed Forces had finally crumbled the Japanese juggernaut on the Philippines, a quick operation really, and the president was ready to inform the world of this success.

But now a wild card floated recklessly about, somewhere, ready to deal a horrifying blow to America. Could they find it? Could they defend against it? What were the options?

"Well, the monsoon has lifted and we need to get a message to our man in the Philippines," Sewell said, then departed.

CHAPTER 55
Manila, Philippines

Prime Minister Mizuzawa held a glass of chilled sake high in the air, clinking it against General Nugama's crystal glass.

"*Banzai* Japan," Mizuzawa said, his voice muffled with an air of disappointment. He had not wanted to send the *Shimpu* on her final voyage but had gladly done so once the situation had turned for the worse. Her traditional enemies surrounded Japan, and he could either sue for peace using the *Shimpu* or let her steam right through the harbor and send a serious message to the world.

"Who could that be?" Mizuzawa asked Nugama, who shrugged his shoulders at the sound of the knock on the door.

"Your Excellency, it is Father Sierra. I wish to speak with you," Matt Garrett said, his voice softened by the thick mahogany door. "The United Nations has asked me to come and speak with you as a neutral party."

"Yes, come in, Father," Mizuzawa said, as a guard opened the door. "But what about Father Xavier?"

"He's here," Matt said as Father Xavier pushed his wheelchair through the entry. Dressed in his black suit with its standard white collar, Matt was an image of holiness. His compassionate brown eyes were set deep on his face. His skin was light brown and tan, his hands callused and rough. He hid his hurt arm by draping his black coat over the sling. The bayonet gash had grazed his side. The shot he had heard was a bullet that had killed his attacker. He was weak, but had enough for one last mission. Also, the sling hid his pistol and IV bag nicely.

"I am Father Sierra, and, of course, you know Father Xavier," Matt said. He remained in charge of the conversation from his end, speaking Japanese and not wanting words to flow through an interpreter. His voice was firm but wavered when he had to dig deep, which the Japanese language often required.

Mizuzawa nodded at Matt, who bowed his head in return. A peaceful gesture.

"The Americans have requested an audience with you, Prime Minister," Matt said.

"What could the Americans want with me, other than to kill me?" Mizuzawa said, almost laughing. "Soon, they will surely want to do that."

Matt looked at the two men as Xavier closed the door to the small office they occupied. The room was filled mostly with clerical equipment: an old computer, desk, bookcase, the two cots the men used for sleeping, and the radio equipment.

Matt scanned the room and the men. Both Mizuzawa and Nugama each had a new Nambu model 60 .38 caliber revolver holstered on his right hip. Nugama's uniform was wrinkled and dirty from days of wear, and Mizuzawa looked comfortable in his olive regalia.

The two men looked at him and Father Xavier, who *was* nervous, and took light sips from their sake.

"Gentlemen, the Americans are concerned about a nuclear weapon that they believe you may have stored on a commercial ship," Matt said. Mizuzawa dropped his glass on the floor, the fine crystal shattering cleanly into thousands of tiny pieces. The clear sake left a dark stain on the tile. After a pause, Matt continued. "While the Catholic Church recognizes your right to political asylum, we cannot harbor a terrorist. So please, if you have designs with this weapon of terror, reverse its course or I must release you," Matt said, eloquently.

"Father, mind your own business. You do what the Pope tells you, understand?" Mizuzawa said. "Where did you come from anyway? We've been dealing with Xavier and have had no problems until now."

Matt ignored the question and continued in Japanese, "The Pope wishes that you would stop the ship and turn it over to a United Nations force for boarding. The *Shimpu*, is it not?" Matt said in a stern voice. Actually, he had never contacted the Vatican but was sure that the Pope would want the ship stopped.

"Well, then, tell the Pope to mind his own business," Mizuzawa said.

"Are you refusing to reverse the course of the ship, Prime Minister?" Matt asked, clear he was not negotiating.

"There is no ship. Now leave," Mizuzawa shot back. His eyes darted between the two "Priests." "Wait a second, sir—" Nugama said, only to be cut off by Mizuzawa.

"Enough!" Mizuzawa screamed, grabbing the capped bottle of sake and cracking it over the computer's keyboard, the alcohol's clear liquid spreading over the gray frame.

There it was. Matt had been looking for an opening. He could sense that Nugama might be willing to deal, though Nugama didn't need to know just yet that he wasn't going to live. Matt slightly nudged Father Xavier in the right thigh with his right elbow as the guard took a step toward them.

"Operations, this is *Shimpu*," said a static-filled voice over the radio receiver positioned next to the computer monitor. "Thirty minutes out from target, I can see the harbor."

Sierra looked at the radio, then back at Mizuzawa, who was pacing back and forth.

"Well, Prime Minister, what are you going to do?"

Mizuzawa turned the jagged edge of the sake bottle up to his lips, drinking the remainder of the liquid from the capped bottle. The sharp glass cut his lips, causing bright red streams of blood to slide down his face. Nugama watched, his eyes darting nervously between Mizuzawa and the two priests.

Biting a chunk of the glass from the bottle, then chewing, Mizuzawa tossed the jagged glass at Matt. Mizuzawa then drew his revolver from his holster, waving it madly in his face.

"The Americans must die! They dropped bombs on Nagasaki and Hiroshima! Now, we drop bomb on Los Angeles! In 30 minutes the Japanese people will have revenge for the most heinous war crimes of all time. *Then* we will be even!" Mizuzawa shouted, spitting wads of blood and glass into Matt's face.

"I ask you one last time," Matt said, calmly, his stoic countenance showing no sign of fear. "Are you going to stop the ship?"

"You idiot! Can't you see this is our destiny?! Soon my generation will go the way of the *Shimpu*. We will all be gone, taking with us the memories of the horror of Nagasaki and Hiroshima. If we do not act now, revenge will never be achieved. The West will have triumphed over the East, an unforgivable sin. I would have you tell the Americans 'no,' but now I must kill you both. I have told you too much already," Mizuzawa said, red spit bubbles forming at the corner of his mouth. He angled the revolver toward Matt's face.

"Prime Minister, you underestimate me. I will tell the Americans nothing," Matt said, his voice like granite.

"I wish I could trust you, but you both are useless to me now."

Matt looked at Nugama, who had turned away, awaiting the blast. He thought he saw a tear streaming down Nugama's cheek, which was a good sign.

Matt's sling angled slightly and his pistol coughed twice, killing the intended target, the prime minister.

"Either you turn that ship around, or you're next," Matt said. Father Xavier's Glock was dangerously close to Nugama's temple.

Matt's Glock was wafting smoke from the bore and still aimed at the dying prime minister.

Nugama picked up the radio handset and said, "*Shimpu,* this is operations center. Reverse course. The worthless Americans have met our demands. Your mission is complete."

After a few clarifications and assurances back and forth over the radio, Admiral Sazaku said, "Roger, *Shimpu* turning now. Congratulations.'

Father Xavier held his pistol level with Nugama's face, then backed away from the Japanese general, nodding at the man's revolver.

Matt saw Nugama reach for his own revolver and Father Xavier let him finish the move. Nugama's hand slid slowly up his side, and he turned the weapon against his temple, pulling the trigger. The bullet bored through his brain, squeezed out the other side, and tumbled harmlessly onto Mizuzawa's body.

Nugama slumped to the floor, draped across Mizuzawa's legs, their bodies forming an X on the concrete.

"Fathers" Sierra and Xavier pulled the starched collars from their black shirts and tossed them on the desk. Xavier wheeled Matt into the hot Philippine sun. Matt removed the brown contact lenses and chucked them aside also. Strapping, combat-ready Marines opened the tall iron gate surrounding the chapel grounds and carried him onto the hospital litter, which they placed in the UH-60 helicopter for immediate evacuation back to the *Mercy.*

"Sir, you okay?" the security detail leader asked.

"Fine. Get me back to the hospital ship."

The Marines snapped to attention and saluted the wounded warrior and his partner as the Black Hawk departed.

CHAPTER 56
Greene County, Virginia

Meredith watched Karen collapse when she heard the news. This time, the green sedan did not carry her, Meredith; rather, it bore the grim reaper.

"Your brother is dead, ma'am. Killed in action. Performed magnificently. Made a difference. Made history." Even in Meredith's mind she only heard broken sentences, or so it seemed, as Karen had collapsed on the wooden porch.

Meredith had lifted her, though, holding her up with her strong arms. "Be strong, Karen," Meredith had said. And so she was.

Reverend Early spoke that day, standing next to the fresh-tilled dirt next to their mother's grave in the shadows of the Blue Ridge. The new hole would receive Karen's brother, and Meredith couldn't fathom the pain she felt, though she burned with sadness as well. There had been no other news, except a report that a civilian had died from a gunshot wound to the stomach. She would pray and be strong though. She would try to believe that the other brother was still alive. Like walking against a gale-force wind, she would force herself to go against the intelligence reports she had heard.

Meredith sat next to Karen in the cold metal chair on the cool spring morning. The fog had only recently lifted, replaced by the smell of fresh-cut hay. The old brick house was perched above them on the hill across from the barn where the horses and cows wandered, oblivious to all of the pain endured in the Garrett household during the past month.

There was more pain to follow. There always was.

Matt and Zachary's father sat on the other side of Karen, and they all peered into the deep hole that would receive their loved one.

They couldn't help it, Meredith and Karen. They cried openly, unembarrassed, with the 100 or so well-wishers standing behind them and paying their last respects to Stanardsville's fallen hero.

"He died in the fury of combat, protecting the world from a heinous enemy. Through his personal efforts and his sacrifice, the world is truly a safer place," Reverend Early said. He spoke eloquently, as all preachers seem to do. He was emphatic at just the right moment and soft-spoken when necessary. His words soothed and at least tried to heal some of the pain.

Meredith watched and couldn't help but think of when she had first met Matt in Palau. She looked away, seeing the angular wings of a dove dart back and forth along the tree line near the stream. A rabbit hopped into a hole near the barn, and the wind churned lightly atop the trees. She felt the Blue Ridge to her back, strong and powerful, full of grace. Yes, amazing grace.

She stood as the gathering began singing "Amazing Grace."

"Amazing grace, how sweet the sound, that saved a wretch like me. I once was lost but now am found..."

The DC-9 Nightingale had landed at Andrews Air Force Base in Maryland less than 15 miles from Washington over three hours ago.

The government car sped down Route 29 until it reached the small town of Ruckersville, then turned right onto a county-maintained road. Passing an outlet store, then Shifflett Exxon, the car sped past a Greene County police officer who did not bother to pursue. The trees and split-rail fences that cordoned the road whipped past. The Blue Ridge stared down upon him from the west, almost seeming to smile. The rolling hills and gradual peaks adorned with trees and shrub and grass opened their arms wide, welcoming him home. It gave him a good feeling, a sense of connection. He remembered the area well, and was glad that he could visit once again.

The car turned off the paved road and dipped once to the right as it crossed the cattle guard, then found purchase in the gravel and hardstand that was the road.

The passenger could see the brick house and he felt secure. Just being on the property, the land, was enough to make him want to stop the driver and let him walk and feel the red clay beneath his feet. If only he *could* walk.

The car stopped in a circular area just outside the wooden porch, and the driver opened the door so that he could give assistance.

"Once was blind, but now can see!"

Meredith looked down, then over her shoulder at the Blue Ridge, rising above her like a strong man but emanating the seductiveness and lure of a beautiful woman. The mountains gave her strength. She knew she could be strong. She had endured.

She looked at Karen, who was also peering over her shoulder, having stopped singing as well. Beyond the throng of well-wishers, their mouths all moving in synch, they could see the source of their strength. Something so beautiful had to develop the character of its people.

A special breed.

They both turned and looked at each other, Meredith's blond hair lying softly on her black dress, Karen's reddish brown hair equally beautiful in its unfamiliar position fanned across her shoulders. Their eyes connected, passing a knowing sign that they would forever endure the tragedies of the past that had created an indelible link between them. Life would go on. It always did.

Meredith looked back at the coffin sitting ominously next to the rectangular hole as she felt the wind brush her face and thought she could feel Matt's presence.

The man used crutches to assist his movement to the graveyard, the rubber tips collecting, then kicking out, red clay. Near the back of the group, he heard one woman gasp.

The singing slowed, then stopped, as the man made his way to the front of the group and placed his hands on the shoulders of the blond-haired woman.

Meredith felt the wind kick at her face again, bringing a smile to her lips. Suddenly, the chorus of "Amazing Grace" grew louder, echoing distinctly through the valley below, then resonating loudly back to the Blue Ridge. It was a proud sound, a comforting one.

Then there were the comforting hands of a well-wisher upon her back. She reached and touched both hands lightly, patting them to say "thank you." Odd, though, that both hands were bandaged.

Why would Preacher Early be smiling so much, singing so loud?

Meredith thought she heard a familiar voice say, "How's my Virginian?"

There he was. Matt Garrett, flesh and blood. Scars and healing wounds ran across his face, white gauze covered his hands, and he looked *tired.*

The singing stopped at the very moment Meredith placed both her hands to her mouth, holding back the tears and the joy and the frustration and the sadness and the happiness. Her emotions tumbled through her body, coursed through her mind, causing her to shake and stretch her hands outward, seemingly unsure of what to do.

Matt managed a weak smile and laid his chin on her shoulder as he grabbed Karen and his father, who were by then standing and holding on to him.

Karen grabbed the back of his hair and held him tightly, saying, "My God, you're back. Thank you." They all held on to Matt's bandaged torso tightly, squeezing so hard it hurt him, but it didn't matter. Then Riley Dwyer, Zachary's girlfriend, was joining the group. And there was Blake

Sessoms, Matt's childhood friend, smiling, his ponytail shaking as he cried and joined the growing throng.

Matt hugged them all, looked over the shoulders and heads burrowed into his strong chest and stared into his brother's grave, weeping. Out of the corner of his misty eyes he noticed a young girl, maybe 14, standing away from the group, near the fence, with her arms crossed, staring at the mountains. Amanda: Zach's daughter.

His father turned his head, looked at Zachary's grave, and said to his God, "My boys are home. Thank you."

CHAPTER 57
Pentagon, Washington, DC

It had been all Matt could do to heal and survive. Being pulled off the hospital ship *Mercy* that was by now situated somewhere in the Persian Gulf to play the wheelchair-bound role of Father Sierra, had been challenging.

He had heard about the big battle at Fort Magsaysay, and a Special Forces general named Rampert had flown to the *Mercy* to give him the news about Zachary's death on the battlefield.

"Nothing left to view, son," Rampert had said.

Matt had looked at the general's chiseled features and buzzed hair. Notably his eyes looked away when he mentioned Zachary.

"How do we know it's him?" Matt had asked.

"It's him," Rampert said.

That verdict from a general had allowed Matt to push adrenaline through his body sufficiently to subdue the pain for one last mission. Later, though, he did question why a special forces general had notified him about Zachary's death.

There was never any doubt that he would perform the *mission*, Matt knew. But the only way to do it was in tandem with Macrini as Father Xavier and Matt as the feeble priest. While the doctors had all said no to the mission, all Matt had to do was think of Zach, and he said, "Yes— make it work."

A full week after Zachary's funeral and a debriefing from Meredith on the Rolling Stones, Matt thought he had pieced it together.

Stone and his cronies were fanning the flames of insurgency in an awkward move to derail the building momentum to fight in Iraq. *Create a war to stop a war?* He thought about Iran-Contra and wondered what this would be called?

But when young men and women were putting their lives on the line, Matt believed, the academic theories of amateur political appointees were best rejected and left in the rough drafts of the professors' dissertations and class notes. *Where and why you went to war mattered,* Matt thought. *Intelligence is central to the whole discussion. And we damn sure didn't need to manufacture a war in the Philippines.* That thought had dropped another tumbler into place on figuring out the true identity of Ronnie Wood.

Every time I'm close, I'm moved.

Matt walked through the E-ring of the Pentagon and passed a man who looked the other way as they approached one another. Matt immediately recognized him as a journalist for the *Washington Post.* The gouge on him was that he was shady at best and dishonest, even up for grabs, at worst. Matt strode confidently past the man and now the final tumbler of the lock fell into place in his mind. He had solved the mystery.

Energized, he stopped in front of Latisha's desk directly outside of Secretary Stone's office.

"You're up next, Mr. Garrett." Latisha smiled.

"Thank you."

Matt was dressed in his usual garb: olive cargo pants, basic tan button-down cotton shirt, and dark windbreaker. His arm was out of the sling and he could walk with minimal pain.

"Matt, come in," Stone said.

Matt followed Stone into his office and sat on a blue leather sofa. In front of him was a small coffee table with an assortment of magazines and newspapers that were current but unread.

"How can I help you?"

Matt tossed the manila folder on the table. "Read it. Then we'll talk."

He watched Stone pick up the file and skim through the pages. Matt had to hand it to Stone; the man's expression never changed. But he guessed that anyone who could pull off the kind of charade that Stone had must have the deadened sense of morality that allowed him to appear unfazed by shocking information. Stone closed the folder and placed it back on the table.

"Okay," Stone said.

"All of this was some game?" Matt asked.

"Everything has its purposes, yes," Stone said.

"Do the people who die matter?"

"Everyone dies eventually, Matt," Stone said.

Matt stiffened and said, "Your compassion is overwhelming."

"You're not here to discuss my compassion. I agreed to see you based upon what you've been through. What we put you through. You know about everything now, and I would ask that you keep confidential your knowledge of Ronnie Wood."

"Why?" Matt asked. He leaned back into the sofa, curious.

"I'll appeal to your sense of patriotism. This is a great country, and we need to avoid further embarrassment."

"I could argue that exposing Mr. Wood would help us greatly in that regard."

"Perhaps, but the short-term pain might be debilitating. We're in a very vulnerable place right now."

"He's just another bureaucrat, but I'll think about it," Matt offered.

"Speaking of vulnerabilities, have you heard about the tragic deaths of my deputy Saul Fox and Dick Diamond?"

"Not even sure I know who they are," Matt said, staring directly into Stone's liquid eyes.

Stone seemed to consider his comment and nodded.

"Yes. You're CIA, and a field agent at that. There would be no reason for you to know them."

"No reason," Matt replied. "But there is this."

He pulled a small tape recorder out of his windbreaker pocket and placed it on the table as he punched the PLAY button:

"This was all so very exciting. So close to Armageddon in Los Angeles..."

Matt let the recording play where the two men disclosed all the bits of the conspiracy to include Stone's participation, albeit coerced.

Stone's hand reached out for the tape, and Matt used his good arm to strike like a cobra against Stone's wrist, grabbing it and squeezing it in a viselike grip. He leveled his eyes on Stone and began to speak.

"Scumbags like you think you can live in your little soundproof world so that nothing circles back on you. I look at it differently. I'm thinking that maybe you and Ronnie Wood will have a similar fight over these matters? Perhaps go the way of Fox and Diamond?"

Matt squeezed Stone's arm so tight he thought he might snap the bone. Stone's eyes fluttered either at the hint that Matt had something to do with the deaths of Fox and Diamond or the fact that Matt's palpable desire for revenge transmitted from Matt through Stone's wrist like an electrical current.

"You send anyone after me and I will know about it, Stone," he said, his voice like granite. "And I will personally come to your little cottage in Orange County. I might be hiding behind the fireplace or perhaps in that nice refinished kitchen. Who knows? Or maybe I'll be at your McLean mansion, where you tried to rape Meredith. But I'll be somewhere. So be smart. And being smart includes calling that slimy reporter you just told to out me and hang the bullshit failures on my back. I know how your type operates. Call him right now," Matt demanded.

"Now?"

"Rathburn was a meticulous record keeper. I've got your E*Trade account that shows you made a fortune shorting stock before 9-11. Now what are you going to do? Think about it because you've got a lot riding on this one."

Stone stared at him for a moment, then looked away toward the window.

"I understand," Stone said. He picked up the phone and dialed a number. Shortly someone answered and Stone said, "Call it off." There must have been a protest because Stone shouted into the phone, "I said call it off, or you're dead, are we clear?"

"Are we clear?" Matt asked.

In the end, Matt knew there was nothing he could do to Stone that wouldn't violate his principles or the law, but he would leave the tape behind as a tangible reminder to Stone of his influence.

And on that thought his mind spun to the night before.

Matt had watched Diamond and Fox from behind the thick curtains in the bedroom. He had lined up the iron sights of his pistol on each of their foreheads with his good arm. He had a steady aim on Fox, then he would move to Diamond, and back to Fox.

When the moment came to pull the trigger, Zachary's face flashed in front of him, saying, "Don't do it. It's not worth it."

As he looked back up, though, he saw the glint of steel in Fox's hand and a pistol in Diamond's.

"What's this letter, Dick?" Saul Fox asked angrily, shaking the white paper at his lover as he walked from the study into the bedroom. His voice raged above Diamond's favorite opera: Puccini's "Nessun Dorma" ... *None will know my name!*

"It's not mine, Saul. It's a plant," Diamond countered, holding up his hands as if to surrender.

The two men were naked except for their underwear. Both men had paunches that overlapped beyond the waistbands of the briefs. *Disgusting and comical at the same time,* Matt thought.

Of course, Matt had planted the letter and the dossier in Fox's study once he'd learned of the Rolling Stones and thought of Dick Diamond's role as Ronnie. Though he knew Ronnie was merely a cutout for a far-more-powerful person, as he had found a different picture beneath Diamond's in the file Meredith had opened. It had been password-protected, and nothing could have prepared him for the image staring back at him.

Still, he couldn't let Diamond or Fox get away with their crimes. Matt knew that, assuredly, the protective cocoon of the political-appointee bureaucracy would shield them from any accountability. Still, Matt had shaken his head at the internecine politics where there were double agents within cliques and power groups inside the Beltway. He figured his ploy might work.

But what did that make him, he wondered?

"And what's this?" Fox screamed. "You're Ronnie? You're a member of the Rolling Stones? You've been double-crossing me? I knew it, you bastard!"

Matt saw him hold the knife the way an orchestra conductor might hold an Uzi. *This should be interesting,* Matt thought.

"I'm not Ronnie!" Diamond proclaimed.

Matt was surprised to see how quickly Fox leapt toward Diamond, brandishing the knife as he shouted, "Double-crossing bastard."

This was as much a lovers' quarrel as it was a dispute about who was supporting which conspiracy. It hadn't hurt that Matt's sister Karen had transposed a photo of Diamond and Stone appearing intimate in conversation.

As Matt had watched Diamond respond, he thought, *Never bring a knife to a gunfight.* He didn't even wince as Diamond's pistol kicked back the moment Fox's knife entered his heart. The bullet from Diamond's gun caught Fox in the middle of the forehead, killing him instantly. The knife in Diamond's heart let him live long enough to say, "But I know who Ronnie really is…"

Matt had closed his eyes and lowered his head. Covering his tracks from Fox's apartment, he stole silently through the night in his old Porsche 944 and did not stop until he reached his home in Loudoun County.

"Yes," Stone said. "Yes, we have an agreement."

Stone's words brought him back to the present. He released the man's wrist, which Stone snatched back.

When Matt departed Stone's office, he put the Pentagon in his rearview mirror and the memories of last night in the recesses of his mind as he drove along the George Washington Parkway to Langley. His thoughts turned to Zachary and the daughter who would never get to know her father now…and the brother he would never see again.

When he arrived at Langley, he walked onto the giant seal of the Central Intelligence Agency in the headquarters building and he blew past the security desk, only to be stopped by two large men in gray suits. One of them was the deputy director, Roger Houghton. They had seen him coming, or perhaps someone had been following him. Either way, Houghton was prepared for him.

"Don't do it, Matt," Houghton said.

"Lantini. Where's Lantini?"

"Gone. Nobody can find him. Now go home and rest."

"I won't rest until he's dead," Matt said. Good operators always relied upon two sources, as opposed to one, to confirm intelligence. In this case Matt had three.

Matt had always wondered why he had received the text to keep his 'feet and knees together' before Peterson's airplane was even shot down. Once he discovered CIA Director Lantini's role as Ronnie Wood by Lantini's photo in the file, hidden by the ruse of Diamond's picture, Matt had developed a plausible theory. Now, the fact that Lantini had fled the country served as confirmation to Matt that the CIA director had conspired with Stone and the others.

Every time I'm close, I'm moved.

Matt's 944 Porsche boiled smoke from the burning tires as he sped out of CIA headquarters and back onto the George Washington Parkway.

He stopped at an isolated scenic overlook, gazed across the Potomac, and leaned over the rock wall. Lifting his head, tears running down his cheeks, he shouted, "Zachary!"

EPILOGUE

A week later Matt stood by himself on a large rock that protruded above the South River at the north end of the 150 acres he called home in Stanardsville, Virginia. He had pushed his rehab a bit too hard, and an admonishing doctor had promised him she would order him to bed rest if he didn't wear the sling. So with one arm back in a sling, with his good arm he flung flat pebbles across the bubbling water giving no evidence of the shortstop he had once been.

Just a few short weeks ago he had been in the Philippines chasing Predators and finding Japanese troops and ships. The text he had sent from his Blackberry on that incident had cued Meredith to convince the National Security Advisor to have the ship interdicted. It turned out that all of his reports had either been received by Rathburn or Lantini, and discarded. Thankfully, the United States Navy had corralled the rogue vessel with a carrier battle group, F-18s circled the sky like buzzards spying road kill. The SEALs had boarded the *Shimpu* and found the skipper on the floor of the captain's ward with a fresh bullet wound in his head.

He skipped another stone upstream, the current causing the stone to flip wildly. Not a good toss. Each time he tried to throw, the stitches in his abdomen screamed at him, pulling at healing skin.

Would the wounds that mattered ever heal?

Zachary was dead, and he wondered if he would ever be able to accept that fact. Life was never what it seemed, he understood, but the unfairness of his brother's death in that remote corner of the world might weigh on him forever. At least he hoped so. Zachary was too great a man simply to be gone. His contributions were too substantial just to be forgotten. No, Matt *would* earn Zachary's sacrifice. Once healed, he would be back in the field taking the fight to the enemy. In the meantime, he would continue in his capacity as a special advisor to the new director of the CIA…until his physical wounds healed.

He would go back to Afghanistan or Iraq and fight there. That was his mission.

On that thought, he wondered exactly what was happening in the world. How could Diamond and Fox be so manipulative and callous? How could Stone not see what they were doing? How could Lantini betray him and call off his shot in Pakistan?

What was in store for the world? Nine-eleven, Islamic fundamentalism, and rogue nationalism were supposedly exploiting the seams of a fractured universe. But what was real and what was manufactured?

The ivory-tower conspiracies of the elite clouded the true heroism of the young men and women fighting so hard, who, in the eyes of the likes of Fox and Diamond, were truly nothing but cannon fodder.

He turned, carefully stepping along the rock, placing the stream to his back.

"Hi, handsome," Meredith said. She was standing on the bank, her arms crossed, perhaps warding off the spring chill. She was wearing a dark blue Northface jacket over lighter jeans. Her hiking boots were crossed one over the other as she leaned against a small poplar tree, growing hopeful and new in the large forest. Matt nodded at her and stepped off the rock. He approached Meredith and took her in his good arm without saying a word.

"It's okay," she whispered, hugging him back.

Matt rested his head on her hair, the sling causing his arm to press awkwardly between them as he looked west into the churning river and the mountains that delivered it.

"Don't leave me," he caught himself saying. Why, he wasn't sure. Maybe with Zachary's loss he needed to fill the empty space quickly. Perhaps it would be less painful that way.

"I'm not going anywhere you're not going," she said softly.

He pulled away and kissed her on the lips, then said, "I refuse to believe he's dead."

Matt's words of disbelief floated like an autumn leaf into the wind, fluttered up the hill toward the house, circled the fresh-tilled grave, and bolted skyward toward the heavens.

From the author of SUDDEN THREAT and HIDDEN THREAT

One year ago, Captain Jake Mahegan led a Delta Force team into Afghanistan to capture an American traitor working for the Taliban. The mission ended in tragedy, his team infiltrated and decimated by a bomb. After killing an enemy prisoner, Mahegan was dismissed from service—dishonored. Now, back in the United States and haunted by the incident, Mahegan is determined to avenge the loss of his comrades. The military wants him to stand down. But when the turncoat who calls himself the American Taliban returns to domestic soil—leading an army of ghost prisoners—Mahegan is the only man who knows how to stop him.

Outside the law. Under the radar. Out for vengeance...

FOREIGN AND DOMESTIC
By
A. J. Tata

Want to read A.J. Tata's National Bestselling Thriller,

Foreign and Domestic

TURN THE PAGE FOR AN EXCITING PREVIEW!

Military Oath of Enlistment:

I do solemnly swear that I will support and defend the Constitution of the United States against all enemies, **foreign and domestic**.

PROLOGUE

September 2014, Nuristan Province, Afghanistan

The generals had labeled the mission: "Kill or Capture."

Though Captain Jake Mahegan refused to consider anything but capturing the target.

With one-hundred mph winds whipping across Mahegan's face, he was running through the checklist in his mind: insert, infiltrate, overwatch, assault, capture, collect, and extract.

Mahegan knew his men were fatigued from days of continuous operations. They couldn't afford any mistakes this morning. He felt the mix of emotions that came with knowing they were close to snaring the biggest prize since Bin Laden: The American Taliban, the one man who had posed the gravest threat to United States security since Army aviators and Navy SEALs had killed Osama. Concern for his troops gnawed at the adrenaline-honed edges of excitement. Mission focus was tempered with empathy for his men.

This morning's target was a bomb maker and security expert named Commander Hoxha, who would lead them to The American Taliban.

Mahegan and what remained of his unit were flying in on the wing seats of MH-6 Little Bird aircraft to raid Hoxha's compound. Doubling as both expert bomb maker and the primary protection arm for The American Taliban, Hoxha had weathered wars in the Balkans, Iraq, and Afghanistan. Mahegan's review of Hoxha's dossier told him this could be the toughest mission he'd ever faced.

No mistakes.

The generals gave Mahegan this mission because they were on a timeline for withdrawal and he was the best. From the start of his special operations career, his Delta Force peers had called him, "The Million Dollar Man." The other twenty-nine of the thirty candidates in his Delta selection class had washed out. Each selection session cost the Army one million dollars.

For a year, Mahegan's outfit was casualty-free with impressive scalp counts of sixty-nine Taliban and al-Qaeda commanders. The better and more consistently he'd performed, the more Mahegan's legend had begun to take on mythical status within the military.

But that had mysteriously changed two months ago. A twenty-man unit had been whittled to eleven men over the past eight weeks during which they had conducted twenty-two missions. The pace had been relentless and Mahegan knew his team was sucking gas.

The brass, however, had insisted on this early morning mission. They had told him that the President wanted The American Taliban captured before the final troops withdrew. His senior officers directed him to press ahead based on what they called "actionable intelligence." Translated to Mahegan and his men: They were on their third night with no sleep as they kept pressure on the enemy like a football team blitzing on every play with the added threat that their lives were at stake.

In the two helicopters, Mahegan's team whipped through canyons so tight the rotor blades appeared to be sparking off the granite spires of the Hindu Kush Mountains. Through his night-vision goggles, Mahegan could see the static electricity produced by the rotors painting a glowing trail, like a time-lapse photo. The helicopters, called Little Birds, were nothing more than a light wind through the valleys. Two canvas bench seats on either side were supporting him and his three teammates with a similarly configured one in trail.

As a backup extraction plan, Mahegan had his protégé, Sergeant Wesley Colgate, leading a two-vehicle convoy from the ground a couple of miles away. The lead vehicle carried Colgate and two more of their Delta Force teammates. In the trailing Humvee was a contract document and detainee exploitation team, known as Docex, from private military contractor Copperhead, Inc. Mahegan had fought Copperhead's inclusion, but the generals had insisted.

The Task Force 160th pilots skillfully flared the aircraft and touched down into the landing zone at a twenty-degree angle like dragonflies alighting on grass blades.

"Blue," Mahegan said into the mouthpiece connected to a satellite radio on his back, giving the code word for a successful offload in the landing zone. He expected no reply, and received none, as they were minimizing radio communications. The two helicopters lifted quietly out of the valley and returned to the base camp several miles away in Asadabad.

It was nearly 0400, about three hours before sunrise. As always, on every single mission it seemed, the fog settled into the valley as if the helicopters had it in tow. He considered Colgate and his two vehicles a few miles away. Moving quickly through the rocky landing zone, Mahegan found the path to their target area.

"Red," he said, as they passed the ridge to be used by the support team. He watched through his night-vision goggles as Tony "Al" Pucino and his three warriors from the trail helicopter silently chose their support-by-fire positions.

Moving toward the objective, Mahegan noted the jagged terrain and ran the remainder of the checklist through his mind: assault, capture, collect, and extract. Eyeing the darkened trail above the Kunar River a half mile to the west, he paused. His instincts were telling him it would be better to walk away from this objective than to have Colgate risk the bomb-laden path to the terrorists' compound.

Registering that thought, Mahegan knelt and adjusted his night-vision goggles. He spotted the enemy security forces milling around. They were not alert. To Mahegan, they looked like a bunch of green-shaded sleepy avatars. The offset landing zone had kept their infiltration undetected. They were good to go.

Mahegan gave the signal; they had rehearsed the assault briefly in the compound a few hours ago. From over fifty meters away, he put his silenced M4 carbine's infrared laser on the forehead of the guard nearest the door, pulsed it twice, which was the cue to the rest of the team, and then drilled him through the skull. He heard the muffled coughs of his teammates' weapons and saw the other guards fall to the ground, like marionettes with cut strings. Motioning to his assault team, he led them along a defile that emptied directly into the back gate of Commander Hoxha's adobe compound. With a shove of his massive frame against the wooden back door of the open compound, Mahegan breached the back wall just as the target was yanking his tactical vest up around his shoulders and reaching for his AK-74. Mahegan knew questioning Hoxha was key to the ultimate mission, so he shot him in the thigh, being careful to miss the femoral artery. Hoxha fell in the middle of the open courtyard between the gate and the back door. Several goats bleated and ran, bells around their necks clanging loudly.

"Target down," he said. "Status."

"Team One good," Pucino reported.

"Move to the objective. Help with SSE," Mahegan directed to Pucino. Not only had they come to capture Hoxha, but Sensitive Site Exploitation usually garnered the most valuable intelligence through analysis of SIM cards, computer hard drives, and maps.

He led the assault team into the courtyard and Patch, one of his tobacco-chewing teammates from Austin, Texas, strapped the terrorist's hands behind his back using plastic flex-cuffs. Two more men were already making a sweep through the compound, stuffing kit bags full of cell phones, computer hard drives, and generally anything that might be used to kill American forces or provide a clue as to The American Taliban's location. Mahegan's agenda included searching for something called an MVX-90, a top-secret American-made transmitter-receiver he believed had fallen into enemy possession.

Mahegan pulled out a picture and a red lens flashlight to confirm he'd shot the right man. He felt no particular emotion, but simply checked another box when he confirmed they indeed had Commander Hoxha, the leader of The American Taliban's security ring.

With the fog crawling into the narrow canyons, Mahegan confirmed his instinct to call off the Little Birds and Colgate's team. They were walking out.

With the terrorist flex-cuffed in front of him and the place smelling like burned goat shit, he radioed Colgate, "We are coming to you. Do not move. Acknowledge, over."

"Roger." He recognized Colgate's voice.

On the heels of Colgate's reply, Pucino radioed, "Team One at checkpoint alpha." This was good news to Mahegan. Pucino's team had completed their portion of the sensitive site exploitation and was now securing the road that provided for their egress toward Colgate's vehicles.

Mahegan checked off in his mind the myriad tasks to come. They were in the intelligence collection phase. He entered the adobe hut, saw his men zipping their kit bags, and then moved outside where Patch was guarding Hoxha.

He heard Hoxha speaking in Pashtun at about the same time he noticed a small light shining through the white pocket of his *payraan tumbaan*, the outer garment.

Mahegan thought, *Cell phone.*

He also thought, *Voice command.* Like an iPhone Siri.

"Patch, shut him up!"

He went for the cell phone in the outer garment, while Patch stuffed a rag in the prisoner's mouth, tying it off behind his head. Fumbling with the pockets, Mahegan grabbed the smartphone, but saw the device had made a call.

His first thought was that the adobe hut was rigged with explosives. He pushed the end button to stop the call and wondered if he had prevented whatever the phone was supposed to trigger. He smashed the phone into a nearby rock, knowing the SIM card would likely be undamaged and still valuable.

"Everyone inside, get out of the house! All outside, get down! Now!" he said to his men in a hoarse whisper. Mahegan landed on top of the bomb maker, crushing him beneath his 6'4", 230-pound frame. He saw Patch and two others digging into the dirt, wondering. Patch silently mouthed the letters, "WTF?"

A few seconds later, he heard an explosion beneath the house as the rest of his team came pouring out of the back door.

"There was a tunnel. Put a thermite in it," Sergeant O'Malley, from southeast Chicago, said.

"Roger," Mahegan replied. A thermite grenade would have only stunned anyone in the tunnel, but Mahegan didn't want to risk going back inside. Two minutes passed with no further activity.

Mahegan stood, pocketed the crushed smartphone, lifted the terrorist onto his back, and said to his team, "Follow me."

Colgate

About ten minutes before Mahegan said, "We are coming to you," Colgate was getting eager. He inched his way forward from the rally point along the raging waters of the Kunar River, assuming the worst when he noticed the weather would most likely prevent aircraft from conducting the extraction.

Colgate kept easing forward, pulling the contractors along behind him. The trail they were on was rocky, filled with potholes. It made the Rubicon Trail look like the Autobahn. His gloved hands gripped the steering wheel, sensing the tires on the Ground Mobility Vehicle pushing dirt into the raging waters fifty meters below as he crept toward his mentor.

He and Chayton Mahegan had been together in combat for two years now. To Colgate, Mahegan was a brave warrior, a throwback to his Native American heritage. Chayton and Mahegan were Iroquois names for "falcon" and "wolf," and Colgate had no doubt Mahegan possessed the ferocity of both predators.

He was proud to be one of Mahegan's Quiet Professionals. Colgate adhered to his boss's motto: "Keep your mouth shut and let your actions do the talking." After two months as Ranger buddies and then being one class apart in Delta selection, Colgate and Mahegan had bonded. Combat had made them closer, like brothers.

Colgate was a big man, a former college running back for Norfolk State University. He had almost made the big time. As a walk-on for the Washington Redskins, he had been cut the last day and enlisted a few hour later. After basic training, he was assigned to the Rangers and graduated Ranger school with Mahegan as his Ranger buddy. They got the same Ranger tab tattoo on their left shoulders and Colgate later made sergeant.

Now, Colgate flexed his left arm, thinking about the Ranger tab tattoo. He inched the vehicles closer. Not all the way, but closer, expecting the call. He was Plan B. Then Mahegan called: "We are coming to you. Do not move. Acknowledge, over."

"Roger," Colgate replied. But on the single lane dirt road with a drop to the violent river beside him, he couldn't turn around. He was committed. He had to continue.

He heard a dull thud in the distance, like a grenade, and stopped momentarily. But he had to find somewhere to turn around, so he continued toward the objective. He leaned forward straining to see through his own goggles.

His gunner was getting nervous. "Colgate, I can't see jack, buddy," he said through the VIC-5 internal communications radio set. "No place to turn around. We better hold up."

But Colgate had state-of-the-art jammers that could detect buried mines and roadside bombs better than cats could find mice. He had passive finders and active jammers. He had a heads-up display and wide-angle night vision that made it seem he was watching high-definition TV as he drove. He could see thermal out to thirty meters in front of his vehicle and he was scanning every radio frequency every second with a jammer so powerful he figured they were sterilizing the men in every village they passed. To Colgate, this vehicle was like the Terminator on steroids. He was good to go and so he kept going. Besides, he couldn't even Y-turn where they were without tumbling into the river. He considered calling Mahegan to tell him he had already committed, but knew his friend was busy.

Then he heard Holmesly say, "Hey, man, big ass rock pile in the road!"

Never a good sign, the rock pile loomed large in the HD viewer. Colgate slowed his vehicle and noticed through his goggles that they had crossed an infrared beam. He knew it was too late and muttered, "Oh shit."

Then he heard his radio come to life. It was Mahegan's voice. "Colgate–"

Mahegan

As Mahegan led his team single file down the road away from the village they had just raided, he stopped. He heard the GMVs moving not too far away, which was not good, not part of the plan.

He pressed his radio transmit button and said, "Colgate–"

A fireball erupted through the night mist. The billowing flame hung in the distance, a demonic mask sneering at Mahegan and his men. Shrapnel sizzled through the air with a torturous wail. Mahegan felt the pain of burning metal embedded into his left deltoid.

The shockwave knocked all eight of them down, plus the terrorist Mahegan was carrying. Hoxha, bound and gagged, was getting up to one knee. The fireball had momentarily destroyed Mahegan's night vision, but he could see enough that the prisoner was standing, squaring off with him. Mahegan calculated Hoxha's options. Run toward the wreckage? Jump into the river rapids with hands bound? Scale the cliffs to the east? Or move back toward his compound?

The fireball receded but still flickered brightly about one hundred meters away. The shadows of the jagged rocks were black ghosts dancing in ritual celebration of more foreign blood spilled in this impossible land.

Mahegan ignored the burning and bleeding in his left deltoid as he fumbled for the weapon hanging from a D-ring on his outer tactical vest. A secondary explosion sent another fireball into the sky, probably the ammunition from Colgate's GMV, he thought. The second blast gave the terrorist more time, but Mahegan still had him in his field of vision. Instead of choosing the three options away from him, Hoxha ran directly at him.

Hoxha faked one way as if he were a football running back and then attempted to get past Mahegan. Mahegan thought about Colgate and the casualties his team had suffered over the last two months. Then a flywheel broke free in his mind.

"Impulsive and aggressive," the Delta Force psychiatrist had said.

Mahegan figured, this time, the man was correct.

He cocked his elbow with his right hand on the telescoping stock of his M4 carbine and his left hand on the hand guard and weapon's accessory rail. He stepped forward with his left foot and propelled the leading edge of the butt-stock forward toward the terrorist's torso. He rotated his upper body and extended his right arm, locking his right elbow as he connected with Hoxha. His aim was high, or Hoxha ducked, and the weapon caught him across the face. The claw of the butt-stock connected with the man's temple. Hoxha crumbled to the ground, dead.

Mahegan saw the flesh and brain matter hanging off the end of his weapon and knew he had unleashed mortal fury onto the prisoner. He sprinted one hundred meters to Colgate's vehicle and found what he'd suspected: burning bodies. He reached in through the fire, his own shoulder burning from the shrapnel, and pulled at Colgate. All he got was charred skin coming off in his hands. He grabbed for Colgate's upper body and wrenched him out of the GMV, placing him on the ground. Patch and O'Malley were crawling over the burnt windshield to grab Coleseed. No one could find the gunner, Holmesly.

"Search away from the vehicle. He probably got thrown into the river. We'll have to search downstream," Mahegan said. Inside, he was a raging storm. Three more of his men were dead.

Eight left.

He stared momentarily at the trail vehicle in the distance, undamaged, with its crew of Copperhead, Inc. contractors standing stunned and motionless in the eerie darkness. Turning back to the burning vehicle, he only cared about piecing back together the bits of Colgate so that he could make him whole again. He was furious. He wondered how all the jammers, scanners, and thermal equipment had failed to defeat a homemade bomb in Nuristan Province, Afghanistan. In fact, there was only one way it could have happened and Mahegan refused to believe what he suspected.

As he stood over Colgate's remains, the charred flesh and the horrific grimace seared onto his face, he asked him, "Why, buddy?"

Pucino approached and said, "I don't know why, but I do know how, boss."

Mahegan, towering over the Italian soldier from Boston, looked down at the box in Pucino's hand.

"An empty MVX-90 box. From the bomb maker's hut. Made in the Research Triangle Park of North Carolina. Several more in there, unused," Pucino said.

Mahegan internalized this information. This was the only device that could have guided an electronic trigger signal past the jammers in Colgate's vehicle. And it had come from the U.S. of A.

The raging storm that had been building inside him for two months, ever since he had lost his first soldier in combat, finally unleashed. Mahegan howled with a primal ferocity that roared through the distant canyons, the valleys echoing with his anguish. Then he turned toward the Copperhead, Inc. private military contractors and stared at them, wondering why they were on the mission at all.

CHAPTER 1

September, 2015, Roanoke Island, North Carolina

Mahegan knew he was being watched. After a year of drifting in eastern North Carolina, they had finally found him.

Which wasn't all bad.

The black Ford F-150 pickup truck had driven past his rented above-garage apartment on Roanoke Island one too many times. Mahegan had noticed the unusually clean exterior of the vehicle the first time. Here in the Outer Banks of North Carolina, a shiny, waxed truck was as obvious as a gelled playboy amongst seafaring watermen. The second and last drive-by, a day later, coupled with a slightest tap of the brakes, confirmed that either the Department of Homeland Security or the Department of Defense had located him.

He kept to his routine.

At five a.m. on a typically warm September morning, he ducked out of the Queen Anne's Revenge, a guesthouse owned by Outer Banks proprietor, Sam Midgett, and walked along Old Wharf Road of Roanoke Island. Mahegan slid around the fence that blocked the pavement a hundred meters from Croatan Sound, and found Midgett's twelve-foot duck-hunting boat. Pausing to listen to the bullfrogs and inhale the brackish odor, he shoved off through the low marshes, pushing through the reeds. A small white-tail deer darted past him, splashing through the knee-deep water. Stepping into the boat, he used the paddle to get some momentum and then he was in the deeper water of the sound, which was to the western side of the island. About one hundred meters out was an orange channel marker. He reached it, pulled a half hitch through a rusty cleat on the buoy, kicked off his mocs, and dove into the black water.

The sun was about an hour from cresting over the horizon of the Atlantic Ocean less than half a mile to his rear. He pulled with broad-shouldered strokes, the lightning bolt scar from the shrapnel of Colgate's vehicle explosion screaming with every rotation. The doctors had removed the embedded metal from just beneath his Ranger tab tattoo on his left deltoid and had told him to swim for rehab.

So he swam. Every day.

He preferred swimming this way, in the darkness. Alone, he was able to rehash the botched mission and its aftermath. And here he was also able to evade the vigilance of the Homeland Security noose that was tightening around him. He let his mind drift again, from being watched now to what had come before.

He latched on to the moment he had turned in his papers to resign his commission as a military officer. His teammates had written seven too-similar statements about how Mahegan had thwarted an escape attempt by the clever terrorist who used the bomb blast as a diversion. The Army Inspector General had balked at the carbon copy testimony of his teammates.

"What my team says is essentially true. But I let my emotions take over," he told his commander, Major General Bob Savage. "Colgate was dead. Hoxha may have given us something useful on Adham. Hoxha *did* try to escape, but he was still cuffed and gagged. I killed him. I failed. And we're no closer to Adham than before. It's that simple."

Mullah Adham was the nom de guerre of The American Taliban. Actually, Adham was an American citizen in his mid-twenties from Iowa named Adam Wilhoyt who had gone native with al-Qaeda.

General Savage nodded, trying to persuade him not to resign, but Mahegan never wavered.

"I could drive on like this never happened, but without my integrity, what do I have?" Mahegan said. Savage stared at the captain like a seasoned poker player.

"You know it was an MVX-90 that killed Colgate, Holmesly, and Coleseed. And I'm sure you have thought this, but once Hoxha was able to make that call to activate the trigger on the bomb, all you had to do was initiate a radio call to initiate the blast. Only the MVX-90, US manufactured and tested, could allow our radio signals, which operate on a very specific bandwidth, past all of the jammers that were operating."

Of course, it was all he could think about. He had technically killed his own men. In order to simultaneously jam enemy trigger signals and communicate to friendly forces, the American Army had developed the MVX-90. The device left discreet, protected gaps in the radio spectrum so that friendly communications could enter and exit while still searching for ill-intended incoming signals to block. The only way to find those gaps and know how to program a trigger device on the American frequency, Mahegan knew, was for the enemy to have an MVX-90 operating in the area. Effectively, it was like finding a programmer's backdoor into a software operating system.

A flash burst in his mind from the fateful radio call: *"Colgate—"*

Running his hand across his face, Mahegan said, "I know I killed them, sir."

After a moment, Savage responded. "Your radio did. Not you." Reacting to Mahegan's silent stare, he continued. "And whoever gave them the MVX-90."

Mahegan looked up at his commander and said, "I have an idea."

He explained as Savage listened, sometimes nodding and sometimes frowning.

"I have a different thought," Savage said.

Mahegan listened to his commanding officer, who pushed the papers toward him across the gray metal desk in Bagram Air Base. Mahegan looked down, shook his head, and pushed the papers back at his general.

"I've got to do this my way, sir," he said.

Savage nodded, saying, "You always do, Jake. But if you stay over here in the sandbox you can get your revenge for Colgate . . . and the rest of your team."

Mahegan grimaced. "You know what they say about revenge, sir."

"What?"

"It's all in the anticipation. The thing itself is a pain."

"Twain," Savage had replied. "Since we're discussing authors, then we might as well state the obvious: You can't go home again. You ought to take me up on my offer."

"I'll think about it, sir. Like I said, it's got to be done my way. And maybe there's another way to do it." Mahegan paused, and then said, "Thomas Wolfe, by the way."

"Roger. And that means you know what I'm talking about. You go back to America, especially with Homeland Security all over your ass, and nothing will look the same. You'll be blacklisted by that new moron they have running the nut farm at DHS and this list of vets she says are threats to society. You've gotten some press over this thing, too. And, Jake, General Bream, the Army Inspector General, is sniffing all around this faster than a Blue Tick Coonhound. He's an ass hamster of the highest magnitude and wants to be Army Chief of Staff. They are calling him the 'Chief of Integrity' or some such bullshit. If you go back, he will be gunning for you."

Mahegan shrugged. "Got a fair amount of that kind over here, too. I'll be okay."

"He's putting on his best indignant performance for the press. He's going for a dishonorable discharge, you know."

Actually, no. This was news to him. Bad news. He had fought with honor, risking his life for his fellow Americans and his teammates. Endless days and nights with no sleep, little food, and unspeakable danger.

"Didn't know that, sir." Mahegan looked away at the maps of Afghanistan on the plywood walls, reminders of firefights, combat parachute jumps, and helicopter raids everywhere.

"Don't sweat it for now, Jake. Cross that bridge when we get to it. Your team covered for you."

"They didn't cover for me, sir. They reported what happened."

Savage waved off Mahegan's statement and continued his sales pitch for Mahegan to stay in the Army.

"For the record, you belong here, with us, doing this," Savage said, pointing his finger at the maps. "This is your home. I took you in despite your psych evaluation, Jake. That counts for something."

Mahegan nodded, recalling how the Army psychiatrist had identified Mahegan's sometimes "impulsive, aggressive behavior," and recommended against inclusion in the elite force. Savage had stood firm and the "million-dollar man" was born. Oddly, Delta Force *had* been Mahegan's home, and he had left all that he loved.

"I just need time, sir," he told Savage. "Then, maybe I can do what you suggest."

Now, this morning, pulling hard through the black water, he wondered whether or not he should have accepted Savage's deal. The general had been right. Someone was looking for him and that General Bream was gunning for a dishonorable discharge. He tried to push the black pickup truck and the Inspector General out of his mind.

His broad shoulders and powerful legs propelled him through the sound. After a shark incident while swimming off Wilmington's fabled Frying Pan Shoals, Mahegan was determined to appear dominant in the water. He swam with purpose, as if he were the apex predator, some kind of savage beast on the prowl.

His mind drifted from Colgate to The American Taliban, Mullah Adham, to his shoulder and to Martin Strel, who owned the world record for the longest continuous swim. Before beginning his swimming rehab, he had researched the sport. Strel swam 312 miles in the Danube River in 84 hours. Mahegan did the math. He was doing 5 miles max each way. Strel had cruised at a sustained rate of 3.7 miles an hour. Mahegan was doing something less than that, but not by much. Plus, Strel had a helping current while he was going cross-current. The tide was either coming in or going out, which was always perpendicular to his axis of advance. Mahegan knew he wasn't doing the miles all at once, of course.

He swam that way for an hour and a half until, on a downward stroke, his hand hit sand, touching the small beach of the mainland of North Carolina. He pulled himself up, strode through the knee-deep water, and sat on the jutting spit of land that was the easternmost point of the Alligator River National Wildlife Refuge.

He sat about twenty meters back from the water, facing east, and watched the dawn appear over the Atlantic Ocean, Outer Banks barrier islands, and Roanoke Island. The sun cast an orange streak along the spreading vee of his swimming wake. The water rippled outward, inviting the coming day. The vee eventually disappeared, and he wondered about his life path. What was left in his wake so far? What more would there be? Would his trail simply blend back into the environment with no remaining signature?

As Mahegan stared at his diminishing path, he felt welcoming eyes surround him from behind.

He smiled. They had learned to come to him, or perhaps he to them.

The red wolves crept from their Alligator River refuge and joined Mahegan as he watched the sun and wondered about life. Mahegan had researched the terrain of Dare County Mainland, and among other valuable lessons, he learned that at one time there had been only sixteen red wolves left in the United States. The National Wildlife Refuge had tried an experimental repopulation program by placing a few of the sixteen in Alligator River National Park. Fierce hunters, the red wolves began to thrive on the abundant wildlife in the remote national park.

They traveled in family packs of adults and cubs. Mahegan turned and saw a youngster lying in some saw grass, staring at him. The pup looked more like a red fox than a wolf.

Mahegan felt a comfort here, removed from even the sparsely populated Roanoke Island. Drifting up the Outer Banks of North Carolina for a year, he had worked the odd job for a couple of weeks before moving on. He was a deckhand on a fishing boat out of Wilmington, a bouncer at a bar in Beaufort, and part of a landscaping crew in Hatteras. Remaining obscure was paramount.

But a year was enough. The one-year anniversary of his failed mission in Nuristan Province was tomorrow, and he was at the end of this particular trail.

Plus, they had found him. He needed solitude to finalize his plans. Today.

The first part of his plan, if he could call it that, was to borrow his new landlord's pickup truck, drive up to Arlington National Cemetery, and visit the gravesites of Colgate and the rest of his men who had been killed in action.

The second part was, well, complicated.

He stood and turned slowly, facing west. He counted the faces poking through the reeds and tall grass. Eight. Just like the remaining members of his team.

They seemed to be staring at his arm, where the scar that looked like a lightning bolt welt ran from his left shoulder to his elbow. Mahegan suspected that somewhere deep down in the psyches of these animals, they knew the threat to their species. Sixteen left. Just as families passed stories from generation to generation, these red wolves, Mahegan was certain, were passing the story of their near extinction to their offspring.

One of the wolves circled past him. He didn't know, but perhaps his kinship with these animals had something to do with being backed into a corner, the very essence of their being whittled to the core. Would they survive or evaporate into thin air? He closed his eyes, becoming certain of his connection with these predators. He relaxed and let his mind drift outward to them, and then opened his eyes. They had slipped silently into the bush, Mahegan catching the flipping tail of the pup.

He turned, waded into the sound, and began swimming.

As he glided into the water that was now showing some chop from a southerly wind, a distant, but enormous explosion shook the water around his body.

He stopped, stood in the chest-deep sound only twenty meters offshore and turned toward the mushroom cloud fueled by a large plume of smoke billowing upward like a miniature nuclear blast. He gauged the distance to be about ten miles away at a two-hundred-degree azimuth, southwest, in the center of Dare County Bombing Range.

Picturing the source of the burst cloud, Mahegan thought, *That's about right.* More than a year ago the Department of Defense had closed Dare County Bombing Range, which oddly enough sat in the middle of the Alligator River Wildlife Refuge. In an attempt to appease a shunned contractor, the DoD had given the dirty job of clearing the bomb detritus to the private military contractor Copperhead, Inc.

As he began swimming back to Roanoke Island, Mahegan suddenly felt better about his decision regarding Savage's offer.

Buy now at http://bit.ly/KindleForeignDomestic
Or new Paperback: http://bit.ly/Foreign_and_Domsetic_Paperback

To find out more on AJ Tata, visit his website
www.ajtata.com

Rogue Threat:	http://bit.ly/RogueThreat_AJTata
Hidden Threat:	http://bit.ly/Hidden_Threat_AJTata
Mortal Threat:	http://bit.ly/Mortal_Threat_AJTata

Brigadier General Anthony J. Tata, US Army (Retired) lives in Cary, North Carolina, with his wife, Jodi. A career paratrooper and infantryman, he commanded combat units in the 82nd and 101st Airborne Divisions and the 10th Mountain Division. He is the author of three critically acclaimed novels, *Sudden Threat, Rogue Threat*, and *Hidden Threat*. He has been a frequent foreign policy guest commentator on Fox News, CBS News, and The Daily Buzz. NBC's *Today Show* featured General Tata's career transition from the army to education leadership where he served as Chief Operations Officer for Washington, DC, Public Schools and then as the superintendent of Schools in Raleigh-Wake County, North Carolina, the sixteenth largest school district in the nation. He has two children, Brooke and Zachary.